# RETURN
# OF
# THE
# FALCON

Also by Satalic

*The Dummy Case*

*A Tribute to Frank Marshall- An Essay*

*The Masque of William Shakespeare - An Essay*

# Ha'Penny Press
## Chicago

HaPennyPress@mail.com

*Return of the Falcon* is a work of fiction. Names, characters, businesses, places, events, incidents, other than historical references, are either the product of the author's imagination or used fictitiously. Any resemblance to actual persons, living or deceased, events or locales is entirely coincidental.

ISBN 978-0-9890346-4-7

Cover art by **J.C. Grande**
http://jcgrande.blogspot.com
http://johnnymorbius.deviantart.com/gallery

First Edition

SATALIC

Ha'Penny Press
Chicago

To Digger, whose belief
became this book.

Yet let him remember the days of darkness;
for they shall be many.
All that cometh is vanity.


Ecclesiastes 11:8

# ACKNOWLEDGMENTS

Thanks to my wife, Ann, who charms the birds and the squirrels and the possums and me. And thanks to my son Digger who has a keen sense of what is cool.

I am especially grateful to cryptology expert Fred Brandes and longshoreman Jose Garcia.

# CHAPTER ONE

*Late Summer, 1946*
SOUTH CHICAGO
*Vookie's Tavern*

The war was finally over. It ended in an orgy of destruction and death unleashed by Fat Man and Little Boy, horrific creations of the new "Atomic Age."

But it brought our boys home.

And with them came a secret. If you looked real hard, you might be able to see it, just behind their eyes. Joe Ganzer knew what to look for. He saw it every morning in the mirror.

Today, Joe Ganzer only takes the easy cases, the cases with no danger, no challenges, no chance to trigger those memories, none at all. Fortunately for *Jos. Ganzer Investigations* a lot of returning GIs were curious about how their lovely ladies had occupied their time while they were away saving the world. Not that they doubted their fidelity, it was just insurance. Joe's policy cost $50, more than enough to guarantee her virtue.

He settled into the complacency of these domestic cases, where his GI clients needed assurance that life was what they thought it was, that the world was essentially good if only a little screwed up.

But Joe knew better.

A couple of bullet holes kept him out of the war, at least that was the story on the street. Rumors surfaced about counter-espionage, about the "Bomb," about hunting down Nazi spies for the FBI. That last one played well with the ladies.

And it was a lady client he would see today. She had called the office to arrange a consultation. He wasn't sure he even wanted her kind of case, too many unknowns. But Joe at least agreed to meet her at Vookie's Tavern, his "other" office. Besides, no sense meeting at his Commercial Avenue command center—it was hot and dusty and a mess. Vookie's was good enough, the kind of place where everyone minds his own business, especially in the quiet of late afternoon.

Her entrance shattered the cathedral's silence and spilled some afternoon heat into the place. Her eyes caught Joe's in the last booth. She walked down the three steps and headed over to Joe's booth and slipped into the opposing side. "How'd you know?" asked Joe with a broad smile, admiring her angular features, blonde hair, and winter eyes, slate-gray with flecks of blue.

"I didn't think you could be that drunk over at the bar or the bartender or that peculiar man with the hat leering at me. So, that left you," she said with only the hint of arrogance in her soft, rich voice. She was bright and knew how to handle herself. She had depth. This case would be different.

*But it's too soon*, he told himself. "So…how can I help you, Miss Kemidov?" Joe asked cautiously.

"I want you to locate my Uncle Yuri…Yuri Kemidov," Polina said almost defensively. "I know this will be difficult, and I'm quite willing to and able to pay for your services, though perhaps not in the way you seem to be thinking."

Joe laughed, "I already like you, Miss Kemidov. May I call you by your first name?"

"Surely, if you would like. It is pronounced Po Lee Na," she said with a corrupted German-Russian-Polish accent that defied Joe's ear for detecting such subtleties. He'd been trained to recognize the regional German dialects and, to some extent, the Russian as well. He just couldn't quite place this one.

He kept looking at her. *Maybe she's learned too many languages.*

"My uncle is a displaced person, you see. He was a general in the Soviet Army during the war. He was more of a figurehead than a field general. More an honorary position, you see. The Germans captured him late in the war, and he was held in a POW camp. The Americans liberated him, and he wrote that he wanted to immigrate to Canada. We have relatives there. That's the last I knew of his locality."

That accent was rolling around in his head when Joe asked, "Last you heard, he was in Canada? That's one big country."

"No—he is not in Canada now. He wrote me that he was *going* to Toronto. That's all I know," she said as she reached in her purse, pulling out a crumpled piece of paper, clutching it in her delicate hand.

"Wrote you from where?"

She winced, and Joe immediately held himself back fearing that he would come off as an interrogator. He followed the question up with a smile that almost wasn't. *She's dancing around that location.*

Polina replied, "He wrote from London, if that is any help." She spoke a little too rapidly, as though she knew the drill, knew that answers had better come without hesitation, almost rehearsed. She glanced down at the paper.

Noting the furtive look, he thought: *She must have been in Europe somewhere under Nazi occupation.* The bad news was the POW repatriation thing was off. The Americans sent Soviet soldiers right back to the Soviet communists. Many had actually fought with Hitler against the communists. *If Uncle Yuri was one of those, he would have been executed by the Soviets. So he escaped or paid his way out.*

"Now, for all you know, Uncle Yuri could still be in London. He could have run out of money or he could have taken ill or....?" Joe suggested, raising his eyebrows in wordless speculation. He paused, leaned his head to the side, looked at that paper in her hand, and gave a slight nod "When was your last correspondence?"

"About three weeks ago, Mr. Ganzer," Polina said. "He was at this hotel in London." She passed Joe the paper with the name "Alhambra Hotel" on the letterhead. The body of the letter was in Russian Cyrillic, which Joe could partially comprehend. He asked if he could keep the letter.

"No, I don't want to lose it. It means so much to me," Polina pleaded. "Mr. Ganzer, I lost my whole family in the war——my mother, my father. Uncle Yuri is my father's only brother. This letter may be all I will ever have of him. I cannot let it go."

"That's fine…it's all Greek to me, anyway." But it wasn't fine. *She doesn't want me to translate that letter. Maybe it's something personal or something else.* What Joe inexpertly translated seemed more like a mundane list of requests, not a personal letter.

"All I need is that hotel name for now," Joe said. "I just want you to know: London is a big city. There are thousands of people displaced by the war who are traveling to all parts of the world… mostly the free world."

What Joe didn't want to say was that most likely General Kemidov was running from the Soviets, that maybe they'd caught up with him. "I may have to go there," he said. "Are you prepared for those kind of expenses?"

She responded quickly, "No, please, Mr. Ganzer. Money is not a problem. I just need to know what has happened to him—that he is all right."

"Skip the 'Mr. Ganzer.' Call me Joe. So... why are you staying here in Chicago... on the South Side?" he asked. He motioned for Eddie the bartender, who arrived just as Polina was answering.

"I have relatives—cousins—that I am staying with on 71st and Jeffrey," she said.

"What would you like to drink?" Joe asked. "Eddie will get whatever you want. Right, Ed?"

"I would like a martini. Not too strong, please," she said. Eddie went back to the bar as Joe assessed this lovely woman across the booth from him, admiring her impeccable taste in jewelry and clothing. Elegant but not ostentatious. Her suit, though, looked a half size too large for her. *She has lost weight,* he thought.

Joe leaned into her. "Now, why did you choose me?" If she answered wrong here, he would drop the case cold.

"I was told you had contacts everywhere," she said. "That you could reach people anywhere in the world."

Eddie returned with the martini and a napkin that had "Vookie's" printed on it in a tropical shade of blue. He set them both down and headed back to the bar. That's when he heard Joe say "Who'd you get that from?" Eddie tensed up. He knew that tone in Joe's voice.

Polina sensed it too. "I—I was at the Blackhawk Restaurant in downtown... in Chicago and—"

"Let me guess: You bumped into a guy who talked me up."

"Yes," she gasped, "but how did you know?"

"I'm a detective. I'm supposed to know things. That's why people hire me."


Two nights ago, Polina had ventured into the Blackhawk Restaurant on Wabash and Randolph, a place made famous all across the country by WGN radio's "Live! From the Blackhawk" on the Mutual Network. The show featured top musicians, like Kay Kyser, Chico Marx, Louis Prima, Ish Kabibble, and others. They even had a telegraph right there in the restaurant to take remote requests from their listeners.

If you wanted to dance between the soup and the entrée, then the Blackhawk was the place. It was at the east end of the "bright lights" area, 139 North Wabash, across from Marshall Field's department store and just a ways from the stairway to Chicago's "L," the elevated mass transit. The sounds of the "L" and the bustle of the street crowd all added to its appeal.

The Blackhawk just happened to be the favorite haunt of a former grifter named Ludko Randelli, a shadowy denizen of the city's underworld and one of Joe Ganzer's best operatives, not to mention his best friend.

Ludko loved the Blackhawk not only for the music, but also for the interesting people you could meet—politicians, gangsters, wealthy businessmen, reporters, janitors, girls from the office, models, actresses. Anybody who wanted a good time could find it at the Blackhawk.

Ludko spotted Polina Kemidov sitting at the bar that night, looking exceptionally beautiful. Of course, he couldn't help but strike up a conversation with her. Ludko was a street-wise psychologist, and in the course of their small talk, he noticed that Polina seemed preoccupied, worried.

"You seem a little troubled," Ludko said.

"Oh... it's my uncle. He is now missing," said Polina in that strange alluring accent. "He is my only living relative. The war took both my mother and father. He's all that I have...." She broke off and turned away.

"Hey, now don't go gettin' misty. Maybe there's somethin' can be done. Where was your uncle last time yuh knew?"

"London...the last I had contact with him."

"London, eh?" said Ludko trying not to sound too impressed. "Listen, I represent a private investigation company. I believe we can locate your uncle without a problem." Ludko's mind went into overdrive. He could impress this beautiful woman and make some money at the same time. "Of course, this will require a little money to open a case, but I feel we can help."

"I have monies," replied Polina eagerly. "Anything to find my Uncle Yuri."

That's when Ludko told her to call *Jos. Ganzer Investigations* and set up a meeting.

◊◊◊

"So tell me what happened with this character you met at the Blackhawk."

"The band was marvelous that night and there was dancing and this fellow who asked me to dance. We had a few drinks."

"Did he pay?"

"Why, yes, he did."

"That's unusual. Go on."

Polina looked at Joe quizzically and continued, "I told him about my uncle, and... and he said you was only one detective in Chicago who could find him."

Joe smiled and let out an imperceptible laugh, "Walter Randelli! Did he get any money out of you?"

"His name was Ludko Randelli— I am almost sure— and, yes, he did get money, but how did you know?" Polina said with that withering tone of someone who knows they have been taken.

"I'll get it back for you," Joe said. "My apologies, that guy is a professional con. He makes his entire living hustling people who are in one form of trouble or another. He's even going to try to charge me a finder's fee for sending in a new client."

Ludko knew Joe had wartime associates inside British intelligence, so he steered Polina to Joe and made a fast C-note in the deal. He figured Joe could use his contacts to help locate her uncle.

But more than that, Ludko knew something was wrong with Joe, something only a lifelong friend could see. He watched one of the best detectives in Chicago become a second-rate domestic peeper. Ludko sincerely believed what Joe needed was a real case again, like before the war, like before those long absences, something to engage his mind again, something to unravel, something to change.

Joe saw through his friend's plan and appreciated his concern, but he wasn't sure he wanted cases like that anymore. He wasn't sure of anything since the war.

From habit, Joe continued, "Now, how can I recognize your uncle? Do you have a photograph?"

"No... No photograph. It has been many years, you see? He is taller than me, but I was a girl then. He had dark hair, gray at the temples. He has a medium build and a scar on the left side of his cheek, near the temple."

"How old is he now?"

"He was a few years older than my father, so I would say 63, perhaps older."

Joe let the conversation drift expertly to talk of Chicago, places to see and things to do while she was in town.

They finished their drinks, and Joe asked her if she needed a ride somewhere. She said she would take a cab. Eddie was given the nod to get her a cab. It was near dusk in South Chicago. Cars were leisurely moving down Commercial Avenue. The scent of coke from the steel mills lightly perfumed the air, and the haze made the setting sun glow red, like the inside of a blast furnace. The cab pulled up.

"Cab's here, Joe," announced Eddie.

"Okay, call me at the office in a couple of days," Joe said as he handed her his card. "I'll see what I can dig up on your uncle, and I'll track down Ludko, too."

"Thank you, Mr. Ganzer. You don't know what a relief this is," Polina said. She walked, almost glided, to the door, giving Joe just enough time to admire her sparse curves and practiced gate.

*She does that on purpose. This might be a good case after all.*

When she got outside the door, Joe went over to the passed out drunk and said, "Ludko, she's gone now. Better get going."

Ludko raised his head from the bar. "See, Joe, I told yuh she'd never recognize me. Not in these clothes," Ludko said with a certain pride. He was one of those people you never really see, even when you're with them for a long time.

"Get going, before you lose her," Joe said. "She's headed to 71st and Jeffrey." He patted him on the back and headed down to the end of the bar. "Benny, you have to stop staring at these girls. You're making it rough on my business."

Benny was one of Joe's part-time operatives, doing odd jobs whenever he felt in the mood or was in need of some cash. "Yeah, but Joe, she was beautiful. I'm sorry. What do yuh want me ta do now?"

"Hang tight, Benny. I've got to get a few things together. I'll call you here later."

Ludko tailed Polina in his unremarkable 1940 LaFayette, but she didn't end up at 71st and Jeffrey.

◊◊◊

Joe left Vookie's, walked around the corner, slid into his 1940 Special Deluxe Chevrolet, a black coupe, and drove to his Commercial Ave office. He found a space down the block and walked leisurely back to the three-story building. His office was on the second floor above the Law Offices of Albert Strugala.

Albert Strugala used to live on the second floor, and he rented the third floor apartment. That was in his early days before his law practice grew. Now he lived on the near north side with all the other lawyers. He had the second floor renovated into a two room office with a private shower and was planning to do the same on the third floor now that the war was over and young businesses were hungry for space.

You entered the upper floors through the small door to the far left of Strugala's impressive plate glass window with only the words "Law Offices" in gold leaf Times Roman lettering in a delicate arc across the expanse of glass. Wood venetian blinds shuttered the office from curious passersby, but occasionally, on quiet afternoons, the secretary would open them to watch the world go by from her desk in front of row of wooden file cabinets filled with documents and records of the practice.

Strugala had two law clerks to do research and help prepare briefs. For now, they were students at the University of Chicago School of Law, hoping someday to become as wealthy as their boss.

Joe first met Albert Strugala through an insurance case a number of years before the war. Strugala represented a real estate man who was suing the insurance company Joe was working for at the time. The case involved a fall by the real estate man at a construction site.

The insurance company had their doubts about the extent of the claimant's back injury, so they had Joe run a routine surveillance. For two weeks, the real estate man did nothing out of the ordinary, nothing strenuous. He didn't take the garbage out. He didn't open the garage door. He even had the next-door neighbor kid mow his lawn. He did nothing.

The insurance company's agent was adamant that the reports from the job site indicated there should be nothing wrong with this man. Joe offered a plan to test the veracity of the claim. He had Wilma Murphy, an attractive secretary at the insurance company, pose as a prospective real estate seller, a girl who had inherited some industrial property near the Crawford Power Station on the city's southwest side, a booming industrial area. The real estate man jumped at the bait.

The claimant told Wilma he would like to help but couldn't drive because of his back—just as Joe had expected. So, she agreed to drive him to the property. On the way there, the real estate man concluded that Wilma was a typical scatterbrain, without a clue about land development or anything else for that matter. She was a good actress.

When they arrived, Wilma just pointed out the boundaries of the property. "I don't want to ruin my shoes on this bumpy ground."

"Oh, that's fine. I'll just take a walk around, survey the area."

"Sure, I'll wait here."

The man walked along the property lines. It was perhaps thirty acres of undeveloped land in what would soon be a factory, as soon as he got it away from "witless" Wilma. While he perused the land, licking his lips at this unbelievable opportunity, she let the air out of her rear tire. When he returned, she said, "Oh, goodness! Look at that darn tire. What am I going to do now? I don't know anything about cars."

The real estate man was hesitant at first, looking around carefully, but with Wilma's pleading and her skirt ruffling in the breeze, he relented and set about changing the tire. Joe was in a warehouse right down the street with a Crown Graphic camera fitted with a telephoto lens. He photographed the real estate man jacking the car up, tossing around the tires, and tightening the lug nuts.

Later, when presented with the photographs, Strugala advised his client to withdraw the law suit and accept a moderate settlement. Out of curiosity, he asked the insurance representative, "Who did this surveillance work?" The agent gave him Joe's name and number. He called Joe that night.

Strugala asked if he would like to moonlight for him, serving summons, surveillance, interviewing witnesses, even acting as a body guard. Joe accepted, and they have worked together off and on ever since.

And when Strugala took up residence on the north side some years before the war, Joe asked if he would be interested in renting the second floor apartment as an office. He was dubious at first, but Joe coaxed him by offering to give "most" of his cases top priority. Strugala smiled at that and agreed. Later, Joe even talked Wilma Murphy into joining his new company. The frosted glass upper panel on the door to his offices read: *Jos. Ganzer Investigations.*

Joe cantered up the stairs to the second floor. When he walked in, he could feel the heat sear into his clothes. Wilma hadn't left the windows open, fearing it might rain. Joe turned on the fans, opened some windows, and a whisper of a breeze came in through the gangway between the buildings. As light perspiration formed on his brow and his dark brown hair formed two semicircles on each side of his head, Joe thought: *In just a few weeks autumn will be here.*

Wilma refused to dust and straighten Joe's inner office. She would tidy up her outer area, but not Joe's. "I'm not your maid. I'm your secretary," she would say every time he asked. So, tonight, Joe laughed and wrote her a note telling her to find them a maid. He dropped it on her desk.

Wilma's outer office was smaller than Joe's because of the stairway, but it had a large window that faced the street below and let morning light in to nourish the plants she had throughout. Alongside her desk and against the wall was a leather sofa. In front was a small coffee table with newspapers and magazines neatly stacked on it. Behind her desk were five tall file cabinets filled with reports and relevant documents for all the cases, past and present.

Joe's office had dark oak wainscoting, with a repeating pattern of recessed rectangular panels capped by a fluted chair rail and plastered walls painted a light beige, an office remodeled by Albert Strugala with a lawyer in mind.

Joe's desk was large with papers and notes strewn all over its surface. On the left-hand side were his phone and the intercom. Sometimes, when he was consulting with a talkative client, Wilma would buzz him on the intercom reminding him he had an appointment with the police or whatever, which was code for "time's up."

On the right-hand side of his desk, along the wall, were Joe's private file cabinets, filled with sensitive information about everything and anything; and only Joe knew how to fathom their depths—but not always.

After an hour pouring through his haphazard files in the heat of his office, he found the current address of his former instructor and associate from the British counter-intelligence agency MI5—Lawrence Hamilton. After the war, Hamilton had been assigned to work surreptitiously with INTERPOL. Joe purposely lost contact with almost everyone involved with the OSS and the Manhattan Project and Die Glocke, including Hamilton.

But now Joe needed him to check into the whereabouts of Yuri Kemidov. He suspected Uncle Yuri was hiding from the NKVD, the ruthless Soviet secret police. As an MI5 agent with ties to INTERPOL, Lawrence Hamilton could surely locate Kemidov without leading the NKVD right to his door. Joe took no chances when contacting Hamilton.

He walked over to his bookshelf and pulled from among his law books a copy of *Telegraphic Code to Ensure Secrecy in the Transmission of Telegrams* by Robert Slater. Slater's Code was a dictionary of 25,000 alphabetized words. Each word was assigned a five-digit number from 00001 through 25000. No one but a cryptographer could decode a message in Slater's Code unless they had the key number, an offset value added to the value of the intended word.

Joe used the number 1776 as his key number offset because he and Hamilton had used it before. Joe came up with it in 1942 during training in Canada. It was the birth date of the United States, it was the number shown at the bottom of the pyramid on the American dollar bill, and it was on the tablet held by the Statue of Liberty. Just a little playfulness on Joe's part to barb his instructor Lawrence Hamilton who lampooned Joe by insisting that the States were still British colonies.

Joe composed his message carefully, looking up each word in the Slater book and its corresponding number. To that number he added his 1776 offset to reveal the number of the new coded word. When Joe had to include the name "Kemidov" in his message, he used a transposition code Hamilton had also taught him at Camp X. After twenty minutes he was finished. He picked up the phone and called Vookie's.

"Eddie? Is Benny there?... Tell him to get over here quick?"

Staying about one hundred yards behind, Ludko saw Polina's cab blow right past 71st Street and continued heading north. *Okay,*

11

*change of plans. Wait'll Joe hears this.* The cab stayed on Stony Island Avenue right past the jazz clubs and then past the Southmoor Hotel. The cab jogged over to Lake Shore Drive into the Hyde Park neighborhood. They cruised by the Museum of Science and Industry, one of the largest science museums in the world, a gleaming white limestone Beaux Arts facade saved from ruin by a Sears, Roebuck and Company president, originally part of the 1893 World's Columbian Exposition.

Somewhere in the back of his mind Ludko promised himself he would visit that place someday, but he never would. He accelerated to keep up with Polina's cab. After a few blocks, they breezed past the University of Chicago, home of Enrico Fermi and Edward Teller, godfathers of the atomic bomb. Beneath the west stands of the abandoned Stagg Field stadium, in the racquets court, the world's first nuclear chain reaction was set off by Fermi at Chicago Pile-1.

Just a few years later they built the atomic bomb, and the world would never be the same, neither would Joe for his role in that mission, which is why Ludko was so relieved that Joe even took this case. It wasn't safe. It wasn't a domestic snoop job for a quick buck. It was formless. It was twisted. It was a challenge. They were back in pursuit.

Polina ended her cab ride at The Drake Hotel, right off Michigan Avenue. Ludko thought: *Far cry from South Chicago.* He'd have to get back to Joe with this as soon as he could. He parked the Lafayette in the first open spot and hurried into the hotel.

The entrance was clad in Carrera marble with oversized glass doors encased in brass with double brass push bars. Ludko entered the marble-floored foyer. Straight ahead was a carpeted staircase that led to the main lobby. He reached the top of the stairs just as Polina picked up what looked to be some mail and headed for the elevators.

She was the only one who entered the elevator, so Ludko calmly sat in one of the many upholstered chairs in the lobby and noted the floor it stopped at. He was delighted he didn't have to run up the stairs or work a scam on the concierge. She stopped at the seventh floor. Ludko waited for the elevator to return. It was empty, except for the operator. He took the same elevator up to the seventh floor, but when he emerged no one was in the hallway. A bellboy walked by and Ludko grabbed a folded paper from his coat pocket and asked him: "Miss Polina dropped this on her way out the elevator. Would you give it to her?"

"Sure," he said and walked directly down the carpeted corridor, inspecting the mail casually. He disappeared into a niche, the entrance to Room 706. For a terrifying second, Ludko thought he'd given the bellhop his electric bill with the paper. He frantically checked all his pockets, then laughed without a sound.

A man answered the bellboy's knock. "What's this?"

"Miss Kemidov dropped this in the hallway, sir," he said as he handed him the folded up form.

The man glanced at it and closed the door. Ludko was already down one flight of stairs by the time the bellboy scratched his head, trying to remember Ludko's face. He shrugged his shoulders and headed toward the elevator.

In the lobby, Ludko phoned Joe's office. He didn't wait for the hello, "Hey, Joe."

"Yeah, Lud."

"Hey, listen. This Polina ain't nowhere on 71st Street. She's at The Drake of all places. Hey, hold it... the bellboy's looking straight at me."

"You are handsome, Lud. Maybe he wants a date."

"Knock it off, Joe. The kid thinks he recognizes me. Nope, he just turned away. Ha..."

"Is she visiting somebody?"

"Nah, she's registered here, but there's a guy in her room."

"You got all that in just this time?"

"What can I say? I'm a professional."

"No more money, Lud; but nice tap dance. I'll put that in your record."

"Where to from here, boss?"

"See if you can get a name on her guy, but don't make it obvious. Be creative and call me about nine tonight at Vookie's." Just as Joe hung up, Benny came nonchalantly into the office. His hand was still on the receiver, "Where the hell have you been?"

"Joe, I was talkin' ta this girl at Vookie's and—" Benny was halted mid speech.

"Look, I want you to go downtown to Western Union and send this telegram. Exactly as I've worded it. Don't screw it up. You got that?" said Joe.

"Yeah, sure, Joe," said Benny looking over the message. "Wow this is like nuts. Is it supposed to read like this?"

"It's an old code, Benny that I use to keep things private."

"Gotcha. And it's going to London, England, huh? Cheerio old chap and all that crap."

"All right. Get going... and thanks."

Benny the Hat left the office with a certain lightness of foot and caught a bus to downtown South Chicago with his homburg hat firmly on his round head. Depending on the day, the mood, or even the hour, it might be a black hat or blue or brown with feathers or sometimes without, maybe even a trilby. Benny liked today's choice.


Ludko went into the men's room off the lobby at The Drake and combed his hair a little differently, added a little wave to the front, dipping it slightly forward, but not quite a forelock. Satisfied with his new look, he walked out and down the hall to just off the main lobby into one of Chicago's favorite watering holes, a hangout for newspaper reporters and politicians and sometimes Outfit guys.

The bar had a ruffled valance right above with a dozen or so stools, like so many soldiers standing at attention. The floor was carpeted with a small square grid pattern of floral scrolls all but obscured by a dozen square tables with four chairs each. Ludko grabbed a stool across from the large arched mirror with fluted molding behind the bar on the far right-hand side. In the mirror he watched the entrance and the lobby beyond. *If that guy shows up anywhere, it'll be here.* Ludko ordered a drink and listened to the radio.

This episode was "The Secret Menace Strikes" on the Adventures of Superman Show sponsored by Kellogg's foods. It was about half over, but Ludko listened as Perry White, editor of the *Daily Planet,* is missing and in possible danger. A mysterious individual has telephoned Jimmy Olsen saying that he has a message from Perry for Clark, Lois, and Jimmy; but he will have to go to the Newspaper Club to pick it up and....


Polina looked at the racing form with a delicate curl at the corner of her mouth. "I don't understand what this is."

"It's a racing form, my dear. You betting on the horses these days?" he asked with a raised eyebrow.

"No…I picked up the mail at the desk. It must have been in there by mistake."

"Look, I've been cooped up in here all day. I'm going down for a drink. Want to come along?"

"No," she said. "I'm a little tired; you go ahead." She walked over to the sofa by the faux fireplace and dropped the racing form onto the glass coffee table and sat down and opened a magazine.

The man rose from the upholstered chair across from her and headed out. He walked down the hall to the elevators and pressed the down button. A few moments later it arrived, and he ambled in and told the operator, "Lobby."

When he entered the lounge, Ludko caught him in the mirror and recognized him immediately. Even though he saw Ludko briefly in the hallway, there wasn't a glimmer of it on his somber face. He just sat down and ordered a Scotch. On the radio now was *The Quiz Kids*, the announcer was just introducing Joe Kelly, the quiz master. Then, the kids introduced themselves one by one. "I'm Lonne Lunde. I'm 13 years old in the eighth grade at Lincoln Junior High School... I'm Joel Kupperman. I'm 12 years old in eighth grade…….."

Ludko said to no one in particular: "Them kids are really sharp. They're all local, yuh know." The bartender smiled and nodded. "And last week they were up against some college professors. They really slammed 'em."

"I never listen to that show," the man said.

"Well, let me tell ya' about this question they had." Ludko laughed uncomfortably, "It goes something like: If a hen and a half can lay an egg and a half in a day and a half, in 5,347 days how many eggs per dozen would 26 hens lay in four days?"

"How would I know?" the man answered as he reached for his drink. His suit was a deep blue with a purple undertone. His black hair was neat with part that looked like it was shot in with a bullet. His eyes were dark brown and dead, and Ludko almost choked when he remembered who this guy was.

"Hey, buddy, it's just a joke. See? There's always 12 eggs in a dozen. Get it?"

The man snickered, and Ludko knew he had him. He began talking about everything: baseball, football, and his favorite topic— horses. After a few minutes discussing the highs and lows of horseracing, it hit him: *Damn… that racing form.* "You staying here at this hotel?" the man asked Ludko.

"Nah, I'm supposed to meet a guy here tonight."

# CHAPTER TWO

SOUTH CHICAGO
*Western Union Office*

Benny the Hat got off the bus, walked about a block, and went straight into Western Union. "I want to send this overseas, to London. That's in England," he said proudly. It wasn't everyday someone in this neighborhood wired London.

Dubious, mostly of Benny, the clerk looked up over his glasses. He shuffled some papers around and then curiously scrutinized the message.

Frustrated, he shuffled more papers around, some landing on the floor. "Western Union has clear, concise rules concerning what is and what is not properly a part of the full address and signature. Is this the proper address?"

"Yeah, that's it all right: the Hotel Cavendish, 75 Gower Street, Bloomsbury, London." said Benny.

"But this message doesn't make proper sense," decried the clerk. The body of the telegram read:

EBENEZER ANGELESEA

OFFENCE ILLIMITABLE LHEU WAYUXBI MISINFORM
MOORED BOIL
SQTSYZES JUROR.

GANZER

"Just send it. Just like it is. Okay?"

"That will have to be full rate, then."

"Naturally." Benny paid the clerk and left. He headed for a phone booth across the street and called Joe. "Hey, I sent off that

16

telegram like yuh said, and you owe me some money."

"Yeah, sure, drop the receipt off at the office when you get a chance. Look, Benny, I might need you later to help me out with something. Will you be around?"

"I'm goin' down to the Trianon Ball Room. When do yuh need me?"

"Not sure—maybe tomorrow afternoon, maybe sooner. That good?"

Benny had planned a late night. "Sure, I should be home by then. Just gimme a call," he said. "And, hey, Joe, that telegram clerk... he gave me some funny looks, like I was nuts or somethin'."

"Maybe it was the hat. Anyway, thanks, Benny." And he hung up and looked at the clock. It was early evening, just about half past seven, but that made it after midnight in London. No chance for Lawrence Hamilton to make inquiries. No chance for the telegram to reach him for at least a few more hours.

Hamilton had worked closely with Joe during the war on a delicate piece of counterespionage involving the Manhattan Project, Chicago, and Los Alamos. Now Hamilton was posing as an international antiquities dealer, using his contacts throughout Europe as part of a counterintelligence scheme in concert with INTERPOL.

Hamilton could locate anyone anywhere in Europe, much less London. Joe suspected, from what Polina told him, that General Kemidov might be fleeing the Soviets or had already been picked up by their agents in London, which might explain why Polina hadn't received any more correspondence from him.

Hamilton could help. He would know what Joe had suspected simply by his name and title in the telegram: ILLIMITABLE LHEU WAYUXBI (General Yuri Kemidov). A Soviet general making his way to Canada or possibly the US could have aroused Soviet intelligence, especially if he were of some importance.

But perhaps the "General" thing was self-appointed, to impress his niece, and he was nothing more than another displaced person, another DP, trying to get to the States. The answer would have to wait until morning.

Joe locked up and headed downstairs, got into the Chevy, and drove to the West Side. He was working a divorce case. He always checked out each side of his domestic cases, regardless of who hired him. His client, a recently wealthy businessman, made his money running an Army post exchange in southern England during the war.

He started out as a thirteen-week wonder in the Army, just like everybody else, but he made them believe he knew mathematics, which got him into Officer Candidate School. Later, the Army found out he had some managerial expertise and immediately assigned him to a PX in the south of England for the replacement men that were coming over. Joe discovered that his client had barber shops, shoe repair, beer, and he even had control over all the Zippo lighters in England. At the end of the war, he parlayed all his PX profits into one of the biggest auto-supply houses in Chicago. Now, for some reason, he didn't trust his wife.

Women usually cheat during the week, not on weekends. It was early in the week, so Joe sat on their house waiting for the wife to leave. This had been the third time. He was almost convinced there was nothing to his client's mistrust. For once he thought there might be someone with some virtue left.

She headed out of their driveway in a new 1946 Lincoln. Joe kept a bunch of different hats in his car. When he tailed someone, he would change his hat every so many miles. The other driver rarely picked up on it, never suspected a thing.

From experience, Joe had to be careful tailing women. Call it intuition or keen perception, but women had an uncanny knack for spotting a tail. He held back almost a block and a half. At one point he almost lost sight of her Lincoln, but noticed her making a turn.

He picked her up again. She eventually made a rendezvous at an elegant motel on Cicero Avenue. Joe used his Contax 35mm camera, the same camera used on Omaha Beach by Robert Capa on D-Day. Joe snapped photographs of her meeting a man in the parking lot, kissing him "hello," entering a room. That's all that a rich man's lawyer would need. Joe headed back to the office to develop the film and print the pictures that would end a marriage.

Traveling down Ashland Avenue, he turned on the radio. "Ole Buttermilk Sky" by Kay Kyser was playing. Later, as he got closer to South Chicago, Frank Sinatra was singing "Five Minutes More." After a few cigarette commercials, they played the Ink Spots' hit "The Gypsy." Bill Kenny opened the vocals with that beautifully clear and emotive voice...

In a quaint caravan
There's a lady they call The Gypsy
She can look in the future
And drive away your fears
Everything will come right
If you only believe The Gypsy
She could tell at a glance
That my heart was so full of tears

She looked at my hand and told me
My lover was always true
And yet in my heart I knew, dear
Somebody else was kissing you
But I'll go there again
'Cause I want to believe The Gypsy
That my lover is true
And will come back to me some day

*Some of them can't come back,* and Joe switched the radio off and continued heading back to Commercial Avenue, with only the warm night air softly mumbling through the side vents.

Joe opened the door to Vookie's and took the three steps down into the darkly paneled barroom. There were horseshoe booths along the wall and the bar ran parallel and just opposite them. At the rear was a small stage where every weekend Eddie booked a jazz band, a tambura group, even promising magicians, comedians and ventriloquists.

Between the horseshoe booths were small rectangular booths for two people, four people on the weekends. On jutting pedestals above each two-person booth were three-foot statues, replicas of Grecian goddesses. Others had artificial tropical plants. The bar was a work of Italian art. The bar top was Sienese marble, yellowish-white that contrasted perfectly with the dark mahogany beneath it. The bar was more ornate than the paneled walls, with fluted wood columns supporting the heavy marble and recessed panels every four feet. It had a brass foot rest and brass-legged stools. The mirror behind the bar was etched with arabesque patterns and framed in rich mahogany.

Vookie's could hold fifty people comfortably and sometimes more when he booked a hot act. Eddie had an agreement with the local cops to stay open past his license in exchange for a white envelop every week. The Chicago way.

"Joe, you're back," said Eddie from the bar. Vookie's had the usual late crowd, a rough bunch if you didn't belong. Joe belonged.

"Hey, Eddie, did Ludko call?"

"No... nobody," answered Eddie shaking his head.

Before he bought Vookie's, long before the war, Eddie used to work for Joe. Joe needed help and Eddie was out of work, so he came with Joe on a few "bar checks." In those days the nightclubs and dance clubs were always packed. Joe and Eddie both loved music, the girls, the atmosphere. It was a dream job.

Club owners, especially lucrative downtown club owners, always suspected their bartenders of clipping the till. They'd hire Joe to check them out on hectic nights, usually weekends. It was just too obvious for one guy to sit alone at the bar and eyeball the cash register all night.

But if two guys came in together, ordered drinks, sat around and shot the breeze, it looked perfectly normal. On the busy nights, piles of money would accumulate on the ledges of the cash drawers. Bartenders would make change quickly from those piles. Waiters and customers were shouting orders. The pace was hectic.

Joe and Eddie would look past each other to see if the bartenders would ring up a sale every time they put more cash on the pile. Sometimes bills would find their way into a "special" pile or under the register. Eddie once remarked to Joe, "Look at this guy. He'll skim off at least hundred bucks tonight." A professional bartender is like a sleight-of-hand magician. He can remove any number of bills off the pile nightly.

But if he sees anyone looking at him, he'll shuffle the stolen cash back into the pile, like nothing happened. Eddie enjoyed the bar checks. They went to exciting clubs with headliners like Kay Kaiser, Stan Kenton, Count Basie, Dizzy Gillespie.

He noticed how much money was being made and told Joe he was going to open a small place of his own someday. Joe found out about a place up for sale on the South Side. Eddie had some money saved but not enough to make the buy. Joe offered to help him out. Eddie bought the place and named it "Vookie's," a corruption of a Serbian word that meant "wolf." He promised Joe he would pay him back—it just took longer than either one of them expected. After a while, Joe told Eddie he could forget the balance if he could use Vookie's as his second office.

Joe headed for his "always reserved" booth in the rear, running the gauntlet of "Hellos" and "Wha'chyuh been up tos" from the bar and the side booths. In a way, they protected him from the outside world. He was a local. Knew everyone, and they thought they knew him.

At the end of the bar "One Two" Johnny stopped him with, "Hey Joe?" That voice—in an instant—closed the gulf of time between then and now, a brown leather boxing glove crashing into the left side of his jaw, splitting the corner of his mouth. The world froze and turned into a soft quiet blur as Joe fell to the canvas.

A shattering glass behind the bar broke Joe's trance. "...Hey... Johnny how are you? Haven't seen you in a while. Are they keeping you bottled up these days?" Joe carried a memento from that boxing match, a little scar on his upper lip, inside corner. Johnny was already a tough ring-wise fighter when they first met in the local ring all those years ago. In the clenches, Johnny would rub the laces of his gloves on Joe's back to get him mad, throw his concentration off.

It worked. Joe started throwing wild punches, only to be pounded by carefully executed lefts and rights. Johnny let a few punches slip just so the laces of his gloves would cut Joe's face and eyes, drawing blood and anger. He skillfully cut the ring off and moved in and landed his famous "one two" combination—a right cross followed by a left hook that changed Joe's mind about a boxing career.

They stayed ring friends after that, but Joe kept at his studies. Johnny fell in with a few Outfit crime members, mostly muscle jobs to collect money, but then they took him on a few burglaries. A job went soar, and Johnny ended up in prison. Not for too long—it was his first offence. It happened again, which is how Johnny got his nickname: he served two prison terms for burglary.

Johnny wanted to believe the nickname was for his wicked combination from his South Side Boxing Club days. A "combination that would rock the nation," he used to say.

But Johnny knew it was a slur. They didn't start calling him that until after his second term in prison. This last stretch was commuted to a term overseas with the army for the D-Day invasion. One-Two Johnny was a truly hard case, and it's going to be "One Two Three" Johnny fairly soon. He was implicated in a liquor warehouse heist about a week ago. He's going to be brought in for interrogation maybe tomorrow.

"I wanted to talk to you about something, Joe. Do you think you could give me a listen?" said Johnny.

Joe already heard about it. "John, you're in an awful way with that 100th Street thing, you know."

"Yeah, I know, but this time it ain't me," complained Johnny in a whisper. "I know who's in on it. I can't rat, and I can't do no more time. That'll be strike three. I'll never get out."

"Step into my office," invited Joe, as they walked over to the rear booth. Johnny had a natural rhythm in his walk, as if he were always listening to music. He was a few inches taller than Joe, well over six foot with broad shoulders and a broad face to match and caramel-colored eyes and a few thousand more miles on his face. Joe was older but didn't look it. He had a stunning smile and the suave look of someone who had seen it all—twice. They slid into the booth. Everybody knew what they would talk about. Not much is a secret in this part of the city.

"John, what do you need me to do?" Joe didn't want to take Johnny's case, another case fraught with complications and a sea of troubles.

"Look, you've been gone for a while. Since I got discharged from the army, I got a job at Wisconsin Steel, the coke plant. I'm straight now. A citizen. That thing with the liquor warehouse ain't me."

"So, how'd you get messed up in it?"

"That's an Outfit warehouse. They hit their own place for the insurance, and their guy Sergeant Kavanaugh in the 103rd Street Precinct is lookin' at me. I been up two times for robbery. I'm tailor-made for the fall," he paused, shaking his head, and added, "My pisans."

"When are they supposed to pick you up?"

"I heard tomorrow."

"John, you know what they're going to do. They're going to tell you to confess. If you don't, they'll put you out on the street...."

Johnny understood that meant a contract would be on him. "You know, I got Tommy in Catholic School. I'm doin' good by him since his ma took off on us," he said and paused for moment, weighing his options. "Joe, if I say anything, that kid is an orphan, and if I don't say anything he might as well be an orphan cuz I'm going down forever for this."

Joe had to take this case as much for Tommy as for Johnny and maybe himself, no matter the trouble. "Okay, you're going to need about two grand for bail. I'll get a bondsman. Can you afford bail?"

"Yeah, I got some money saved," Johnny said with a look just short of hope.

"Okay, drop it off at my office tomorrow morning. Wilma will be there. She'll know what to do, and I'll have her sister take care of Tommy." He looked at him with his clear steel blue eyes. "John, I'm not going to sugar this pill—it won't be easy. I'll do my best, and if I pull this off, I'll need most of that bail money."

"I know you will, Joe, I know. If you get me out of this, I won't need the bail money."

Joe looked across stone-faced at Johnny and said, "Now in a few seconds I want you to get up from this booth and shake your head, like you just got bad news. Act like you're mad, like I turned you down flat. Then, later, talk me down at the bar. Tell everyone I wouldn't take your case, that I won't do anything for you."

Johnny knew what was coming, so did Joe. He gave Joe a grave look, got up from the booth fast, turned toward the bar, threw his hand down in disgust, and went back to the end stool to finish his beer. After he sat down, Eddie went from behind the bar over to Joe's booth.

"Anything wrong, Joe?"

"Nothing at all."

"Hey, Ludko called. He's got some important info for you." Eddie handed him the paper with the Drake Hotel's number and a man's name. "Page him here and ask for this name. Use the backroom phone, if you want."

Joe left the booth and headed for Vookie's backroom. It was dingy, but spacious, and often the venue for middleweight poker games, games the Outfit didn't care about. He sat down and made the call to The Drake Hotel Bar.

Looking at the scrap of paper, "Yes, I'd like to talk to a Philip Orsini," Joe asked. He laughed to himself at the countless names Ludko's had invented for himself over the years. The bartender handed the phone to Ludko.

"Hey, you'll never believe who is rooming with our little Miss

Kemidov," challenged Ludko. He didn't wait for an answer. "Frankie Ferrel. Remember him?"

"Yeah, yeah... Frank Ferrel. Wasn't he one of Dixie Monahan's guys? If I remember, Monahan was one great gambler with wild streaks of awfully good luck," Joe said.

"Not too gooda luck. Somehow Monahan ended up owing two-hundred grand to the Outfit. He jumped the states to the Orient with another guy way before the war. Some say Ferrel killed Monahan in Turkey or somethin' like that," added Ludko.

"Lud, be careful of that guy," he warned. "What the hell is she doing with Ferrel?"

"Look, I talked to that sourpuss for over an hour. I couldn't get anything out of him, just his name. I thought he almost made me when I started talking about horses."

"How would he make you on that?" Joe asked incredulously.

"It's a long story, but he's not too bright, so nothin' came of it," said Ludko.

"You're sure he's not brighter than you think?" asked Joe.

"Nah...positive." Shaking his head, "Nobody that ugly could ever have any brains."

"You better hope," said Joe. "He's nobody to mess with. Anyway, Philip, get over to the Trianon, pick Benny up, and meet me at Commercial Ave. Ferrel has changed the plan."

"Yes, boss, be glad to." Ludko handed the phone back to the bartender along with a tip and said, "Thanks." He walked out of The Drake Hotel and over to Michigan Avenue where his Lafayette was parked, an unremarkable car that looked like every other car and was a perfect fit for an unmemorable guy. He took off for the Trianon Ballroom on 63rd and Cottage Grove.

He pulled out on Lake Shore Drive and headed south. He rolled down his window and let the warm night air rush through his car. A couple of scraps of paper started to wrestle around in the back seat. He turned on the radio and was enjoying the dazzling light show that the city and the lake put on after dark. Cruising along the lake on a warm summer's night, radio on, listening to Bing Crosby sing *Day and Night*, it was a little piece of pleasant. He wouldn't see the car tailing him until he made the turn on to Cottage Grove Avenue. For now, he simply enjoyed the music and the cool night air.

He made the turn and spotted the tail. Lights in his mirror.

"So, that ugly rat made me after all," Ludko said out load. "But he can't know me." He tried to remember: Had they ever met before? *No, he must have remembered me from the hall by their room.* He sped up, so did the other car. The stop light up ahead was about to turn red. He blew the light hoping that that would shake the tail.

It didn't.

Ludko picked up speed, so did his pursuer. The street lights were flying by and the night air rushed in through the open window. He made a right turn so sharp, everything in the front seat slued over against him—racing forms, newspapers, shoes, hats. He slammed on the brakes and hit the lights. Pitch black.

The pursuer sped past him into the night. He drove slowly to the next block made a left then another left, turned on his lights, and got back on Cottage Grove heading toward 63rd Street and the Trianon, his heart still pounding so hard he could feel the beat in his ears. *I shook 'em.*

He eased into the parking lot and took a deep breath. He entered the Trianon's lobby with its candelabra chandelier and grand staircase leading to the ballroom. Tex Beneke's *Hey-Ba-Ba-Rebop* was playing, and the dance floor was packed.

The Trianon was the most expensive and extravagant dance hall in the country. Decorated in Louis XVI-style decor and elegant furnishings, it gave its patrons the fantasy of wealth and sophistication. The dance floor could accommodate three thousand dancers and had six floor men to keep the guests in line. Management banned smoking by its female patrons, but not male patrons. Smoking by women contradicted the ballroom's image as a dance establishment that upheld traditional, middle-class behavior in a way that less highly regarded dance halls and cabarets did not. Still, some women insisted on smoking, and the floor men would routinely remind them: "Ladies, please, you are not permitted to smoke. *This* is the Trianon."

After about twenty minutes, Ludko spotted Benny on the floor with what appeared to be a beautiful girl, at least from the back. Despite his extra weight, Benny the Hat was an outstanding dancer, one of the best on the South Side. Ludko went over and tapped him on the shoulder and said, "We gotta go."

"Who the hell is this guy, Benny," she asked.

"Uh...he's like my boss, sorta," replied Benny. "I hav'ta go, but I'll catch yuz here next week, right?"

She squeezed her eyes down thin and said, "Well, I don't know. We'll see. Go on with your boss here."

"Ahh come on. I'll teach yuz some other steps. What do yuh say?" pleaded Benny.

"I don't know," she said and walked off.

"Boy, this better be good. I don't get to meet girls like that every day yuh know," complained Benny as they went down the grand staircase toward the door. Benny stopped at the coatroom to pick up his hat. He gave the girl his ticket.

"Thanks," he said as he handed her a liberal tip.

"Boy, you sure throw the money around," remarked Ludko.

"Hey, she took good care of my Stetson. It's a Whippet, cost ten bucks."

Ludko filled Benny in on the way to Joe's office—about the tail from The Drake and how cleverly he ducked it. Benny was moderately impressed. As they made their way south, Benny kept talking about the girl he just met, how beautiful she was. They arrived at Joe's building and went right up to his office. When they got there, Joe was on the phone with Detective Donnelly from the Grand Crossing Police District, a longtime friend. He hung up. "Hey, that was Donnelly. I told him about Frank Ferrel. Have a seat." They each brushed off the dust from the chairs in front of Joe's desk and gave him a "look."

"What?" said Joe. "I'm getting a maid already."

Ludko said, "About time. Hey, Joe, somebody tailed me from The Drake. I ducked him at Cottage Grove."

"It had to be Ferrel," said Joe.

"Who's Ferrel?" asked Benny.

Ludko turned to him and answered, "He's a killer. Works for the Outfit."

Benny took his hat off.

"It ain't what you think," Ludko said. "Don't get excited. He ain't *in* the Outfit, just works for 'em."

"Oh, yeah, like that makes me feel any better," moaned Benny. "Joe, what's goin' on here?"

"He's somehow involved in this Polina case. Ludko found out about him only today," said Joe. Looking at Ludko he continued, "I talked to Detective Donnelly. He thinks Ferrel probably killed Monahan, and being with Miss Kemidov can't be good news." The windows behind Joe's desk were open, and the cool night air glided into the office.

"Monahan? The gambler? That guy killed him?" Benny asked in a strained, high-pitched voice.

"Well, that's what Donnelly thinks. He's a contract killer probably hired by the Outfit to even the score with Monahan, but I can't figure why he's with Polina."

Ludko said, "I don't know, maybe Ferrel's her bodyguard, just like he was for Monahan. Hey—she ain't tied up with the Outfit is she?"

"I doubt it," said Joe, leaning back in his chair. "I'll have at least a few answers tomorrow when I get a reply back from London. But Ferrel puts a new drift on this thing. We have to find out why and how he's involved. That's where you come in, Benny. You have to be at The Drake in the morning."

"Me?"

"Yeah, you."

With a turned down smile, Benny reluctantly nodded his head. "Okay."

"But for tonight, Benny, you have to fill in for me. Ludko's going to take you to the Blue Moon Club in Beverly."

Benny perked up and said, "Hey, that's a good Jazz club. Lotta pretty girls in there."

Joe handed Benny a photograph of a would-be politician. "See this guy?"

"Yeah," answered Benny. He passed the photograph over to Ludko.

"He's an up-and-coming politician, supposed to be at the Blue Moon tonight. If you spot him hanging on any of those girls, get pictures with this camera." Joe handed him a tiny Minox camera loaded with high-speed film for low-light conditions, like inside bars, restaurants, or clubs.

"Hey, now this assignment *really* spins my hat. Who we workin' for?"

"Alderman Clancey," Joe answered. "And get pictures of the guy not pictures of the girls, okay?" Joe shook his head. " You have to be at The Drake in the morning. Pick up the shadow on Ferrel."

"Sure thing, Joe," said Benny. He looked over impatiently and said, "Come on. We'd better get goin', Lud."

Before they left, Joe said, "Ludko, you can help Benny for as long as you want, but drop by tomorrow morning." They both headed out the door and down the stairs.

Joe stepped into his darkroom, a large converted closet, and started to develop the film of the businessman's wife from a few hours ago.

In the darkroom, in the total blackness, in the silence, Joe carefully removed the film from the Contax camera. He groped in the blackness for the stainless steel developing tank, about the size of a large coffee cup. He opened it, felt inside for the film reel, and removed it. As he wound the film around the reel, Polina occupied his thoughts. What was her connection to Ferrel? To the NKVD? Why had he let himself into the kind of case he swore he wouldn't take again, not ever again, not after the Manhattan Project matter? What compelled him? He wanted no more smoke, no more involvement with professional killers working for governments, friendly or not.

The film was completely on the reel now. He dropped it back inside the little tank. He put the lid back on. It was safe from light now. He pulled the dangling chain and light flooded the closet. He opened the door. Joe went over to his bathroom sink and mixed a dilution of Rodinal developer. He measured out what he needed, made a dilution, and poured it into the tank. It always amazed him that the developer could enter the tank but not the light. He started the rhythmic agitations of the tank, which would reveal the images on the film now safely rocking inside. Every thirty seconds he would invert the tank a few times and set it back down on the shelf by the sink.

Now, in the light, looking at himself in the mirror, he justified the Polina case as one where he could actually help someone, a case where he could bring some good out of a war that brought so much evil into the world. Maybe Ludko was right—Ferrel was just a bodyguard—a frightened woman, desperately trying to help a family member escape a network of ruthless Soviet agents, agents Joe knew were capable of everything.


It was getting too late. Joe decided to sleep in the office instead of going all the way back to his apartment in Hyde Park. The couch had served as his bed many times before; besides, he wanted to be in the office in case Hamilton sent a response.

He had been asleep for maybe an hour, on the edge of dream, when someone kicked the door to his office open, and there in the dark of early morning stood a black figure with a gun.

Joe woke with a start. He was up on his feet instantly. Adrenalin surged through his body. Instinctively he went toward his desk to put a barricade between him and what he now saw was a gun.

"Get away from that desk," he shouted. "Stand over there."

Joe didn't recognize the gunman. "Hey, what's this all about?" Joe asked groggily, knowing that he had to get over to the file cabinet where he kept another gun.

"You got someone tailin' me, snooper?"

"What are you talking about? I don't even know you." Joe said. *So you're Frankie Ferrel.*

Ferrel waved his gun. "Don't know me? Well, here's my calling card." He came closer to Joe. "You put a tail on me, and I ain't no monkey. See?"

"I've never seen you before," said Joe, "and get that gun out of my face. You're giving me a complex."

"I'll give you more than that if I don't get a straight answer," said Ferrel. "I tailed a guy that was at our hotel right here to this office, just a few hours ago," Ferrel said. "What do you say to that?"

"That someone is one of my clients, and I cannot give you his name," Joe said defiantly.

"What's he want with me?" Ferrel demanded.

"Nothing that I know of. I'm doing a tail job on his wife. I told him she's meeting someone at The Drake Hotel. Maybe he took a look for himself. Maybe he didn't believe me. I don't know. So much distrust these days... don't you think?"

"Drop it. I want to know what he's doin' sniffin' around my hotel."

"Are you saying you want to hire me to double cross my client and investigate him for you?"

No sooner had Joe said that, Ferrel's gun hit him on the side of the head so hard he lost his balance and fell back into the file cabinet. "No, peeper, I want you to give him that message. Understand?" Ferrel closed in and hit him again. Joe slumped to the floor.

## CHAPTER THREE

LONDON, ENGLAND

*Hotel Cavendish*

Lawrence Hamilton was a fastidious man, rising early, morning calisthenics, breakfast, and start the day. Today would begin with a knock at the door. He was met by a youthful bellhop with a telegram. Hamilton took the telegram directly, gave the boy a two shilling tip, and closed the door. The years of stress from receiving such telegrams showed on his face, the wrinkles darkened, the mouth sagged. He steeled himself for whatever the contents might be.

The relief at seeing "GANZER" at the bottom of the message gave this jaded MI5 agent a rush of excitement, a sense of the old drama. Hamilton met Joe as a trainee when he was assigned to the Toronto division during the war. His thoughts turned now to the message and saw it was in the old Slater Code with a couple of substitution codes thrown in. *Must be names*, he thought.

His rooms at the Hotel Cavendish were just short of elegant, a ruse in his current role as an antiquities dealer but also a reward for risking his life for the Crown. He walked past his desk and the chaise longue to a large bookcase against the wall. He removed a heavy tome and opened it to reveal its hollowed-out, inner compartment. Hamilton removed the Slater code book, sat at his desk, and went to work decoding the message. He knew Joe would use "1776" as his offset number. He smiled at that, and some of those years returned to him. His hair was mostly gray now with some stragglers of black, which belied his age, an asset at times when enemy agents underestimated his speed and strength.

He had that part of the message decoded. "Now, to those

names—" and he laughed out loud, remembering the transposition code word: SNAFUWY, concocted by Joe when Hamilton trained him at Canada's Camp X outside Toronto.

Camp X was only 30 miles west of Toronto, but it was a world away from any ordinary Canadian city. Its denizens included Italians, Hungarians, Croatians, and Germans, all recruited as spies for service throughout occupied Europe. Men like Hamilton would train them in the art and craft of espionage.

Being only miles from the United States made Camp X perfect for training US agents like Joe Ganzer. The Office of Strategic Services (OSS), the US wartime intelligence agency, handpicked Joe Ganzer for their X-2 branch of counterintelligence. His journey behind the veil began there.

Camp X was the Allies' university of espionage with Lawrence Hamilton one of its professors. Joe was one of their star pupils, top of his OSS class. The school had an extensive library, weapons, enemy uniforms, insignia, a shooting range, a 90-foot jump tower, and a telecommunications center (code named HYDRA) which received top-secret coded data from around the world. A spy factory.

Those Camp X days seemed so long ago to Hamilton. He smiled now remembering Joe's transposition key, and how they used it later during operations in the States. The code worked by placing the word SNAFUWY beneath the regular alphabet and skipping every other letter:

```
A B C D E F G H I J K L M N O P Q R S T U V W X Y Z
S   N   A   F   U   W   Y
```

Then, the coder put the rest of the letters back together in reverse order, so it looked like:

```
A B C D E F G H I J K L M N O P Q R S T U V W X Y Z
S Z N X A V F T U R W Q Y P O M L K J I H G E D C B
```

TRYING TO LOCATE GENERAL YURI KEMIDOV
LAST KNOWN ADDRESS ALHAMBRA HOTEL.

Not a sophisticated code by any means, but one that would prevent anyone except a cryptographer from knowing its contents. Hamilton arranged the clear text on a sheet of paper with the "Hotel Cavendish" discreetly printed across the top, he wrote out:

He memorized the message without delay and set it ablaze in an ashtray on the writing desk. The Alhambra Hotel was only a few miles from the Cavendish. He grabbed his coat and headed downstairs for the lobby and the street. He hailed a nearby cab. "Alhambra Hotel, please," he said as he entered the back seat.

He watched out the window at the remnants of unimaginable terror, now in neat piles of what was once London. *We'll rebuild*, he thought. Londoners were mounting an intense reconstruction effort, but the scars, both external and internal, would remain.

He arrived at the Alhambra on Argyle Street. Hamilton got out of the cab and went straight to the front desk. "I am to meet a Mr. Kemidov here for business this morning. Is he in?" asked Hamilton. The clerk looked over his glasses at Hamilton in that suspicious and curious manner that only a hotel clerk can manage.

"No, I am sorry Mr. Kemidov left rather abruptly. Let me see...." The desk clerk looked in his registry and added, "Yes, here it is. He left over two weeks ago under disturbing circumstances."

"Why do you say disturbing?"

"Well, delicately, sir, he departed without settling his account."

"I see," said Hamilton. "Of course, he left no forwarding address."

"No, I am again sorry. He left late in the evening. I was not at the desk, or I would have challenged him directly." Leaning toward Hamilton, the clerk offered his personal analysis. "He did not appear the sort to leave his account open, but one never knows."

Hamilton, sensing suspicion by the clerk, asked, "I have never met Mr. Kemidov, only through correspondence. You say he appeared trustworthy?"

"A distinguished gentleman, yes. About your age, I would imagine, gray hair, impeccably dressed. I was curious about that scar at his temple. Perhaps a war wound."

"Well, Mr. Kemidov may have been called away on some immediacy. These days, you know. Perhaps he will return to right his account."

Then spoken like a dedicated employee, the clerk added, "We can only hope, sir."

"Yes, I am sure he left many loose ends in his business affairs—mine being one of them. If he returns, would you give him my card." Hamilton handed him his card, which read:

Lawrence Hamilton, Esq.
Antiquities
Hotel Cavendish

The clerk studied his card carefully. "Indeed, Mr. Hamilton, I will tender this to Mr. Kemidov should he return." Impressed with Hamilton's credentials, the clerk offered, "You are now the second person to inquire upon Mr. Kemidov of late. They did not receive the news of his departure as candidly as you, sir."

"Perhaps a relative?" suggested Hamilton wanting more information, knowing the clerk's quibbling, polemic nature.

"Hardly," replied the clerk. "This inquirer seemed more alarmed than remorseful, bordering—it seemed—on anger."

Hamilton, goading him, "This war has affected so many of us in so many different ways. It could simply be he wished to reunite with a wartime comrade and was disappointed."

"He?" exclaimed the clerk. " No, it was a woman that inquired after him, only days after Mr. Kemidov absconded."

Hamilton countered, "A jilted lover?"

"Not likely, she was so much younger...." Reconsidering, he added, "Of course, he certainly appeared wealthy, so perhaps. She left no name, no card. Simply turned and walked out."

Hamilton shook his head. "Curious." He hesitated tapping his finger on the counter, knowing the clerk would fill the emptiness.

Glancing again at Hamilton's business card, the clerk remarked, "I see you are in a similar business as Mr. Kemidov."

Hamilton was off guard now. "Well, in a manner of speaking."

"But, it was my understanding he dealt with art, not antiquities, like you, sir."

"Yes, he was expanding his pursuits," said Hamilton, deliberately vague.

"A number of his visitors were gallery owners here in London, some from abroad. In fact..." He looked in his record and produced a card. "Ah... here we are. Michael Cooper Gallery, very prestigious." He proffered it to Hamilton.

"Yes, I do business with them occasionally." He glanced at it for a moment and handed it back, his photographic memory capturing it all. "Well, thank you so much for your help." He handed him a 10-shilling note and asked, "May I impose upon you to call a cab?"

Without hesitation, the clerk said, "Certainly, Mr. Hamilton." He turned and picked up the phone.

Outside the Alhambra, across the street in a dark alcove, something moved in the shadow, like someone hiding. Hamilton came out of the hotel and entered the cab. He was heading for the book store.

As Hamilton drove off, a tall gaunt man with pale skin and deep-set dark eyes emerged from the shadows of the doorway. He crossed the street to the hotel and would soon ask the presumptuous desk clerk the same questions as did Hamilton, but for entirely different reasons.

Hamilton told the driver to proceed immediately to Blacklands Terrace and King's Road. They sped off, past the rubble and bombed-out buildings. At those crossroads, the cab came to a halt. Hamilton emerged from the cab and walked two blocks toward Treadwell Bookseller. The building looked like any other shop in London—small, two-story, charming with multiple glazed windows showcasing stacks of books inside. The upper story had two windows facing the street each with flower boxes brimming with vivid deep reddish-purple geraniums.

Throughout the war, Treadwell Bookseller was a "double cross" center for MI5, run by the unassuming Harry Treadwell. As many as thirty Nazi espionage agents were apprehended and placed under direct control of MI5 as double agents. Harry Treadwell, from inside the Treadwell Bookseller store, directed a number of these double agents, sending disinformation to their Nazi controllers. Harry even had a wireless transmitter on the second floor of the bookstore to send deliberately inaccurate information sprinkled with accurate (but useless) intelligence to the Nazis, as if from their own agents. Harry was a rather good "piano player," the term used for radio operators. He could impersonate the "fist" of almost any wireless operator. He carried on this charade until the end of the war. Harry was an integral part of the Twenty Committee, taking its name from the Roman numerals "XX," the double-cross system. He was one of the lead coordinators, using the turned agents of the Nazi Abwehr and Sicherheitsdienst (the dreaded SD), to misinform their handlers back in Germany. Today, Harry is the case officer for an elite group of MI5 operatives in Britain and the broader United Kingdom.

Every agent has a case officer, the man who "runs" him. The case officer is the agent's accountant, keeping track of all the details so that there will be no miscues, no contradictions. Harry Treadwell was more than that: he was his agent's liaison, backup man, big brother, and father. Spymaster Harry Treadwell became their one reality in their world of illusions.

Hamilton pulled open the door. The bell chime announced him. As he entered, there was that unmistakable musty smell of old books. Harry Treadwell greeted him. "How may I help you?" Harry was perplexed to see one of his agents arrive unannounced.

Hamilton could see the store was empty. "I took no chances if that's what you imply," he said defensively. "I am pressed for time and need to access our books and identify a possible NKVD agent."

"Let's go upstairs to my office," said Harry, concerned at Hamilton's request. As they walked to the rear of the store passing rows of book shelves, Harry asked, "Do you have a name?"

"General Yuri Kemidov is what I was given. It is an alias, I believe."

"How did you come by that name?" asked Harry as he climbed the stairs. Harry was in his early 70s, hair nearly all white, with unruly eyebrows above black glasses, a man of books. The stairs creaked as they ascended them, carefully engineered creaks intended to announce a visitor who should somehow bypass the door chime.

"I had a request to locate Yuri Kemidov from a former OSS colleague, Joseph Ganzer, in the Colonies."

Harry furrowed his white brow and said, "Ah, I do recall, you and he knew each other."

"Indeed, he was an outstanding agent, a star pupil. He returned to civilian life after the war, after his last assignment. He only contacted me to discover what I could about the situation of a General Kemidov."

As they entered his office, Harry remarked with barely a smile, "This all sounds quite intriguing, Lawrence."

That tone in his voice and that smile told Hamilton that Harry questioned the relevance of this investigation to MI5. "Joseph suspects NKVD. He sent his inquiry in code via telegram. I received it this morning."

Satisfied with the explanation, Harry walked over to the top bookshelf beside his office desk. "Then let us proceed from there. We have a book here of known NKVD agents in Western Europe. Look through them. See if you can find our General."

Hamilton went through page after page of photographs and dossiers. Nothing. The door chimed. Harry abruptly left Hamilton to attend his customer in the bookstore. Hamilton could hear their lively discussion about James Joyce and Ernest Hemingway and authors he did not recognize. He resumed his search and found an entry describing a NKVD operative known only as "The General," an informant working in Switzerland before the war. He heard the door chime as the customer left. The stairs creaked as Harry labored back up them.

Winded at the top, Harry asked, "Any luck?"

"Just this entry for a low-level NKVD informant known as 'The General'. "

Harry went over to the desk and read the account. "It states here this chap is dead."

"Yes, but see here, MI6 didn't eliminate him."

"NKVD kill their own quite often, you know," Harry said with the whisper of a lament.

"The report says that he was killed by Corsicans over some art swindle."

"It's not unusual for NKVD field agents to line their pockets whatever way they can. This one just chose the wrong people to swindle."

"The General I'm looking for is very much alive," said Hamilton, "or at least he was until about two weeks ago when the desk clerk at the Alhambra Hotel said he absconded without paying his bill. He also said Kemidov was an art dealer of sorts, even had business with a representative of the Michael Cooper Gallery."

"Well, the swindle sounds like your man, as does the involvement with the art world. I seem to recall a bulletin on that gallery, though. Michael Cooper was it?"

"Yes, that's what the clerk said. I saw the card myself."

Harry pulled a report from his files and studied it. "Just what I thought."

"What?"

"It seems we have an MI5 agent inside the Michael Cooper Gallery, gathering intelligence on a group of former SS members converting stolen art into cash to finance some new campaign. I'm afraid that is all we have in here."

"Can we find out who he is?"

"That is a separate operation, Lawrence, outside of my purview. I shall try, but I think I have a better ploy," said Harry as he read further in the report. "It states here Scotland Yard also has the Michael Cooper Gallery under surveillance. Apparently, they have Cooper under investigation for trafficking in stolen art."

"And you think we can get more information out of Scotland Yard than our own agency?"

"Not more, Lawrence, just sooner. MI5 is at cross purposes with the Yard on this, obviously. We don't know and can't know what another MI5 unit's mission entails, but we can extract what we need for *our* purposes from the unsuspecting Yard."

"Quite right."

"I shall need to contact Scotland Yard and arrange for a 'friendly' exchange."

"The cops do not trust the spooks," said Hamilton.

"And vice versa, it seems, considering our agent is inside that gallery. We must tread carefully," said Harry.

"How can we get the Yard to cooperate?"

"An exchange of intelligence, my dear Lawrence," said Harry with his calming baritone. "Scotland Yard will be thrilled to learn that their investigation has unearthed the living dead."

Hamilton laughed, "A real spook, eh?"

"Surely. Now I must ring some bells to wake them at the Yard." Harry took the phone and started making calls. Another customer arrived. Hamilton looked at Harry, who nodded. He hurried down the stairs to assist. Hamilton looked out of place in the Treadwell Bookseller store, too virile, too polished, someone unaccustomed to books.

His customer, a portly woman in her fifties, asked for help locating a copy of *Leaves from the Journal of Our Life in the Highlands, from 1848 to 1881* by Queen Victoria. Hamilton was lost. From the second floor, Harry shouted at the top of the stairs, "It's in the last bookcase at the rear. I think on the third shelf."

They walked to the rear of the store, through a labyrinth of bookshelves so narrow the woman could hardly squeeze between them. Then in the last case, sure enough, there it was on the third shelf. The woman looked admiringly at Hamilton, as if he had personally located it for her. She inspected the book carefully, nearly every page, for what seemed an eternity. "Thank you ever so much, my dear man. I shall have it." They moved back through the bookcases to the front of the store, where she paid absentmindedly, looking slyly at Hamilton as she tendered the money. The door chimed as she left, and Hamilton lit up the stairs to Harry's office.

"Quite a good sale I must say. Do I receive a commission?" asked Hamilton.

"After I extract my finder's fee, I'm afraid you will owe me a fiver."

Hamilton loved the old man. "So where are we now?"

"You have an appointment with Inspector Raynes, who is not altogether willing to share findings in their investigation but will hear what you have to offer."

"How accommodating the Yard is."

Harry leaned forward, placing his elbows on his desk. "You meet with him. I have a few more calls to make, but I assure you he will give you whatever they have by the time I'm through." Harry smiled and added, "Your cab will be here any minute."

"Excellent, Harry. I may even pay you the five pounds."

"Off with you now. Don't keep the Inspector waiting."

The black cab pulled up to Treadwell Bookseller. This was no ordinary cabby but one of Harry Treadwell's "East End Tommys," trustworthy citizens from the working class who were Harry's eyes and ears outside the espionage community. Usually, the intelligence officer gathers information unfettered by his case officer, but Harry suspected that MI5 might become entangled in a problematic international situation with the American OSS. So, he attached one of his East End Tommys to report on things from another perspective.

Hamilton got in the cab and said, "Scotland Yard, please."

"Right, suh, Whitehall Place it is then. No trouble, I 'ope," said the driver.

"No. I'm meeting a friend for lunch, an inspector," said Hamilton. The cab pulled away from the curb.

"I been there meself a few times under curious circumstances," said the driver.

"Curious, how?" asked Hamilton.

"Seems, the police thought I was involved in a series of robberies. This is way before, when I was a younger man."

"I see."

"They hadn't a thing on me, you understand? Had to lets me go."

"I'm sure they had the wrong man."

"Indeed they did, suh. Indeed they did. Mickey Browne never committed no robberies. No, suh." They drove on in silence. Hamilton watched as the city flew by, past Hyde Park and Piccadilly toward Westminster.

In Chicago, in the small dark hours past midnight, a phone is ringing. It is Benny the Hat calling Joe Ganzer's apartment to tell him he and Ludko had just captured that would-be politician on film flaming drunk and hanging all over two girls at the Blue Moon Club.

"Hey, Ludko," Benny yelled over the din of the crowd, "there's no answer. I know it's late but—"

"He's probably still at the office. Try there."

"Okay, yeah." Benny hung up the receiver and the coins jangled into the return slot. He grabbed them and tried again.

The phone rang and rang and rang.

Benny shrugged, "No answer."

"Let it ring, he's probably in his little darkroom or somethin'."

But there would be no answer.

Hamilton arrived at Whitehall Place, the suite of buildings making up Scotland Yard, the headquarters of the London Metropolitan Police Service. He paid and tipped the driver,

"Why, thank you kindly, guv'nor," said Mickey Browne. He tipped his hat and drove away, like a man possessed.

Hamilton smiled, turned, and looked up. Two large Romanesque male statues stood above and either side of the equally large entrance doors, all meant to inspire and intimidate the criminals and miscreants with the power and grandeur of law enforcement.

Hamilton went through the doors to the central desk and asked for Inspector Raynes. He was directed back into the bowels of Scotland Yard. Door after door he passed until he reached the rather small office of Inspector Raynes. His secretary stopped him.

"I'm here for an appointment with the inspector."

"Name please?" she asked perfunctorily, looking down at the appointment book.

"Lawrence Hamilton."

"Yes, I have you right here. One moment, please." She left her desk and entered the inner office and announced him. "You may go right in, Mr. Hamilton."

"Thank you." He walked past her through the door into an unimpressive office that looked like any other bureaucrat's office anywhere in London.

"Good morning," greeted Inspector Raynes, thrusting his hand out. They shook hands. "Please have a seat." Hamilton sat down across from Raynes, a bulbous man, balding, dark eyes and complexion, putting on more weight, a bureaucrat well suited to his office, but his crooked nose and small facial scars told of his days as a bobby.

"I understand you have the Michael Copper Gallery under surveillance," said Hamilton getting straight to the matter.

"What can I help you with, Mr. Hamilton?" said the inspector, not committing to anything.

"You understand, I do not have any interest in your investigation, per se," said Hamilton, allaying the inspector's concerns that the security services were out to railroad his investigation. "We are looking to establish the identity of someone who may be involved with the gallery now under your investigation."

"Who are you looking for?" asked the inspector, still trying to limit what he would reveal.

"A representative from the Michael Cooper Gallery contacted our target at the Alhambra Hotel approximately two weeks ago."

"Why should that concern Scotland Yard?" remarked the inspector as he leaned back smugly in his chair.

"The target is thought to be a NKVD agent operating here in London. We need to locate him."

"Go to the Alhambra. I'm sure you'll find him there."

"If I walk out of this office without obtaining the information that we need, I promise you, within a year you will be back in a bobby's cape standing in the rain wondering why you didn't help us when you had the chance."

The inspector looked stunned. "You blokes don't have that kind of power."

"Shall I leave and let us roll the dice?"

Inspector Raynes straightened up in his chair, "Does your target have a name?"

Hamilton said unemotionally, "Yuri Kemidov...which may be his alias."

"That name hasn't come up in our investigation, not a single time. Do you have a description of the *target*." He said "target" with a taste of sarcasm that angered Hamilton but didn't deter him.

"He is middle-aged, well-dressed, salt-and-pepper hair and a scar at his temple."

"Well, that narrows it down to just about every client going in or out of that gallery, except for the scar."

"May I see your surveillance photographs?"

"What good will that do? I just said that just includes about everybody coming—"

"I want the photos from the Alhambra."

"What makes you think I have any from that location?"

"Despite your abrasive character, I believe you are an excellent policeman. You put tails on the representatives of the gallery, I am sure. Let's have a look, shall we?"

The forthright compliment warmed the inspector, who reached behind him for a thick album of annotated surveillance photographs. He opened it on his desk. Hamilton stood and went over to look at them. "Let's see," said the inspector leafing through pages of surveillance photographs. "Well I'll be.... Here's one of Cooper's men entering the Alhambra Hotel."

"Do you have any of this fellow leaving the hotel?"

"I'm sure we have. Be patient." He turned more pages, then paused. "This is the Cooper man leaving."

"Indeed," said Hamilton. They both looked carefully at the photograph of the Michael Copper representative leaving, almost to the street, with a thin rectangular parcel under his arm. Further back in the picture, at the door, about to leave the hotel, was a man fitting Kemidov's basic description. "This might be our man here," said Hamilton as he pointed to man at the door of the hotel.

"Here, let me have a look at it," said Inspector Raynes, taking a magnifying glass out of the center drawer of his desk. "Let's have a closer look at this gentleman." The inspector stood over the photograph with the glass. Then, as if startled, he stood erect, looked Hamilton in the eye and said, "I know this chap."

"Who is he?"

"Not your Kemidov, I'm afraid. That's Mr. Hugo Morand."

# CHAPTER FOUR

LONDON, ENGLAND
*Scotland Yard*

Hamilton looked at the inspector intensely. "Who is Hugo Morand?"

"He is an international art swindler and quite possibly a murderer. It's a good thing you came along with this. We would have completely overlooked this photograph."

"It's not like Scotland Yard to overlook anything," Hamilton said with an invisible smile, raising his eyebrow, as he inspected the man in the photograph.

"Now see here," protested the inspector, "we are understaffed, and the war is still having its effect upon us."

Hamilton looked up benignly, "Of course, of course...." Having had his fun, he asked, "Tell me about Hugo Morand."

"Well, we have been alerted about him by the French government. It seems Morand was a reptilian Swiss art dealer who swindled Parisian Jews out of their art and then turned them over to the Gestapo. For his kind help in locating enemies of the Reich, the Gestapo agreed to split any money they confiscated with him. In most cases, that was more money than he had paid for the art."

Hamilton added, "Jews were indeed desperate to escape the Nazis. They sold anything and everything to have money to buy their way out of Occupied France."

Inspector Raynes said, "Morand selected only wealthy Jews who had fine art worthy of his beneficence."

Nazis were looting art all over Europe, but nowhere were they more rapacious than France. The art markets of France and the Netherlands were hives of vermin, teaming with collaborators, opportunists, and shady middlemen, like Hugo Morand. Thousands of objects, even entire collections, were seized or swindled by the likes of Morand and stored at the Jue de Paume Museum in Paris. At the bottom of this barrel of human garbage was Hermann Goering, the ruthless and powerful Reichsmarchall. Goering was amassing a fortune in stolen art at his lair outside Berlin named Carinhall, after his wife. Goering's collection rivaled most all the museums in Europe.

"Let me get the file on this bird," The inspector said and stepped out of his office, leaving Hamilton to study the photograph. Although grainy, he could see that the man at the door of the hotel fit the description, at least generally, of Yuri Kemidov. He could not tell if there was a scar. The image lacked sufficient clarity. After a few minutes, Raynes returned.

"I have it now," said the inspector opening the file. "The name 'Hugo Morand' turned up in Goering's records of all places, discovered by Joop Piller, the resistance fighter, after the Allies liberated Paris. They also found these photographs of Goering in Paris at the Jue de Paume. Inspector Raynes pointed out in the photograph. "See here—from right to left—it shows this German art dealer Bruno Loshe and Hermann Goering. And look here, in the background, none other than our Hugo Morand.

"And see, it states here Loshe was arrested in May of 1945 and testified against his fellow looters, including lurid details about Morand. Loshe claimed that Morand had, by way of murder, obtained a statue of a bird that once belonged to the Knights Templar, going all the way back to the Crusades. Can you believe that? A golden falcon, it was. 'Encrusted with jewels' it says here. I don't know how much truth there is to that tale."

Hamilton interjected, "But they never got their hands on Morand, then?"

"No," replied the inspector. "They apprehended all the other sewer rats but not him." He paused and added, "In fact, Goering's in Nuremburg right now awaiting the gallows."

"Yes, I know."

At first the inspector looked surprised that Hamilton would know about Goering, but then realized he was MI5 and dismissed the thought. "How Morand arrived here in London is not Scotland Yard's concern, but we will definitely expand our case to include him now. We'll turn him over to the French when we catch up to him."

"But how Morand got to London is *our* concern, inspector," said Hamilton. "He had to have had considerable help."

"Who would help a Nazi collaborator?"

"That is what we need to discover," said Hamilton abruptly. "Thank you so much for your time, Inspector. I shall include your diligent assistance in my report." He shook the inspector's hand. "Good day, then." Hamilton exited the office and headed out of Scotland Yard to Whitehall Place. He motioned for a cab.

A cab pulled up immediately. "Where now, guv'nor?" said Mickey Browne. Hamilton was amused to see him. He got in the cab. "I felt bad takin' off on you like that, so I stuck around in case you needed to get away in a hurry."

"Well, thank you, Mr. Browne; but I hardly need to escape the police. I am trying to help the police, Mickey."

"Uh oh! Me and me bloody big mouth. I knew I should keep quiet about me past."

Hamilton laughed. "It's not what you think. I'm helping the police apprehend a Nazi collaborator."

Mickey let out his breath. "I fought the Jerries in the Great War, but these Nazis were bloody worse, I say." He turned and looked out the driver's window and said, "Look what they've done to us."

Hamilton said, "Would you like to help us locate this collaborator?"

"Me? How?"

"Do you know any cabbies who work the Alhambra Hotel area?"

"I surely do."

"Excellent. Could you try to find out if one of them had a fare about two weeks ago fitting the description of a middle-aged man, graying hair and a scar at his left temple."

"I'll ask about...but, no offence, fares all start to look alike after a while."

"I'm thinking this fare may have been harried, disconcerted, and it would have been late at night."

"Unglued, eh?"

"Yes, if anyone remembers him, I can be reached at the Hotel Cavendish." He handed Mickey his card over the seat.

"I'd certainly rather deal with you than Scotland Yard. Not that I have any trouble, mind you."

"No...No." Hamilton just smiled.

"Did I tell you about how I almost got barred from picking up fares from Euston Station during the bombings?" Mickey didn't wait for an answer. "I was in the taxi rank, and I sees this couple. Must've come in from Manchester. Everybody was goin' there to escape the bloody bombings. This couple had two suitcases, a pram, and a little baby. The line must have stretched around the station. So, I gets it in me head to just drive ahead and get them. So's they don't have to wait in the queue for hours. The porters were yelling as I pulled up. They had First Class passengers and officers, but I went right past 'em. Picked that couple up and took 'em all to Waterloo. Wouldn't even take their tip. No, sir. Course threats were made by the station staff. Tried to bar me, they did."

"We need noble gestures like yours in times of war."

"My feelin's precisely," replied Mickey. "We're almost to Treadwell Bookseller." He turned the corner and pulled up to the door.

Hamilton exited the cab and paid Mickey with a handsome tip.

"Awfully generous of you guv'nor—ah—Mr. Hamilton."

Hamilton leaned into the cab and said, "Help me locate that man, Mickey."

"I'll try me best."

"Thank you." Hamilton turned and entered the bookstore. The door chimed merrily.

Harry greeted him and said, "Well, how did you get on with Scotland Yard?"

"Frosty at first, but they came along. They gave me the name of Hugo Morand, an art dealer in Paris. I believe our Kemidov is actually Mr. Morand. He is a Nazi collaborator. Do you think we have anything in our files about Morand?"

"Let's go check the files." Harry headed up the steps slowly as Hamilton followed. When they entered the office Harry walked over to his file cabinets. "Paris, you say?"

"Yes."

He opened one cabinet drawer after another, searching through files. Then, grabbing a file, "Here it is—Hugo Morand. Let's see here. Identified as a double agent working for the Nazis and the NKVD. He posed as a Swiss art dealer as his cover. He was a minor player, we thought, and didn't justify additional surveillance, but our MI6 boys captured some photographs of him in occupied Paris. One here with his morbid-looking henchman, identified in the dossier as 'Molyneaux—the butcher.'" He leaned over his desk and showed Hamilton the pictures.

Hamilton scrutinized them and remarked, "A scar at the temple."

"What's that, you say?"

"The scar. See here," said Hamilton as he indicated the left temple. "Hugo Morand is most assuredly Yuri Kemidov, aka 'The General.'"

"I believe you're on to something," said Harry as he inspected the photo again.

"A clever deception. Kemidov is not only a master criminal but a double-crossing spy as well."

"Is there a difference?" Harry said with a stifled laugh. "And I suppose Scotland Yard wants the criminal."

Hamilton smiled at his case officer's joke. "They think he is Hugo Morand and are planning to turn him over to the French government if they ever apprehend him."

"We cannot let them have him, Lawrence. He's worth far too much to us."

Hamilton nodded knowingly. "I understand."

Harry added, "Unfortunately we have no leads on Kemidov's current location."

"Something hastened his departure from the Alhambra, but I believe he is still in the city."

"As do I," agreed Harry.

Hamilton continued, "He is not working with the NKVD. He is using them. They smuggled him out of Paris, for whatever reason, and dropped him here in London. Now he resurrects his identity as The General, art dealer, connoisseur, and collector. According to Scotland Yard, Morand stole a fortune in art while in Paris."

"And you think it's here in London?"

"Not for long, if my guess is right," said Hamilton as his brow arched. "Kemidov was selling art to Michael Copper Gallery to finance his escape. I'm sure of it."

Harry's face grew dark. "It is quite possible, like Operation Sunshine, Kemidov is working with the remnants of the OSS against the communists in yet another deception. This inquiry did come from your colleague and former OSS operative, Joseph Ganzer. Am I right?"

"You think, then, this is an OSS operation gone bad, and they are using us to clean it up?

"It is quite possible," said Harry.

Operation Sunshine began near the end of the war. Nazi General Karl Wolff, commander of the SS and Gestapo in Italy, contacted the senior OSS officer in Switzerland. Wolff and other Nazi leaders were seeking amnesty and escape for themselves and an extensive roster of SS and Gestapo personnel. In exchange, General Wolff offered to shift allegiance of 5000 former Nazis of Eastern European and Russian descent to anti-communist activities. They were given extensive espionage training at a camp located in Oberammergau, Germany.

This army of spies flooded Europe, undertaking covert operations against the communists. As part of the agreement, the Nazis were permitted to keep the booty they had collected during the war—gold, cash, precious jewelry, art and antiques, most of which had belonged to Jews who fell victim to the "Final Solution." Thousands of high-ranking Nazis were now fleeing through "rat lines" to South America and elsewhere.

Hamilton weighed the possibilities. "There is no conceivable way Joseph Ganzer would work an operation on me, Harry. He knows I would discover it straight away. No, Yuri Kemidov may be using the OSS or the NKVD or both, but Joseph is not part of Operation Sunshine nor is he any longer part of the OSS. Of that you can be assured. No, Kemidov is nothing more than a cunning opportunist who is just about out of rope. I am convinced he is now running for his life."

"Elimination?"

"Precisely, but not for his double cross—for his art treasures. Case in point: Scotland Yard has a report alleging that Kemidov has a bejeweled golden falcon once belonging to the Templars. Surely, some NKVD operatives in the field have learned of Kemidov's treachery and his treasures. Once they locate him and have a little discussion as to the location of his art collection, they will report back to their control, and then they will kill him."

"Rouge agents? Yes, yes," agreed Harry. "Even communists can become capitalists if there is enough money. I fear, then, your friend in America is in considerable danger."

"I agree. Someone approached Joseph Ganzer to track down Kemidov. That someone believes Kemidov will flee to the United States or Canada." He paused and realized, "They know our operation, Harry."

"Yes, it seems they know us quite well."

"We must get to Kemidov before they do."


Hamilton sat at his desk in his rooms at the Hotel Cavendish, considering his next move. He had to warn Joe Ganzer about the danger he might be in, but he had so little to report, no concrete intelligence. He didn't even know if Yuri Kemidov had already fallen prey to the Soviet agents trying to assassinate him. He didn't know where Kemidov's stolen art was being stored. Was Joe Ganzer being used by OSS to locate Kemidov for them? Was Joe part of that operation?

The phone rang. Hamilton reached over and picked up. 'Hello."

"Sir, this is the desk clerk. There is a gentleman." The clerk paused and looked at the man standing across the desk from him. "Your name please?"

"Mickey Browne... with an 'e'."

The clerk repeated, "A Mickey Browne with an 'e' is here to see you. Shall I send him up?"

"Yes, of course, of course."

"Very well, sir." The clerk hung up and said to Mickey, "You may take the lift to the third floor. Mr. Hamilton's suite is—"

"Yeah, I know, guv'nor," and Mickey was off to the lift. He pushed the button and ascended to the third floor.

A brisk knock. Hamilton rose and headed to the door and opened it. "Come in, Mickey."

"Blye me...that desk monkey was a real uppity type."

"Have you some news?" asked Hamilton anxious for any piece to the puzzle before him.

"Indeed I do," said Mickey. "There's a cabbie friend of mine—I ain't seen him in quite a while—but when I asked around his name comes up as a cabbie that works the Alhambra area. His name is Charlie Cuddy, an Irish bloke. He thinks I'm Irish, too, 'cuz of me last name. But mine ends with an 'e,' you see. That makes it English, but I don't tell anybody until I knows 'em good."

"Very discerning of you, Mickey. Continue."

"I thought he was killed in the bombings. Hadn't seen 'im around the pubs. Turns out he was in hospital for a time, then changed his route. He's fine now."

Hamilton was impatient. "What did he tell you?"

"Well, I asks 'im if he had a fare out of Alhambra fittin' the description of the bloke you told me about."

"And...?"

"Well, he said he took a gentleman one evening, very late, from the Alhambra to The Strafford Hotel. Can you imagine?"

"The Strafford? My that is a considerable move up."

"Quite right, guv'nor," said Mickey. "That's why it stuck in ol' Charlie's memory. Not many fares make a change of address like that."

"Are you sure it was our man?"

"Positive. He had the scar on his temple, just like yuh said."

"What else do we know?"

"Charlie tells me he knows the bloke's room number, but he won't give it up unless I pay him a quid."

"So...?"

"So, I paid out of me own pocket." Hamilton reached in his suit coat pocket for his wallet and handed Mickey a two pound note. "Thank you again, Mr. Hamilton."

"Now, how did your friend learn his room number?"

"Turns out this fare had luggage, and Charlie lugged it up to his room expecting a generous tip, which he didn't get," said Mickey with contempt. "Imagine a rich bloke like that, at The Stafford Hotel, tipping a farthing?"

"Atrocious behavior."

"Yes, sir. He lugs these three bags up to his rooms. Suite, it was. Fancy, too. Charlie said the smallest case must've had lead in it, it was so heavy. The fare kept telling him to be careful of the small case."

"Go on."

"Then, when he gets inside Room 436, there's a big fellow already in there. Charlie claims he was a real gruesome sort."

"I see. Anything else?"

"No...Charlie left directly after that measly tip. He was done with 'em both."

"Could you take me to The Stafford now?"

"For that extra quid yuh gave me, I'll even take you back to Scotland Yard."

With that, they were on their way down Gower Street, then to Bedford Square through Soho, finally arriving at The Stafford Hotel at St. James Place. The street was crowded. Mickey had a difficult time negotiating his cab down the cramped passage, jumbled with people and other cabs picking up fares and dropping them off.

"Mickey, let me out here," said Hamilton. As he exited the cab, he added, "But wait for me, no matter how long it takes."

"Whatever you say, " and Mickey lit out and looked for a parking space just off Piccadilly close to Green Park.

Hamilton walked down the street. The entrance to the hotel was palatial. Four Doric columns supported a heavy canopy of black marble. Hamilton reached the arching carved wooden doors and entered the hotel. As Hamilton approached the front desk at the end of the long entranceway, one of the clerks asked, "May I help you?"

"Yes, I was told to meet a party here for business."

"Would that be a guest of The Stafford or perhaps you are meeting at our dining room or one of our private rooms?"

"No, a guest in Room 436."

The clerk consulted the registry and said, "Yes, Mr. Kemidov. He has one of our suites overlooking the courtyard. Shall I ring him, sir?"

"Yes, please. Tell him an associate of Bruno Loshe, Lawrence Hamilton, is here to see him." Hamilton used Loshe's name to assure Kemidov he would meet with a colleague in the underworld of stolen art, one scoundrel validating another. Hamilton did not expect Kemidov to meet him cold, not now, not with NKVD searching for him.

As expected the clerk returned to the desk and said, "Mr. Kemidov regrets that he cannot meet with you right now, but if you leave your card, he will contact you sometime later."

*Cautious*, he thought.

If Hamilton were a NKVD agent, he would certainly not have a calling card, but if he were truly associated with Loshe, he would definitely have one, the semblance of legitimacy in an unsavory business. "Very well," said Hamilton and handed the clerk his "Antiquities" calling card.

Reading the card he said, "Certainly, Mr. Hamilton, I will tender it to him when next I see him."

Hamilton chummed the waters hoping it would attract the interest of his quarry. Right now he needed to call Harry and let him know his progress and get additional support. He found a comfortable sitting room just off the main lobby. No one was there.

All the world's major newspapers were carefully arranged on oval tables opposite green and brown leather couches. Photographs of famous guests covered the green walls above the dark brown wainscoting. Hamilton sat in one of the upholstered chairs next a house phone. He picked up the receiver and placed a call through the hotel switchboard to Harry.

"Treadwell Bookseller," answered Harry.

"Harry, I have located our quarry. Could you send someone to keep an eye on him?"

"Of course, where shall he be dispatched?"

"The Stafford. Room 436, a suite."

"Excellent accommodations in the business of art, I see."

"Perhaps we can put an end to that," said Hamilton.

"Anything else?"

"No, when my replacement arrives, send him to the sitting room off the main lobby. Then I'll head back to the Cavendish."

"Very well then," and Harry hung up and immediately placed a call to summon another agent. Harry would brief him on Kemidov, show him the photograph, and send him to The Stafford.

An hour and a half later, Hamilton's replacement arrived. They surreptitiously acknowledged each other. Hamilton remarked how wonderful the weather had been of late. The MI5 agent smiled and said, "Better than at Gloucester," which was the signal for the change of guard.

Hamilton rose and left the sitting room, heading for the front doors. The doorman held the door as Hamilton exited. He walked a short distance toward the intersection at Little James Street. Mickey pulled up alongside, and Hamilton hopped in. "You waited after all."

"Where to now?"

"Back to The Cavendish."

"Right, sir," said Mickey as he pulled away from the curb. "Have any luck with your Nazi collaborator?"

"He is there alright, but we have to be patient now."

As they drove along Pall Mall on their way to the Cavendish, Hamilton tried to formulate a plan that would ensnare Kemidov. Having worked with the NKVD and important Nazis, Kemidov had a wealth of intelligence that would be invaluable to MI5.

However, they needed criminal charges to detain him in Britain; otherwise, he would have to be turned over to the French for almost certain execution.

Mickey could see that Hamilton was lost in thought, so the ride was kept quiet and uneventful. Even when Mickey was cut off by a careless motorist, he stifled his swearing. After a few more turns, they arrived at The Cavendish. Mickey pulled up to the entrance, stopped, and waited....

"Sorry to disturb you sir, but we're back at your digs."

"Ah...so we are," said Hamilton. "I'm afraid I was too preoccupied to notice."

"That's all right. I know you have important things on your mind."

Hamilton exited the cab and went to the driver's window and handed Mickey his fare plus a handsome gratuity.

"Thank you again, sir."

Hamilton smiled and said, "Give my regards to Harry Treadwell, would you?" For less than a breath, Mickey was caught off guard but then smiled, gave a little wave, and pulled away from the curb. Hamilton walked into The Cavendish. As soon as he got to his rooms, he placed a call to Harry. He listened impatiently as it rang.

"Treadwell Bookseller."

"Harry, I'll need some expensive art work, preferably paintings, smallish, if you can manage to procure them."

"Pray tell, what is this all about?" asked Harry.

Hamilton laughed. "Sorry, old boy. I am setting out a little bait out for our quarry. If I can lure him here to The Cavendish with stolen art, we will have some serious charges to hold over his head."

"I like it," said Harry. " Once he takes possession, we will have him alright. But are you sure he will even bite?"

"Get me something he cannot resist, something to appeal to his greed and his aesthetics."

"Tall order, but I shall do my utmost. An old schoolmate Lt. Col. Leonard Maycott is one of the Monuments Men. I can see whether he has something we may borrow."

"Quickly, Harry," urged Hamilton. "I'm afraid we have little time."

"I appreciate that fully," said Harry. "I learned from C that our

MI5 agent inside the Michael Cooper Gallery is gathering intelligence on a network of former SS members liquidating stolen art to finance Die Spinne or 'The Spider.' Lawrence, they are planning a Fourth Reich in South America...."

"Heaven help us."

Harry hung up and began trying to track down Lenard Maycott.

They hadn't seen each other since their days at King's College. Maycott had gone on to become an important art historian but volunteered for duty with the Monuments, Fine Arts, and Archives (MFAA) to help save as much of the culture of Europe as they could during combat and thereafter. Lenard Maycott was one of the "Monuments Men."

General Eisenhower worked in coordination with the MFAA in France and Germany to salvage and protect cultural treasures, but the MFAA soon discovered that the Nazis had planned and were executing cultural theft on a scale unprecedented in world history. Hitler's focus remained on stealing the greatest artworks of Western Civilization. No object was too small or too large to ignore, and all the better if it could correct the wrongs of history and humiliate those responsible. The Nazis had created an enormous web of deliberate deceit that stretched across all of Europe.

Between 1938 and 1945 Nazi thieves stole millions of items, nothing of value was left unplundered. It was the job of the Monuments Men to at first protect and later to return the art treasures of Europe. Lt. Col. Leonard Maycott was still on the project, identifying and cataloguing art objects, hoping to return them to their rightful owners.

The phone rang in Lt. Col. Maycott's temporary office at the British Museum, a cramped room barely large enough for a desk, not to mention art objects of all shapes and sizes, stacked precariously in every available space. "Hello."

"Lenny? Is that really you?" asked Harry Treadwell.

"Who's calling, please. I'm quite engaged at the moment."

"This is Harry... Harry Treadwell."

"Good heavens," said Lenny. "I haven't heard from you in years. How have you been? I've heard rumors about you."

"They're all true, especially the ones about my amorous adventures."

Laughing, Lenny said, "A little old for that aren't you?"

"Not yet. Just slowing down."

"We must get together soon, over some tea."

"I agree, but over some brandy. It's been too long. The war and all."

"Yes, it has. But I understand you are in a very unusual business these days," Lenny said having learned of Harry's work with British Intelligence. "How may I help you?"

Harry had always admired Lenny's acumen. "Let's call it a unique business, shall we? And I do need something special from you fellows at the MFAA."

"What might that be, Harry?"

"Lenny, I need some paintings. Important. Valuable. Not too large."

"We have hundreds and hundreds here at the museum, but they are under catalog and will be returned to their true owners in due time."

"Perhaps there are some that meet our criteria that have no owners."

"Unfortunately there are some we fear their owners have perished in the death camps. Orphans as it were."

"I need at least one of great value. I'm thinking a modern artist."

"We have a Van Gogh that would be quite valuable and a Renoir. Would those do?"

"Not to press the issue, but do you also have a minor work by a recognizable artist?"

"Oh, indeed, there is a lovely Picasso that we believe is lost."

"That would be excellent," said Harry. "Can you dispatch the paperwork without delay and assign them to us at MI5?"

"I shall send this up the ladder, and I am sure we can help. However, there is the problem of their return," cautioned Lenny. "Eventually we hope to discover their rightful owners and return their art. Therefore, they must be protected at all cost and returned."

"I understand completely. They will be in the best of care."

"Wonderful."

"May I send a man over to transport them?"

"Where to, Harry?"

"I am not at liberty to say, you know."

"You can't blame my curiosity, Harry."

Harry laughed, "Someday, my friend, when we're old."

Lt. Col Lenard Maycott turned three paintings over to the young MI5 agent with a warning: "See to it that nothing happens to these."

"Right, sir," said the agent as he signed for the transmittal. He left Maycott's office with a package not much larger than a suitcase but worth a small fortune. The agent stowed the package in his car and headed the short distance to the Hotel Cavendish. Lawrence Hamilton was pacing the floor when the agent knocked. Hamilton opened and greeted the agent.

"Your package, sir."

"Thank you so much," said Hamilton, delighted that Harry was able to make the arrangements.

"There is a letter here, sir, from the Monuments fellow. Harry said the name is Martin Ruddock at the Michael Cooper, and he knows your target."

Hamilton took the letter and thanked him and opened it as the agent left. The letter explained the nature of the paintings and their worth in the present art market. Hamilton was impressed by the value of the paintings. He burned the letter in the ashtray.

He took great care removing the paintings from the small crate and prepared to hang them in his office adjacent the main room. He hung the Van Gogh in the center of the wall opposite his desk, a delightful landscape in muted greens and ochres, a field of wheat in the foreground and a distant village with aqua rooftops in the background, all in Van Gogh's bold unmistakable brushwork.

Hamilton placed the Renoir to the left of the Van Gogh. A delicate little painting of a child with a ball in a garden that was radiant in its palette of pastel blues, reds, and yellows. The Picasso placed on the right of the Van Gogh seemed somehow out of place, almost grotesque. The painting itself was a contradiction. Although the canvas size was moderate, the subject was an oversized woman looking contemplatively at flowers in her hand and dressed in a white tunic. The arrangement of these paintings was a tableau of the development of art over the past 50 years, all of which the Nazis abhorred.

Many such modern paintings were actually burned by the Nazis in Paris to make room at the Jue de Paume modern art museum for "more desirable art" looted elsewhere in Europe. They declared such art "degenerate," unworthy of German standards of excellence and beauty. Some were treated as devalued scrip and traded for other paintings coveted by the Nazi elite. These three escaped the Nazi bonfires. Hamilton surveyed their placement with a certain pleasure and recalled Sherlock Holmes with a smile and thought: *"The game is afoot"... now to warn Joseph."*

Hamilton took no chances with this message. He used a poem to encode his message. The poem, "The Life That I Have," was written by one of England's most brilliant cryptographers, Leo Marks, and both men knew it by heart.

The life that I have
Is all that I have
And the life that I have
Is yours.

The love that I have
Of the life that I have
Is yours and yours and yours.

A sleep I shall have
A rest I shall have
Yet death will be but a pause.

For the peace of my years
In the long green grass
Will be yours and yours and yours.

Choosing the second stanza at random, Hamilton selected the last line and used the next five words as his key: ISYOURSANDYOURSAND. He used this sequence in a double transposition of his message. The encryption had to be strong. Hamilton suspected Morand/Kemidov was darkly entangled with the NKVD; nothing else could explain how he got out of Paris and arrived in England. With the kind of money involved in stolen art, even a dedicated communist could be driven to neutralize a fellow agent and abscond with his loot.

So, if Kemidov was indeed a Russian, he reasoned, then he has been working with the NKVD throughout the war. He was probably using them now to smuggle a fortune in art out of Europe to the US or Canada.

The phone in Hamilton's room rang. "Yes," said Hamilton.

In a cultured Russian accent, the voice on the other end said, "Mr. Hamilton, I believe you left your card at my hotel. I see that you are an antiquities dealer. How may I help you?"

"I am an acquaintance of Bruno Lohse. He told me some time ago when I was in Switzerland that you were someone to approach about disposing of certain objects discovered during the war."

"If I may be so direct, how did you know to contact me here, at this hotel?" asked Kemidov.

Hamilton was ready. "I spoke with Martin Ruddock."

"Ah, yes, Martin. Well, what can I do for you?"

"I have some paintings that were acquired recently, but they are not in my area of expertise. They are works by the Spaniard Picasso and a work by Van Gogh and one by Renoir."

"Do you have these paintings in your possession? I would like to view them as soon as possible, as I am departing very soon."

*Greed never fails*, Hamilton thought."Yes, they are here in my rooms at The Cavendish. Are you familiar with it?"

"Yes, I am. May I visit you later this afternoon?"

"Of course. I'll order dinner for us, if you don't mind?" said Hamilton.

"That would be most gracious of you. Thank you," said Kemidov. "I'll see you in an hour."

"Indeed, 'til then," Hamilton said as he hung up. He at once dialed Harry Treadwell and asked for an agent to send a telegram. A young man arrived a short while later and took the coded message with orders to send it to Joseph Ganzer, 8112 Commercial Avenue, Chicago, Illinois, USA. The message read:

```
GCHSU EODDV WVINE BJSIT EETEH
PEOMR VWNEP EAITI RTTNI ERNSD
DNLSR PSKAH VEMUR MPIWE AHYYN
HSEEE ERIFA ELRTO SBEAO ATAEI
OIDII HOKRW TTUIL UYEEE OHCAD
SRWAS NAAWA OLRHO VBHGV IIERS
EADMC UASND OAXMN MARHF OFLEG
CNOTR RNNPT EMIBW AERNN ODAHI
YAYAH
```

(See Appendix *Cryptography* for a brief description of message encryption.)

# CHAPTER FIVE

## SOUTH CHICAGO
### *8122 Commercial Avenue*

"Joe...Joe...Wake up, man. You been drinkin' ?" One-Two Johnny said, shaking Joe gruffly by the shoulder.

"Wha..., Johnny? What time is it?" Joe asked.

"It's eleven o'clock in the morning. How long yuh been here like this, huh? All night?" Johnny said.

Joe felt the left side of his head. There were two walnuts there now. "No... uh... it was ... I don't know... two a.m.? This morning... when this guy, Frankie Ferrel, came in here and tapped me on the head."

"Here le' me get you up. Man, you better see a doctor, Joe."

"Nah, I'll be all right. Just let me sit down here on the sofa for a while." Joe tried to clear the static from his mind.

"Hey, who's this Ferrel? Sounds familiar."

"Remember Dixie Monahan?" Johnny nodded as Joe continued, "Well, Frankie Ferrel was one of his guys. Took off with him to the Orient way before the war."

Johnny said, "Yeah, yeah. Now I remember. Monahan owed the Outfit a lot of money, I remember. I know some guys that would like to plumb that guy up."

"I heard that Ferrel plumbed Dixie up permanent quite a while back."

"Ferrel ain't lookin' for me is he, Joe?"

"What?—No!" said Joe."It's another case entirely."

"You know, I got some friends say they're gonna lock me up today."

"I figured that, too," Joe said as a rush of pain went down the side of his head into his neck, making it hard to pronounce his words. "They can only hold you for 48 hours. I'll... aggh... see what

I can do before they file charges—if they file."

"Here's some money for the bond." He handed Joe $2000 in cash in an envelope. "Joe, see a doctor. You're no good if you're messed up."

"Yeah, okay, maybe. I'll see you tomorrow. Wilma will be here in an hour. We'll take care of Tommy, so ah, don't worry."

"See yuh, Joe," and One-Two Johnny walked out of the office but without his natural swing. Joe watched him leave and leaned back in the sofa.

After Johnny left, Joe fell asleep. And he had the dream again. It was different, yet always the same. He woke in a sweat, disoriented, and breathing heavily. Just as he dozed off again, a quick hard knock on the outer office door woke him. Joe labored to get up as the knocks grew louder. He got to the door and opened it. The boy handed him the telegram. Joe gave him a look and reached in his pocket for a tip. "Gosh, thanks Mr. Ganzer," said the boy, and he ran out of the outer office slammed the door and galloped down the stairs. Joe closed the door, rubbed his eyes, walked back to his desk, and opened the telegram.

"What?" he asked out loud.

Then he answered himself. "This is that old poem code we used during the war."

Strange, he thought: *Why would Hamilton go to such lengths to send a reply?* An odd feeling came over him, one he hadn't had since the war, a thrill, a rush, the game. He sat down to decipher the message. It would take a while. It had been almost two years since he decoded a message like this. He took his time.

Joe looked first for the twenty-fifth letter. It was indeed an "H," for Hamilton. This would appear as a mistake in the decoded message and guaranteed that Hamilton had actually written it. Another clue confirmed it was genuine.

The last six letters (five plus one) were I-Y-A-Y-A-H. The "H" at the end was Hamilton's signature. The other five letters represented words from the poem "The Life That I Have." After a little work remembering the poem, Joe had the words. Now for the hard part: deciphering the message. It came back to him with a little effort, and as he worked on the message, he remembered long hours at Camp X, working with codes and ciphers until it became second nature to him.

Agents like Joe Ganzer and Lawrence Hamilton owed their lives to the cipher men, a group of dedicated mathematicians and technicians at Betchley Park whose codemaking and breaking shortened the war by as many as two years.

Joe made some mistakes decoding and had to start over. He was rusty, but then the clear text slowly emerged. The final clue, the last letter, was indeed an "H":

```
KEMIDOVISAWARPROFI
TEERANDCRIMINALALI
ASHUGOMORANDWANTED
BYTHEFRENCHWHOEVER
HIREDYOUISINVOLVED
INARTSTOLENFROMPAR
ISIANJEWSWHOWERESE
NTTOTHEGASCHAMBERS
WEMUSTAPPREHENDAND
EXTRADITEUSECAUTIO
NKVDMAYBEINVOLVEDH
```

Joe tore up the telegram and his transcription, dropped it in the waste basket, and set it on fire. *So now it begins again.* He sat back in his chair, exhausted from the effort of decoding, and fell asleep again.

Wilma entered the outer office. At first she didn't notice the splintered wood around the door that led to Joe's office. Routine makes people follow familiar patterns until something breaks through the murk. *The wood... it's broken and the frosted glass... cracked.*

Panic flooded her. *It's all wrong.* She ran to Joe's door without thinking that whoever kicked in the door might still be in Joe's office. She didn't care. She threw open the door, and there was Joe slumped over in his chair.

"Joe...Joe," she screamed and flew over to the his chair. Tears ran down her cheeks as she grabbed him in his chair. "Joe, come on, come on. Don't be dead. Oh, God."

Joe's eyes struggled open. He saw a blur that he thought was a woman. The dark-haired woman slowly came into focus. "Wilma...?"

"Joe, I thought you were dead," she said.

"I'd have to feel better to be dead."

Wilma tried to hide her tears as his focus improved. "What happened? I'm calling the police."

"No, don't. Frankie Ferrel came in here and telegraphed a message on my head. I don't want him to finish it. Let it go."

"Who's Frankie Ferrel, and why does it smell like smoke in here?" she asked.

"He was one of Dixie Monahan's guys. Remember him? Probably killed him. A contract killer. Now he's back in Chicago."

"What's he doing here and why did he hurt you?"

"Ludko found out he's Polina Kemidov's guy now, and he came here to force me out of the picture."

"Every time you get involved with one of Ludko's so-called clients something goes wrong. When are you ever going to learn?"

"Hey...I must be a mental case. Get Ludko on the line for me would yuh?" Joe asked with a smile that made his head crackle.

Wilma walked to the outer office and murmured, "You're all idiots." She dialed Ludko's number while glaring at Joe, then switched the line over.

Ludko answered, "Yeah."

"Guess what? Frankie Ferrel stopped here early this morning to tap out a message on my head. He wants me off the case, and you brought him here."

"Joe, I was sure I lost that tail. Nobody could have followed me. Nobody."

"Well, he did and I got the receipt to prove it."

"Joe, I'm sorry. I'm sorry. I didn't—. It won't happen again."

"It can't. He'll kill me next time. Look, I got a telegram from Lawrence Hamilton this morning. There's enough money in all this to kill anybody who gets in the way. Ferrel's going for a double cross on Polina. I'm sure of it. Her loving Uncle Yuri was an art swindler in Occupied Paris and a Nazi collaborator. He's running from the French government, the NKVD, and who knows who else. His only chance is to get out of England, maybe to the States, maybe to Canada."

"So, then Polina figured the double cross and hired us," Ludko said.

"She might be legit about her uncle. She may not even know about what he did in Paris. He operated as an art dealer under the identity of Hugo Morand, so she might not know. But Ferrel knows for sure. He might have just glommed onto her to get to the art, wherever that is. And Ferrel doesn't know she even talked to me. He just knows about you, and you led him here. He must think we're after the art, just like him."

"Hey, Joe, what are we talkin' about here—Rembrandts, da Vincis, what?"

"Maybe, I don't know," said Joe. "All I know is Kemidov flimflammed desperate Jews out of their valuable art, then turned them over to the Gestapo."

"What a stinkin' puke," Ludko said. "So what are we talkin' about in money here?"

"I'd say millions, Lud." Joe heard the phone drop. "...Lud, you still there?"

Ludko juggled the phone back to his ear. "Yeah, sorry, no wonder Ferrel hammered yuh. So what do we do now? And what's the NKVD got to do with this?"

"I'm guessing that Kemidov worked with the NKVD and was giving them intelligence on the Nazis all the time he was operating in Paris. A reptile like that would play both ends. The Soviets aren't stupid. They figured it out. They knew he stole a lot of art, so they're just following the money. And money is important even to communists—especially that kind of money."

"Joe, we dealt with those guys before, during the war. They're damned ugly. Can't we just let *them* take care of Ferrel?"

"They'll get Polina, too. I can't take that chance."

"Sounds like the old Joe."

"What do you mean by that? She's my client."

"She's beautiful, too. That'll be your undoing someday."

"Get back to the hotel. Do you think you can tail Ferrel without him knowing it or should I just send Benny?" Joe asked.

"Aw, Joe, you really know how to hurt a guy," Ludko said with a phony lament.

"Look, I'm the one with the bruised ego. Now call me when you get something."

"You can count on me," Ludko said as he hung up the phone.

Joe called to Wilma, "Wilm, could you have your sister pick up Tommy Della Penna? Could she watch him for a couple of days?"

"Where's his dad?"

"He'll be in custody, but not for long. You're going to bail him out after they charge him. Maybe tomorrow." Joe reached into his top desk drawer. "Here's two grand that Johnny brought here early this morning."

Wilma came in and took the money from Joe and said, "What are you doing dealing with losers like Johnny?"

"He's being pulled in on a burglary charge for hitting a liquor warehouse over on 100th Street. The guy is trying to go straight. He's got a job at the mills, and he's trying to take care of his kid...."

"And you're trying to help him out. What's he paying you with, the liquor he stole?"

Joe was disappointed, "I'll tell you this, but don't you breathe a word of it to anyone. That warehouse is owned by the Outfit, and they robbed it themselves for the insurance. Johnny's their fall guy."

"Damn, Joe, first that Ferrel guy might kill you and now if you get Johnny off, the Outfit will make a nice hole for you in Chicago Heights. What's the matter with you? Why don't you stick with the domestic cases, like you have been?"

"Say—can your sister get Tommy or not?"

"Yeah, sure," and she went into her office to call her sister.

Joe went into his bathroom to see what he looked like. He combed his wavy dark brown hair and winced when the comb ran over the left side. He thought the knots beneath his thick hair made the wave stick out too much. *I've looked worse.*

He grabbed his keys. On his way out he whispered, "Don't worry."

Wilma was talking to her sister and looked up disapprovingly and smiled and shook her head.

◊◊◊

Joe got in the Chevy and headed over to 100th Street to see if he could find something—anything—that might help Johnny. He drove the twenty blocks to the warehouse district. There were new houses going up on nearly every street. GIs were picking up their lives after four years of madness—starting families and businesses, building homes.

In the warehouse district, the story was the same: new buildings going up on street after street. The total creative energy that won the war was now unleashed on the American business landscape, not only in Chicago but all across America. GIs were starting machine shops and auto mechanic garages and cabinet shops. As Joe made his way into the older sections along 100th street, the buildings were worn and needed repair, buildings of all shapes and sizes, and all ugly. After a few more minutes, there it stood—Marcello Liquor Warehouse—right on the corner. Joe pulled along the curb, opened the glove compartment and pulled out a pair of glasses. He put them on, grabbed a notebook and his hat, and got out of the car. He walked to the man door that probably led into the office. He opened it and walked in. It was a little room with a metal desk and a fat dark-eyed guy sitting behind it.

"What do *you* want?" said the dark-eyed man.

With his faint practiced lisp, Joe said, "I'm here investigating the robbery. I'd like to see the damage caused by the intruders."

"You with the insurance?"

"Yes, could you show me the damage and do you have the inventory account?" Joe asked, not believing how easy it was. Show a little authority, even to a thug, and they respond accordingly.

"Sure, come on with me," said the fat man, relighting a cigar. They walked into the warehouse from the office and over to the door where the burglars had entered. There had been some amateur repairs done to the back door. "Right here. See?"

"Yes," Joe said, looking interested in the door frame, "I see. Must have made a great noise. Did you hear anything?"

"I wasn't here. It was at night. Nobody was here."

"Did anybody see anything?" Joe asked.

"Nah, like I said nobody was here."

"Yes, you said that before. May I see the account of what was stolen."

"Yeah, come on back to the office." They made their way

through the maze of stacked boxes of every kind of alcohol imaginable. The little fat man handed Joe the list of beverages that were stolen, all expensive products.

"I see that these thieves knew what they were looking for. These are the most expensive spirits on the market," said Joe.

"Yeah, it was a big haul. They done good."

"What do you mean by that?" Joe snapped.

The fat man stammered, thinking he'd said something wrong, "You, you know, it was all expensive. Like you said, '...expensive spirits.'" The fat man laughed uncomfortably.

"Yes, indeed. Well I shall include that in my report. Thank you, sir." And Joe headed back to his car. The flunky watched Joe carefully and picked up the phone. He'll tell Marcello that an insurance guy came snooping around.

Still wearing his glasses, Joe took a little cruise in the Chevy around the neighborhood of drab. Two blocks away from the Marcello Liquor Warehouse was a small, shabby warehouse that looked out of place with a new Cadillac parked in front of it. He parked and walked up to the door and tried it. Locked. He hammered on the door.

After almost a minute, a muscular thug, late thirties, opened the door and said, "What do *you* want?"

Joe smiled at that. *These guys must all read the same books on hospitality.* "Oh, I'm so sorry to disturb you, but I'm quite lost," Joe said with a small bookish voice, pulling out his notebook and reading the blank page. "Do you know where, uh, the Marcello Liquor Warehouse is located?"

As Mr. Friendly answered, he let the door open a bit more and Joe spotted stacks of liquor crates inside, "Yeah, it's two blocks over on 100th street, right on the corner. Can't miss it."

"Thank you so much," said Joe and got to his car and left. He thought how brazen these guys were, storing their heist only a few blocks away. Took guts and connections—and "Mr. Friendly" was definitely a crew member. Sgt. Kavanaugh must be in thick with this crew to overlook that place. Joe headed for Vookie's Tavern.

"Hey, Joe, how's it goin'?" asked Eddie wiping the bar.

"What have you got for a headache and a growling stomach?" Joe replied.

"Hung over?" Eddie insinuated.

"No, a real headache, but what's to eat?" Joe asked.

"I got my famous egg sandwiches. Want some aspirin?" Joe nodded and headed for his booth.

Before he got to his booth, the lone old guy at the bar said with the slightest of slurs, "I usually have a little bit of peppermint schnapps for my hangovers. Works like a ch-chaaarm."

"Thanks for the advice" said Joe, his head throbbing.

Eddie filled a beer mug of water, a couple of aspirin, and an egg sandwich and brought it to Joe at his private booth.

"Thanks, Eddie."

"Joe, you don't look too good."

"I feel even worse," said Joe. "I got to ask you something. You get your liquor from Rossi, right?"

"Yeah, not that I want to deal with those people, but I sort of have to, yuh know." Eddie said.

"I figured Rossi had the lock on booze down this way. What's with that Marcello's over on 100th Street?"

"That's one of Rossi's places. He's got it all down here, all the way to Calumet City. Why, what's up? Hey, you ain't messin' with that guy are you? Cuz, if you are, you're gonna loose."

"No, I'm just following a lead for Johnny. You know, they got him up for that heist."

"Damn, I didn't know it was that place. Johnny's had it. You can't do anything there, Joe," said Eddie, his eyes and expression showed genuine concern for his friend and silent partner.

"I was afraid of that." As he took the aspirins and downed them with the water, he let out a melodious: "Thank you, Eddie." Then he lowered his voice to a whisper and said, "You can't say a word."

"I won't. Take your sandwich."

He took the egg sandwich off the plate and and tore into it. Halfway through the sandwich Eddie's phone rang.

"Joe... it's Wilma."

Joe hopped out of the booth and headed to the bar. "Yeah, Wilm?"

"Ludko called and said Ferrel's on the move. He said he'll call back when he's got more."

"Thanks. When he calls back, tell him to try to keep Ferrel away from The Drake as long as he can. I'm going there to talk to Polina."

"Okay, Joe. How's your head?"

"Eddie's the best doctor. I'm doing fine. Still a little blurry," Joe said.

"Well, if it gets worse, see a doctor. Please, Joe—I mean it," Wilma said.

"I will, I will. See yuh," and Joe hung up, put money on the bar when he left, and headed for Lake Shore Drive and The Drake Hotel.

# CHAPTER SIX

DOWNTOWN CHICAGO
*The Drake Hotel*

As he walked from this car to the door of The Drake Hotel, Joe could feel the heat rising up off the sidewalk. It made his head throb. The doorman at The Drake opened the door, and Joe felt the cool of the lobby wash away the heat. He went straight to the elevator, entered, and told the operator "Seven, okay?"

"Yes, sir. Awfully hot today?"

"Enough to boil my brains."

The operator gave Joe a sidelong glance and closed the door and engaged the elevator.

At the seventh floor Joe exited and went straight to Room 706. He knocked on the door, in the way that only a maid or bellhop would knock—gentle but demanding. Polina came to the door.

Joe startled her. She gasped. "Mr. Ganzer, how did you...?"

"That's why you hired me. May I come in?" He walked in past her.

"Why... uh... yes, please."

"Where's your boyfriend?" Joe asked without missing a beat, looking around the room.

"You know about—he's not my boyfriend. He's a friend," Polina said.

"Yeah, I met your friend this morning, and I'm still giggly from all the fun we had."

"How could he? I never—never told him anything about you," Polina insisted.

"You mean to tell me, he just picked me out of the phone book and decided to come and hammer a message out on my head?" Joe said. "A message about staying away from The Drake?"

"I said nothing at all about you or our meeting," Polina said.

"Well, he found me and that's a problem. And another problem is you lied to me about where you were staying. This sure doesn't look like 71st Street to me," Joe said.

"I can explain," she said. "My cousin truly lives on 71st Street, but I didn't want to impose on them, and I hadn't decided where I was going to live so I gave that as an address where I could be reached."

"You've been in this hotel for a while."

"But I didn't know if I was going to stay here or move elsewhere. I may...."

"Yeah—where's the boyfriend now?" Joe said.

"I told you he's not my boyfriend," she repeated.

"Then what's he doing living here with you?" Joe demanded.

"His room is down the hall at 715. Check the desk," she snapped back.

Joe continued the interrogation, "Then what are you doing with Frankie Ferrell?"

"You know his name?" she paused.

Joe didn't answer.

"He's my bodyguard."

"From what?"

"The people who are looking for my uncle," she explained.

"What people?"

"Do you know who are NKVD?" she asked.

"Just three letters to me," Joe said in a convincing tone of ignorance.

"They are the Soviet intelligence organization. My uncle is a former general. He loves Russia, but he hates the communists. He is trying to immigrate to the United Sates to escape them. He told me that NKVD are trying to apprehend him and that I am not safe from them. He said they would use me to get to him. He has certain informations that could be valuable to the West."

"So where does Ferrel come in?" Joe asked, as he mulled over that unusual accent of hers.

"I met him in Toronto while waiting for my uncle," she said. "My uncle never arrived so I came to Chicago to be with relatives."

"Met him? How?" Joe asked.

"You don't understand. There are people in our community who have fled the communists, and they know how to help their sisters and brothers. They told me of a man—an American—who could help and protect me."

"Why didn't you stay in Canada with your 'community'?" Joe said.

"They said it was becoming too dangerous. The war, Mr. Ganzer, is not over... not for some. They said I should go to my cousin's in Chicago. It would be safer for me. Then I met your associate Mr. Ludko, and...."

Joe felt he had gone too far. "Please, let's sit down here." Joe put his hand on her shoulder and guided her to the sofa in front of what was meant to look like a fireplace. "I'm on your side. Remember? I'm not your KGD or whatever. I'm your investigator, and stop calling me Mr. Ganzer. I've got some information on your uncle."

Polina reached over and embraced Joe, "I'm so glad. Where is he?"

"Well, he's not at the Alhambra," said Joe, who knew Hamilton would have already apprehended him. "But I have a colleague in London working on it." Joe put his arm around her. She reached her arms around him and held tightly. He could smell her hair. She leaned her face toward him and kissed him, deeply and tenderly.

"Oh... please... please excuse me. I was... just so happy," she said as she stood up immediately from the sofa. That moment hung on Joe, entered his mind through a side door that he rarely opened. He stood up. Time to leave.

"I don't have much yet, so don't get your hopes up. " Joe said. He couldn't possibly tell her what he had learned about her uncle. The NKVD may surely be trailing him, but so was INTERPOL and the French government and now MI5. Thousands of Nazi war criminals and profiteers were fleeing prosecution through "rat lines" operated by the Vatican, but Uncle Yuri had plunder enough to kill for. Anybody who knew him as Hugo Morand would be interested in acquiring his wonderful art collection. Joe figured that's where Ferrel came in.

"I've got a few things to look into. I'll call you when I have something concrete. In the meantime, leash your dog before I cripple him," Joe said.

"Surely, I will... Joe," she said in her apology.

Joe headed for the door and Polina followed him part of the way, but not all the way. Joe closed the door behind him trying to reason out what had just happened when he bumped into the bellhop in his daze.

"Hey, watch where you're goin'. What are you, punchy?" the bellhop squawked.

Joe was just about to snap at him when he saw that it was Ludko. He pulled him aside, "What are you doing here? I thought you were on Ferrel?"

"Ferrel's at the Ambassador Hotel drinkin'. I got Benny on him."

"That's a little early, don't you think?" Joe said worried about Ferrel's next move.

Ludko sneered, "He ought to drink himself to death."

"Where'd you get that uniform?" Joe asked as they walked together down the hall toward the elevator.

"Right in the supply room in the basement. I thought you might need some help in case there were more Ferrels around."

"There's only one—that I know of," Joe said. "I just can't figure how Ferrel made you. I didn't recognize you, and I've known you for twenty years."

"He's got the instincts of a tiger shark. Guys like Ferrel live by 'em. They have to. He won't get that close again. I got his number now."

"Let's hope so, or next time I'll have to really rough him up," Joe said smiling. "Hey, keep an eye on her." He looked toward Polina's door.

Ludko continued down the hallway, and Joe stood waiting for the elevator. It opened, and Joe got in. "Lobby."


When it reached the lobby, the elevator door opened slowly, like a vaudeville curtain, to reveal Benny the Hat. Joe was glad to see a familiar face, only Benny had a look of horror. Joe lost his smile. A thousand things ran through his mind that ended in panic.

Frankie Ferrel stumbled into the elevator. Joe turned slightly, angled away from the door and pulled his hat down. Ferrel was drunk. "Sevvnnth... seventh floor."

Joe said, "Two, please." The operator looked at him quizzically, shrugged and actuated the control. Joe intended to take Ferrel apart right in the elevator.

Ferrel weaved and turned and looked blearily straight ahead. Joe got control of himself but thought how delightful it would be to pummel Ferrel in this elevator and leave him bleeding on the floor curled up in agony. The door opened at the second floor. Joe edged past Ferrel and added this to a list of regrets running back decades.

He got to the stairwell and flew down to the lobby. Benny looked worried, just standing at the elevator doors. Joe came up behind him and said. "Waiting for someone?"

"Joe, I for sure thought there was gonna be trouble. I didn't know what to do," Benny said with what looked like relief or constipation on his face.

"Ludko's up there. He's in a bellhop's uniform... don't ask," Joe said. "Stay here and let me know immediately if he leaves. Understand?"

"Yeah, I got it, Joe," Benny said. "Want me to tail him out o' here, too?"

"Yeah, but be careful. If he makes you for a tail, drop him and come to the office."

"Gotcha," Benny replied.

Joe took off for the door, negotiating his way through a group of conventioneers invading the hotel lobby. He got to his car, opened the door, and the heat plumed up at him. His head began to throb, and he regretted not hammering Ferrel even more. He cranked the driver's window open, got in, and headed back to the office. On the way, he thought he'd stop at the Grand Crossing Police Station on Cottage Grove and South Chicago Avenue to talk to Donnelly, a good cop and an even better detective.

Joe pulled into the Grand Crossing's parking lot just off South Chicago Avenue. He got out of the car and headed to the doors. He asked for Detective Donnelly. The desk sergeant said, "He's in. Just go down that hall and...."

"Yeah, I know. Thanks." Mike Donnelly was busy typing up a report when Joe stole into the chair at his desk.

Donnelly looked up, "Joe, you son of a gun, what brings you here?" He stuck out his hand and shook Joe's like a lost army buddy. "Damn, it's been a long time since you actually came in here."

"Yeah, I've been busy."

"I heard," Donnelly said and looked up at him smiling. "You need a little help?"

"Mike, it's about Della Penna. Can we talk?" asked Joe.

"Hey, let's get out of here. I'm sick of typing. Let's go to that Polish diner on South Chicago Avenue." Donnelly didn't want anyone at the Third eavesdropping. So, they left in Joe's car and headed down a few blocks to a sleek fluid-looking silver structure that didn't have a single hard edge, not even the corner windows, all sensuous curves. Above this streamlined eatery, in bold letters, was the name "Warsaw Diner."

Inside, the place was immaculate and cool. The booths were framed in chrome tubing, The counter was curved, too, with stools and two-inch square tiles on the floor echoed by four-inch square tiles beneath the counter. A tasteful lightning bolt logo hung above the gleaming visible open grill.

"What do you think, Joe? Let's take this booth at the end here."

"Man, like Flash Gordon's rocket ship," Joe said as he took the place in.

As they got settled in the booth, Donnelly added, "Yeah, the guy who owns this place bought it with a GI loan. He was wounded in North Africa."

"How's he doing with his rocket restaurant?"

"We're early, but this place will be packed in about ten more minutes. We're here just ahead of the shift change crowd."

"I'm glad for him," Joe said. "We owe a lot to these guys."

"Yeah, we do. And we owe more to the guys that didn't make it back."

Joe just looked out the window for a moment until a beautiful girl with blonde hair and blue eyes took their orders.

After she left, "You can see why Hitler invaded Poland," Donnelly quipped.

Joe laughed and said, "Mike, Johnny Della Penna's in trouble. He asked me to help him."

"Joe, I know what you're asking, and I can't get involved," Donnelly said "That's South Chicago's department."

"But that's the problem. The detective on that case is hanging a wrap on Johnny for Rossi. You know what I'm talking about. Right?" Joe asked, confirming that Donnelly understood Detective Kavanaugh was handling the case.

"Look, if you think I can go after another detective outside my house, you're nuts. It ain't gonna happen," Donnelly said. "But I can tell you this: One-Two Johnny will have to go down for it. There's nothing I can do."

"Kavanaugh is no detective. He's a stooge for Rossi."

"Even so, I can't do anything," Mike said.

"I understand." Joe let it go and turned instead to the White Sox. "Hey, what do you think of Ed Lopat?"

Lopat was a young pitcher who only broke into the majors with the Sox two years ago, and he was making quite a reputation for himself.

"Yeah, he's had a good year so far," said Mike. "Not much of a hitter though."

"No, you're right there, but he can throw."

They continued discussing the Sox halfway through lunch when Joe turned the subject back and made one more request, "Mike, is there any way you could pick Johnny up and hold him at Grand Crossing?"

"Why?" asked Mike munching on his fries..

"Maybe to avoid a murder," Joe answered.

"You're not saying they're going to kill him are you?"

"That'd be my guess," Joe said.

"I draw the line there," Mike said. "I'll pick him up. When and where?"

"I'll get it set up and call you later today," said Joe. "How long can you hold him?"

"I could squeeze three days... maybe more," Donnelly said.

"Aw thanks, Mike. I owe you one," said Joe with some relief.

"Just get lunch and we're even," Mike smiled.

"Okay, but I need to pick your brains a little on another topic," asked Joe.

"Go ahead, but it'll be slim pickin's."

Joe smiled at Donnelly's attempt at humility. His knowledge about crime and especially criminals was truly impressive. He was a savant and could remember details of crimes all over the city. That's one of the reasons why he made detective.

"Mike, what more do you remember about Frankie Ferrel?"

"Not a whole lot more than I told yuh. He is rumored to have done a contract job on Dixie Monahan and his bodyguard for the Outfit. It seems Monahan was running a past-posting scam on some of their bookies. He hit them for around $250,000, is what I heard."

Dixie Monahan was a crooked gambler who tried to outsmart the Outfit bookies. He figured out a way to bet on the winning horse after the race had already been run. He did it by having an accomplice at the racetrack while Dixie was at the bowling alley or tavern or social club where the bookie took the bets.

His accomplice would watch the race. As soon as the results were known, he would place a phone call and ask for a "Mr. Edward Brown." Of course there was no Mr. Brown there—it was a signal that meant the number 2 horse in the sixth race had finished in second place. They had a whole series of signals for all kinds of bets.

Monahan knew better than to pick race winners, just place and show bets. He would even place other boxed bets with other horses just to make it look good. After he heard the "Phone for Mr. Edward Brown" announcement in the bowling alley or tavern, he knew exactly which horse to bet.

The bookies didn't have direct lines to the track and didn't know sometimes until late in the evening which horses had won which races. Dixie Monahan had discreet cohorts working other bookies throughout the city, all for a piece of the action.

By the time the Outfit guys wised up, Monahan had hit them for almost a quarter of a million dollars. Then they placed a hit on him, but Monahan had already skipped with his gunman and accomplice, Floyd Thursby.

Donnelly continued, "The contract went out, but Dixie cut out to the Orient—Constantinople, I believe. I know Frankie Ferrel went after him and got him. Got his bodyguard, too, but later."

"What do you mean... later?"

"Well, you know how particular the Outfit is—if the contract is for two guys, two guys better end up dead. It seems Ferrel missed the bodyguard, a guy named Thursby. This Thursby ends up dead in San Francisco, something like a year later. It even made the papers back here as I recall. I'm loose on the details. It's been a long time. Hard to remember." Donnelly laughs as he thinks about it: "I was on a beat back then. Anyways, as I recall, all of a sudden Ferrel comes back here to Chicago. Getting the rest of his money, I'd bet. And that's all I know."

Then, like an electric jolt, he remembered something, an out-of-place detail, Donnelly blurts out "You know what? You know what? I remember that some broad got the wrap for that Thursby hit. How Ferrel arranged that is beyond me, but funny crap happens in San Francisco."

Joe thought about that; let it sink in for a bit. Then, he said, "Ferrel's acting as a bodyguard now for one of my clients. You've got me worried."

"He's dangerous, Joe. But he's just a contractor, not mobbed up. But he knows where a lot of bodies are, I can tell you that. Your client might be in some real trouble. Maybe you too, Joe."

"Hey—with you looking out for me, what have I got to be afraid of?"

"Right. Now, get me back to the house before they miss me."

Joe dropped Mike Donnelly off at the Grand Crossing Station, thanked him again, and headed back down Cottage Grove Avenue toward the office. On his way, he thought now he could at least keep One-Two Johnny alive until he could figure out a way to get him out of the fix he was in. His thoughts went back to Polina and Ferrel. That wasn't working out so well either. He pulled to the curb in front of his office and sat in the car for a long time. He finally got out of the car and went in.

The heat was oppressive inside the office, even with some windows open. Joe turned his fan on. Wilma's too. There was a breeze, lightly scented with steel mill coke fumes, which made him think how some of his school pals had ended up in the mills, in the coke ovens a few miles away, and how they must be suffering today. The room was cooler now. He picked up the phone and dialed Vookie's.

Eddie answered. "Vookie's."

"Eddie, is Johnny Della Penna there?" asked Joe.

"Yeah... hold on. John, it's for you," Eddie called out.

After a moment, "Hello."

"John, it's me, Joe," he said. "Listen, I'm going to have to put you in jail for a while. Is that okay?

"Hey, Joe, I thought you were gonna help me," Johnny complained.

"It's for your own good," Joe explained. "I got a friend at Grand Crossing that's going to arrest you on a burglary charge. Capisce?"

"Hey, you said it with the 'e'," Johnny remarked with a smile."Where'd you learn Italian?"

"I grew up here, remember?" said Joe. "Anyway, you won't be in that long, I promise. See, if you're in jail in another division under another charge, Kavanaugh can't interrogate you. Let me work things out, and I'll call back. "

"Joe, I think I get it, but this jail thing is not my style, you know."

"John, it's all I can come up with right now," Joe tried to explain, without letting him know what he suspected. Joe figured Kavanaugh might arrange for a little accident for Johnny while in custody over at South Chicago Station, maybe a jail break and a bullet in the back. That would clear the case, and the insurance company would pay and drop the whole thing. "John, wait at Vookie's for my call. Okay?"

After an awkward pause, Johnny said, "Sure."

Joe hung up and called Mike Donnelly at Grand Crossing Police Station. "Mike, where do you want to apprehend our burglar?"

"There's a tavern on South Chicago Avenue called 'The Last Stop'," said Donnelly. "I'll pick him up on a tip about the burglary of a jewelry store right nearby." Donnelly knew the owner of the jewelry store, Jerry Engel, and told him what was going to happen and part of the "why" but not all of it. He needed some room in case things went wrong.

Donnelly was streetwise. Joe trusted him and knew everything would be set up right. "Thanks, Mike," Joe said. "Johnny'll be there in thirty minutes." He hung up fast and called back over to Vookie's. Eddie answered. "Put Johnny on, Eddie."

"Joe, he left right after you guys hung up," said Eddie.

"Damn it," Joe yelled.

"Was I supposed to do something, Joe?" Eddie apologized.

"No... no... if you see him, tell him to go to The Last Stop, a tavern, on South Chicago Avenue right away," Joe said and hung up. He called Donnelly back and explained that Johnny skipped. That meant there was a two-time loser with two new raps, both phony, hiding out from everyone, probably on his way out of town.

Wilma walked in from her post office errands. "You look like crap. What's the matter? Your head?" she said.

"Where's Johnny's kid?" Joe asked.

"Over at my sister's. Why?" she asked back.

"Johnny's on the run... from everybody," Joe said. "I just want to know if the kid is okay."

"He's fine, Joe," Wilma reassured him. "I just came from there. We had lunch together. Sweet little boy."

"Call your sister, tell her what's happened, and tell her to watch out for Johnny," Joe said sternly. "He may try to grab the kid before he heads out of town." Joe didn't think that at all. When Rossi finds out their pigeon has flown, they would grab the kid. Johnny would turn himself in, just to protect his son. Sicilian ransom.

# CHAPTER SEVEN

*Earlier that same day*
LONDON
*Hotel Cavendish*

L awrence Hamilton heard the knock at his door. It was Yuri Kemidov. "Please come in Mr. Kemidov. I had just ordered dinner for us. I hope you don't mind Welsh rarebit and Chorley Cake for dessert?" Kemidov nodded his approval. They shook hands perfunctorily.

"That sounds delightful," Yuri replied. "Lovely rooms you have here. I'm wondering if we could review the paintings while we wait."

"Of course, of course, they are here in my office," said Lawrence as he directed Kemidov to the adjoining room. Near the center of the room was a French Provincial desk laid out with the care only Hamilton could bring to his role as an antiquities dealer. The paintings were hung on the opposing wall. The entire ambience was meant to give the air of dignity to the insidious business of stolen art. The practitioners like to think of themselves as erudite sophisticates dealing in the nuanced business of art. Kemidov had swindled art from desperate, unsuspecting Jews trying to flee the gas chambers by selling their art treasures to Kemidov and his ilk. In Kemidov's case he would turn them over to the Gestapo right after the deal was struck, tying up any loose ends and splitting the money with the Gestapo.

Hamilton played his role well. His cover was antiquities, but this time paintings were the bait to lure a potential NKVD informant into MI5's double-agent program. Kemidov, however, did not look the part of the reprobate swindler. He had salt-and-pepper hair, graying ever-so-elegantly at the temples. His eyes were piercingly ultramarine, and his clothes were exquisite. He was tall and of good build for his age without any outward signs of arthritis or malady whatsoever. He had the look of an aristocrat. A perfect specimen.

"Indeed, these are remarkable paintings," Yuri exclaimed. "What, pray tell, is the provenance?"

"Are you doubting my integrity?" Hamilton protested.

"Well, you understand, today, the traffic is high in such matters. I don't want to make a purchase and have the authorities later discover that the works were stolen, you understand," said Yuri in his most convincing appeal to decency.

"I acquired these pieces from a banker in Amsterdam by the name of P.J. Reinstra van Stuyvesande. I have his card," said Hamilton while searching the drawer of his Provincial desk. "Ah, yes, here it is."

Yuri took the card and scrutinized it, knowing full well who Reinstra was. He said, "Indeed, I have had some dealings with his associate Alois Miedl. Have you met him as well?"

Miedl was a friend of Herman Goering. He was, during the war, an active art dealer and one of his nation's most voracious collectors. By 1945, he had purchased nearly 1,800 works for Goering's private collection. But he also ruthlessly exploited his substantial political weight in order to put pressure on his business partners. Jewish art dealers and collectors, who sold on Meidl's conditions, would be allowed to flee the country with little more than their lives. Goering traded paintings by Van Gogh and Cezanne from Miedl for classical works by Vermeer and Rembrandt as represented through Rienstra.

Hamilton knew who Miedl was but feigned ignorance, "No, I'm afraid I haven't made his acquaintance, but I hope to some day soon." Criminals like Miedl and Rienstra were sought after by Dutch authorities for collaboration and treason, and the Reichsmarschall was now on trial in Nuremburg .Yuri would know this and would understand that the paintings before him were plunder from the war. Relief fell over Yuri Kemidov; he was now confident he was dealing with a fellow profiteer and criminal.

Kemidov said, "This Van Gogh is exquisite. Not the bold palette of his later years, quite unique in its styling don't you think?"

"Yes it is a lovely work, but my favorite is the Renoir."

Kemidov inspected the Renoir, leaning very close to the canvas. "So delicate the brushwork, and the colors are so vibrant. My

English fails me, but it is sparkling with light."

"Excellent description, Mr. Kemidov. I would say almost poetic," said Hamilton playing the sycophant.

"Why thank you. Now, this Picasso is a minor work. Even so, it will fetch a good price in the proper gallery. These paintings should be moved to another venue. Wouldn't you agree?" asked Yuri, intimating that their mere possession could lead to arrest and prosecution by any number of governments seeking to right the injustices perpetrated under the Nazis. This also was a not-so-subtle petition for a drastic price reduction.

Hamilton let Yuri believe he was desperate to dispose of these paintings, pacing back and forth, stammering when he said, "Surely, surely we can agree on a price today, as I will... will be traveling abroad shortly." He had just the right amount of quaver in his voice to confirm his anxiety.

Kemidov, sensing his prey's fear, made a proposal: "I am prepared to offer you ten thousand pounds and my fidelity as you take your leave silently into the night."

"That is considerably less than even one of these paintings is worth, let alone all three," pleaded Hamilton.

"Do you really have a choice in this matter?" countered Kemidov. "I am taking all the risk and you have your profit." Yuri assumed that Hamilton had acquired these paintings from collections somewhere in Europe and was now attempting to flee to South America.

In this game, the target must always feel in complete control. Hamilton let him believe the tale he'd spun for himself and agreed, "Yes, I suppose that is all I can hope for, considering the circumstances."

"Excellent, then I shall send an associate over with the funds and take these paintings from you. Then you may be on your way," said Kemidov smiling, like a satisfied predator over his kill. Hamilton donned the pallor of the vanquished when they feel the boot on their necks, a certain helplessness that comes from acceptance.

And it wasn't all an act. Hamilton had hoped to ensnare Kemidov in this charade, but Yuri was an accomplished criminal, far too cunning to make the transaction himself and then take possession of stolen art. No, he would leave that unpleasantness to an accomplice.

Hoping to at least elicit more information from him but knowing the deal was over, Hamilton asked, "Will you not stay then for some dinner?"

"I'm afraid I have some other pressing business to attend to and must be going. Thank you, nevertheless," and Kemidov made his way to the door.

Kemidov took the lift down to the lobby of the Cavendish and hurried through the doors to the street. He had an imperceptible smile, quit pleased with himself and his conquest. He summoned a cab and got in and ordered the driver to head to The Stafford Hotel. As the cab pulled away from the curb, an MI5 agent in a late model Flying Nine family car followed him. His orders were to record Kemidov's movements and report back to Harry Treadwell. What the MI5 agent didn't see was another car, further back, stealthily following them both. The driver, a cadaverous man, and his companion were silent as they tailed the two cars, weaving through the traffic, staying just far enough back to where they would not be spotted.

Not too much later, Kemidov arrived at The Stafford. He paid the driver. The doorman opened the door for him. Kemidov brushed past him without so much as a glance and walked to the lift. The operator asked, "Floor, sir?"

"Four."

When they reached the fourth floor, the operator jogged the car to flush up with the floor and opened the door. "Four, sir. Watch your step."

Kemidov got out and headed down the hallway to his rooms. A dark figure came towards him with his head down. Kemidov paid little attention. They seemed to be timed to cross paths at his door. Kemidov paused and used his key to open his door just as the man passed. The next second he felt the hard steel of a gun muzzle stab into his ribs.

"Get in," ordered the man in a distinct accent. "Don't turn around."

Kemidov gasped and looked up in dread. He thought he had eluded them when he left the Alhambra. Now they were here at The Stafford.

The man shoved Kemidov through the door and kicked it closed behind them. "What is the meaning of this?" protested Kemidov.

"Sit down." The man pushed Kemidov toward the lounge.

In a strong Russian accent, but speaking exquisite English, the man said, "We have some business to discuss, Mr. Hugo Morand."

"What are you talking about? Who is this Hugo Morand? You have me confused with someone else, I say."

The man stood across from Kemidov pointing the gun squarely at his chest. "I have a complete dossier on you, Comrade Yuri. I know everything there is to know about you. My mission is to eliminate you."

"Your mission? What are you talking about?"

"Stop playing the innocent. I am with the NKVD. I was sent to Paris to check the veracity of your intelligence reports. Of course they were bogus, just like Hugo Morand. You played the same game with the Nazis as you did with the NKVD. A Nazi agent would be in my place right now had they won the war."

"This is absurd. The NKVD helped me escape Paris after the liberation."

"That is because I never told them about your deceptions. You fed them useless intelligence through your spy network, a network that only existed in your imagination. It worked, Yuri. You made a grand living off the NKVD and the Nazis, playing one against the other. Brilliant."

"So, if this were true, why didn't you inform your superiors of my blatant treachery?"

"Because I learned of your other business—the art business. You have a fortune in stolen art somewhere. I arranged for the NKVD to get you and your cache out of Paris, out of France. We had to clear up a few other loose ends as well."

Kemidov could feel the rush of fear wash over him now. This NKVD assassin knew his quarry well. Perspiration appeared on his forehead. He pleaded with him, "What is it that you want? Money? Art? Tell me. I will give you anything you want."

"One word from me, Yuri, and there will not be a safe place for you anywhere on Earth. This you know. The NKVD will find you no matter where you hide. They are everywhere, you know."

"Please, please, name your price. I will pay anything you ask."

The assassin smiled and said, "I thought you would comply, once you understood your circumstances."

"What do you want from me? Tell me your name?"

"Let us say that my name is Semyon Tatarov. What we want is the location of your art treasure. But what I want now is something you have owned for a very long time."

Color drained from Kemidov's face, his breath grew shallow, meekly he said, "Whatever do you mean?"

"You know what I want, Yuri." He paused and looked Kemidov straight in the eye and said menacingly, "I heard a fantastic story of an ancient relic, a golden falcon. Where is it?"

"Whatever are you talking about? I have no such object. I have paintings, yes; but no golden statue. I have recently acquired a Van Gogh of great value, perhaps you would like that."

Semyon's laugh turned into a sneer. "Do you think me a fool? That golden falcon is worth ten of your Van Goghs."

"You have been misinformed," said Kemidov. "I have collected art from worthless Jews, I admit; but I have no such object that you speak of."

"One transmission from me to Moscow, and I will have the order to eliminate you. Do you understand that?"

"Yes, yes. But how can I give you something I do not have?"

"I am going to use your phone now to call my associates and have them make a transmission." Semyon picked up the phone with his free hand. "An outside line, please." He waited for the tone and then laid the receiver down. He began dialing a number. He picked the receiver back up, all the time keeping the gun trained on Kemidov. "You will be dead within the hour, Yuri."

"Put the phone down, please. I will get it for you. But it is not what you think it is."

"What do you mean by that?" asked Semyon.

"It was a ruse I used years ago. An imitation. A fraud."

"A ruse? How?" Semyon hung up the receiver. His treacherous plan to get the golden statue all to himself had failed. He listened as Kemidov explained.

"I circulated an extraordinary tale about the golden Falcon of Malta to lure art collectors. I sold them each a worthless lead statue, painted in black enamel. I assured them it was indeed the lost Falcon of Malta, the precious tribute of the Knights Templar. It was all an elaborate fraud."

Semyon looked puzzled and incredulous. His eyes narrowing and murderous.

Kemidov pleaded, "Please look. I have one of the frauds here in the next room."

"Let me see it," demanded Semyon.

Kemidov rose from the lounge and headed for the adjacent room.

"Wait," warned Semyon. "Not too fast. " He followed closely behind Kemidov who opened the door to the next room of his suite. He walked over to a bureau against the far wall and pulled open the top drawer. "Stand back, Yuri. I don't think I shall let you reach in that drawer."

"No, of course," Kemidov said as he moved back from the bureau. "Please see for yourself it is merely a forgery." Semyon passed by Kemidov to look in the drawer.

"These are nothing but clothes. Do you take me for a fool?"

"Please—no—look beneath the clothes."

Semyon removed the top layer, and there it was glimmering— the golden bird, the precious statue. He was transfixed by the brilliance of the jewels and the gleaming gold,  enveloped by thoughts of the legend, the Falcon of Malta, the priceless bird of yore.

*My god, it exists,* he thought. *It is real. The stories are true. I am rich.* He reached in frantically to grab the Falcon. As he did, his face twisted in anguish.

Kemidov's lips curled back viciously as he now twisted the dagger. The NKVD man could only gasp as Kemidov had pierced his lung and his heart with the dagger always hidden in his suit coat. In a bizarre choreography, Kemidov wrenched the gun from his hand. Semyon rattled, gasping for air as his heart stopped beating and his blood pressure fell. He collapsed toward Kemidov.

The NKVD assassin looked up at Kemidov. His eyes dulled, and Kemidov let him drop to the floor.

In complete disgust, "And *you* were going to eliminate me?"

Kemidov rushed to the bathroom and grabbed some towels to absorb any blood. He pulled the dagger from Semyon's body and cleaned the blood on the assassin's clothes. He pressed a towel to the wound and placed the other beneath his unfortunate victim. Then... a knock at his door.

Kemidov's eyes grew wide. *An accomplice?* Kemidov picked up the gun, put it in his right hand and went into the sitting room and opened the door a few inches with his left.

"I've come to make the bed and tidy up."

"I am in an important phone conversation, please come back later."

"Well, it won't be 'til tomorrow then, sir."

"That will be fine," Kemidov said and slammed the door. He went back to the bureau, stepped over the body, reached in the drawer, and removed the little golden falcon. Even he marveled at this stunning treasure, solid gold and beset in jewels. Radiant. The only one of its kind in the world. He took a pillow case from another drawer and wrapped the bird carefully. He placed the statue in an oversized attaché case and carried it into the sitting room and set it near the door.

He picked up the phone and placed a call to Evrard Molyneux, known affectionately to his friends as "the butcher." Kemidov met "the butcher" in Paris during the Nazi occupation.

Working both sides of the espionage game while amassing a fortune in stolen art presented certain problems. Kemidov needed a man like Evrard Molyneux to take care of the loose ends that would invariably arise in his business. After questioning his contacts in the French underworld, he located Molyneux, a career criminal whose specialty was murder.

"Evrard, get over here as soon as possible. You will need two trunks," ordered Kemidov. "...Yes, another problem we need to take care of."

Evrard understood what had to be done. He had been working with Kemidov in his guise as Hugo Morand for a number of years. Now, because of that alliance, Evrard, too, was running from the French government and prosecution as a traitor. Evrard picked up his saw and his knives and a length of oilcloth and put them in the suitcases. He arrived at The Stafford within the hour and went directly to Kemidov's rooms. They both set about the ghoulish task of hanging the NKVD agent by his feet from the shower head and slitting his throat to drain the blood.

Evrard asked, "Who is this?"

"He called himself Semyon Tatarov," answered Kemidov, "an NKVD assassin who has been stalking us for quite some time. He had a great deal of intelligence on our operations with the Gestapo and NKVD."

"I think I remember that face," said Evrard.

"He will bother us no more," said Kemidov. As an afterthought he warned, "But there are sure to be others."

Kemidov didn't tell Evrard about Semyon's shakedown over the golden falcon. That would put thoughts in Evrard's head that might prove troublesome at this point. As it stood, Evrard knew little about the art and antiquities business and cared less. He was content with the large payments Kemidov provided for his services.

The two retired to the lounge and listened to classical music, drinking fine cognac, smoking Kemidov's expensive cigars. Neither said a word. Each lost in his own thoughts. Evrard dozed off occasionally. It took little to satisfy Evrard Molyneux.

But Kemidov was worried. The implications of this rogue NKVD agent making such a bold play foreshadowed a menacing storm. The NKVD dossier on Yuri Kemidov, alias Hugo Morand, must have grown thick with details that could tempt even the staunchest communist. Yuri's stash was now easily over a million pounds. Added to this was his double cross of the NKVD.

Kemidov considered himself a cultured person, a refined art dealer, not a scurvy little spy. As Hugo Morand, he had developed a reputation in Switzerland as a dealer of considerable skill and influence who could find a buyer for any art regardless of its provenance.

The Nazis were more than happy to use him to dispose of art looted by them in the occupied territories. Most were modern works by what Hitler termed "degenerate" artists. Hugo Morand made frequent trips between Paris and Switzerland to unload the Nazis' stolen works by Picasso, Dali, Pissaro and others in exchange for Rembrandts, Titians, and Rubens. For an art criminal like Kemidov, times like these would never come again, and he made the most of them.

Watching this spectacle of industrialized looting on a scale the world had never seen before made the NKVD very uncomfortable. Not fully trusting their sometime-agent Yuri Kemidov, the NKVD attached an "observer" to monitor his activities. Semyon Tatarov was that agent, and he soon learned of Kemidov's duplicity.

Kemidov decided early on to work both sides of the street, enriching himself in the process. He would feed interesting but worthless information to the NKVD about the Nazi military organization in Paris in exchange for a handsome salary to pay his "operatives." Kemidov created an entire network of fictitious spies, gathering intelligence from all over Paris and greater France. He played the same game with the Nazis: gathering and providing harmless intelligence on Soviet military and NKVD activities in the East.

Had Semyon reported any of this, the NKVD would have ordered him to eliminate "Hugo Morand." But Semyon had reasons to let Kemidov live. He had uncovered Kemidov's rapacious theft of Jewish art collections and his dealings with Goering and other members of the German High Command, all acquiring art for their personal collections. His diligence unearthed yet another fantastic story.

It seems Kemidov, through murder, had come into possession of the priceless Golden Falcon of Malta, a treasure of the Knights Templar, and it was hidden somewhere in Paris. No... Semyon would not be informing the NKVD spymasters of Yuri's offenses, not just yet anyway.

When the Allies liberated Paris, Semyon kept silent as the NKVD helped Kemidov escape from Paris and the reprisals of the French government. They established Kemidov as one of their NKVD operatives in London using his real name along with most of his art.

Semyon was ordered back to Moscow. Instead, he and his accomplices chose to trail Kemidov to London, to the Alhambra Hotel and to the art and to the Maltese Falcon. Ever the wary criminal, Kemidov sensed the wolves at the door and slipped out of the Alhambra late one night and moved to the exclusive Stafford.

Semyon eventually tracked him down at The Stafford, but the pursuit ended in the death of the predator instead of the prey. Kemidov smoking his cigar was satisfied with the outcome but thought: *Semyon was not alone.* His thoughts were broken when, without a word, Evrard "the butcher" rose and headed to the bathroom to dismember the body of Semyon Tatarov.

"Be careful there is no blood on the carpet, Evrard," ordered Kemidov. "When you're finished, dispose of it and take this envelope over to one Lawrence Hamilton at the Hotel Cavendish. He waved the envelope with his hand. There you will pick up three paintings. They should fit well in these suitcases after you dispose of the contents, but make sure there is no blood to stain the paintings. Come back here immediately. Do you understand?"

"Oui," said Evrard.

Kemidov headed for the door, preferring to entrust the butchering to his Frenchman. He turned back and said, "I'll leave this here." He placed the envelope on the table at the door as he left the room. He picked up the attaché case and headed for the lobby. Kemidov left The Stafford in a cab taking him to Limehouse Dock, Pier 23. The MI5 agent in the family car picked him up just as the cab pulled away from the hotel.

Evrard removed the saw and knives from the trunk and spread oilcloth on the bathroom floor. He removed his own clothes and lifted the body from the shower and laid it on the oilcloth. He always began by severing the head. He took great pleasure in starting at the head, with a few deft strokes of the saw it was severed from the body. He carefully wrapped it in oil cloth and placed it in one of the suitcases, which looked more like small trunks.

Evrard removed the legs below the knees followed by the upper thighs, wrapping and packing them into the cases. He was quite an efficient meat cutter and packer, having worked in an abattoir for many years in Paris. He proceeded to remove the arms at the shoulders, folded them, and wrapped them neatly in oilcloth. He arranged the parts carefully in each suitcase. He wrapped the torso and placed it into the larger trunk.

He scrubbed the shower spotless. Evrard smiled as he admired his work. He washed himself and his tools and put his clothes back on. He picked up the suitcases as if they were empty and headed toward the door. On his way out, he looked back double-checking everything. Satisfied, he walked to the lift and descended to the lobby.

Evrard walked casually through the lobby of The Stafford carrying the suitcases. The doorman held the large door as Evrard approached and said, "Good evening, sir."

Evrard did not acknowledge him. He left the hotel and walked a block to his rented car and placed the cases in the trunk and slammed it shut. He drove a distance to Newgate Street. London had been so savagely bombed during the Blitz, every block had at least one building in rubbles, an excellent place to dispose of the body.

Evrard spotted a dark and secluded area. He carried the cases into a building whose roof and two walls had collapsed, forming a grotto away from the street. He tossed aside some rubble to form a shallow pit.

Evrard opened the cases, delighted by the contents, which looked like some grotesque ventriloquist's dummy folded into its compartment. He removed the body parts. *Bon, pas de sang.* Relieved. The suitcases were clean.

He shoved what was once a NKVD agent in the crater and threw the debris back over him. No one would discover that body any time soon. The suitcases were still fine. Evrard now made his way to the Hotel Cavendish to meet Lawrence Hamilton.

He drove from Newgate Street to Farmington Road then on to Clerkenwell Road and made his way to the Hotel Cavendish. With suitcases in hand, he entered the hotel and asked the clerk to ring up Lawrence Hamilton. The clerk picked up the phone and dialed Lawrence Hamilton's rooms. "Yes, sir," said he clerk, "there's a mister..." and looked questioningly at Evrard and raised his eyebrows.

"Molyneux," replied Evrard.

"A Mister Molyneux for you, sir," he reported.

"Send him up," said Hamilton who recalled the dossier on Hugo Morand mentioned a Parisian handyman named "the butcher." A killer as he recalled. After what seemed an eternity... a knock at the door.

"Lawrence Hamilton?" demanded Evrard.

"Yes, indeed, come in," said Hamilton, "and you are Mr. Kemidov's man?"

Molyneux looked at Hamilton with those dark empty eyes and handed him the envelope and stood there beside the suitcases. Evrard was just now considering a plan to kill this Englishman. *I will keep the money for myself and deliver these paintings to Yuri. Who will know?* But he feared Kemidov's intelligence and brutality and decided to remain standing there. He let the thought pass.

Lawrence took the envelope and opened it. He counted the money, and the count was short £200. *Always the predator,* he thought. "The paintings are here in this room," he said, and motioned for Evrard to enter the adjacent room.

Evrard went right to work like an obedient dog, placing the paintings cautiously in the suitcases, separating them with linen cloth. Evrard did not know the value of the paintings only that Yuri Kemidov would fly into a rage if anything happened to them from careless treatment.

Hamilton observed, "I see you are quite efficient and experienced at handling art."

Evrard nodded his head without saying a word. After packing them, Evrard headed directly to the door and left. As the door closed, Hamilton thought: *Quite a gruesome chap.*

An MI5 agent waited outside in a car ready to follow Molyneux wherever he went. Evrard led the MI5 agent on a lengthy circuitous journey through London, an old habit he developed in Occupied Paris, always leery of the Gestapo. Molyneux finally arrived at The Stafford.

He parked the car about a block away, another precaution from his days amid the Nazis. He carried the suitcases along the street and into the hotel. He went up to Yuri Kemidov's rooms and stayed there until Yuri returned. He cautiously removed the paintings and set them leaning on the lounge. He looked at the paintings and saw nothing more than some bright colors and what he thought were crude renderings of everyday things. He ignored them and lit a cigarette, turned on the radio, and listened to music, waiting for his master to come home.

# CHAPTER EIGHT

## LONDON, ENGLAND
*Limehouse Dock, Pier 23*

At Limehouse Dock, Pier 23, sat a Portuguese cargo ship, over 400 feet long and about 60 feet wide with a 26-foot draft named *Ponta Delgada*. When Kemidov arrived, the fog was heavy and yellow. It slithered into your clothes. You could feel it on your face. He boarded the ship with his attaché and went straight to the captain's cabin without raising even an eyebrow of the busy crew readying the vessel for her voyage. He knocked on the cabin door. An English speaking voice said, "Come in."

"I'm here to inspect my cargo, I am Yuri Kemidov," he said while handing him his card.

Taking the card and inspecting it, "I'm Captain DiGiacomo, your cargo is secure below."

"May I inspect it nevertheless?" demanded Kemidov.

"Certainly, I'll take you personally," said Captain DiGiacomo as he motioned for Kemidov to exit the door and continue down to the cargo hold. They went below deck, and Captain DiGiacomo grabbed a manifest from the office below. "Here they are, over here," he said as he read the manifest and pointed toward the bow of the ship. They both walked over. The Captain absently noted how Kemidov seemed to list slightly to the right under the burdened of his attaché. He dismissed the thought as they reached the area where his crates were stored. Captain DiGiacomo patted the crates, "Here they are."

"I see," said Kemidov as he looked over the crates. "I would like a few moments to inspect the contents of my shipment."

"Take all the time you need. We don't shove off until midnight," he said with a smile. "I'll be in my cabin if you need anything else."

Once the captain was out of sight, Kemidov got out his keys and feverishly opened each crate. He scrutinized the contents of each, checking them against his records. The criminal trusts no one.

The looting was exceptional, mostly oil paintings. There were works by Picasso, Braque, Matisse, Modigliani, Pissarro, Van Gogh, and Degas, as well as lesser French artists.

Kemidov opened a smaller crate and removed two paintings by Cezanne, one by Pissarro and one by Monet. He reached in and lifted up a false floor and removed a small crate. He had the crate builder make these special provisions for his most precious acquisition. Kemidov gently removed the bird from his attaché and unwrapped the linen. He marveled, as he always did, at the beauty of the priceless Falcon of Malta.

"You shall be safe in here for your long voyage to Canada," he said as he guardedly wrapped the falcon back in its linen and placed it in the little crate. He found a hammer and nails nearby and nailed the crate shut. He lowered it into the secret compartment. His eyes shifted from crate to crate all around the ship's hold, searching for some imagined intruder or meddlesome deck hand. Satisfied no one was watching, he replaced the false bottom and repacked the paintings, sealing and locking the crate once again, and then he nailed it shut. He did the same to all his other crates, sealing and nailing each one of them.

Kemidov patted the last crate affectionately and headed above deck and returned to Captain DiGiacomo's cabin. "I have perhaps one more crate to bring aboard," he said. "I shall, of course, pay the additional shipping fees."

"Is it a large crate? As you can see, I'm nearly full, and I have more freight due in this evening," cautioned Captain DiGiacomo.

"No... not at all. In fact it wouldn't be larger than two suitcases," he reassured the captain. "I will send it with my associate later."

Captain DiGiacomo said, "Yes and I'll have his room ready when he gets here. The accommodations aren't the best, but we won't be at sea that long."

Evrard would be aboard to insure that nothing happened to Yuri Kemidov's art trove while en route. Kemidov hurried back to The Stafford to pack and catch his flight later that evening. The MI5 agent noted the name of the ship and its dock and followed his cab back to the hotel. What he didn't see was that he too was being followed.

From a side street emerged a car with the same two men as before. The gaunt man was still driving and his companion was still silent as they weaved through traffic trailing their targets with the precision and stealth of a panther.

Evrard stared up at Kemidov as he entered the room.

"Did you get everything done as I asked, Evrard?"

"Oui," said Evrard almost dozing.

"Ah...these are marvelous paintings, wouldn't you say, my friend?" remarked Kemidov, admiring the paintings displayed on the sofa, not expecting an answer.

"I don't know. I suppose they are fine," remarked Evrard.

"They are fine, indeed, and will make us a handsome profit when we finally get them to Canada," said Kemidov. "You may pack them up carefully and get to the *Ponta Delgada* on Pier 23 at Limehouse Dock, leaving tonight at midnight. I have booked passage for you to Montreal. When you get there, I have rooms for you at the Le Saint-Sulpice hotel, 414 Rue Saint-Sulpice. Here I have written it down for you." He proffered the address and an envelope containing Canadian currency.

"A great deal of money, Yuri. How long before I hear from you?" he asked, slowly turning toward Kemidov with his head cocked.

"Not long, my friend. I have to take a Pan Am Clipper across to the United States and meet an art dealer in New York. Your job is to watch our investments aboard the *Ponta Delgada* and make sure nothing goes awry," said Kemidov, and while writing an additional note said, "When you arrive, rent a truck and transport our shipment to this address." He handed Evrard the paper. "The Montreal docks are a few kilometers from Le Saint-Sulpice hotel in old Montreal. The area is somewhat dangerous at night, but perhaps you are the one to cause that fear, eh, Evrard?" Kemidov laughed at his humor. Evrard folded the paper.

And at the Hotel Cavendish, Lawrence Hamilton had been briefed by the MI5 field agent of Kemidov's activities. The agent told Hamilton how Kemidov went to Limehouse Dock and how he boarded the *Ponta Delgada*.

Hamilton thought: *Kemidov is about to make his move.* Wherever his trio of paintings were headed, Kemidov couldn't be far behind. Hamilton rang Harry Treadwell and told him of the ship and its possible contents. Harry assured him they would get the ship's logs and manifest, but this case was not a priority. Hamilton would get the information, but it would be too late.

Early the next morning an agent called Hamilton and told him the ship left port at midnight and was bound for Montreal, Canada. They discovered there was a passenger aboard but had not discovered his name. Hamilton thought it might be Kemidov.

Ever since the end of the war, sections of MI5 had been cooperating with the International Criminal Police Organization (INTERPOL) pursuing cultural theft and its collaborators. That alliance brought on its own inefficiencies and rivalries. Just a few years earlier, the *Ponta Delgada* would have been boarded and searched. Now, there were too many channels to go through.

Hamilton received word that the agent surveilling Kemidov had not seen him leave The Stafford at all last night. Hamilton was relieved that his quarry was still at hand, but dismayed that the evidence and an accomplice were now out to sea. Hamilton rang up Harry Treadwell and told him that Kemidov was about to flee and should be apprehended at his hotel at once.

Harry dispatched another agent immediately. Together with the surveillance man, he was to apprehend Kemidov. The surveillance agent entered the hotel, flashed his credentials at the desk clerk and headed up the stairs to Kemidov's rooms on the fourth floor. The MI5 man outside watched the rear exits and the fire escape. They had orders to shoot if Kemidov resisted in any way.

The agent knocked politely on Kemidov's door. No answer. He tried the door handle—it opened. The agent drew his gun and cautiously entered the room, his eyes darting everywhere to catch a glimpse of a trap. The sweat beginning to bead on his forehead, his stomach muscles hardened, his breathing became rapid— anticipating that flash of panic that comes with....

Nothing.

The room was empty. He searched every closet, under the bed, behind the sofa, in the shower—no one. Kemidov had vanished. He went back down to the desk clerk.

"When did Kemidov check out," he demanded.

"Why, he hasn't," replied the clerk. "In fact, he has yet to settle his account."

The agent left the bewildered clerk and headed immediately to the exit door. Outside, he motioned for his partner to get in his car. They headed back to their headquarters to turn in their report to Harry Treadwell and the head of MI5 's INTERPOL liaison unit. Across the street, as they drove away, was a tall pale man dressed plainly watching them intently as they left. He crossed the street and entered the hotel. He, too, asked the clerk about Kemidov.

"Why is everyone so interested in Mr. Kemidov?" asked the clerk. "Apparently he has left without paying his account." The tall man simply turned around and left The Stafford and disappeared into a waiting automobile.

An hour later that morning, Harry rang up Hamilton at his hotel, "Lawrence, I'm afraid your pigeon has already flown, and we have no idea where."

"He couldn't have simply vanished. He's aboard that ship."

"Lawrence, we know that ship docks in Montreal. You'll get him there."

"What about my operations here?" said Hamilton. He had been working on two other cases before this one came up.

Harry said, "We shall never get them all, you know; but Kemidov was one of Reichsmarschall Goering's curators and a valuable asset for MI5." After a short pause sorting through some papers, he continued, "We will maintain your situation here. Inform your concierge you have business in Paris and that you will return shortly. We will have a contact in Paris take care of anything that transpires in your absence. I'll send over a packet with full details. Besides, we have to retrieve our expensive bait, " said Harry with a playful grin. "Good luck, Lawrence."

"Thank you, sir," said Hamilton and hung up. He pulled writing paper and a pen from the drawer and began to code a message to Joe Ganzer. If he could have Joe meet that ship in Montreal, perhaps Joe could discover who was on board. If it was Kemidov, Joe could apprehend him. If not, at least he could pursue the illicit cargo. He used the same poem code as before, except he used the third stanza to key the message. It read:

```
KUIAM  EEOLO  AGCHA  MIINB  DAMCH
RLLEK  CNAEL  ORRVE  SVOOD  TTOAR
UOCFA  TRRDC  DEGDN  MHIDA  PPTAF
JRGOA  ETPIB  EPISE  OSORT  PAGTO
EKRON  BALEN  DDRCT  LFIOE  ARISH
```

He sent it off immediately, but it would take a number of days before he could arrange his departure without causing disruption to his other cases. He had time. The *Ponta Delgada* would not make Montreal for at least a week.

# CHAPTER NINE

SOUTH CHICAGO
*Jos. Ganzer Investigations*

Wilma had been calling every dive and gin mill on the South Side trying to get a lead on One-Two Johnny. She made off that she was his girlfriend, that he stood her up, and that she was mad. No luck.

Wilma opened the door to Joe's office. "Joe, I can't come up with anything. Johnny's just gone," said Wilma. "I'm sorry."

"That's okay. Look, it's getting late," Joe said despondently. "Why don't you go home."

"Sure, see you tomorrow... right?"

"Maybe, I don't know. Things are nuts."

"Hey I could—"

Joe interrupted her, "No, go home. Everything will be fine."

Wilma left reluctantly. Joe started pacing around his office. After about ten minutes he laughed at himself. *Where am I going in here?* Fed up with waiting for something to happen, Joe grabbed his suit coat and hat and left. He got in his car and headed over to Vookie's Tavern. Even with all the people, Vookie's was the one place he could relax and think. It was as if Joe drew strength from the clamor, from the controlled chaos of people, the glasses clinking, people talking, music playing.

When he got there, One-Two Johnny was already in Joe's office booth waiting for him. Joe went straight to the booth without even saying "hello" to Eddie or anyone else. He sat opposite Johnny.

"Where the hell have you been?

"I was over by Cal Park, lookin' at the lake. I had to figure things, yuh know?"

"So what did you figure?"

"Joe, I know you're good at all this. I heard things about you. During the war."

"That's all bullshit."

"Not what I heard," said Johnny and paused. "I gotta trust you. You don't wanna say what you think, but I figure I'm walkin' dead anyway."

"Not yet," said Joe. "Look, I've got to get you over to the Grand Crossing District and get you arrested. Mike Donnelly is going to pick you up on suspicion of burglary. You'll be in jail for the next three days. That's all he can hold you for. In the meantime you won't be on the street."

"Yeah, I follow."

"John, I think you're in a lot of trouble. The rap will stick if the perpetrator is dead."

"What about my boy? What about Tommy?"

"He can keep staying with Wilma's sister. She has a boy Tommy's age, and there won't be a problem."

"Joe, I'm gonna owe you if I get out of this."

"I'll send you the bill," Joe said. "Now look, I've got to go out of town for a few days on another case. Don't panic. I'll be back and get this straightened out."

"Okay, Joe."

"I have to call Donnelly. So just walk out to my car. It's just around the corner." Joe went into Eddie's back room to put in a call to Detective Donnelly. Johnny left a few moments later, his head down.

Joe exited the backroom and looked at Eddie on his way out and just pursed his lips. Eddie got the message: things weren't looking too good.

As Joe reached his car and got in, Johnny hesitated, looked around. "Come on, John."

Johnny got into the passenger's seat and rolled the window down. "It's still hot."

"Yeah, summer can't end soon enough for me."

"Me neither."

Joe drove north toward Grand Crossing. Joe turned into the alley behind a jewelry store on 77th and Cottage Grove Avenue. He got out of the car and walked over to the rear entrance door of the Engel's Jewelry. He kicked the door in.

Johnny leaned toward the driver's side window. "Hey, Joe I

don't... uh didn't... work like that. I usually go in through the roof."

"Yeah, I'm a lousy burglar, but I'm setting you up for the rap anyway," Joe said.

"Story of my life."

"Here comes Donnelly, right on time," as Joe pointed down the alley. Donnelly pulled up, killed his lights, and got out of the car and walked over to the jewelry store's rear door.

"Nice work you did here, Joe."

"I'm kind of proud of it myself, but why didn't the alarm go off?"

"I had the owner turn it off. I told him I was setting a trap," Donnelly said. He looked at One-Two Johnny. "Johnny, I'll have to take you in on suspicion."

"I never thought I'd say this to a cop, but: Thanks for arresting me," Johnny said as he walked with his musical swagger to Donnelly's car and got inside. Detective Donnelly smiled and got back behind the wheel.

Looking at Joe from the driver's seat, Donnelly said, "You know, I can only keep him three days on a suspicion charge, but I'll file it late. That'll give you more time."

"Thanks, Mike," said Joe. "Tell the owner the damage will be paid for."

"Sure," said Donnelly as he thought for a moment. "You know, I could book him and send him to Cook County. Might get us some more time, but his chances there would be worse."

"Yeah, probably right," said Joe and got in his car.

He gave One-Two Johnny a little nod as he drove past them heading back to his office.

Very late that evening a telegram arrived at Joe's office. The door to his office was open. The boy just walked in and handed it to Joe. "Wow, Mr. Ganzer, you sure are an important detective with all these telegrams."

"Don't let that fool you. It's probably from my landlord threatening to evict me if I don't pay up," and he took the telegram from him and gave him a dollar tip.

The young man looked at the money and said, "Maybe if you didn't tip so good, you could pay your rent." The kid smiled.

"Yeah, you'd better give it back."

"Well if you think—."

Shaking his head, "Get out of here. Take your girl out to a movie or something." The young man left with a smile, and Joe opened the telegram. "The poem code again?" he muttered to himself. He sat at his desk and began decoding the message. It took quite some time. When he finished, his paper read:

KEMIDOVFLEDSTOL
ENARTBOUNDFORMO
HTREALINTERCEPT
SHIPPONTADELGAD
AACCOMPLICEORTA
RGETABOARDKGBCO
NFIRMEDIARRIVEA
SAPGOODLUCKJOEH

Joe didn't like it. It was getting complicated. Hamilton needed Joe to apprehend and detain whoever showed up to collect that art. *And then what?* he thought. He had to level with Polina and tell her that her uncle was an international criminal and war profiteer. He had to show her that Uncle Yuri was just using her to shield himself and provide safe harbor while he disposed of his art.

The NKVD evacuation crew that managed to get Kemidov out of Paris did so not realizing the extent and value of his stolen art collection. But someone in the NKVD knew. Joe understood their operations. Hugo Morand definitely had a permanent "shadow" courtesy of the NKVD. This shadow knew everything, and he did not work alone. They were waiting for Hugo Morand to become Yuri Kemidov safely established in London. Then, when the time was right, the shadow and his confederates would strike.

Joe couldn't figure why the NKVD shadow hadn't killed

General Kemidov by now and made off with his art trove. He could have informed Moscow that Kemidov had been captured or had defected. Then they could dispose of his collection through any number of galleries and disappear wealthy men.

During the war, and after, most of the black market in Soviet Bloc countries was operated by the NKVD. They had volumes of experience in stolen property and contraband. For them, a man like Yuri Kemidov would be an easy mark, or so they thought. Kemidov had somehow slipped away from the NKVD and MI5 along with his art and right before their collective eyes. The magician vanished. Now they were all in a race to get their hands on him.

Joe locked up and drove over to Stony Island Avenue, heading toward his apartment in Hyde Park. He lived near the University of Chicago on 57th and Drexel Avenue, a pleasant neighborhood, brownstones, porches, tree-lined. His building included university professors and administrators. They were pleasant and cordial but kept to themselves. He parked the Chevy and trudged up the stairs to the second floor. He took a quick shower, laid on the bed, staring up at the ceiling. Something wasn't right.

He couldn't see MI5 getting involved merely to apprehend an art swindler, even if he was a Nazi collaborator. No, they had other plans, and Joe was now grudgingly back behind the veil on another unknowable mission. His sleep would be restless and the dreams would return.

Next morning, back in his office, Joe studied the telegram from Hamilton again. He memorized the contents and set it on fire in his ashtray. As it was smoldering in the ashtray, Wilma came into work.

"What are you cooking now?" said Wilma.

Joe said, "My lunch. Hey, I'm headed to the Heights on that summons thing for Albert."

"You'd better," she said. "We owe Mr. Strugala the rent this week."

Joe smiled, "Maybe I can skip the rent if I get that summons served."

"What, that skinflint?"

"Now, now. We mustn't speak poorly of our landlord."

"How long?"

"Couple of days tops."

"Okay. Call me."

Joe grabbed his hat off the coat tree. "I will." He cantered down the stairs and on to the street. He got in the Chevy and drove over to Vookie's for lunch before he made the long trek to Chicago Heights. Ludko and Benny called in while he was there. Joe told them to keep the shadows on Polina and Ferrel. He said he would be back in a couple of days. Joe left Vookie's and drove to Halsted Street heading south. He had time to think.

The "Heights" was dominated by organized crime. The Outfit had its tendrils in every aspect of the city, slowly bleeding it to death. Capone had one of his hideouts in the Heights back in the bootleg days. He was the visiting unofficial mayor until the FBI put him in a box in Alcatraz. Today he's sitting by a pool in Florida blathering like an idiot. The Outfit's "capo" in the Heights these days is Frank LaPorte. He developed gambling, vending machine, and prostitution rackets in South Cook County, Will County, and Northwest Indiana.

But Laporte thought himself too good for the Heights. He lives in Flossmoor, an exclusive community of lawyers, doctors, and businessmen a few miles and a world away from the Heights. That's where Joe was heading first, to the Idlewild Country Club in Flossmoor to meet Albert Strugala's client, Howard Schneider, a banker.

Idlewild Country Club has been around since 1908, built by a group of wealthy men. They wanted a club nestled in secluded surroundings where men of influence could escape Chicago and spend a day on a championship 18-hole golf course with their friends and business associates. It had watered fairways, a swimming pool, even air conditioning. And it had a long waiting list. Joe wasn't on it.

He maneuvered off Halsted and headed over to Western Avenue, still heading south. It would be quite a ways. He drove leisurely. Lost in his thoughts.

Joe was trying to figure an angle for Johnny Della Penna, a way to get him out of the jamb he was in without getting himself and Johnny killed in the process. As thought swirled into thought, he ended up back to the Polina case.

But Polina conjured up feelings he struggled to forget, not just the attraction to his client, but a kind of psychological dementia tremens brought on by loose ends and lies and contradictions, flashbacks to those days with the OSS and Hamilton. He thought he had left that all behind when the war ended. Now it was back.

Jolted from the flashbacks—Joe felt something. The third eye, a guardian angel, something moved his feet to the clutch and brake pedals. The tires now screamed in agony as the wheels locked, the rubber grinding into the pores of the asphalt. The tail lights of the truck at the stop up ahead grew larger, closer, brighter.

Joe snapped out of it. Instinct took control. Joe stood on the brakes and the clutch. He drew in a breath, ready for the impact.

The driver inside the truck heard the tires wailing. He looked in his side mirror. Joe's Chevy was hurtling toward him. The driver grabbed the wheel hard and then... nothing. Quiet. The engine of his truck was all he heard.

He checked the side mirror. He saw Joe's face behind the windshield. The driver got out of the truck. His adrenalin hit hard, almost a panic. "What the hell happened? You been drinkin'?"

"No," yelled Joe. "I was going to ask you the same thing."

The driver was confused now. "Whaaa...?

"What do you mean parking that truck in front of me? Another coat of paint and I'd've hit you." Joe flashed that smile.

"Buddy, you gave me quite a scare," said the driver. "I thought you was gonna smash into the rear of my truck. Mighta cut your head off."

"Might not of mattered," Joe said.

The truck driver laughed, let the tension dissolve. "Well be careful. Where yuh headed?"

"I'm from Chicago. I'm a little lost." Joe lied to cover his distracted mind.

"I'll say," said the driver. "So where yuh headed?"

"I'm looking for Idlewild Country Club."

The driver knew all about the exclusive club; he had made deliveries there. He gave Joe and the Chevy the once-over. "You don't look the type."

"I'm not. I have to meet someone there."

"Well, it's about another coupla miles or so. You can't miss it. Big huge entrance. Just stay here on Western Ave. It turns into Dixie Highway about a mile down. No signs."

"Okay, thanks," said Joe. "Sorry if I gave you a start."

"No problem, buddy; but be careful. There's a lotta stops and cops around here."

"Sure. I will. Thanks again."

The truck driver gave a little wave and smiled as he headed back to his truck. They were both relieved. He got in the truck, revved the engine, threw it into gear and took off. The Chevy had stalled. Joe didn't even know it until just now. He took it out of gear, turned the key off, and just sat at the stop.

This close call made Joe realize he was losing. He needed to control those thoughts and memories that invaded him. So he focused instead on the matter today. *Got to make that meeting.*

Joe turned the key. The Chevy tried but didn't start. *Great.* He tried again. The engine cranked but nothing. *Don't flood it. Just wait.* On the third try, "Thank you, old boy."

He continued on to Idlewild Country Club. Joe pulled up the long drive to the clubhouse and parked, getting looks from some of the men exiting the golf course. Joe's Special Deluxe Chevy stood out among the Packards and Continentals.

The clubhouse looked almost like a Swiss Chalet except with a definite Prairie School influence. It reminded Joe of some of the homes he'd seen in Oak Park. Graceful lines and field stone. Two massive doors separated by glass greeted its members. Joe opened one and walked in.

The attendant at the cloakroom on the left said, "Your hat, sir?"

"Nobody else's?" Joe just continued past the cloakroom and the lobby heading toward the center where a row of large, floor-to-ceiling, wood columns guarded the entrance to a dining room. On the right of the columns was the entrance to the bar where Joe was to meet Howard Schneider. He went in and walked over to a bar that had to be forty feet long with two bartenders. *Eddie ought to see this.*

Joe asked one of the bar tenders, "I'm here to meet Mr. Howard Schneider."

"He's seated at that far table, sir." He pointed to a table off in the corner.

"Thanks." Joe walked over to the table. The banker was thick-bodied, glasses, curly silver hair, thinning with a few scattered black strands.

"You're Joe Ganzer," said Schneider.

"I'm out of place here, right?"

"Not at all. Albert told me what you looked like," said Schneider while sipping his martini. "You're late."

"Do you want another detective?"

Schneider laughed. "Albert told me you're somewhat intolerant. Sit down, please. And call me Howie."

"We're not friends, Mr. Schneider. I'm here to do a job."

"Exactly, I appreciate your professionalism. I'll get down to cases," said Schneider. "I became involved in a land development deal with a contractor who seems to be... how shall I say this?... disingenuous."

"He's mobbed up?" Joe asked.

"I see you understand the possible situation," said Schneider. "But I'm not sure. He is a Chicago Heights contractor. We were going to build affordable homes for returning GIs as part of the Park Forest development in cooperation with American Community Builders, a major builder. This village would provide a variety of housing options for over 5000 families, an entire community with parks and shopping, even a library."

"Where's Park Forest?"

"It will be south of here about five miles or so. Is that important?"

"I like to know as much as I can Mr. Schneider."

"It hasn't been built yet, just the planning stages. We were to be part of this 'GI Town' development. There will be an announcement at a press conference scheduled for perhaps October at the Palmer House in Chicago, if all goes well. Unfortunately, Mr. Marino seems less inclined to participate these days. So I've filed a lawsuit against him."

"Let me guess: You can't get the Cook County Sheriff to serve the guy."

"That's it entirely," complained Schneider. "They say he can't be reached."

"Where does he live?"

"That I don't know, but his construction yard is in South Chicago Heights. Closed, though."

"What's his first name?"

"Anthony."

*It would be.* "Can you describe what he looks like?"

Schneider thought for a moment. "He's about five feet ten

inches tall. Dark bushy hair. Dark eyes. About forty-five years old, I would say."

"Is he married?"

"Why is that important?"

"We might be able to serve his wife, instead of him."

"Yes—yes—of course," said Schneider. "He is married, but I do not know her name. Sorry."

"That's okay," said Joe. "How much is he into your bank?"

"Two hundred thousand."

*That's a lot of money even for a banker.* "Do you know where he hangs out, drinks, anything like that?"

"He did mention in passing a place called Hilltop Lounge."

"Mob hangout?"

"I wouldn't know."

"This construction yard that Marino owns. What's the address?"

"It's 3120 Chicago Road, South Chicago Heights."

Joe looked Schneider in the eyes and said, "I'm not promising anything, but I'll do what I can."

"I knew I could count on Albert to engage a good man. I would appreciate any help in this matter. I genuinely wanted to help build homes for the men and women who stopped the wholesale slaughter of my people. Hitler would have destroyed all the Jews in the world if he'd had the chance."

"We'll see," said Joe. "Maybe you can build those homes after all."

"Thank you, Mr. Ganzer."

"Call me Joe."

"Alright, Joe," said Schneider as he handed Joe a card. "Here is a number where I can be reached any time, day or night."

"Thanks, Howie." Joe winked, took the card. They shook hands, and Joe walked over to the bar and asked for the phone. He placed a call to Detective Donnelly.

"Hello, Mike, I'm almost afraid to ask another favor."

"Let me guess: you want me to hold Johnny a little longer."

"That's why you're such a good detective."

"How long, Joe?"

"Two days."

"I sorta figured you weren't ready, so I held up booking him. That gave me one full calendar day. I'm going to release him—"

109

"Mike, you can't you have to keep—"

"Hold on, hold on," Mike said. "I can release Johnny on the burglary charge and hold him for three more days on another charge. But that's it, Joe."

"That's all I need. Thanks, Mike."

"Hey, I did some checking on that Frankie Ferrel and Floyd Thursby thing. I was curious. you know how I am. So, I called San Francisco. Talked to a Captain Tom Polhaus."

"What'd he say?"

"Turns out a women really didn't kill Dixie Monahan's bodyguard, that Floyd Thursby guy."

"Oh no?"

"But get this—she killed a private detective, instead."

"Uh, oh! Anyone we know?"

"Nah, some guy named Miles Archer. His partner is still around but not in the business anymore. A guy named Sam Spade. Couldn't reach him. You know, Spade cracked the case for Polhaus back when Polhaus was a detective. Led to him making captain."

"I can't help you there, Mike."

"I didn't think so," said Donnelly sparing with Joe. "But guess what this was all about?"

"No idea."

"It was all over some golden, jeweled-up statuette."

"A statuette?"

"Not just any statuette, Joe, a falcon that once belonged to the Knights of Templar."

"That's quite a relic, then. Must be worth a fortune."

"Well, sort of. Some wealthy collector, a fat man named Kasper Gutman was behind the whole thing. Funny, a fat man should have a name like that... Gutman," said Donnelly with a laugh. "The guy spent nearly twenty years looking for that golden bird. Ended up being killed by his own boy gunman, a little punk by the name of Wilmer Cook."

"All over this falcon?"

"Yep, but here's the rub—the statue was a phony."

"A phony? Sounds like a nightmare."

"It gets better... or worse," said Donnelly. "Polhaus actually had Ferrel under investigation during this whole matter. Seems Ferrel had trailed Thursby all the way from the Orient. I'll bet money he was chasing that little statue. Otherwise, he'd've killed him straight off."

"Yeah, you're right, Mike. He could have done the contract hit on Thursby anywhere, so why track him half way around the world?"

"Exactly," said Donnelly. "The SFPD didn't have anything on Ferrel, so they dropped that part of the investigation and concentrated on the woman, Brigid O'Shaughnessy, and the boy gunman, little Wilmer Cook. Both were found guilty of murder, you know.

"Brigid O'Shaughnessy was convicted of killing that private detective, Miles Archer. Wilmer Cook was convicted of killing a ship's captain named Jacobi on orders from Gutman and for killing Gutman, the fat man, the collector. In court, Gutman's teenaged daughter, Rhea, testified that her father did not order Cook to kill anyone, that Cook was a homicidal maniac. Turns out Gutman's daughter was the maniac. Ended up in a mental institution over this whole affair. Poor kid—lost her father and then her mind.

Donnelly paused and added, "But you know what's funny? Cook and O'Shaughnessy blamed each other for killing Floyd Thursby. There just wasn't enough evidence, so they were both acquitted of Thursby's murder but not the others. So it's possible that Ferrel got Thursby in San Francisco, then skipped."

Joe shook his head and added, "A lot of blood on that little statue."

"That ain't the end of it," predicted Donnelly.

"What do you mean?" asked Joe.

"Just where is the real McCoy and who pulled the switch?"

"Don't lose any sleep over it," said Joe.

"Call me, wiseacre."

"I will. Thanks again, Mike." Joe hung up smiling and headed out of the country club.


When Joe got back to the Chevy, there were a couple of paunchy silver-haired golfers leaning against it talking and laughing.

"Gentlemen, I hate to interrupt, but I have a meeting with President Truman, and I'm already late."

They looked at him trying to digest what he'd just said. Was it a joke? Was he for real? In unison the two men bolted from the car, fearing they might be dealing with a dangerous lunatic. They darted directly toward the servants' entrance at the rear of the club, looking back as they did, muttering to each other.

Joe opened the door to the Chevy and got in. He drove out along the same long road that exited to Dixie Highway. He turned south, on his way to Chicago Heights. When he reached the city limits, he spotted the Skyline Motel on the west side of the street. The looks of such a modern motel impressed Joe. It had a streamlined car port as the main entrance. Two round columns came together at the base and formed a "V," which supported one end of the car port. The other end merged and became the motel office roof.

Joe stepped out the car and walked through the glass doors into the office. The manager was standing behind the desk dressed in a white shirt with the name "Skyline" above the pocket and a blue tie. The office was spacious, painted in pastel blues, and smelled of cleaning chemicals. It had a small couch for waiting guests or family. Three walls were glass. Even at night it was bright.

"May I help you?"

"Yes, I'd like a room for two nights."

"Surely. We have a number of rooms open. Would you care for a certain side of the building?"

"Yeah, the inside."

It took a moment, but the clerk smiled and said, "Of course, I just meant—"

Joe interrupted, "How about the north side?"

"Yes, sir," said the clerk. "Room 126. It's on the ground floor. Will that be okay?" He pointed to a small map of the motel layout. "Right here."

"Sure. That'll be fine."

"Is there anything else?"

Is there a phone in the room?"

"Yes there is and a phonebook as well."

"One more thing—do you know of a place around here called Hilltop Lounge?"

"That's rather a nice place. It's up on Lincoln Highway, just south and west of this motel."

"Do they serve dinner?"

"Yes they do, and there are a few family restaurants a little further west on Lincoln Highway. I suggest the Taste of Italy. Excellent food and good prices. Just tell them Steve at the Skyline sent you."

"Thanks," said Joe, knowing the clerk would get a kickback from them. "I might just try it."

"You won't be disappointed."

"Oh, I meant to ask, where is the township records office?"

"I think that would be right in the courthouse building on Chicago Road just a mile or so from here."

"Well, thank you."

The clerk handed Joe the key to room 126. He drove the Chevy around to the north side and parked right in front of his room. Joe always had a change of clothes in a suitcase in the trunk of his car. He grabbed the suitcase, opened up the room, and turned on the lights. *Nice,* he thought. He hung up his extra suit and shirt and straightened them on the hanger. Satisfied, he sat on the bed and picked up the phonebook. Sometimes locating a person was as easy as looking him up.

*Nope, that would've been just too easy.* Joe threw the phonebook on the bed and picked up the phone. "Outside line, please." Joe placed a call to Wilma at home.

"Hello," said Wilma.

"Hey, Murph, it's me," said Joe playfully.

"Who?"

"Is that any way to treat me after I almost got killed in a car wreck?"

Wilma gasped, "Are you alright?"

"Yeah, I'm fine. Not a scratch. No damage either."

"What happened then?"

"I don't know. My mind was drifting, and I about ran underneath the rear end of a truck at a stop sign."

"It's that hit on the head, Joe. I told you to see a doctor."

"It's not that, really," said Joe, considering just for a second that Wilma might be right, but he dropped it. "Look, can you get your sister's kid and Tommy and drive down here day *after* tomorrow around ten o'clock in the morning?"

"Are you staking a place?"

"Yeah, I might stand out too much in this town."

"Where?"

"Meet me at the Skyline Motel on Dixie Highway in the Heights, just north of Lincoln Highway. I'll be in their coffee shop."

"I'll use a map."

"Good. Now what are the guys up to?"

"Ludko said Ferrel's just hitting all the night spots. Benny's shadowing him and having a great time."

"And here I am sweating out a summons job."

"This is the way you want it, Joe," said Wilma. "Now, Ludko also said that Polina—ooh I don't like that woman—she has only gone to see a movie, *Notorious*, with Ingrid Bergman."

"I saw that one. It's about a woman who everyone mistrusts but turns out to be a heroine."

"Don't get me started, Joe Ganzer."

"Is that it?"

"Detective Donnelly called to say Johnny Della Penna will be safely behind bars for at least five days."

"Good." Joe paused and added, "Okay, sweet pea, I'll see you later. I'm going to dinner. I'll call if anything changes."

"Okay, Joe, see you soon."


That night Joe had one of the dreams again. They rarely changed. He is an observer, watching himself being interrogated. The questions always change, but there are never any answers. They are a fabric of lies too intricate for him to hold together, and just before the threads all break, he wakes in a sweat, panting. It is pure swirling madness, and then it dissolves. Sleep engulfs him again, until the next time.

Next morning Joe was up early. He had breakfast in the Skyline's cafe and brooded about finding Marino. *It's a job*, he convinced himself. He got up, left the waitress a liberal tip, and headed out the door on his way to the Bloom Township Records Office. It wasn't a long ride, just up Dixie Highway at the Lincoln Highway intersection. A sign there proclaims it's "the Crossroads of the Nation." It says the city fathers back in 1916 had persuaded the Lincoln Highway Association to route the first transcontinental highway through their city. The Crossroads brought more than the city fathers had bargained for.

The Heights became notorious back in prohibition, a regular stomping ground for bootleggers. During the war it became famous for all its factories running day and night producing everything from chemicals to steel for the military.

Joe passed the "Crossroads" and a block later turned into the municipal parking lot. He walked into the records office. A heavy-set, middle-aged woman was at the front receiving counter. "May I help you?"

"I hope so," said Joe. "I need the survey books for an address my company is interested in. We are considering developing a property at 3120 Chicago Road."

"That's in South Chicago Heights. Those records are back here. One moment." She disappeared into the rows of towering shelves in the records office. When she returned she had two books. "You'll have to look yourself. It's one or the other."

Bureaucrats don't really care to help commercial operations. Joe preferred he looked them over himself anyway. He needed no help. "Thank you," he said and took them over to a nearby table and sat down. He scanned the survey layout and located the address in the second book. He wrote down the number of the parcel. He returned the books and asked, "Could I see the tax records for this number. I want to make sure there are no delinquent taxes or liens."

The woman gave a cleansing breath and took the two books and returned with the tax records. "Here it is for last year."

"Thank you, you've been so very helpful." Joe handed her a five-dollar bill. She took it with a smile so broad it almost cracked her makeup. Joe opened the book and turned to the page with the matching tax identification number. There was the owner's address: Anthony Marino, 1287 Edgewater Avenue, Chicago Heights. *Found you, Tony.*

"Did you find everything you need, sir?"

"Yes. Thank you." Joe returned the book and smiled. "Could you tell me where Edgewater Avenue is?"

"That's right down Lincoln Highway—that's 14th Street—about a mile on the right, going west."

"Thank you, again." Joe smiled again and began to leave.

"Come back any time."

Joe waved and smiled and left. He got in the Chevy and headed toward Edgewood Avenue to have a look. *With some luck I'll find him home.* He reached the address, a beautiful tree-lined street. The large two-story house was clad in sandstone with a turret at one side of the entrance and a steep roof. The driveway was long. Joe parked on the street and put on his hat and glasses and walked up to the door.

A teenager next door was shooting baskets by the garage. He missed most of the time. When Joe got to the door, he rang the bell. No answer. He didn't expect one. He rang again. Still no answer.

He walked away from the door and over to the low hedges that separated all the properties in this neighborhood. "Could you tell me if Mr. Richardson is home?"

"Richardson?" said the teen. "You have the wrong address."

"I hope not. This is 1287 Edgewood, right?"

"Yeah, but that's the Marino House."

"Oh, I see. Well maybe it's the right address but the wrong name. There's no one home."

"Yeah, Mr. Marino's gone somewheres. I don't know, but Mrs. Marino will back later this afternoon, I think."

"Yes, well, I'll try back then perhaps."

"Sure," said the teen, not paying any attention to what Joe said and continued to shoot baskets and continued to miss.

Joe turned away from the young man quickly. He didn't want the boy to recognize him later when he returned to actually serve the summons. He headed toward the Chevy, just down the street and out of sight of the house.

# CHAPTER TEN

## CHICAGO HEIGHTS
*Lincoln Highway*

Builders and real estate people were always getting served papers in one type of civil action or another. Marino might be just another contractor in a legal dispute or he might be an Outfit guy with a phony construction company. Joe had to find out before he made another move and involved Wilma and the kids. He headed back toward Lincoln Highway and stopped at a phone booth.

I He looked up the Hilltop Lounge. It was nearly noon. he called and paged Anthony Marino. Not there. *Okay, strike two.* Joe decided to go to the Hilltop Lounge and have lunch anyway. Perhaps he could discover something about Marino and his associations.

It was about half past noon when Joe reached the Hilltop Lounge. It wasn't the Idlewild Country Club, but it was still an impressive restaurant and lounge. There were a number of businessmen having lunches with their clients or employees. Joe went to the lounge, sat at the bar, and ordered a beer and a Rueben sandwich. He watched the other customers.

*All citizens*, he thought. The bartender came over and asked if he wanted another beer. Joe took the chance and said, "Yeah, I was supposed to meet a contractor here today, but he doesn't seem to be here."

"Who are you looking for?"

"Mr. Marino."

"Are you the fellow who paged him?"

"Why yes. I was running a little late and just wanted to let him know, but it seems he's the one who's late. Too bad too, I had a check to give him on a project we just completed."

117

"A number of people seem to be looking for him these days, but not to give him money."

"Very busy man I assume."

"Well...." The bartender just trailed off.

"Nothing serious is it?"

"Well, he told me the other day he had too many projects running now that the building boom has started, and he owes quite a lot of money."

"That happens from time to time. I certainly would like to tender this check to him. It may help the situation. Do you know where I might reach him?"

"No, I don't, but he could sure use the money. There are some people he owes money to that you *don't* owe money to—if you know what I mean?"

"Oh my, but this is Chicago Heights, isn't it?" said Joe with a few understanding nods.

The bartender added, "Not a lot of money, you understand, but it could be dicey."

"I will stay here a while longer then, in case Mr. Marino shows up late."

The bartender nodded his head and walked over to attend another customer.

*So, Marino is probably not an Outfit guy,* Joe thought. *Okay, then.*


Joe was already in the Skyline Motel's coffee shop the next morning when Wilma pulled in. She wrangled the boys out of the car and went in. Joe smiled broadly.

"Good morning, sweet pea," he said. "And let's see—this is Tommy and of course this is Henry." He grabbed the boys and gave them a hug.

"Hi Uncle Joe," said Henry. "Are we on a real stake out, like in the movies?"

"Yes, we are," said Joe. He stooped down and whispered to both of them, "Now, you can't say a word to anyone. Okay?"

In unison they said, "No way!"

"Good. Now let's have some breakfast."

Wilma gave Joe the "uncle" moniker back when Henry was born. Her sister, Maggie, and her husband were having a hard time financially. When Joe heard about it, he outfitted their whole nursery from Sears, Roebuck & Company's catalog. He made a few mistakes, like ordering too many diapers and some toys Henry wouldn't need until he was five years old. So, he became an honorary uncle.

"Can we get waffles?" begged Henry. "I'm tired of Corn Flakes"

"Sure, you can have anything you want."

"You're gonna spoil them, Joe," scolded Wilma.

"Have whatever you want, boys," said Joe. "Wilm, I want them happy and just a little crazy." He looked at the boys and said, "Let's sit over in this booth, you guys."

They sat down and ordered. Joe went over his plans with Wilma while the boys dug into their waffles. This was just a typical summons drop. Wilma could see that Joe was merely going through the motions on this case. Ever since Polina came into the picture, Joe was different, more like he has was before the war, before his work with the OSS. It had been well over a year since he returned to his private investigation practice. At first, he seemed satisfied with the domestic "peeper" cases, getting sworn statements, serving a summons.

But about three months ago, he started becoming increasingly detached and moody. Wilma thought he was brooding over some woman, but Joe never mentioned anyone. He would spend hours in his office just looking out the window. He'd been like that when he first returned from out West. Now he was reverting, and it worried her.

Joe announced, "Okay, boys, we have to get going."

"Sure thing, Mr. Ganzer," said Tommy who hesitated and added, "Henry said you're not really his uncle, just a fun uncle."

"That's right, Tommy."

"Well, on this stakeout can I call you 'uncle' too?" asked Tommy.

"Sure thing, Tommy. I'd like that."

They piled into Joe's Chevy and headed to Edgewood Avenue. On the way, Wilma tugged on Joe's shirt and asked, "Where'd you get these construction worker clothes?"

"In the trunk," he said. "This guy's a contractor. If he sees a suit approaching his house he's not going to answer. I already tired that. If he thinks I'm a guy looking for work with his construction company, he might answer the door. Or maybe his wife will answer the door."

"You look the part. Kind of rugged," admired Wilma. "Where's the hat?"

"I used that yesterday. He shouldn't recognize me without it. Not in these clothes, for sure." The boys were already getting a little rambunctious in the back seat. Joe didn't mind at all.

"Okay, but here—" Wilma messed his hair up a little bit. Joe winced a little when she hit the goose egg on his head. "Oh! I'm sorry."

"Forget it," Joe smiled and looked at himself in the rearview mirror. He liked the look, a little disheveled.

"Is that what I think it is?" Wilma glimpsed the outline of Joe's gun beneath his shirt.

"Part of the wardrobe," said Joe. "Nothing's going to happen. Trust me. Just a summons drop, remember?"

"I understand," she said.

"We're almost there," Joe said. "Now, boys, I want you to play a game of catch in the back seat there. You can yell a little if you want but not too crazy. Okay?"

"Okay," said Tommy.

"Yeah sure," said Henry.

Joe pulled the Chevy up in front of the house. He got out. Straightened his clothes a little. He felt someone looking at him through the curtains of the front picture window. He walked a little slump-shouldered up the drive. He could hear the boys going at it in the car. He knocked on the door. This time it opened. It was Anthony Marino.

"Hello, I was told that you might be looking for a good carpenter."

"I might be," said Marino. He looked at the car with the two kids going crazy and the wife in the passenger seat. He felt at ease. "What kind of work have you done."

"I was working on a bungalow crew the last four months, and I've done a lot of concrete work, too. Foundations mostly."

Marino looked at Joe with tape-measure eyes, sizing him up, the height, the build, the muscles. "Yeah, I might be able to use you."

"You are the owner of the company, Mr. Marino?"

"Yeah, that's right," said Marino.

"Then you're the right man." Joe reached into his pocket and pulled out the summons and handed it to Marino.

Marino took it and said. "What is this your resume?"

"No, it's a summons, Mr. Marino," Joe said and turned around and started to walk back to the Chevy.

"You son of a bitch," yelled Marino.

Joe just waved his hand in the air as he walked back to the car, looking over his shoulder just to make sure. He got in and heard Marino slam the door so hard he thought it might fall off its hinges.

"Let's go." He looked over at Wilma while he started the engine and added, "That's the last of these cases."

"That guy called you a bad name, Uncle Joe," said Henry.

"I'm used to it."

While driving back to the motel, Joe looked up to see the boys in the rearview mirror and asked, "Hey, boys, what do you say to a trip to Riverview?"

In perfect screaming harmony, they yelled, "Riverview?"

"Yeah? And what do you think?" said Joe and he looked at Wilma and added, "Yeah, you too."

"Gosh, I've never been to Riverview. I heard about it." said Tommy.

Grabbing Tommy's shoulder, Henry said, "Hey, I been there with mom and dad. They got roller coasters and even a crazy fun house."

"A fun house?" said Tommy.

"Yeah, and all sorts of other stuff, too," said Henry. 'That'll be great, Uncle Joe."

"We'll get your car, Murph, and drop it off at your sister's, then head to Riverview."

Wilma looked at Joe and said, "You're going on the roller coasters with them—not me."

"Sounds good to me," said Joe. "Right boys?"

Two resounding "Yeahs" sang from the back seat, and Wilma shook her head side to side with a broad smile. They continued heading back to the Skyline Motel while the boys chattered like monkeys about Riverview.

Wilma dropped her car in front of her sister Maggie's house, ran in and told her where she was taking the boys, and rushed out to join Joe and the crew in the Chevy. They were off to Riverview.

After a long while up through the city, watching from the back seat, the boys spotted the hazy peaks of a giant wooden roller coaster. They stuck their heads out of the back windows for a better look.

Henry blurted out, "Uncle Joe, there it is!. There it is!"

"I see it, too," said Tommy, "What is it?"

Joe said, "In a little bit, we'll be there. Tommy what you see is the fastest, scariest, wildest roller coaster in the world—The Bobs."

Wilma said, "Don't even look at me. No!"

Joe laughed, "The Bobs goes over fifty miles an hour, but it feels like a hundred. There's a vertical drop that plummets eighty-five feet straight down."

The boys' eyes lit up. "Hey, Uncle Joe," Tommy said, "Are those parachutes hanging from that big tower?"

Joe beamed at Tommy calling him "uncle." He explained, "That's 'The Pair-O-Chutes,' Tommy. They lift up to six giant parachutes with seats attached way up to the top, almost two hundred feet in the air, and then they let you drop."

"I want to go on that," said Henry.

"Me, too," agreed Tommy. "I can hear people laughing and screaming."

"I hear 'em too," said Henry.

"Riverview looks really big. We'll get lost." said Tommy.

"I think I read that it covers something like seventy-four acres, almost as big as downtown South Chicago; but I know my way around. We won't get lost."

"Wow," said Tommy. "Are we almost there yet?"

"Not too much longer, but there are a lot of stop lights so maybe ten more minutes."

As they made their way up Western Avenue, they could hear the clank of the coaster cars. Riverview Park sat at Western and Belmont Avenues and was bounded by the North Branch of the Chicago River, which is how it got its name—Riverview Park. It had over 120 rides, which included six coasters: the outrageously famous and most feared of all being The Bobs, and for the less adventurous there was the Zephyr, the Blue Streak, the Jet Stream, and the Flying Turns. Riverview Park bought the Flying Turns coaster from the Century of Progress Exposition held in Chicago back in the '30s. But none matched The Bobs.

Riverview was a maze of wonders and noises with the smell of popcorn and cotton candy scenting the air. You could tell the park was old but hauntingly beautiful. There was an air of old world charm about Riverview.

In 1908 Riverview brought in an ornate seventy-horse carousel made by the Philadelphia Toboggan Company. From a distance it looked like a wedding-cake-style state capitol building with a white picket fence surrounding it. Up close you saw the elaborately carved horses each one was a work of art. Encircling the horses was an elaborate frieze with scenes from ancient Greece and Rome. Joe wouldn't go on the carousel, though. He would get so dizzy, it made him sick.

Aladdin's Castle, an enormous walk-through fun house, had to be everyone's favorite attraction. The forty-foot giant head of an Arabian mystic in a turban with piercing black eyes and a goatee guarded its entrance. It delighted visitors with the hall of mirrors, a rolling twelve-foot barrel, and the Magic Carpet.

Joe parked the Chevy and everyone bailed out. The entrance to Riverview Park looked like the Taj Mahal, two square towers linked by an archway and topped with two minarets, painted in bright red, white, and blue. The entrance fee was almost free. This was a working class amusement park so families on a budget could pick which rides and attractions they could afford. Joe paid for everyone.

When they all got inside the gate, Wilma said, "Oh, look at the flower garden here. Isn't it beautiful?"

"Yeah," said Henry, "but look at the Silver Flash coaster, right there. You could go on that one, Aunt Wilma. It's slow."

Wilma, said, "Not slow enough."

"There sure are a lotta people here," said Tommy, looking around bedazzled and giddy.

"Okay, we can only spend about three hours here... agreed?" said Joe.

"Yeah, let's go to the Bobs first thing," said Henry.

Tommy said timidly, "Alright, I guess."

"Don't worry, Tommy. I'll be with you guys," said Joe, and he looked at Wilma. "There's room for four."

Wilma just glared at him.

Joe and the boys stood in line at The Bobs waiting to get tickets for their turn. They waved to Wilma when they got on. The coaster took off. Wilma just stood watching and gasping—the speed and twists and turns. When it finally stopped, the boys begged to go again.

And they did. The same with the Jetstream, the Blue Streak, and the Zephyr.

"Come on, Auntie Wilma, go with us on the Zephyr. It goes real slow," pleaded Henry.

She looked at Joe. "Did you put him up to this?"

Joe raised his hands and shook his head.

Wilma grudgingly tried The Zephyr. Each car was totally enclosed and she felt safe. When they got off the Zephyr, Wilma said, "Okay, let's go again. What do you say?"

Wilma even gave the Tilt-O-Whirl a try.

Joe looked at the boys and said, "I've created a monster."

Then they came upon the carousel. Wilma wanted to go on, but Henry said, "Aw, that's for sissies, right Uncle Joe?"

"Absolutely."

Wilma said, "Well, this sissy is going on. Come on, Joe."

"No—I'm with the boys on this one."

So they waited and waited as Wilma waved to them each time the carousel whirled past them, turn after turn. the ride ended. Finally.

"Come on guys," Joe said, "We just have time for Aladdin's Castle and maybe the Palace of Wonders."

"No freak show—and that's final, Joe Ganzer," ordered Wilma.

"Okay, okay."

Right inside Alladin's Castle was a maze with dozens of identical screen doors. "Look at all these doors," said Tommy.

"We have to try them all," instructed Joe. Only a few would swing open which led to a room filled with mirrors.

"Wow, look at me, Tommy," said Henry. "Look at my head." The mirrors distorted your size and shape in the most delightful ways.

"This one takes about ten pounds off me, don't you think?" said Wilma admiring herself.

"Yeah, but look at these muscles," said Joe with his bulging distorted arms the size of his entire body. "Remember guys, things aren't what they seem to be in the fun house."

They moved on to rooms with slanting floors where they could hardly stay upright. In a dark hallway the boys stepped on a disc in the floor that started spinning and made them stumble. Tommy laughed, "Hey, Mr. Crackey walks like this on Saturday night."

The boys loved what came next. Just ahead, they had to get through a huge rolling barrel. A few could walk through it but most had to crawl. The boys made it after a few stumbles and laughed like crazy when Wima and Joe tried.

Wilma fell over and rode with the barrel up one side then back on her feet.

Joe said, "It's like being in a cement mixer."

"Come on Uncle Joe, you can make it," cried Henry.

Tommy went back in the barrel to help Wilma get through.

She finally made it through, then said to Joe, "Well, we're waiting."

Joe had tears in his eyes from laughing as he went down again. Tommy stuck out his hand, and Joe pretended to miraculously find his footing and make it to the end.

"Tommy, I couldn't have made it without you. Thanks."

After a trip under Alladin's beard which took them briefly outside in the light, they entered more dark passages and had a bumpy ride down a series of padded rollers to a metal seat. When you sat on it, the seat collapsed and sent you cascading down the Magic Carpet, an undulating cloth that passed over more rollers.

Somehow Joe got turned upside down as he slid down the Magic Carpet and came to the end head first. The boys ran over and helped him up.

"We got yuh, Uncle Joe," said Tommy as they both helped him get to his feet.

"Hey, are you guys hungry?"

"I'll say, huh Tommy?"

"Yeah."

Joe bought everyone hot dogs and pops, and they ate in the park area at a picnic table right under a tree.

The boys were ravenous but couldn't stop talking to eat and couldn't stop eating to talk.

Wilma said, "Thanks, Joe... for everything."

"You are very welcome."

"But I am glad you didn't buy them hot dogs before you went on The Bobs."

He looked at Wilma knowingly, "If I had, I'd be wearing hot dogs right now."

On the way back home, Tommy said, "Gosh, thanks Uncle Joe. I sure had a good time today."

Henry agreed, "Yeah, it was real fun."

"We all needed a little change," said Joe.

He drove them all home and headed back to the office.

When he made it back to his building, he noticed the lights on in Albert Strugala's Law Offices on the first floor. He parked and went in. The receptionist had gone home. "Albert, are you here?"

A voice from deep within said, "I hope you have good news."

Joe walked back to his friend and landlord's office. "Sorry, I'm going to be a little short on the rent this month." They shook hands. Joe sat across from Strugala's massive desk.

He looked at Joe's construction clothes with a frown. "Moonlighting in construction these days?"

"I needed this getup for your summons drop."

"Bad news, then?" said Strugala.

Joe smiled. "No, I got him."

"I thought for a moment you were losing your touch, Joe."

"So was I. Still think it."

"You do seem restless, preoccupied," said Strugala. "Do you want to discuss it. No one is here."

"Can't, Albert. Professional ethics. You know that."

"Well, I'm always here, you know." He paused and added, "If there is anything I can do. Do you want more work? I could inquire among my colleagues. Perhaps I can help that way."

"Thanks, Albert, but I need less not more."

"You mean less of this picayune, don't you?"

"Maybe."

"I was wondering when you would drop all this 'unfaithful spouse' poppycock and get back to work."

"I *am* working," said Joe.

"No you are not," intoned Strugala with his deep courtroom voice. "You are hiding." It got quiet. He let that sink in and added, softer, "The wounds will heal, Joe. Give it time."

"It's been almost two years—" Joe said and stopped himself.

"And it might take ten years," said Strugala leaning forward in his overstuffed chair, "but you cannot hide from who you are. The proverb says: 'This too shall pass.' Let it, Joe."

Looking down at the floor, Joe said, "It's what I became."

"It was war, and it's over now."

"For some."

"In my business I have to judge people and understand them in order to help them. I understand you better than you realize."

"Yeah?"

"No one sees men like you. There are no 'welcome home'

parties, no parades, no medals. The battles you fought, you fought alone. Your victories can never be celebrated."

"What makes you think I did all this?"

"When an investigator of your caliber disappears repeatedly for months and months on end, and no one knows where, it's not hard to surmise what our government was using you for."

"Conjecture, you honor. Pure supposition."

Strugala leaned back in his chair, smoking his expensive cigar, playing with his Sheaffer fountain pen. "In the morning, after a gentle midnight shower, everything is somehow fresh and clean and new, and no one bothers to ask why or how. Life goes on, but a few of us see the telltale."

"Thanks, Albert."

"No... thank you and all those others we'll never know," said Strugala.

"And all the ones who died alone."

Strugala laid his cigar carefully on the ashtray and said, "It was Emily Dickenson who wrote: 'The cavalry of woe. Who fall and none observe.'"

Joe paused, then said, "We'll talk again, maybe."

"I know where you work."

Joe smiled, got up, and shook Albert's hand again, more firmly this time, an agreement without words was made as they looked each at other. Joe left the Law Offices and took the stairway entrance up to his floor. He felt a whisper of relief rustle the "veil," as he liked to call it. Joe sat at his desk, feet up, enjoying the cool breeze coming through the windows. He could focus more clearly now. He gazed out at the street below. A plan was emerging.

# CHAPTER ELEVEN

SOUTH CHICAGO
*Jos. Ganzer Investigations*

The next afternoon Joe finally got around to scribbling out his report describing all the relevant actions taken for the summons drop in the Schneider Case for Albert Strugala. Only Wilma could read his handwriting, and she always complained about it. When she got back from lunch at her sister's, he would have her type it up.

The outer door opened just as he dropped the finished report on her desk. Joe looked up and said, "Oh, good, I was just about to leave."

Wilma countered, "So now that I'm here, you have a *reason* to leave?"

"No, I just meant—"

"What's that?" pointing at the report.

"Oh, I need you to type up this report on the Howard Schneider Case for Albert and bill him."

Wilma walked over to her desk and picked up the long report. "You expect me to make sense of these hieroglyphic scratches? I should get hazardous duty pay."

Joe smiled and without missing a beat, "When you're done, would you walk it downstairs to Strugala's office."

Albert genuinely liked talking to Wilma and would try to get her to quit Joe and come and work for him. She always refused, but thanked him anyway.

Joe left the office for Vookie's. He took the long route, listening to the radio, watching the pedestrians, letting the world play on.

He sat in his booth and mulled over what he would say to Polina, about how he should make her understand what had to be

128

done. He sipped a cool beer, undisturbed, scribbling thoughts on a napkin, putting the last pieces into place in his plan for One-Two Johnny, like planning the moves in a chess game. Only at this point, not all his men were in their proper positions, but they were all en route. At dusk, as the night crowd started to wander in, Joe got up, waved to Eddie, and left.

He was heading to The Drake Hotel to tell Polina what he knew about her uncle. Mentally, he was rehearsing what he would say and how he would say it. He drove up Cottage Grove from Vookie's to catch Midway Plaisance and get over to Lake Shore Drive. As he passed the Museum of Science and Industry, the lights on the building made it look like an ancient Greek temple. The museum originally housed the Palace of Fine Arts during the 1893 World's Columbia Exposition and now was the largest science museum in the Western Hemisphere. *I should take Henry and Tommy here some day soon, when this is all over.*

A breeze came rushing in off the lake through his windows as he sped up Lake Shore Drive. Joe pulled on to East Walton Street and parked about two blocks from The Drake Hotel. He sauntered to the door. A gust of wind blew in off the lake. He entered the hotel and immediately spotted Benny the Hat sitting in the lounge, but no Ferrel. Joe cautiously walked into the lounge, sat next to Benny, and ordered a Scotch.

"Lo, Joe," exclaimed Benny with relief and delight. "Ferrel ain't moved. He's still up there. Can I go now?"

"Where are you headed, Benny?"

"I'm going to the The Blackhawk Restaurant for dinner and some dancin'. Tonight should be great—Ted Fio Rito's band will be there."

"I don't think I know him, Benny."

"Sure you do. He wrote 'Toot, Toot, Tootsie, Goodbye.' You know."

"Yeah, yeah, now I remember. Wish I could go, Benny."

"Well come on. I'll teach you some real steps."

"Don't tempt me. Is Ludko still employed here as a bellhop?"

"Yeah, I saw him, maybe twice."

"Take off, Benny, but call me tomorrow because after that I'll be going to Canada."

"Canada! Man, way up there?" Benny said.

"It's for this case, so don't forget to call me. Hey, I might need a traveling partner...," Joe said smiling.

"Sure, tomorrow," and Benny left the lounge and headed for the door.

Joe nursed his Scotch and thought about how to tell Polina about her uncle. She seemed vulnerable to him in a way that only long periods of hardship can bring. Almost everyone in that horrible war was affected whether they knew it or not. For all the relief that VE and VJ day brought, it left behind humility and despair. This masque of barbarism and savagery left scars that you could not see but you knew were there just the same. Joe sipped his drink. A voice said, "Do you need anything, sir?"

It took a second, but Joe saw the face behind the voice—it was Ludko still in his bellhop uniform. "Lud! Let's get out of here." Joe left his drink and walked out of the lounge to a nearby hallway. Ludko followed dutifully. "Is Ferrel still in his room?"

"Yeah, last I checked."

Joe looked dubiously at Ludko in his bellhop outfit holding someone's clothes.

Ludko frowned and said, "What?"

"Nothing."

"Hey, a guest caught me upstairs and asked me to take these shirts to the laundry. Don't give me that look—I get good tips on this little stakeout."

"I'm going up to give Polina some bad news, and I want you in the hall. If Ferrel comes out of his room, distract him whatever way you can. I don't need another problem to deal with."

"Sure, I'll take care of Ferrel, even if I gotta use a blackjack."

Joe laughed, "Or just hit him with something heavy."

"Be glad to, boss."

"I'm going up after you drop off those shirts, so hurry."

"Okay, it'll only take me a second. I'll meet you at the elevator," and Ludko went down the hallway to the laundry.

They got on the elevator together and took it to the seventh floor. Joe walked down to room 706 and Ludko the bellhop continued down the hallway and turned the corner to Ferrel's room. Joe knocked on 706. He heard it unlatch.

"Yes?... Oh, Mr. Ganzer, please come in," Polina said as she opened the door wider. Joe entered.

"Please sit down," said Joe. "I have something to tell you concerning your uncle." She walked silently over to the sofa and sat down. Joe drew up the wing chair close to her. A single table lamp warmly lit the room. The windows faced the lake and sparkles danced on the water. Joe took off his hat with a slight wince and said, "You're not going to like this."

"My uncle hasn't been killed has he? Not NKVD?" she said with tears in her voice.

"No... nothing like that. It's just that my contacts in London have discovered something disturbing about your uncle."

Her relief gave way to new concerns. "What? What is it? What could have happened?"

"Polina, your uncle has been identified as a war profiteer and Nazi collaborator. He's being sought by the French government."

Polina pleaded, "What has he done?"

"He is accused of swindling French Jews out of their valuable works of art and selling them to high-ranking Nazis. The exact details—I don't know." Joe scanned her face.

"This cannot possibly be," Polina said, as she turned away and stared at the floor. "They must... must have the wrong man. My uncle is a war hero and a general, I tell you." Tears welled up in her eyes. There was a throb in her voice, "This is propaganda by NKVD. Your associate is wrong. They have the wrong man. Not him."

"Polina, my source is unimpeachable. There is an entire operation underway to apprehend these criminals."

"Don't call my uncle a criminal," she demanded, turning back to look at Joe. "Can't you see, he is being—how do you say—framed up by NKVD?"

"I'm headed for Montreal shortly to intercept a shipment of stolen art that your uncle is smuggling out of England."

"I hired you to find my uncle and now you are working with the authorities to arrest him? Why don't you help me to clear him?" she pleaded. Joe didn't answer and she added, "Now I am glad Mr. Ferrel hit you. I should never have hired you. Never." Tears fell from her eyes.

Joe moved over to the sofa and put his arm around her and comforted her by saying, "Okay, I'll tell you what I can do. If I find him, I'll safeguard him long enough to give you a chance to talk to him. And I'll make damn sure that the charges are legitimate. If he's innocent, I'll do everything I can to help you and your uncle."

"Oh, thank you, Joe. Thank you. I will be forever grateful to you...." At that, she put her arms around him and kissed him on his face, then his lips. Joe kissed her back. A torrent of memories came flooding back. He was enveloped now, not by Polina, by someone lost, a wraith.

Joe pulled back from her. He shook his head to break the spell. "Polina, I'm sorry. You are a very beautiful woman, but not... but you are my client. This can't be this way, not now." He rose from the sofa and grabbed his hat. "I will help you all I can. I have to do my job, and this is not part of it. I'm sorry."

Polina pushed her blonde hair off her face. With her eyes half shut and her pale skin flushed, she said, "I understand. It's just that I—"

As he shut the door, he caught a glimpse of Polina as he closed the door, through the crack. She was smiling. He turned and saw Ludko down the hall with his hand in his bellhop jacket. He had a blackjack.

He walked briskly over to him and said, "Lud, come on." Ludko turned in less than a beat and headed toward the elevator with Joe.

As they exited at the lobby, Joe tried to marshal his thoughts. Polina boiled in his mind. Ludko could tell something was off, "Hey, what's the matter with you?"

"Nothing, nothing. I just gave Polina some bad news about her uncle. I'll tell you back at the car."

"Oh, boy?" said a guest, a fat man in an ill-fitting suit chomping a cigar, "Would you take these bags up to room 326?"

Ludko looked at Joe and shrugged, "Hey, it's a livin'." He looked back at the portly guest and said "Sure thing, mister."

Joe said softly, "I'll meet you by my car on East Walton Street." Ludko nodded and Joe left the hotel. He walked halfway to his car and stopped. He stared out at the lake. It was beautiful in twilight, he thought, and his mind shot back to Polina. He felt the rush again—anxiety overcame him.

Ludko came up behind him on the sidewalk. "Joe, what the hell is wrong with you?"

"I think Polina's in trouble."

"Why what's goin' on?"

"It's beautiful out tonight."

"Joe, you sound like you're nuts. What's up?"

"First thing—what did you get for that last tip?"

"That cheap fat squeak gave me a quarter."

Joe started laughing, "You'd better quit that job."

"Okay, okay, fill me in."

"Polina's uncle is a war profiteer, Lud. He was working a scam as an art dealer in Paris. He found wealthy Jews and offered to buy their art for a wretchedly discounted price. They needed the money to get a visa out of France to save their lives. As soon as he made the deal and got their art, he turned them over to the Gestapo. I figure the Gestapo split the money with him as a reward for turning them in."

Ludko looked at Joe, a slight frown surfaced. "Yeah, Joe, you already told me all this before." He was worried that Joe actually suffered a concussion and wasn't thinking straight. *Maybe, he's just talkin' to himself.* He played along. "So, the Jews get the gas chamber, this weasel walks away with a fortune... and no witnesses."

"Exactly," said Joe. "Hamilton telegrammed that Kemidov is shipping his stolen collection from London to Montreal aboard a ship named the *Porta Delgada*. Hamilton wants me to meet that ship and follow the art. He figures that Kemidov can't be far behind. But Polina thinks it's a mistake, that her uncle is being set up by the NKVD. They're not much better than the Gestapo. They run the black market in all the Soviet bloc countries. They're even more powerful now that the war is over."

"Why would they set her uncle up?"

"I don't think they would. They know what Kemidov is and what he has, and they want it. Hamilton believes there are only two, maybe three, NKVD agents involved in this operation. After they get the art, they will eliminate Kemidov and defect or maybe retreat down to South America and never be heard from again."

"You can do anything you want with that kinda money."

"You sure can," Joe said absentmindedly.

"But it can't beat bellhoppin'," Ludko said as they both headed for their cars.

Early the next morning, before Wilma got in, Joe sat at his desk, tapping with a pencil, trying to figure out how to intercept that ship and discover what was really aboard. He had no license in Canada. He wouldn't go to his former contact in the FBI. It was up to him to lay a plan and somehow reunite Polina with her uncle—if only for a brief time. He had to know where that ship would dock and when.

Joe was a member of the International Longshoremen's Association from back in his days in college. College didn't last too long, but his union card with the Longshoremen did. It was Joe's "ace in the hole" in case his sleuthing days ever came to an end. If all else failed, he could always go back on the docks at Calumet Harbor. The first part of the plan started to take shape. Joe went downstairs, got in the Chevy and drove over to the Longshoremen's union hall.

It was early when Joe walked in. A few old-timers recognized him. "Hey, Joe Ganzer, where the hell yuh been? We missed yuh," said Jake, one of the jitney drivers always looking for work. The union took care of him because of his age, but he couldn't hold a job for long because of his drinking. He was already a little tipsy this morning.

"Jake, how are you? It's been a long, long time," Joe said.

"You lookin' for work, too, Joey?"

"No... I'm looking for my old partner Sean Cullen."

"He's our president now, don't yuh know?"

"Yeah I know. I can't believe it. Where is he?"

"Come on... follow me to his lordship's office," old Jake boasted. They walked down the narrow hallway passing the business agents' offices and some secretaries. On the last door, a small brass plaque that read: President Sean Cullen. They walked in and Jake said, "There's someone here looking for work, Sean."

Sean Cullen didn't look up from his desk when he said, "Have him sit out in the hall like everybody else. Who does he think he is?" He looked up with a scowl.

"I'll be damned... Joey Ganzer. You're a welcome sight around this hall." He rushed from out behind his desk with a broad smile and shook Joe's hand like a thirsty man at a water pump. They had worked side by side for two long hot summers on Chicago's docks when Joe was going to pre-law school. They stole girls from each other. They drank together, and for a while they even lived together.

"Sean, I can't believe you're president. I should have stuck around. I would be one of your favorite pets now, getting all the gravy jobs. I might have even been a business agent."

"Joey, you're way too smart for that. You'd have had my job. So what are you up to these days? I ain't seen you around since before the war."

"I'm still a detective."

Sean laughed uncomfortably, "You're not here checking into me now are you?"

"No, Sean, I'm here to get some information," Joe said as he looked over at old Jake.

Jake caught the drift and said, "Well, I'll leave you two. I have to see if I can pick up some work today." He left the room and went back down the hallway.

"Hold on a second, Joey, I have to tell Sammy something." He called Sammy, a monster of a man, a Longshoreman business agent, into his office.

Sean said to Sammy, "You make sure you give something to Jake today." Sammy nodded obediently and went back to his office.

Sean explained, "I try to give the older guys a break if I can."

"I can see why you're president of this union."

"What can I do for you, Joey?"

"Sean, I need to know when a ship is coming into Montreal and where she will dock."

"That ought to be easy."

"I also need you to get me a job on that dock in Montreal."

"I don't know how easy that'll be. That's another local union, in another country."

"It's important, Sean. Can't you pull some strings? It's just a job after all."

Sean looked at Joe suspiciously, "This ain't illegal? This ain't smuggling, is it?"

"No, nothing like that. I'm working for an insurance company. They've had a number of losses with this one shipping company, and they just want to make sure they're not being defrauded." Joe couldn't really trust Sean Cullen, president or not. Shipping smuggled goods from overseas is a huge racket. There were too many longshoremen with criminal backgrounds and too much mob influence to let it be known that a fortune in stolen art was soon arriving in Canada.

"I hate the shippers. They always blame missing cargo on the longshoremen when most of the time they damage it or they steal it themselves and blame us. Anyways, Joe, I know the president of that local. We met at our big convention in New York last year. I'll call him up and give him your name. I'll tell him you're helping the longshoremen on a little matter. He'll be okay with that."

Joe let out his breath and said, "Thanks, Sean. You're really helping me out here."

"Yeah, next election come in here and vote for me, will yuh? Now, hey, what's the name of that ship?"

"It's the Ponta Delgada."

"I'll get in touch with the Port Authority here. They'll know exactly when and where."

"That's great," Joe said. "Here's my number when you find out." Joe handed him his card.

Sean Cullen looked the card over and smiled. "Who'd have thought we'd be where we are today, huh Joey?"

"Yeah, but sometimes—usually after a bad day and a few beers—I actually miss the work and the guys. We had a lot of laughs on those docks, Sean."

"Yeah we did. I miss 'em too, but my back doesn't." They both laughed as only those who've shared a hardship can—soldiers in agony.

"You know, Sean, I'm not surprised you ended up president. You always stood up for the men. We had some rotten business agents back in those days."

"We sure did, but the war changed all that. Those guys needed us and couldn't play favorites anymore. It was too important, and they had Feds everywhere. Man, they shipped everything imaginable out of here.

"The Jeeps and tanks were all made right here in Chicago and the surrounding area. And there was all the training up in North Chicago at Great Lakes Naval Training Station."

Joe added, "What's funny is the U.S. Navy trained all those sailors up there a thousand miles from the nearest ocean."

Sean added, "Hey, they even had an aircraft carrier in the lake."

"I didn't know that."

"Sure," added Sean proudly. "I bet you didn't know over 1,400 companies produced everything from field rations to parachutes to torpedoes, and new aircraft plants employed a hundred thousand workers, making engines, aluminum sheeting, bombsights, and all sorts of other components."

Joe let Sean give him a union pep talk about how the Chicago area contributed to the war effort.

"Joe, did you know that the Douglas-Chicago plant turned out over six hundred C-54 Skymaster transports in only twenty-five months? Can you believe it? Over half of all military electronics used in the war came from local plants. And most all of it shipped out of *our* docks." Sean paused, took a breath, and said, "Joey, I heard somewhere you went out west during the war. I heard you were 4-F."

"Yeah, I was."

"No you weren't, Joey. I worked with you day in and day out. That's the hardest work a man can do."

"I can't say much more than that, Sean."

Sean Cullen understood, but curiosity got the best of him, "You can't say... anything? Come on, it's me. I won't blab."

"Let it go, Sean."

"Sure, sure...," Sean relented. For the next hour they talked about everything—mostly lies about women and their cabaret days.


Finally, Joe stood up and said, "Sean, this has been a true pleasure and thanks."

"Don't mention it. I'm glad I could help, but your dues better be paid up."

"More than paid up," Joe said as he stood up and shook Sean's hand and walked out of his office. Driving on his way back, he stopped at Vookie's for one of Eddie's egg sandwiches and some Irish coffee.

"What'll yuh have, Joe?" said Eddie. "You know I don't open for another hour."

"Then you should keep the door locked."

"I'm not open for the city license inspectors, if that's what you mean. Besides, the shift at the mill comes in pretty soon and my license really doesn't cover it."

"I know, Eddie. All I need is one of those egg sandwiches and a cup of real coffee."

"Right with yuh, Joe." Joe went to his office booth and sat down heavily. Eddie came over with his coffee. "Your sandwich will take a few minutes. I got Willy the Whip on duty in the kitchen today."

"No hurry." He just sipped his coffee and mulled over Canada and Polina and Rossi and One-Two Johnny. He grew pale.

Eddie noticed that when he brought the sandwich. "You look bad... and you haven't even *tasted* Willy's sandwich yet."

"Oh," Joe replied as he came back from his thoughts. "I'm alright. Thanks."

Eddie glanced over his shoulder as he went back to the bar. Joe fell back into his reverie. Then something clicked. He ate his sandwich fast, gulped down the rest of his coffee, and got up fast.

"Was it the sandwich?" Eddie asked in earnest.

"Everything was great," and out the door he went. In a few minutes he pulled up to the office and ran up the stairs. Wilma was already there in her outer office. Joe breezed past her.

"Hey—the president of the Longshoremen's called. A guy named Sean Cullen. He said everything's set, but you have to call him today."

"Good work, Wilm," Joe said. "How is little Tommy doing with your sister?"

"Maggie said he's doing fine. My nephew and Tommy are having a blast together."

"Do you think she could keep Tommy a few days more?"

"I don't know. I have to call and ask Maggie, but I'm sure there won't be a problem. But, why? What's up?"

"I have to go to Canada—Montreal—for a few days."

"Canada? What?"

"It's part of the Polina Kemidov case."

Wilma looked disapprovingly at Joe, "You do what you want, but she's trouble I tell you." She grabbed a letter out of her in-box and said, "And, by the way, here's a letter from your Miss Kemidov... special delivery, no less."

Wilma handed it to Joe. He opened it. "Look, here's a certified check for $3000."

"Okay, maybe she's not so much trouble."

"Would you get Sean Cullen on the line for me?" Joe walked into his office. Took off his suit coat and hat and looked over some mail Wilma left on his desk.

"He's on now, Joe."

"Hello, Sean... Okay, got it. It arrives in three days... Portugese?... King Edward Quay... Yeah, London Global Cargo... I've got another favor to ask... Would you get a Longshoremen's working permit under the name John Della Penna?... Yeah? Good!... Thanks, Sean."

Wilma overheard, "You're getting One-Two Johnny a job with the Longshoremen?"

"Not exactly, not here—in Canada. But you can't tell a soul, not even Maggie."

"Okay, I understand, but you'll let me know where you are, right?"

"I love that concern, Murph," Joe said with affection. "As soon as I know anything, I'll call you here or at home."

"I mean, because I have to know—in case something should happen," Wilma said, thinking that maybe he was moving too fast.

Joe walked into her outer office, went behind her desk, bent down, and kissed the top of her head. "Don't worry. I'll be fine." He hugged her from behind. "Now would you get me Detective Mike Donnelly at the Grand Crossing Station?" Joe went back into his office. *Morning and already getting warm.* He opened the window.

"Joe, I have Detective Donnelly."

Joe picked up the phone, "Hello, Mike. How's our suspect?"

Mike Donnelly said, "He's doing fine. I think he likes the food and accommodations here at the 3rd."

"Mike, I'm sorry you had to keep Johnny on ice for so long, but you can release him tomorrow night. Okay?"

"Sure, right, there was insufficient evidence to hold him anyway, but—honest—I think One-Two Johnny likes it here."

"I'll bet he does. Could you hold up the paperwork for the release? Make it look like he is still in custody?"

"Paperwork foul ups happen all the time, but not too long."

"No, not too long. Just one day later."

"I'm working on something that I'll need a little more help from you."

"Joe, you're stretching it."

"This will be a great piece of detective work for you. You might even get a department citation for it."

"Whoopey doopey."

"You might even make captain," said Joe, smiling. "I'll be there tomorrow night. I'll fill you in when I know more."

"Sure... see you then." Mike Donnelly hung up and thought about the change in plans. He figured Joe Ganzer knew what he was doing, but letting Johnny Della Penna out on the street would only give Rossi's people a chance to dispose of him without a messy trial, without all the testimony that might come out about Rossi and his operations.

Joe then called Benny the Hat.

"Hey, Benny, wake up sleeping beauty. Listen, I want you to get back over to The Drake and keep surveillance on Ferrel."

"Sure thing, Joe, and I ain't sleepin'."

"Benny, lose the hat today before Ferrel recognizes you."

"Aw, Joe, can't I wear the Fedora instead of the Homburg?"

"Sure, yeah—just don't be conspicuous."

"Hey, if that means what I think it means....."

"It doesn't. Now get over there as soon as you can. I think Frankie Ferrel should just be over his hangover by now and be on the move."

Ludko burst through the door, went right past Wilma and toward Joe's office door.

"And good morning to you, too, Mr. Randelli," said Wilma as he breezed past her.

"Oh, sorry, Murph. Yeah, good morning," Ludko replied. He opened the door to the inner office and noticed the frosted glass was cracked and the jamb was splintered. Just as he saw Joe he asked, "What's up for today?" I'd like to go to the racetrack this afternoon, if you don't mind."

"Close the door, Lud," Joe said.

Ludko gently closed the door. "Hey, you gonna have Ferrel pay for this door?"

"Polina just sent in full payment. Three grand should cover it."

"I'll say. I sent yuh a good client, then." Ludko sat in the upholstered leather chair in front of Joe's desk.

"I don't know how good, but I like her money. Listen, I have to ask you something."

"Uh oh, no goin' to the track then, eh?"

"Maybe. Tell me if you think I'm crazy with this idea."

"Let's hear it."

"Okay, you know I'm trying to help One-Two Johnny on that liquor warehouse heist."

"Lost cause. Rossi's behind that."

"I know, but what if the swag gets recovered?"

"Now, how is that gonna happen? Rossi's got that shipment somewhere safe. He'll find it when the insurance company pays off, and not before."

"Lud... I know where it is."

"Then you better forget where it is. Look, Joe, you mess with that Rossi and he'll kill you without a second thought."

Without even hearing what Ludko said, Joe continued," You know that little dump of a building over on 100th Street about three blocks from the Marcello Liquor Warehouse?"

"I think so, yeah."

"Well, that's where they stashed the liquor," Joe said as his face lit up with delight.

"Why don't you just go over there real nice like and ask them to return it to its rightful owner? Case closed."

"You're a mind reader, wise guy; but I was thinking more of stealing it."

"Now I know you're nuts. Rossi will know it's you, and he'll contract you out. Then tomorrow, next week, next month—you end up dead."

"I was hoping you'd help me steal it."

"Not a chance. Word'll get out that I was in on it, then I'm dead, too. And I don't like being dead," Ludko said and then added, "You've been nutty ever since Ferrel clobbered you."

"I'm going to move the liquor over to the Grand Crossing district, in one of Santori's places. Detective Donnelly will make the discovery. It will look like one of Santori's crew pulled the job to even up over that whorehouse dispute. Neither one will believe the other. There's been bad blood between them since the Nitti days."

Ludko pursed his lips and shook his head up and down slowly. "It don't sound bad."

"And, get this: Paul Santori gets the rap for the heist. The insurance company doesn't have to pay off. Rossi isn't out a dime, and One-Two Johnny's off the hook because Donnelly will testify that the liquor was probably stolen by a local Outfit crew."

"Okay, quiz kid, but how do we steal that much swag and not get shot in the process?"

"I haven't worked that out yet."

"Oh, great," Ludko said, tossing his arms in the air.

"That's what I need you to do."

"Me?"

"Lud, you were burgling places not that long ago, as I recall. Don't tell me you can't figure a way to get into that place."

"Why don't you just tell the insurance guys where it is?"

"Come on, Lud. This is Chicago. Someone inside the insurance company will tip off Rossi long before the police arrive at the booze dump. The place will be empty."

"Okay, okay. Then who's in on this?"

Joe answered slowly, "Well... you, me, and Benny."

"We're doomed."

"Okay, then who should we get?

"Nobody—I ain't doin' it," Ludko said as he leaned back defiantly in the chair.

"Just think about it would you?"

"I ain't promisin' nothin'."

"Then I'll do it without you. It'll just be me and Benny."

"You'll end up dead, and for what...for One-Two Johnny?"

"Just like you, Lud, he's straight now. He needs a break, and he's got Tommy."

"You don't stop, do yuh? Alright I'll cook somethin' up, but I'm goin' to case it myself. What's over there?"

"Just one of Rossi's guard dogs with a bad attitude. 'Mr. Friendly' drives a new Caddy. It'll be parked out front if he's there."

Ludko smiled and said, "Mr. Friendly, eh?" Ludko got up to leave. "When we doin' this?"

"Tomorrow night."

"What? Tomorrow night?" Ludko complained. "Alright, I'll get over there and case it this morning. Yuh gotta have a truck."

"I know a guy."

"Okay, see yuh," and Ludko was out the door, waved to Wilma, and blew her a kiss.

Joe picked up the phone and dialed Lucky Motors Trucking, owned by his friend and former light heavyweight contender "Bobcat" Bobby Mann, pride of the West Side.

Bobcat answered with the voice of a guy who gargled with battery acid, "Lucky...."

"Bobcat? It's Joe Ganzer."

After a moment to wake his memory, Bobcat replied, "What's goin' on, Joe. I—I ain't seen yuz around much. Where yuz been?"

Joe had just talked to him last week. Bobcat Bobby simply had too many fights. "Mothballed, Bobby. Listen, I need a favor."

"Anything...." Bobcat meant it too. Joe had helped him navigate the torturous process of filing all the proper registrations and certifications as a motor carrier in the City of Chicago. Bobcat tried many times to repay him for his legal help. "What can I do, Joe?"

"Have you got a box truck *without* a sign on the door?"

"Oh brother, sounds illegal, but—yeah—I got one I can pull the sign off. It ain't too big, though."

"A delivery truck is perfect."

"Why no sign?"

"In case it gets spotted."

Bobcat's croaky voice deepened and slowed, "What are you doin' here, Joe?"

"You shouldn't know, Bobcat."

Bobcat hesitated and said, "Then okay, you'll have to steal the truck. I'll leave the keys in it over by the fence. You got other license plates?"

"Way ahead of you, Bobby."

"You always was sharp."

"Thanks, Bobby. When do you close?"

"Every evening at 6 o'clock I close up and then lock the gate on my way out."

"You'll get it back soon, I promise. Report it stolen when it's gone, okay?"

"Sure. How long do you think?"

"Couple of days at the most."

"Okay. Hey, after this, why don't you and me go over by Callahan's Gym and spare a few rounds, like the old days. I could use the exercise."

"Me, too; but you got to take it easy on me."

"Awh, just love taps."

"I'll give you a call in a couple of weeks."

"Okay, Joe. I'll be seein' yuh," and Bobcat Bobby Mann hung up and answered his other phone. It was a load of steel headed for the train yards.

# CHAPTER TWELVE

## SOUTH CHICAGO
*Near 100ᵗʰ Street*

When Ludko left Joe's office, he drove to the rundown warehouse on 100th Street. He coasted past the front of the place slowly, but not so slowly that he drew attention to himself. He was memorizing the layout.

*So that's our Mr. Friendly's Caddy, eh? Parked in front of the overhead door, just like Joe said.*

An Outfit guy would keep watch over the loot until the time was right. Ludko thought they would have to deal with him properly; otherwise, Rossi would think he was in on the deal and kill him straight off. Ludko really didn't care, but he knew Joe would, so they would have to rough him up enough to convince Rossi he fought valiantly for his stashed liquor.

He drove to the cross street looking everywhere and at everyone. This was a neighborhood on good terms with Rossi and his crew. They would give up anybody if they thought it would please the Outfit's street boss, Nick Rossi.

Ludko turned down the alley behind the warehouse. It was narrow with the rear of other small shops along the alley, a car repair shop, a small cabinet shop, and then the swag dump. The back only had a man door leading to the alley. That meant they would have to go through the overhead door street-side. Not good, not easy.

Ludko drove slowly out of the alley, just like someone who was lost. He drove around the front one more time. His LaFayette looked like every other car and wouldn't draw suspicion—just another car. He didn't drive down the alley again. If Rossi got wind of someone casing his liquor hideout, there would be a machine-gun welcoming party for whoever showed up, and nobody in the neighborhood would have heard or seen a thing. Ludko drove away and headed for the racetrack. He did his best thinking at the track, surrounded by his friends and the excitement. As he drove, a plan was taking shape in his mind. It was harder than he thought getting back into the robbery business. It's not like riding a bicycle—you lose the instincts of a predator.

Benny the Hat made it to The Drake Hotel about a half an hour after talking to Joe. He went to the front desk and asked, "Is Mr. Ferrel in?"

The clerk looked over the board, turned and replied, "Yes, he is sir. Would you like me to ring his room?"

"Nah," Benny said, "I'll just go up and see him." Benny made his way to the elevator and figured he'd go up to the eighth floor, walk down to the seventh, and waltz by Ferrel's room, then come back down and sit in the coffee shop or the barber shop.

But the operator stopped the car at the seventh floor. When he opened the elevator door, Frank Ferrel walked in. He looked beat—bloodshot eyes, a sick pallor. Benny had ordered the eighth floor when he got on, just in case his mark got on with him. Ferrel said to operator in a slur, "Lobby."

Benny laughed nervously and said, "Sorry, looks like you'll have to go up to go down, I guess." Ferrel said something unintelligible. He didn't even look directly at Benny. When the door opened on the eighth floor, Benny flew out. No sooner had the door closed, Benny ran down the hall to the stairway and started down the stairs as fast as he could.

Benny was overweight but still very athletic. He leaped three stairs at a time. He reached the fifth floor breathing heavily. He ran down the hall to the elevator and hit the down button. *That'll slow 'em down.* Benny looked at the other elevator. It was on its way up. *Just my luck,* and he sprinted back to the stairs and continued down. The Ferrel's elevator came to a stop at the fifth floor and the doors opened. He stepped out woozily, and after a moment he realized it was only the fifth floor. He got back in and resumed his descent to the lobby. The elevator operator just shook his head.

Benny hit the lobby floor just as Ferrel exited the elevator and made his way to the doors and the street. Benny ran to catch up, nearly out of breath. Ferrel was on his way to his car parked on Walton Street.

Benny couldn't call Joe and tell him that he misplaced Frankie Ferrel. He flailed his arms for one of the taxicabs always lined up at The Drake. A cab sped to the doors. Benny got in and said, "See that Buick over there?" He pointed from the back seat. "Follow it wherever it goes."

The cabby hit the meter and said, "This is like in the movies, ain' it?"

Benny said, catching his breath, "I think that's a buddy of mine from the army. At least it sure looks like him. There he goes!"

Ferrel was heading south on Michigan Avenue. "Now, don't lose him. That's his car right there," pointing vigorously to Ferrel's car up ahead.

"Yeah, I see him. Don't worry, buddy" the cab driver assured him. The cab was only about two blocks behind Ferrel as they made their way along Michigan Avenue, Chicago's "Magnificent Mile." They drove past the eccentric Tribune Tower, with walls inlaid with stones from the most famous monuments in the world and the gleaming white Wrigley Tower. Ferrel turned west on Adams Street. If you know the US Presidents, you can navigate fairly well in this city.

Ferrel turned south to West Van Buren Street across the Chicago River to Canal Street and then headed back north on Canal Street. He pulled over and parked his car. "He's goin' to the train station," Benny blurted to the cabby.

"Just let me off at Union Station," Benny said. He hastily exited the cab, paid the driver, and waited while Ferrel parked his car in one of the long-term lots. *I'll catch him when he goes in the door.*

Eventually, Ferrel showed up and footslogged into Union Station with Benny not more than fifty feet behind him. Ferrel mixed into a small crowd as he went through the doors, not nearly as many people as back during the war when three-hundred trains a day and almost a hundred thousand people passed through Union Station.

But it was large enough for Benny to lose Ferrel. He looked frantically, moving swiftly through the crowd on tip toes searching. *Where'd he go? Joe'll sure be hot if I lose him.*

Benny made it to the Great Hall, a 110-foot-high atrium capped by a large barrel-vaulted skylight. Around the Great Hall are many smaller spaces, mostly small restaurants and services, and a wide passageway leading to the concourse. Above the headhouse are several floors of office space. There were people catching trains, buying tickets, struggling with luggage. It seemed to Benny that everyone was late and in a panic.

He couldn't find Ferrel anywhere. He paraded past every ticket counter. He finally spotted Ferrel purchasing a ticket. Benny stayed back, buffeted by the crowds but still out of eye-shot of Ferrel.

Benny, still watching Ferrel, went up to the ticket window and asked, "Hey, the guy who just bought tickets here—where was he going?"

"What's that to you?" croaked the ticket clerk.

Benny said, "Well, he was supposed to pick me up a ticket, see?" and he dropped a five dollar bill on the sill.

"Well, in that case," the clerk said as he grabbed the five, "you're in luck. He bought only one ticket to Buffalo, New York. You'd better hurry that train leaves in two hours."

"T'anks, I will," Benny responded happily and left the ticket counter and headed for a phone booth. He dialed Joe's office.

"Joseph Ganzer Investigations," Wilma answered.

"Hey, Wilma, it's me—Benny—put Joe on."

"Sure," Wilma said as she buzzed Joe and said, "It's Benny on the line."

"Thanks." Joe picked up the phone, "What's the matter Benny?"

"I'm at Union Station. Ferrel's bought a ticket for Buffalo."

"Damn her...," Joe grumbled, "Polina must have told him. Benny, when is he leaving?"

"In two hours. What'd she tell him?"

"I'll fill you in later, but Ferrel is headed for Montreal. There is a shipment of stolen art due to arrive there in a few days. Polina's uncle might be aboard the ship. I think Polina sent Ferrel there to help her uncle go into hiding."

"From who?" Benny asked in complete bewilderment.

"From me."

"Now yuh lost me."

"Never mind. Let him go. We've got a robbery to pull. I'll meet you at Vookie's for lunch."

◊◊◊

Joe was already in his booth at Vookie's when Ludko came in. He dashed over and sat down.

"What do you want for lunch?" Joe asked.

"Just an Italian beef and a beer. You buyin'?"

"Of course." Joe always bought. Benny the Hat finally walked in, but more like waltzed in, this time topped with his bowler hat made famous by Charlie Chaplin.

"Lo, Joe," Benny said as he edged into the booth right next to Ludko.

"Yur lucky I'm so skinny," Ludko complained when he scooted over to the inside of the booth.

"Joe, what's this about a robbery? I ain't sure about somethin' like that. It don't spin my hat." Benny asked, ignoring Ludko's crack about his weight.

"We're going to steal some liquor tonight, a lot of liquor in fact, over on 100th Street," Joe explained.

"What if we get caught? Ain't you doin' good in the detectiving?" Benny said.

Eddie walked from the bar over to Joe's booth and said, "Something's up—the whole crew is here. What can I get yuz?"

"Three Italian beefs and three beers. Thanks, Ed," said Joe.

"Make that four beefs and four beers," added Benny.

Eddie wrote a note on his pad and asked, "You're going to let me in on it... right, Joe?"

"Can't Eddie."

"How about later?" asked Eddie, forever curious about Joe's cases. Sometimes he helped out, but Joe couldn't let the liquor heist get around, not to anyone outside the crew.

"Trust me... not this time," Joe said.

Eddie nodded. He understood and said, "Sure, Joe. If you need help, you know— I'll get your orders, right away." He went back to the kitchen window and hung the order.

Joe turned to Benny and Ludko and said, "This goes nowhere."

In unison, "Got it."

"Lud, I want you to go to Lucky Motors—you know, over on the West Side—and steal a truck. The keys are in it, but take along the bolt cutters because the gate will be locked. The truck will be along the fence."

Ludko turned to Benny and said, "Come with me and then you can drive the truck to wherever we're meetin'. Hey, Joe, where *are* we meetin' up?"

"I'll get to that," said Joe.

"Is that what you want, Joe?" Benny said with pleading eyes.

"You're in on this heist with us. We need you. We're stealing a truck load of expensive booze from Rossi and ditching the truck near one of Santori's warehouses, just as Detective Donnelly is about to close in."

Benny looked incredulously, "Joe, those are Outfit guys. We'll get killed." He paused and took in a breath and added, "Oh, brother this is trouble."

"No it's not. Those two thugs will be at each other's throats over this. They'll never know we did it."

"So, why do it at all?" Benny asked earnestly.

Ludko whispered, "It's for One -Two Johnny. See, Rossi and that crooked cop Jerry Kavanaugh are trying to pin that heist on him. It's nothing but an insurance scam."

"Ahh, I get it," Benny said as the little light went on. Lowering his voice, he said, "But won't Santori know somebody set him up?"

Joe broke in and said softly, "No, not at first. He's going to think one of his crew is pulling a job off the record and not kicking a taste up to the boss. But he'll have enough trouble trying to avoid a turf war over this."

"I... I really don't like getting involved with Outfit guys. You sure nothing can go wrong?" Benny asked meekly.

"Don't worry, Benny," Joe said, trying to console him. "You're going to be the wheel man on the truck. No one'll even see you. Lud, Johnny, and I will do the break in."

Ludko said, "I cased the place, and there was a Cadillac right in front of the overhead door, just like you said. That's Rossi's guard dog. We gotta get that car out of the way fast and get the truck inside that front overhead door before anybody sees anything. Then we gotta get the Caddy back like nothin's wrong."

Eddie approached with a platter of sandwiches and beer.

"Man, I'm hungry," Benny said as he grabbed two of the sandwiches and almost upset the whole platter.

"Take it easy, Benny.... Joe, don't you feed these guys?" Eddie quipped as he did a little dance trying to balance everything—not spilling a single drop.

"Eddie, you oughta be in the circus with an act like that," Ludko said.

"What?... and give up this wonderful place?" countered Eddie.

He carefully passed out the rest of the beers and sandwiches and headed back to the bar.

Not saying a word, they ate—each mulling over what had to be done. Benny broke the silence. "Hey, these are delicious." He started in on his second beef.

Ludko said, "Would you take that hat off while yur eatin'?"

"Oh, certainly. Didn't even know it was on."

"Well, you better not wear it tonight. Somebody might recognize yuh." Ludko cautioned.

"Hey... yur right." Benny took off the bowler and reached back, putting it on the ledge behind the booth.

"Lud's got a point, Benny," Joe said. "We'd all better have masks when we hit the place."

Benny and Ludko nodded. Ludko added, "I got an idea about getting rid of that guard dog. See, I figure he's nuts about that Caddy of his. Right? It's new. So, how about I go and knock on the door dressed as a mechanic and say: 'I'm here to tow a Cadillac to the shop. Sign here please.'? He gets nuts about his car and he comes outside, see? That's when one of you guys puts his lights out."

For a moment they just looked at each other, then Joe said, "Ludko, you're a genius, but I'm thinking maybe you should play a Greek or a Mexican guy...with the accent and everything. That way, he won't ever recognize you later on someday."

"Yeah, yeah. I even got some dark theatre makeup I could use. Might be too dark... I'll figure somethin'."

Benny joined in, with his mouth full. "That sounds good, Lud."

Joe agreed "Yeah, it does. Hey, it gets dark about nine o'clock, so you two should be at Lucky Motors and get that truck. Then meet me at the rear of the Southmoor Hotel on 67th and Stony Island Avenue in the parking lot at half past ten. We'll head out from there."

"Hey, there's a good jazz club in that hotel, the Venetian Room," added Benny. "Yuh ever been there? It's hot."

Ludko said, "Thanks for the tour."

They talked more about the job, but the conversation eventually got around to the Cubs and the Sox. "Hey, Benny," asked Ludko, "Wrigley Field is in Wisconsin, ain' it?"

"They just beat Pittsburgh, you know," said Benny defending his team.

"That was a squeaker—2 to 1. You know, you can make good money bettin' the short side of the Cubs."

"Better stick with the ponies, Lud. The Cubs are gonna break yuh."

"Wanna bet?"

"Give up, Benny," said Joe. "Ludko is a professional."

"Joe, you always was a Sox guy," accused Benny.

Joe smiled and thought: *If you only knew*. He couldn't tell them about his mission with Moe Berg, a former White Sox player recruited by the OSS. They both spoke fluent German and were part of a team to unveil Nazi Germany's atomic capabilities. Despite graduating magna cum laude from Princeton, Moe Berg chose a career in baseball but ended up a spy. In 1942, before the United States entered the war, he and Joe made a trip to Zurich to determine the progress of Nazi nuclear science.

Unlike Joe, Moe Berg remained an intelligence agent for many years after the war. He would visit Joe whenever he passed through Chicago, and they would always take in a Sox game.

Joe said, "They look awfully good this year, Benny."

Ludko said, "Yeah, the Sox have won seven out of the last ten games."

"I'm outnumbered here."

After finishing their lunches, they left together. On the way out Joe nodded to Eddie and said, "Put it all on the account. I'll settle up in a week." Joe was letting Eddie know he was still a trusted friend, and he would explain what he could later.


Joe drove back to his office, going over everything in his mind. When he got upstairs, Wilma had just settled behind her desk back from a lunch with her sister.

"I just saw Tommy over at Maggie's. He's doing fine. We all had lunch. Those boys couldn't stop talking about Riverview, especially Tommy. Gosh, he's such a good kid."

"Oh, that's great. Johnny will be proud to hear that. I'm going to pick Johnny up pretty soon." As he went into his office, he turned back and said, "Would you bill out that Stevenson case. It's been taken care of."

"That was the surveillance on the store clerk putting his hands in the till, right?"

"That's the one. Bill them for three days' time for two operatives."

Wilma asked, "Catch the guy stealing?"

"No—it was the store owner's wife."

"Hmm, you never know. You write it up, and I'll get it out in the mail tonight."

"Wilm, would you get Mike Donnelly on the phone for me?" Joe walked over to the window behind his desk and put his head out to catch a little fresh air. His phone rang. He pulled back in and bumped his head. He winced and remembered Ferrel's love taps.

"Hello, Mike," rubbing his head.

Donnelly said, "I almost have none of the paperwork done on Johnny Della Penna, would you believe?"

"Good. Then I can come and get him."

"Sure. When?"

"Right along."

"Come to the station. My office first, okay?" advised Donnelly.

Joe said as he hung up, "Okay... about an hour then." He spent the next half hour working on the report for the Stevenson case. He handed it to Wilma on his way out.

She looked at it, then at him as he left the office. She shook her head.

Joe drove over to the Grand Crossing Police Station. When he got inside, he asked for Detective Donnelly and was told he was expected.

"Come on in. Have a seat," said Donnelly.

"Thanks." Joe sat down, removed his hat, and asked, "Mike, I've got another favor of sorts to ask."

"Okay, what now?"

"Don't get defensive," said Joe with a broad smile. "Do you know of a warehouse or building connected to Santori or operated by one of his fronts?"

"Take your pick. He's into everything around this district."

"I thinking now one that's empty."

Donnelly, leaning back in his chair, looking up at the ceiling, after a few moments he said, "Yeah... yeah... there's one on 61st Street just east of Indiana Avenue. It was billed as a furniture store. Always under renovation, you know. It's been closed for months now. Santori's crews were rumored to be using it for a dump of swag from their truck robberies around the city. We did a set up on the place, but *somehow* it leaked out and nobody's been there since. What do you need it for?"

Joe explained, "Well, I have it on good intelligence that it will be loaded with stolen liquor tonight."

"Now that wouldn't be all that booze supposedly stolen by Johnny Della Penna would it?" surmised Donnelly.

"In fact it is... and Johnny's going to help put it there."

Mike Donnelly leaned back in his chair and it squeaked its disapproval. "That's a piece of work, Joe."

"Thanks. Now I have to get my accomplice out of jail, so he can commit another crime."

"I'll lose the paperwork on his release until tomorrow." Then, Donnelly remembered something, "You know, one of Santori's burglary crew smokes expensive cigars. They found a Sancho Panza short in that warehouse after it was shut down."

"Good to know, thanks," Joe said and thought: *Albert Strugala smokes those.*

"Let's get your accomplice." They both went down to the lockup and got Johnny Della Penna released. Johnny went to the window to pick up his belongings. Donnelly told the holding officer that he would handle all the paperwork personally. The officer looked relieved and went back to his desk.

Joe shook Detective Donnelly's hand and thanked him again. So did Johnny, which struck Johnny as outrageous—shaking a cop's hand for locking him up. The two headed out of the station.

Johnny got into Joe's car and breathed a sigh of relief. "I'm sure glad to be outa that place. Honest."

"I believe you, John," agreed Joe. "Now, listen, we're going to hit Rossi's warehouse where that liquor is stashed tonight, and you're in on it."

"I didn't think you was—"

"I'm not," Joe said. "We're going to move that stash over to one of Santori's places. Capice?"

"Uh, no capice."

Joe explained, "We're stealing the stolen liquor and planting it on Santori."

"Wow...now I get it. Rossi will think Santori's crew hit his place."

"Right, and Santori will think one of his crew has gone rouge on him, but he won't be able to do anything because Rossi will be coming after him hard." Joe smiled and said, "And he'll need all the men he can get."

"Yeah...and Santori's crew will get the rap instead of me. Then I can get Tommy and go back to a normal life. Go back to work." Johnny turned away from Joe and looked out the window as his eyes glistened and his voice trailed off. "Yeah...." After a moment, with the wind blowing at his face, he turned back to Joe and said, "I can't thank you enough. I mean...."

"Don't thank me yet. We haven't made the heist."

Joe said, "Now, if anybody ever asks why I was at the Grand Crossing lockup with you, tell them I was arranging bail."

"Got it, Joe," said Johnny. On the way back to Joe's office, "Yuh think I can I see Tommy?"

"Sure, John, but I'll have to have Wilma's sister bring him over to the office. I can't have anyone spot you on the street. You're still in jail—remember?"

They continued on to the office. Joe turned down the alley behind his building and let Johnny out at the rear entrance. He hopped out of Joe's Chevy and ran in the back door and up the back stairs. Joe drove around and parked on the street in front of his building.

As Joe walked up the stairs and entered his office, Johnny was talking to Wilma about Tommy. She was filling him in on everything that had happened.

Joe walked past them and said, "Come on in, John. I want to go over our plans for tonight." They went into Joe's inner office. It was still disheveled from Frankie Ferrel's visit. There was a peculiar chaos to his surroundings that belied Joe's seemingly organized demeanor. "Have a seat, John." One-Two Johnny didn't fit into rooms very well. He looked somehow out of place, awkward. Johnny lit a cigarette.

Joe walked out to Wilma's desk and asked softly, "Would you call Maggie and see if she could get Tommy over here right away. Don't say why."

"Sure, Joe." Wilma picked up the phone and dialed Maggie. It started ringing.

Joe said, "I need you to do one more thing. After we leave, would you—" but Wilma shushed him.

"Hi Maggie... Yeah, it's me..... hold on...," Wilma held her hand over the receiver, glared at Joe and said, "What?"

Joe put his hands up, then grabbed a pad and pencil, and started writing.

Wilma continued with Maggie, "Would you mind driving over here with the boys... No, I need some help with something...."

Joe slid her the note. Wilma looked at it and nodded, "How soon, Maggie?..."

He walked back into his office, closed the door, and sat down. "Okay, here's the plan so far. We located where Rossi stored that liquor. Ludko is going to impersonate a tow truck driver and knock on the door of the place to get Rossi's guard dog outside. This guy looks mean, tough." Joe paused thinking about the guard for a moment. "So, anyway, we get this Mr. Friendly out of the building, and I put his lights out. Then we get our truck inside and start loading up the cases of booze into our truck, fast."

"Who's drivin' the truck?" Johnny asked.

"Benny."

"Does that guy even drive? All's I seen him is taking cabs or the bus."

"Yeah, he drives. He's just too cheap to own a car."

Johnny laughed nervously and asked, "How long yuh think it'll take to get it loaded?"

"With the three of us, I figure about fifteen minutes, maybe longer. Then we get out of there and head for a warehouse on 61st Street. We unload there, and Ludko and Benny will drop the truck off on a side street somewhere.

"Sounds good."

Joe tapped his pencil on the desk. "But after the heist, you and I are headed for Canada."

"Canada!" Johnny exclaimed.

"You can't be around here when all this starts to unravel. I want Rossi and Santori to go at each other and leave you out of it."

"So, Tommy stays with Wilma's sister?"

"Yeah, just for a while, John."

"How long, yuh think?"

"I'm not sure. I'm working on a case in Canada that you can help me with. I don't know how that will play out." They heard a drum roll of feet pounding out a chaotic beat coming up the stairs. As only boys can do, Tommy burst into Joe's office.

"Daddy...."

# CHAPTER THIRTEEN

## CHICAGO, WEST SIDE
*Lucky Motors Trucking*

Ludko and Benny pulled up in the LaFayette at Lucky Motors on South Archer Avenue, near the rail yard. It was twilight, about eight o'clock. Benny said, "This is Bobcat Bobby Mann's place, huh? He done alright for himself."

"Get the bolt cutters in the trunk, Benny. I'm gonna go see where that truck is." Benny got out and opened the trunk and pulled out the bolt cutters. Ludko spotted the box truck along the far fence line. "Hey, I see it over on the left." They both went to the gate. Ludko held the chain with the lock at the crucial spot, and Benny cut it with the bolt cutters. The chain parted, and they opened the gate just enough to let themselves in.

"That was easy," Ludko said as he closed the gate behind him. "Benny, go put them cutters back."

"Oh, yeah." Benny put the cutters back in Ludko's trunk and returned.

Ludko opened the gate slightly letting Benny inside. "Now, go over by that truck and get it started. As soon as it's started, drive over here, and I'll open the gate so's you can drive out. Then head straight to the Southmoor Hotel. Okay?"

"Got yuh, Lud. I'll see you there." Benny was wearing a beat-up Irish flat cap. He chose it to look like a real Chicago teamster, almost a part of their uniform. The keys were not in the ignition. Benny panicked and looked on the dashboard, then under the floor mat. He looked out the windshield at Ludko, put his hands up and gave a shrug. Ludko put two fingers up to his mouth and patted his lips a few times. Benny looked at him quizzically, and took off the cap. He saw Ludko yelling something. He smiled broadly, all teeth, and nodded. Benny looked in the ashtray. There they were. He started the truck.

As the engine engaged and began running, a police squad car slowly pulled up at the gate. Ludko approached the squad car and asked in a mild, convincing Mexican accent, "Si, officer."

The cop in the squad said, "Hey, what are you guys doing here?"

Ludko had his garage mechanic's clothes on and had used the juice from coffee grounds to slightly darken his olive-colored skin. The question made him pause. If he said the truck needed repair, then how could it be drivable. The next thought he had, "The boss say to take theez truck to the garage and install a power take-off unit. And to have it ready for work tomorrow morning." Ludko had heard something about trucks and power take-off and figured the cop wouldn't know anything about, and it sounded legitimate.

The cop came back with, "Oh, a PTO, eh? What is he using it for one of those lift gates?"

"Lift gate, si." Ludko had no idea what the cop was talking about.

"Okay... don't forget to lock the gate. This isn't the best neighborhood." The squad pulled back on to Archer Avenue, and Ludko let his breath out all at once.

Benny watched the whole thing play out, all the while biting his lip. Ludko motioned for him to drive out. He drove the truck straight for the gate, which Ludko swung wide open and Benny was out and on his way to 67th and Stony Island Avenue and the Southmoor Hotel parking lot.

Ludko swung the gate closed and wrapped the cut chain around itself in such a way that it looked normal, even the lock was hanging in front. He admired his handiwork. He went to his car, hopped in and headed for the Southmoor rendezvous.


A breeze swept in off the lake, cool, refreshing and twilight had just lost its battle with the night. Ludko was the last to arrive at the parking lot behind the Southmoor Hotel. He drove to the far rear corner of the lot, parked, locked up his car, and went over to the truck where everyone had gathered. When he saw Ludko, Joe said, "Ludko, I would swear it wasn't you."

Ludko smiled and said with his accent, "Si, señor." He dropped the accent and said, "How yuh doin' Johnny?"

One-Two Johnny said, "I'm okay. Man, I'd"ve never known it was you, either."

Joe asked, "Did you have any trouble stealing the truck?"

"It was just like you said—right by the fence."

Benny added, "But there was a nosey cop, and Lucky Motors is going to need a new chain."

Ludko said, "Yeah, I got rid of the cop. No problem"

Joe said, "You know, I'm glad a cop showed up. When Bobcat Bobby reports the truck stolen tomorrow, there will at least be an embarrassed cop to say he saw something."

"Yeah, but me and Benny almost had a heart attack."

Joe gave them last minute orders. "Benny, follow us to the 100th Street warehouse but stay two blocks back. When we get there, turn your headlights off and wait for our signal."

"Gotcha, Joe," said Benny. "What's the signal?"

"Look for a flashlight in the street, then drive down and back into the warehouse."

Benny answered hesitantly, "Okay."

"Walter, are you ready for your entrance?"

Benny broke in and said, "Who's Walter?"

Joe answered, "Ludko is Walter. Didn't you know that?"

Astonished, Benny said, "All these years, and I thought 'Ludko' *was* your name."

"Better stop thinkin' Benny. I can smell the wood burning," Ludko cracked.

No reaction from Benny.

"Come on... It's time we took off. Everybody got gloves and a mask?" Joe said as he looked them over. "Benny, put these plates on the truck." He handed Benny a set of license plates. "Okay, let's go."

"Hey, what about them license plates, Joe?" Ludko said pointing to the Chevy's plates.

"Those are off a junked car. My real one's are in the trunk," said Joe. "You're really on the ball."

"Just keeping you on your toes, boss," said Ludko, not letting on that he thought Joe might still be suffering from that game of tag he played with Frankie Ferrel.

Joe, Ludko, and One-Two Johnny pulled out in Joe's Chevy and headed south down Stony Island on their way to 100th Street. Benny followed in the truck, staying about two blocks behind.

Stony Island Avenue was the center of the jazz scene in Chicago. There were jazz clubs and bars on every block, and Benny had been in most of them. Gene Kruppa, the fabulous drummer for Benny Goodman, had lived in this neighborhood; so had Mel Torme, "the Velvet Fog," who started singing when he was only four years old. Louis Armstrong recorded with his "Hot Five" and "Hot Seven" ensembles right here on Stony Island with songs like "Potato Head Blues" and "Muggles" with all its allusions to marijuana. Stony Island set the standard and the agenda for Chicago-style jazz.

And the father of Chicago Blues, Muddy Waters, stepped off the bus from Mississippi and landed on Stony Island, playing his Delta Blues. Last year Muddy's uncle bought him his first electric guitar, which let his music be heard above the raucous crowds in the clubs on Stony Island. Benny the Hat was well known in these clubs. With his innate sense of rhythm, his love of music and dance, Benny became one of the few white men welcomed in the black jazz and blues clubs on Stony.

Benny strained to see if he recognized anybody going into the clubs as he passed by while following Joe. On 95th they took a left and headed toward Torrence Avenue and the industrial area. Through a series of side streets, they approached the 100th Street warehouse. Joe waved out his window for Benny to pull over and wait. Joe passed right by the warehouse. Ludko said, "Hey, Mr. Friendly's Cadillac... and there's a light on in the office. Let me out here at the end of the block. I'll walk back."

Joe slowed and stopped. As Ludko got out, Johnny said, "Good luck."

"Gracias."

Joe drove ahead and turned down the unpaved alley, stopping about a half block away from the warehouse. Ludko could see them and got ready. As he approached the front office door, he could hear that the radio was on inside. It was NBC's *Lights Out*, the voice on the program said, "Welcome back to tonight's episode 'The Signal Man.' " Ludko smiled at that and laughed softly through his nose. He knocked loudly on the door.

No answer. He knocked again, only harder. He heard someone on the other side of the door unlocking it. The door opened and a large man filled the doorway, the same man Joe had met on his first visit.

"What do you want?"

In his best accent Ludko said "Señor, I am here to tow the broke car, por favor."

"What're you talkin' about?" he said with the onset of rage.

"The uh carro," said Ludko pointing to the Cadillac. "I tow it to de chop, no?"

"You ain't touchin' that car, spic" he yelled as he pushed Ludko aside and stormed over to his car as if to protect it from this Mexican bandit. Joe and Johnny were just out of sight behind the two front corners of the building. Ludko had to get Mr. Friendly's back to them. He hurried past him to block his way to the Cadillac and started speaking rapid Spanish, mostly swear words that everybody knows, including guys like Mr. Friendly.

Ludko made it to the front of the car mixing English and Spanish. Mr. Friendly angrily grabbed Ludko by the shirt; then grabbed his neck with his left hand and started squeezing. He lifted him off the ground. Ludko gasped for breath. *Where the hell are those guys?*

Mr. Friendly's right fist hit Ludko so hard he was almost out, but he stayed in character, speaking in Spanish, "Halto, halto, por favor...."

Joe ran from the corner and grabbed Mr. Friendly from behind just as he was about to hit Ludko again. He had Friendly in a headlock, squeezing with all his strength, but it wasn't enough. Mr. Friendly twirled around, and Joe was airborne. Ludko fell to the ground as Friendly let go of him. Joe whipped around like a tether ball and slammed into the brick wall outside the office. Still holding on, Joe tried to apply more pressure, but one or two of Joe's ribs had cracked. The pain shot through him as he tried to squeeze harder.

A few seconds later, Johnny Della Penna, two-time South Side Athletic Club champ, aka "One-Two Johnny," came from the other side of the warehouse and landed a full right hook to Mr. Friendly's jaw followed by a left uppercut. Mr. Friendly collapsed straight to the ground with Joe still hanging on to his neck.

Rising from the ground, Joe cried out, "Get Walter." Johnny went over and picked Ludko up as though he were a doll. "Get him inside," Joe said as he coughed and spit out some blood.

Joe used his tongue to check all his teeth. He wasn't sure what happened when he hit the wall. At that point it was all instinct and adrenalin. Joe scuttled inside right behind Johnny and Ludko. Johnny went back out and dragged Mr. Friendly into the office. A commercial for Eversharp-Schick was playing on the radio.

Joe turned to Johnny and said, "It's lucky that Ludko and I softened him up for you."

"You didn't even need me, Joe," said Johnny.

Taking a hard breath, Joe said, "John, get the keys and move the Caddy so Benny can back in." Joe went over and turned the radio up.

Johnny found the keys on the desk. He flew outside, jumped in the Cadillac, and backed it into the street. A moment later, Joe was in the street with the flashlight and gave Benny the signal. As Joe headed back to the warehouse, he spotted a light go on at a house down the block. Johnny passed him sprinting back to the warehouse. He opened the overhead door just as Benny backed the truck up and into the warehouse. As soon as he was in, Johnny closed the door and ran out to move the Cadillac back in front of the door as though nothing had happened.

Ludko was coming around, and his jaw ached as he said, "Did that lummox run over me with the Caddy?"

Joe's ribs hurt when he laughed and said, "No, Benny ran over you with the truck."

"See, I told you Benny couldn't drive," Ludko said as he walked over and joined Benny at the back of the truck.

Joe said, "You and Benny get up inside the truck. Johnny and I will carry the crates to you. Just stack 'em up inside."

"Okay, sure," said Benny, as he and Ludko hopped up inside the truck.

One-Two Johnny worked like a madman, picking up two crates at a time, but Joe was falling behind, each lift sent searing pains across his right side. They moved as fast as they could. It was hot inside the warehouse.

The truck was almost loaded. There was a knock at the door. They looked at each other.

Then came another knock, this one more demanding. "Hey, Gino, where yuh at?"

Joe's mind raced. He remembered, *That light down the block. Somebody called....*

Ludko sprang into action. "How do I look?"

"Like somebody I don't even know," answered Benny.

161

Ludko jumped down from inside the truck and ran to the front door. He opened it. Standing there was another large, Brunswick-haired, sloe-eyed monster, just like Mr. Friendly, only bigger.

Ludko said, "Hola, hola, sí, he is in de back. Come thees way señor." Ludko turned toward the rear door of the office that led to the inside of the warehouse, all the while laughing lightly, motioning his guest to follow him. The radio was still broadcasting *Lights Out.*

No sooner had Ludko's monster passed through the door, One-Two Johnny hit him in the kidney, then a hard right cross to the jaw. The monster only groaned and lunged toward Johnny. He had him in a bear hug. Lifted him right off the floor. Johnny felt his vertebrae separating. This python forced the air out of his lungs.

Ludko spotted a dolly handle on the floor, about the size of a little league baseball bat. *This'll do.*

He ran behind the monster and hit him sharply on the ankle, an old trick the cops use to rouse bums. The monster groaned in agony and let up on Johnny just enough to where he could break free. Then Ludko hit the other ankle. The monster shrieked like a little girl.

Johnny moved back in and delivered a flurry of rib and kidney punches. The blows sounded like a machine gun with a sandbag silencer. Ludko moved behind him, but the monster caught him with a left. Johnny pulled back and started on his head with a left then a right, then another right. He got a blow in on Johnny, a roundhouse punch that almost floored him. He pushed Johnny aside and retreated toward the front door, trying to escape. From the darkness, a fist like a knife caught him in the throat.

The monster started choking, bending over to breathe. That's when a swift, hard chop hit him in the back of the neck. He fell hard on the concrete floor, unconscious. Joe stood over him breathing heavily. "I should have done that to your partner too," Joe said to the hulk, now motionless on the floor.

Ludko came over to Joe. "Hey—you alright?"

"Yeah. I'm sore though," said Joe grabbing his ribs.

"They taught you some delightful tricks in that school, eh?"

"A few, I guess," said Joe holding his side. Then, pointing to the mass of flesh collapsed on the floor, "Hey, where do they get guys like this?"

"I think they make 'em in a basement out of spare parts."

One-Two Johnny went back to loading the last few liquor crates, as Benny positioned them inside the truck.

Joe went into the cab of the truck and got some packing rope. "Let's tie him and Mr. Friendly up and get moving." Ludko and Joe tied them up. Joe said, "Do they look bad enough that Rossi won't suspect they were in on this?"

Ludko said, "Nah...." and he kicked Mr. Friendly in the jaw. "Now they do. That's what yuh get for calling me spic."

Johnny was already outside starting the Cadillac. He backed it up just as the overhead door was rolling up. Benny drove the truck out fast, turned on to the street, and headed for the Grand Crossing address. Johnny pulled the Cadillac right back into place. The overhead door was closing. The NBC radio announcer was saying, "Alright, you can turn them on now...."

When Johnny got back inside, Joe closed the front door and locked it from the inside. He said, "Come on, let's go."

The three of them left through the back door and walked down the alley, still with their masks on. Joe got behind the wheel, Ludko in back, and Johnny in the passenger's seat. Joe drove slowly down the alley with his lights off. When he hit the cross street, the lights went on, the masks came off, and they headed north to Grand Crossing.

"How are you doing, Lud?" Joe asked he looked at him in the rearview mirror.

"My jaw aches from that guerilla," complained Ludko.

"How about you, John?"

Guys like Johnny never complain. All he said was: "I should've got that guy first, before he slammed you into that wall."

"Forget it, " said Joe, "If you hadn't clocked him, Ludko and I might not be here right now, but I think he broke a rib."

Johnny asked, "Where'd you learn how to hit like that Joe? I don't remember anything like that from Clancey's Gym."

"Let me answer for yuh," Ludko broke in. "If he tells yuh, Johnny, he'll have to kill yuh, see? I got that maybe a thousand times." Joe chuckled at that and winced and drove north toward 61th Street, toward the Grand Crossing district. The night breeze felt good rushing through the car. You could just barely catch the fragrance of the steel mills that scented the night air when the east wind blows in off Lake Michigan.

Joe said, "When we get to this furniture place on 61st Street, we can slow down unloading the liquor. We just can't take all night."

"Yeah, that's Santori's area. He's worse than Rossi," said Johnny shaking his head.

"Maybe you guys should put your masks on when we get there—just in case," proposed Ludko.

"He's right," said Joe.

When they arrived at the warehouse, Benny was already parked in front. Joe pulled up alongside him. He leaned out the window and said, "Benny, we'll get you inside in a second. Hold on."

"Sure," said Benny. "It's almost cool out tonight." Joe put on his mask and took his burglar's kit to the man door and worked on it. In a less than a minute they were in. Joe opened the overhead door, and Benny backed the truck right in. He closed the door just as fast.

"Remember," warned Joe. "Everybody keep your gloves and masks on."

They took their time unloading, but Johnny worked as before, taking two, sometimes three cases at a time. Joe said, "John, take it easy. We have some time now."

Johnny answered, "I don't want yuz to think I ain't grateful or nothin'. I want everybody outa here quick like."

"We understand, but let's make Benny do a little extra. He could use the exercise," Joe said.

"Sure, put it all on me, just cuz I wasn't in on the action," protested Benny.

"Benny," Ludko observed, "somehow you're never in on the action. Why is that?"

"Well... cuz maybe I don't want to mess up my hat." Benny took his hat off and inspected it for damage and returned it to his round head. They all continued unloading the truck. When they were finished, Joe had them drape tarpaulins from inside the truck over all the crates.

Joe took a Sancho Panza cigar butt out of his pocket and dropped it on the floor near the crates. "There—that ought to cause a little ruckus."

"A cigar butt? You don't even smoke, Joe," said Benny.

"Yeah but one of Santori's guys does," explained Joe. "Ludko, ride with Benny and go pick up your car at the Southmoor Hotel and clean that truck thoroughly. I don't want anything linking us to this and drop the truck off anywhere you want, but put Bobcat's plates back on."

"Sure, boss, then what?" asked Benny.

"Well, for one, take the mask off while you're driving."

"Oh yeah, yeah," said Benny.

"And for the next few days, until I get back, you two keep a shadow on Polina."

"Where yuh goin'?" asked Benny.

"Johnny and I are headed to Canada on the Polina case."

"Ah, yeah, that's right. But I didn't know it was for that case," said Benny.

"I'll get in touch with Wilma if anything comes up," Joe said, "and thanks to both of you guys. You did great."

"Sure thing, Joe."

Ludko only nodded. His jaw ached, but he managed to say: "Adios, mis amigos." He gave a little wave as he and Benny got into the truck and headed for the hotel.

At one point, while Benny was driving back to the Southmoor, he turned to Ludko and said, "I think Joe's getting better. Don't you?"

"Benny, for some, that war is gonna last thirty more years. For guys like Joe, it might never end. It's the haunts."

"I think yur wrong. I see a change. More like the old Joe. Honest."

"I hope you're right, Benny. I really do."

Joe and One-Two Johnny were driving back on Cottage Grove Avenue towards Joe's office. It was getting late.


Even though it was after midnight, Joe parked in the alley in case someone spotted them. They climbed the back stairs together. Joe said, "I've got to wrap my ribs before we go." He unlocked his front office door and turned on the lights. There, on Wilma's desk, were the train tickets. *Thank you, Wilma.* He smiled and picked them up and went into his office. Johnny sat down.

Joe said, looking in his office bathroom medicine cabinet for some cloth bandages and tape, "Ah, here they are." He removed his shirt and started wrapping the cloth bandage around his ribs. His side looked worse than it actually was. The bruise was dark red but turning blue on its way to black.

"That looks horrible,' Johnny said.

"Feels that way, too."

"Joe, you're still in fightin' shape, I see."

"I have to be. You meet some nasty people in this business." Joe put on a new shirt. "There, that looks better." Joe walked over to the closet and got out a few things, mostly work clothes and boots. He packed them in a suitcase along with his gun.

"What's that for, Joe?" Johnny asked casually.

"For those nasty people I was talking about."

"Are we going to work? Looks like you're packin' work clothes in that other suitcase."

"Johnny, you and I are going to work on the docks as longshoremen in Montreal. I've had a Longshoremen's union card since I was out of high school, and I swung a permit for you to work with me."

"What's happening in Montreal?"

"We're going to work the docks waiting for a certain ship to come in from England. Aboard that ship is stolen art, stolen in France with the help of the Nazis. If we're lucky, we might be able to nab a guy named Yuri Kemidov, the mastermind behind it all and close out a case I'm working on."

"Hey, I don't know a thing about bein' a longshoreman."

"You were doing some of it tonight."

"You mean pounding those two guerrillas?"

"No... loading and unloading freight."

"Oh, I follow."

"John, do you know crane signals?"

"Well a couple, from the mill. Lift and lower. You know."

"I'll give you a crash course on the train, which leaves for Buffalo at two o'clock this morning. So we'd better get going. Look, we can't go near your place to get anything, so for a couple of days you'll have to wear some of my clothes. Okay?"

"Yeah, we're about the same size. You're a little smaller," Johnny said and smiled slyly.

"Uhm huh. Well, you won't look any worse than the rest of us dock rats," Joe said with a pause. "Hey, we better go. Grab the suitcases, will ya?" Joe went over to his desk, picked up his Eversharp Skyline fountain pen, which looked like Flash Gordon's rocket ship, and dashed off a note:

Wilma,

As soon as you get in, call my favorite detective and tell him we're done.

I'll call you as soon as we get to our destination.

Joe

Just in case, Joe didn't give specifics. He locked up. He and Johnny went down the back stairs to the alley. Johnny loaded the suitcases in the trunk. Joe had Johnny switch the plates back on his car. Then they headed downtown for Union Station.

On the way, Johnny said, "I'm sorry about your ribs, Joe. If I coulda got there sooner—"

"Forget it, John. We pulled it off. That's all that counts. When Rossi gets the news that his stash was hit, he's going to be furious. Then when he gets word the Marcello Warehouse liquor turned up in one of Santori's places, he's going to be murderous.

"And Santori's going to hear about that cigar butt and start looking inside his own crew for a double-dealer. There will trouble for months," Joe said laughing and hurting. "I just opened up some wounds from their days with Frank Nitti. If Chicago's lucky, maybe they'll kill each other."

Johnny said, "I hope those two fireplugs didn't hear anything. You know, like names or anything."

"I don't think we said anything until their lights were out," Joe said, but he tried to replay the scene in his mind as he drove. He dismissed it. When they arrived at Union Station, Joe let Johnny off and had him take the suitcases inside. "Here—get us some coffee." He handed Johnny some money. Johnny went inside, and Joe found a week-long parking lot just down the street. He told the attendant, "It'll be a week." The attendant nodded and directed him to park along the back. Joe paid on his way out and walked back to the station.

At night, Union Station looked forsaken and alien. The 103-foot-high ceiling windows were now black as night, making it feel like some ancient Roman Catholic church at midnight mass. He spotted Johnny leaving one of the all-night coffee shops. He walked over. Johnny looked up and said, "Hey, here's the coffee. Can I keep the change."

"You know, I'd expect that out of Benny the Hat or Ludko, but you...?"

"They must be rubbin' off on me," Johnny said and handed Joe the change. They walked over to the benches. There were people there, but not enough to change the feeling of loneliness.

Johnny said, "This place reminds me of church. I think."

"A few years back this place was busy all day, all night, every day. A lot of military travelers. It's slowed down a lot since then."

They sat together silently for almost a half hour when the loudspeaker squawked, "515 Lake Shore Express for Cleveland, Buffalo, and Albany, boarding on track eight."

"That's us," said Joe with a start. He had almost fallen asleep waiting. They got up and headed for track eight. By the time they got there, chose their seats, and settled in, the train jerked ahead, on its way out of Union Station. Before too long, despite the coffee, the rhythmic movement of the train rocked them both to sleep. As he dozed off, Joe thought about Frankie Ferrel and what he was planning in Montreal... and the *Ponta Delgada*...and Lawrence Hamilton and....and Kira.......

# CHAPTER FOURTEEN

## BUFFALO, NEW YORK
*New York Central Terminal*

They pulled into Buffalo a little after lunch. Joe said, "John, we have some time. Let's get some lunch here at the station instead of on the next train. Trust me, you don't want the Toronto train's cuisine."

"It's bad, uh?"

"I'd rather eat Benny's hat."

Johnny asked, "You been up here before, Joe?"

"Yeah, it seems like a thousand years ago instead of four."

"Up here during the war?"

"For a while."

They ordered. Joe just had a Ruben sandwich, but Johnny had a hot roast beef dinner. "Are you that hungry, Johnny?"

"Starvin'."

During lunch Johnny asked, "Now, don't think I'm stickin' my nose in, but can you say what you were doin' up here?"

"Well, not exactly, but I *can* say I was getting some special training from the British."

"They was over here?"

"John, Canada is part of the British Commonwealth."

"Oh yeah, yeah," said Johnny remembering that Canada was a British province. "You forget that sometimes, yuh know." Johnny finished off his meal and said, "Yeah, I was getting some special training, too—at Statesville."

"Are you serious?"

Mocking Joe, he said, "Well, not exactly, but I *can* say they offered to commute the rest of my sentence if I went into the army."

169

Joe smiled. The load speaker came on and announced their Toronto departure. "You done, John? Let's go."

Johnny grabbed the suitcases, and they headed for the platform to board the train. They took their seats at the rear of the train.

"You know what I just noticed? It's cool up here," said Joe.

"Hey, yeah, you're right."

They got settled and after a few miles Joe asked, "John, I *am* stickin' my nose in. How did you get mixed up in all that?"

Johnny understood and said, "I muscled up a couple of deadbeats for Rossi. Good pay. I wasn't goin' anywhere with my boxing, you know."

"You moved on to burglary?"

"Not at first. I was still club fightin', but it was starting to get to me. I heard of a job where they needed a lookout for one of the crews working the warehouse district on the far west side," said Johnny and added, "I took the fall on that one."

"What happened?"

"I was watchin' outside in the back of the place while they were grabbing furs from inside. They just flew out of there and left me. They forgot me. I didn't even know they was gone. Then two squads pulled up," Johnny said shrugging his shoulders. "They had me."

"I can imagine what happened," Joe said knowing how the police operated on a grand larceny case.

"They beat on me for hours, but I never gave nobody up, yuh know."

"And I take it your partners never gave you your cut."

Johnny just laughed. "All's I got was two years." Johnny sat there quiet for a while, looking out of the window. "When I got out, yuh know, I couldn't get no job, so I did some work for Rossi. Then I went on my own. I was doin' jewelry stores. Through the roof—no alarms. Rossi got a cut, and he had fences that paid twenty percent. Not bad. I was livin' pretty good."

"You got married, too."

"That's what ruined me. Sherry liked spending money, lots of it. Then the baby came along, and I got to thinkin' this can't go on. So I was gonna do one last big job and call it quits. Then I get busted casing a jewelry store downtown."

"They can't prosecute based on that."

"Joe, I had the tools in the trunk of the car, and I had a burglary prior."

"Yeah, but that wouldn't be big time."

"It was six years. Woulda been fifteen if I'd been caught inside." Johnny paused and added, "But the war come along, and I got a deal."

"Not *that* good of a deal," said Joe.

"I made it back."

"Yeah, you did."

"You know, I was gonna hire you to check out Sherry. I heard some things around about her."

"John, I'm glad I didn't have to take your case."

"I already knew. She was different after I come back from overseas. I didn't need a detective to know that."

Joe understood. Except for the worst of them, he would certify most all wives as virtuous. He would have done the same for One-Two Johnny.

"But Tommy changed everything. He was gettin' so big. Sherry told him I was a hero in the war. He looked up to me, Joe. I couldn't go back to the life."

"I understand, John."

"So, I took the only job I could get. I hired on at the coke plant on Torrence Avenue."

"That has to be the worst job in all of Chicago."

"I been there for goin' on two years, but that wasn't enough for Sherry. She wanted more—more clothes, more shoes, a better house, a better car. I told her they were gonna make me a foreman. That wasn't enough. She just walked out on me and Tommy. Some other guy, I'm sure. And now all this happens."

"John, you'll be cleared of those charges."

"Yeah, but I've missed so much work already. I don't even know if they'll take me back now."

"It's got to be this way for now, until it all blows over."

Looking down at the floor, he said, "Yeah, I guess."

"Look, I'll think of something," said Joe, almost believing it himself.

They fell silent. They gazed out the window and listened to the clack of the rails, jostled by the sway of the train car. Later, in Toronto, they switched trains one last time.

◊◊◊

Evening came, and Joe and One-Two Johnny were on the last leg of their journey to Montreal. The train was nearly empty. They sat opposite each other, Johnny looking forward and Joe looking back. They were still silent.

"Ever been married, Joe?" asked Johnny.

"No, but had things turned out differently maybe, I don't know." Joe paused and added, "But they didn't."

Joe couldn't tell Johnny how it happened or where or how it ended or how she returned to him in his dreams some nights or that she was Russian.

Johnny broke in, "Well, you ain't missin' nothin'."

"I suppose you're right," said Joe, hoping he was wrong.

Joe changed the subject and started to teach Johnny how to signal the dock cranes when unloading and loading freight. It got their minds off everything. He needed Johnny to look like he had at least been on a dock before.

"Okay, you know that raising your hand with the index finger pointing up means 'raise' the load. Right?" Joe said raising his hand and pointing at the roof of the car. "And dropping your hand with the index finger pointing down like this...." Joe lowered his hand and pointed to the floor, "That means 'lower' the load."

"Right, right. I know that."

"Now to get the crane boom of the crane to move up and change the placement of the load, you stick your thumb up with your fingers clenched, like this...." Joe had his thumb up, fingers curled in a fist, and motioned upward a couple of times. Johnny aped his gesture, and Joe said, "Yep, that's it. When you give that signal the crane will move the boom up and the load will move toward the crane and away from you. We call it booming up."

"Got it."

"To boom down and move the load closer to you and away from the crane, you turn your hand over and point your thumb down toward the ground."

Johnny turned his sledge-hammer fist over with the thumb extended and pointing down and gave a little downward motion. "Like that, Joe?"

"You got it, John."

Johnny said to himself, "Boom up, load away. Boom down, load comes in."

Joe said, "Okay, now show me the load-up and load-down signals."

Johnny pointed up with his index finger and said, "Load up." He pointed down and said, "Load down."

"Good. Now here's the easy ones—If you want to move the load to the left, point to the left. If you want to move the load to the right, point to the right."

"Aw, that's easy."

"Sure it is." As Johnny continued to practice his signals and talk to himself, Joe looked at Johnny's hands. They were almost a knuckle wider than his. His fists looked like softballs as he motioned with them. He noticed the bruised knuckles from the night before.

He turned and looked out the window, watching the scenery pass by. *Polina told Ferrel about Montreal.* He turned back to Johnny. "You know, John, we might come up against Frankie Ferrel in Montreal."

"What's he doing there?"

The train rocked sharply as it switched tracks. Joe said, "He's looking for the same person we are."

"Is he gonna hit him?"

"I'm not sure what his play is. I don't think so. I think he's playing some kind of double-cross on my client, but if the guy we're looking for gets in Ferrel's way, he'll kill him for sure," Joe said and added, "But I think he just wants the stolen art."

"Who's the guy we're looking for?"

"His name is Yuri Kemidov, about 60 to 65 years old. No pictures."

"What's Ferrel look like. I never met the guy, just heard of him."

"He's about your size, maybe a little bigger. Dark hair, brown eyes. He has a small Irish nose, ruddy complected. He has a hangman's look about him.

"I know what you mean. There was a couple of guys like that in Statesville, I remember."

"John, listen, you don't have to be any part of this. I don't want to put you in any danger."

Johnny ignored what Joe said and asked, "This Ferrel, will he be gunned up?"

"I'm positive. He let me taste one of them in my office, remember? I still have some lumps on my head to remind me. If he spots me, I expect a lot of trouble. So I'm going to let my beard grow and wear a hat while in Montreal."

"Did you borrow one of Benny's hats? They'll never fit you with Benny's balloon head."

Joe laughed and said, "Ferrel doesn't know you, and that's a plus... and I brought my own hat. Benny tells me his head is big because of all his brains."

They both laughed. Two passengers took the seats immediately in front of them, so their conversation returned to dock work and crane signals and comments about the scenery.

The route to Montreal skirted Lake Ontario, and the views at sunset were breathtaking. The sun, low on the lake, glinting off the water, looked like a cache of diamonds. Johnny said, "Man, it's beautiful up here, ain' it?"

"It sure is." Joe had a window seat. He recalled how he was struck by the beauty when he first arrived in Toronto on his way to Camp X. It now seemed so long ago, so much had happened. He gazed out the window, lost in thoughts he shared with no one.

The train made a brief stop in Ottawa. The two men who sat a few rows in front of them got off. Later, when the train resumed its journey to Montreal, the two men chose the exact same car as Joe and Johnny. Joe didn't like the feeling he got from them. He felt they looked out of place somehow, but after hearing them speak, he dismissed them as French Canadians.

When they reached the outskirts of the Island of Montreal, in Senneville, on the western tip of the island, the homes were luxurious. "Not like South Chicago," said Joe.

"Is all of Montreal like this?" asked Johnny.

"Just wait."

The affluent homes gave way to the industrial-commercial area. There were factories, grain elevators, warehouses, mills, and refineries. As they came closer to Montreal's Central Station, located in Ville-Marie, a borough in the heart of Montreal, in the old part of the city, they saw centuries-old buildings rising from cobblestone streets, a blend of French and English history and culture. Like Manhattan in the Hudson River, Montreal is an island in the St. Lawrence River, making it one of the largest inland ports in the world and a major transportation center.

Their train rattled to a halt, and they disembarked. Johnny went to get the luggage, and Joe headed for a phone booth. He found one and looked in the book for a hotel near the docks. Everything was in French. He found the Le Pèlerin Hôtel on Rue Saint-Sulpice. The address matched the street he saw in the phone book's map. *Close enough*, he thought. He called the number. When a voice answered with the name of the hotel, Joe immediately asked, "Do you speak English?"

"Yes, I do, monsieur," the clerk answered.

"Do you have any vacancies?"

"Oui...yes, we do."

"Good, I'd like to reserve a room double bed, double occupancy."

"I can accommodate you, monsieur. Your name please."

"Joseph Ganzer."

"Excellent, Monsieur Ganzer. When will you arrive?"

"In less than an hour."

"Fine. I will be here when you check in."

"Thank you—merci."

The clerk chuckled and said, "Good bye," and hung up.

Joe hung up. Johnny was already standing outside the phone booth, waiting. "Hey, Joe, everybody's talkin' French around here."

Joe replied, "I know. I hope that's not a problem for us." He tore the map out of the phone book, and they both headed outside for a cab, which is when it hit them—it was almost chilly.

"Man, that sure feels good," Johnny said.

"It sure does. Yes, it does." They caught a cab and headed to the Rue Saint-Sulpice.

The two men from the train watched Joe and Johnny as their cab pulled away. A moment later, they were joined by a third man. The two from the train bowed discretely to him. They exchanged embraces. The third man appeared to give an order to one of them, who immediately got into one of the waiting cabs and left.

The Le Pèlerin Hôtel is in the waterfront district. Give it a few more years, and it would be a sleazy hotel, with vagrants in the lobby and hourly rates. Their taxicab pulled up in front of the hotel. Joe paid the meter amount in American dollars. The exchange rate made the cab driver grin with approval, and Joe's tip got a "merci beaucoup."

They walked into the hotel, Johnny carrying the bags. When they got to the desk, Joe introduced himself. After he signed in, he asked the clerk, "Could you tell me where the International Longshoremen's Association is located?"

"Certainly, it is three blocks west and one block north of here," the clerk explained, pointing to a map on the lobby wall. "You gentlemen are longshoremen then?"

"Yes we are," Joe said without elaborating. He and Johnny headed to the room and unpacked what little they had. "Johnny, you want to use my razor? I won't need it."

"Sure, I want to look my best for my new job," said Johnny.

Joe handed the shaving kit to him. He had a heavy day's growth. The dark shadow made him look heavier, darker, older, and threatening.

After they cleaned up, Joe suggested, "It's only half past seven. There's a restaurant I spotted across the street. Let's get some dinner. Anything would be better than that train food."

Johnny said, "I'm buyin'." They went downstairs and across the street and halfway down the block to the L'Enoteca, a little family restaurant. When they got in, the hostess and owner led them to a table by the window. Before they were even settled, a plainly pretty girl was saying something in French as she handed them menus. They looked at each other and laughed. Joe said, "I'm sorry, we don't speak French."

Without hesitation and with barely the hint of an accent, the waitress asked, "Would you like wine or coffee?"

Johnny answered first, "Coffee. Yes. Please." Joe simply nodded. She left to get a carafe and cups. When she was out of earshot, Johnny remarked, "Now that's a beauty." Joe nodded again. Johnny looked the menu over and said, "Hey, look here, this restaurant serves mostly Italian. They got pasta and truffle risotto. They even have tiramisu. How do you like that?"

Joe read the menu and nodded.

The waitress returned with their coffee and gracefully poured each of them a cup. She set the carafe in the center of the table and asked, "Are you ready to order, messieurs."

Joe went first. "I'd like the chicken parmesana."

Johnny said with proper Italian pronunciation, "Sugo all'arrabbiata, please and your name."

The waitress hesitated, then looked up from her pad. "My name?" She smiled at him, embarrassed, pushed back her auburn hair and said, "My name is Zoé."

Johnny repeated her name: "Zoh ay... that sounds beautiful."

Zoé asked, "You are Italian, no?"

Johnny replied, "I'm American, but my old man was from Italy."

Zoé said, "Ahh...," understanding now his correct pronunciation. "Where are you from in America?"

Joe interrupted, "We're from Cleveland, Ohio."

Johnny slyly glanced at Joe and looked back at Zoé. "Yeah... Cleveland."

"Are you working on the docks?" asked Zoé.

Johnny said without looking at Joe, "How'd you know? We're longshoremen. I'm a signal man."

Joe just rolled his eyes. His mind made seemingly random associations and connections, he recalled that "Signal Man" was playing on the radio at Rossi's swag warehouse the night of the heist. Replaying that night, Joe now recalled that he had used the name "Walter" while outside the warehouse in earshot of Mr. Friendly. Joe thought, *Maybe Mr. Friendly heard that name before he was knocked out.* He was trying now to replay the entire night, searching his memory for mistakes when....

"Excuse me. Would you like our house wine with your dinner?"

"What... oh... yes," Joe said clearing his mind. "I'm sorry, I was thinking about something."

Zoé left their table to attend a couple who were just seated. She returned later with a bottle of Barbera and two glasses. She poured the wine, leaving Johnny's glass for last and asked him, "What is your name?"

"It's Johnny... Johnny Della Penna."

"Your name sounds beautiful, too, like music." She giggled and headed back to the other table to take their order.

"Nice girl," Johnny said.

Joe hadn't even heard him. "Yeah, listen, we have to get down to the longshoremen's hall by five o'clock in the morning," Joe said, ending the romance.

"Sure, Joe." They ate without another word. Johnny left a tip too large to be misunderstood.

The night was cool and clear as they walked back to their hotel. Along the way, Joe tugged at Johnny's elbow and stopped him. He pointed to the sky.

"You see that constellation right by the Little Dipper? It kind of winds around." Joe traced out the line with his finger in the night sky.

"Oh, yeah, I see it."

"That's Draco, the dragon," explained Joe. "The early Christians saw Draco as the serpent who tempted Adam and Eve in the Garden of Eden."

He looked at Joe out of the corner of his eye and smiled.


They arrived at the Longshoremen's hall early. Joe went to the day window and said, "Sean Cullen from Chicago said for me and my partner to see the president or business agent here. My name is Joe Ganzer."

The day window man looked up unimpressed, pulled the cigar from his mouth, shuffled some papers, and disappeared through the door at the back of the office. The hall was beginning to fill up with men looking for work. They were talking, mostly in French, laughing, roughhousing.

A door opened into the hall alongside the day window, the Cigar popped out and said, "Joe Ganzer?"

"Right here."

"Come with me."

Joe motioned to Johnny, and they all disappeared through the door. They walked down a hallway, down to an office that read: CHARLES ANGUINE. The Cigar held the door open for them and they walked in and were greeted by a stocky man in his early fifties.

"Sit down, here, fellas. I'm Charlie Anguine," he said, shaking their hands." Sean Cullen from the Chicago local told me all about you. Good recommendations. I really like Sean. We met last year at the International meeting in New York. Now who's who?"

"Well, I'm Joe Ganzer, and this is my associate John Della Penna. We're looking to work a few days on the docks on an insurance case. This shipper has been making claims against our client for lost freight due to theft by longshoremen. We don't believe that's true at all. Our investigations to date reveal the shipments are diverted to phony carriers, truckers mostly, under false Bills of Lading."

Charlie asked, "Which shipper are we talking about?"

"The ship is the *Ponta Delgada*, due in port shortly. They sail for

London Global Cargo," Joe said.

Charlie looked in his books. "Oh yeah, here it is... from London. In port tomorrow morning at ten o'clock at Dock 17, at the King Edward Quay. I'll put you two on that crew. You'll start at six in the morning. I hope you know your way around a dock."

"I still have my card, and I can vouch for my associate."

"Good then," Charlie said and extended his hand. He shook Johnny's hand first, then Joe's.

Joe said, "Thanks, Charlie."

"Get these sons o' bitches that are ruining our union's good name."

"I aim to." With that, they left Charlie's office and returned to the hall.

Joe said to Johnny in the hall, "Let's just hang around here and get the feel of these guys." So, they moved around. There must have been about fifty men there, some speaking French, others English. They stayed for another hour, then headed back to the hotel.


When they got back to the hotel, Johnny said he was hungry and continued down the street to a little cafe to get a late breakfast. Joe headed straight into the hotel and went to the lone phone booth in the lobby. He made a collect call to his office. Wilma accepted the charges.

"Joe! Where have you been? I've been worried sick about you. Ludko said your ribs are broken, and what with your head. I just—"

"Don't worry. I'm fine, a little sore now but fine. Did you call Donnelly like a asked?"

"Of course I did, and he called that same evening and said they have everything. Joe, what is going on?"

"I can't go into details, but Johnny Della Penna is going to go free on that liquor burglary charge. And what have Benny and Ludko reported?"

"Ludko said his jaw hurts and that you owe him big time, and that Miss Kemidov is making travelling plans."

"Did he say where to?"

"Ludko said she booked a plane ticket for Canada. He didn't know where."

"I have a good idea where."

"Joe this case is just crazy. Call it woman's intuition or being around you too long, but I don't trust her at all, honest. So please be careful."

"Of course I will. So long, Murph."

"Good bye, Joe," Wilma said as she hung up and gave a brief sigh of acceptance.

Joe sat in the phone booth. *So Ferrel called her. He must know everything and so does Polina. She's going to try to save her uncle from a sure trip to prison. She doesn't trust me now or maybe she never did....*

A knock at the phone booth door by an anxious man in a business suit woke Joe from his reverie. He looked up, saw it was nobody, and exited the booth. "Sorry, I was just thinking about my girl."

"You've got it bad, buddy," said the man. He pushed past Joe into the booth without even looking back.

Joe walked up two flights of stairs to their room. When he got to the door, he noticed that the little piece of tape he placed on the hinge side of the door this morning was broken. It was still early. The maids came in around noon. He looked down the hallway and pulled out his gun. His heart pounded and his breathing became erratic. His ribs ached. He opened the door slowly with his left hand, the right holding the gun close to his chest. He expected someone behind the door. He looked into the right-hand corner of the room. Then Joe pulled in a deep breath and with his right foot kicked the door as savagely as he could. As it flew open, he swung around the door, aiming the gun at whoever was behind it. No one.

*Damn!* Joe cursed himself. Before he kicked the door, he should have checked through the hinged side for the left-side far corner of the room. He immediately looked to that corner over his shoulder and swung his body aiming his gun. He saw a backlit figure seated at the small desk in the corner of the room. His mind racing, his heart pounding out of his chest.

"Really, Joseph, did you need all the theatrics?"

Joe was still flooded in adrenalin, his pulse still racing. He breathed out heavily. "Damn you, Lawrence." He put his gun away and quickly closed the door.

Lawrence Hamilton said, "I expected something a little more convivial... tea, perhaps."

"I could have killed you."

"I trained you remember? I had nothing to fear. I knew you

wouldn't shoot, even if instinct told you to. How have you been, my boy?"

Joe went over to Hamilton with his arm extended and a smile on his face. "You're a sight for sore ribs." They shook hands and Joe put Hamilton in a bear hug. A little too high-spirited for an Englishman, but he hugged him back. "Lawrence, you look good."

"You've looked better, Joseph."

"I've had a couple of rough days, but it fits my role as a longshoreman, don't you think?"

"Indeed, an admirable disguise. I take it you are on the docks waiting for our ship? ... Excellent, excellent."

Joe didn't ask Hamilton how he got into the hotel room or even how he discovered their hotel. He went and closed the door. "The ship comes into port about ten o'clock tomorrow."

"Good work, my boy."

"But there's a problem—a hired killer, a guy named Frankie Ferrel. He knows what's on the ship, and he's figuring to get it."

"Is that how your ribs were injured?"

"Broken—but, no, that's a leftover from another case."

"You should have stayed with OSS, Joseph, instead of all this private investigation business."

"No, I had my fill of that. You can get killed in that line of work."

"Seems you are headed down the same path regardless."

"Yeah, but in that world, reality is created by someone else. In this world, I am in control—right or wrong."

Lawrence dropped his solicitation and asked, "Now, your friend, Mr. Ferrel, he is not on the docks, is he?"

"I don't think so. It takes some clout to get on the docks, and he doesn't have any of that up here."

"I see," said Hamilton knitting his brow and pacing the room. "My quarry, Hugo Morand or Yuri Kemidov, gave us the dodge in London. He left incognito by plane. We believe for here in Montreal, or perhaps New York. In any event, he is most assuredly headed here now. We also believe he has an accomplice, who may very well be aboard the *Ponta Delgada* or perhaps it is your Mr. Ferrel."

"I don't think so. I've had a shadow on him for quite a while. As soon as he heard about this ship, he left Chicago and headed up here."

Hamilton looked incredulously at Joe. "And how did he hear about this ship and its cargo?"

"Now don't look at me like that. My client is Kemidov's niece," Joe said in protest. "She hired me to locate him, which I did with your help. I was supposed to get them back together, a reunion. I couldn't do that, so I had to tell her what he'd done and why I had to help apprehend him and send him back to France for prosecution. I couldn't very well lie to her. She had to know."

"How did Mr. Ferrel enter the picture?"

"My client hired him as protection from the NKVD. She was deathly afraid that they would find her uncle and kill him or take him back to the Soviet Union. She felt they might even use her to bait him into surrendering. So she hired Ferrel."

"I see," said Hamilton accessing what Joe had said. "So you think now your Mr. Ferrel is going to double cross your client? By the way, what is her name, if I may ask?"

"Polina Kemidov... and, yes, I think Ferrel is operating for himself and always has. She didn't find him, he found her."

"Is she still back in Chicago?"

Joe's eyes widened. "No, she's headed up here any time now just to warn her uncle about me."

"She cannot succeed in alerting him, Joseph," said Hamilton looking gravely concerned.

"She won't. I would like to at least give her time to see him before he's extradited."

Noting Joe's commitment to his client, he said cautiously, "That could be arranged, I believe, provided we net this blackguard before NKVD agents get their hands on him or even your Mr. Ferrel."

"I'm more concerned about the NKVD."

"As well you should," said Hamilton pulling a dossier from his briefcase. "I have here Morand's file. He is a master criminal, Joseph, who has operated in Europe and the Orient for many years. Our intelligence on him only leads us back to Switzerland in his guise as Hugo Morand.

"Your inquiry regarding General Kemidov had MI5 puzzled for a time. Our intelligence had him listed as deceased or eliminated by the NKVD. The link between Morand and Kemidov surfaced when I interviewed the desk clerk at the Alhambra Hotel."

"That's the hotel name I sent you in my telegram. What did you find out?" asked Joe, wanting to learn everything about the case to help Polina.

"Your General Kemidov had dealings with a London art gallery suspected by Scotland Yard of trafficking in art stolen by the Nazis. While I reviewed Scotland Yard's surveillance photographs, I recognized the General in the corner of a photo exiting the Alhambra Hotel, just behind the suspected gallery agent. Scotland Yard knew him only as Hugo Morand, an art criminal wanted by the French.

"But I realized Morand was, in fact, General Yuri Kemidov, a NKVD double-agent operating in London. We thought he was with the NKVD in Paris, feeding intelligence to them about Nazi operations. It turns out he was also working with the Nazis providing intelligence on the NKVD's activities."

"A very dangerous Danse Macabre."

"Indeed, it was. He was being paid, rather well I might add, by both sides while at the same time fleecing Jews of everything they owned, including their lives. He was feeding the NKVD mostly worthless information, and the Nazis got little more. In the meantime, our Yuri Kemidov was making himself a fortune, now probably in numbered bank accounts in Switzerland.

"Why is he going to so much trouble for this art?"

"Because, my dear boy, the art is worth far more than all the money in those accounts. Moreover, I believe it is his weakness, his obsession. In point of fact, he went out of his way to acquire the supposedly stolen art I had to offer. He took my bait voraciously. A tragic flaw to be sure, one I hope we may exploit to undo him." Hamilton paused and added, "You see, Joseph, MI5 plans to use him."

Exploiting his loyalty to Polina, Joe realized MI5 had finessed him back behind the veil into *their* house of mirrors. "So now I work for MI5?"

Hamilton said, "But it will save Kemidov's life, and your client will have her uncle."

"And those NKVD agents from Paris, the ones who helped him escape to London, to change his identity, they're now here in Montreal?"

"I am not sure who they are, but they know what we know, Joseph. And we *must* get to Kemidov before they do."

# CHAPTER FIFTEEN

MONTREAL
*Le Pèlerin Hôtel*

The door to Joe's hotel room opened, and Johnny Della Penna walked in. At first, he didn't notice Joe and Lawrence Hamilton at the corner table strategizing their next move. As soon as he saw Hamilton, he said, "Is there a problem, Joe?"

Joe laughed and said, "Not at all, John. This is my friend and associate, Lawrence Hamilton. We're working together on this case." Hamilton turned and stood up to greet Johnny. As he rose, Joe said, "Lawrence, this is my friend, John Della Penna."

"How'd you do," Hamilton said, bowing slightly and extending his hand.

Johnny looked a little confused and replied, "Glad ta meet cha." He shook Hamilton's hand and added, "You want me to get lost, Joe?"

"No—this concerns you too, John. You're part of this case."

Johnny didn't ask any questions about Lawrence Hamilton. All he knew was something was planned, and he was glad to help Joe any way he could.

Joe continued, "Lawrence, Johnny and I will be on the docks tomorrow. The *Ponta Delgada* floats in at ten o'clock in the morning. We'll be on Dock 17 waiting to unload her."

Very pleased, Hamilton said, "Excellent, Joseph. What is your approach and how may we assist you?"

"You can't at first. We need to identify Kemidov's cargo. Once I know that, I have an idea, but—"

"What is it?" asked Hamilton worried that a crucial step is now left to chance.

Joe explained, "Once I know which crates belong to Kemidov, Johnny and I will come back late that night and empty one of them. I'll get inside that crate and take a little ride to Kemidov's hideout, wherever that is."

"Why not simply put a tail on whoever picks up the freight?"

"That won't work," said Joe. "They'll spot the tail."

Hamilton frowned and said, "If you are discovered, my boy, it will surely upset our adversaries, not to mention cause some consternation on your part."

"I won't be discovered," Joe insisted, "because that loot is headed for somewhere other than Montreal. This is just a layover. The crates will remain sealed."

"Perhaps, but what if Montreal is Kemidov's new base of operations? You may not be able to exit your stealthy conveyance without being discovered."

"I'll get out of there... trust me."

"Might be awful tight in there, Joe," said Johnny. "What about your ribs?"

"You're injury may present a problem, Joseph," said Hamilton concerned that Joe might not be able to defend himself.

"I'll be okay. Now I have something to remind me I'm not Superman."

"Shall I send up a physician to look you over?" suggested Hamilton.

"Won't be necessary. I'm getting better every day."

"Very well then. In order to track you, we have a device that we can use to locate your position from a safe distance. It is not wholly accurate but will keep us close. I can have it here some time tonight."

"Leave it to you guys at MI5," Joe said admiring their ingenuity. "I would really appreciate that." Truly relieved that he wouldn't be alone, "At least now you won't lose me in traffic."

Lawrence went on, "I will track you myself, along with two other agents."

Joe asked, "Why only two?"

"I would like more, of course, except this is essentially a police action. MI5 is not entirely convinced they can use Kemidov as a double agent, given his background. However, I believe Kemidov would be of inestimable value to MI5, and so does Harry Treadwell. There is a new kind of war brewing now that will be played out in the shadows. We need Kemidov.

"But, for now, we must endeavor to apprehend a war profiteer and his stolen art. As such, this operation does not have high priority. Thus, we have limited resources.

"Nevertheless, we *will* make an arrest as soon as you are out of the box, as it were. You can assess their strength from within and report the details to us via the tracking radio."

"What do I do, Joe?" asked Johnny eager to help.

"John, just go to work the next day like nothing happened. Tell the dock pusher I was on a bender or something. And when the truck comes to pick up Kemidov's freight—and me—get the plate number and description of the truck and driver, just in case Lawrence's radio tracker doesn't work. At least we'll know something about the truck that takes me away. I figure they'll schedule shipment for late morning or early afternoon, so I won't be in my coffin for very long."

"You are lucky it ain't hot up here," Johnny said trying to find a highlight in Joe's plan.

Hamilton continued, "Joseph, if you could locate the crate containing MI5's paintings that would be most advantageous. That crate would have been the last aboard and, as such, may not have seals or locks on it. Then, when we make the arrest, only the stolen art will be inventoried by INTERPOL and not our bait. It will save us a great deal of bureaucratic falderal."

"So, look for the odd crate? Okay," Joe said considering the possibilities.

Hamilton added, "We know our paintings would have been the last on board. They left us in two large suitcases. They may still be in them and placed in a larger crate when it was brought on board the ship."

"I'll do what I can."

"Marvelous.... I knew I could count on you."


Joe and Johnny reported to the longshoreman boss at Dock 17. "I'm Joe Ganzer. This is John Della Penna."

"Oiu, I have your names down here. I am Marcel. I run this gang," he said firmly and with a moderate French accent. Marcel was short and shaped like a whisky barrel, balding with dark brown hair, a weathered face from years on the waterfront. "We have this ship to finish up. It's a load of coffee beans. Grab two hooks and start on the pallets at the whistle."

Joe grabbed two hooks from inside the gang boss' shanty. "Okay, come on, John." They both walked down onto the dock. There were four large piles of coffee bean sacks. The longshoreman waited for the whistle, laughing, speaking French, and giving Joe and Johnny—the look. Men who work together in a gang rarely welcome newcomers, especially when they don't speak your language. You've crossed tribal boundaries.

The gang sized them up. Joe looked threatening, dark two-day growth of beard, disheveled hair. His denim coat showed signs of wear as did his boots and pants. The pain on Joe's face from his ribs registered with the men as something sinister, a man to be watched. Johnny genuinely impressed the other longshoremen, with his size and muscular bulk and his signature walk came across as carefree.

One longshoreman approached them. "Bonjour, messieurs. We have an easy day today. We dispatch the last of this ship and another break-bulk comes in at ten o'clock. My name is Rémy." He extended his hand.

Joe went first. "I'm Joe Ganzer, and this is John Della Penna." They shook hands. The others watched.

"Ah, Monsieur Della Penna is good for the sacks, not like you and I, eh?" Rémy said with a smile directed at Joe. Rémy was wide-shouldered, like a boxer. He was perhaps 45 years old, medium height, shorter than Joe, not as muscular. He looked bright with dark blue-gray eyes and an aquiline nose.

"Oh, I can manage," Joe replied.

"There is the whistle," said Rémy. "We begin."

The men attacked the pile of coffee bean sacks, each man hooking an 80-pound sack and carrying it on his shoulder to the warehouse. Joe had to switch shoulders because of his ribs. The contortions on his face read as anger with the other longshoremen. Joe kept up with them but just barely. Johnny tried to lessen the load for Joe by taking the sack off his shoulder as they reached the warehouse, sometimes lifting it with one hand while carrying his own sack.

"You okay, Joe?" Johnny asked.

"Yeah, I can manage," Joe said without believing a word of it.

Rémy had noticed Joe hesitating and said, "Monsieur Ganzer, come with me and help land these crates." They walked further down the dock to one of the main cranes. "I see you are favoring your side."

"I got into a little ruckus, but I'm recovering."

"Charlie Anguine, our business agent, told me to watch out for the two new men. You can signal the crane, and I will land the loads. You can do that, no?"

Joe said, "Oui, Monsieur." Rémy laughed at that, and Joe was not quite so threatening to him anymore. Joe excelled at crane signaling, one of the best on Chicago's docks. He could pinpoint a drop spot with deadly accuracy. Joe and Rémy placed nearly a dozen crates in record time.

"You are an excellent signal man. You have the je ne sais quoi," said Rémy complimenting him on his work.

"Thanks, merci," said Joe, proud he could still make the grade in a dock gang.

"You're friend, the Italian, is strong, a good worker, but not so experienced."

"He's just a 'casual', helping me," said Joe. Casuals are day laborers, the grunts of the waterfront. Johnny was more than adequate for the job, and he got along with the other longshoremen, despite not speaking French.

The work was hard, but the morning went by fast. Johnny felt good. He was working again, without a single thought about prison or the Outfit or anything. The other longshoremen had even given him a nickname: Petite Jean. As they finished the coffee beans, the *Ponta Delgada* came to port. Right on schedule.

The *Ponta Delgada* was a Liberty ship, built in the United States during the war. Almost three thousand of them were fabricated between 1941 and 1945 to carry cargo and personnel. The ship was 441 feet long, and the beam was just over 56 feet with two oil-fired boilers powering a triple-expansion steam engine offering 2,500 horsepower and could carry 10,000 long tons of cargo. The *Ponta Delgada* was one of many purchased after the war by the Goulandris brothers, Greek shipping magnates capitalizing on the war surplus.

Joe watched as it floated into Dock 17 and said to Rémy, "Man, that's one ugly ship."

"Most are, mon ami," agreed Rémy. "This is a break bulk ship. We will have her company for maybe two, three days. Then, maybe, she will look beautiful when she sails away."

"Like some women I've known," remarked Joe.

That got a laugh out of Rémy. "I will tell Marcel to make you the signal man."

"Thanks, Rémy," Joe said as Rémy walked to the shanty. Joe kept an eye peeled for any sign of Ferrel or worse—NKVD agents. He suspected Ferrel knew by now what ship the art load was on and when it made port, and so did the NKVD.

No one could recognize Joe with his two day's growth of beard and his longshoreman's work clothes. He and Johnny simply melted into the gang.

As the *Ponta Delgada* was moored and ready for unload, Rémy said to Joe: "You are worried about somet'ing?"

"If you see an ugly guy let me know," Joe said appreciating Rémy's astute observation.

"That would be almost everyone in this gang, except moi," said Rémy with a faint smile.

"This guy won't be a longshoreman, maybe like an inspector or dock official, snooping around," explained Joe. "And, no, he won't be handsome like you, Rémy."

"Now I know you will make it in this gang," announced Rémy, "and I will be as you say—'on the lookout'—for your ugly man."

"Thanks."


Crate after crate was unloaded, cargo from all over Europe and North Africa. Joe was in his element. He was fast. He could land almost every load spot on, every time. Johnny watched and learned the practical applications of the signaling lessons he'd had from Joe on their train ride to Montreal. Once in a while, Joe let Johnny signal while he and Rémy landed the loads.

As they were landing a load of crates, Rémy spotted someone at the gunwale of the *Ponta Delgada* near the stern. "If you are looking for an ugly man, there is one on the ship," said Rémy as he pointed. "There... the big one."

Joe looked up casually and saw Evrard Molyneaux toward the stern of the ship, pacing. Johnny signaled a load to another spot. Two longshoremen positioned it as Evrard watched intently. Evrard's clothes announced he wasn't part of the crew nor was he the captain. *That's got to be Kemidov's accomplice,* Joe thought and then said to Rémy, "I have to go over and help those guys with that load. Keep an eye on our menacing watchman."

"Oui, oui."

Joe went to where the load was placed. He noted all the crates on the skid. There were various crates with seals and locks, each with a serial number containing the prefix "VEK." On the next load of crates, nestled among the larger ones was a small poorly fashioned crate also marked "VEK." Joe recalled that if crates and containers were damaged en route, the ship's carpenter could build another out of materials aboard ship. *Hamilton, you were right again.* The last paintings had been crated hastily by the carpenter on board ship. After landing that load, he went over and relieved Johnny.

"Thanks, Joe, I was getting a little flustered with how fast this goes."

"Ah, you'll get the hang of it in no time," Joe assured him. "Listen, there's a small crate in that last group with the letters 'VEK' on it. When you get that into the warehouse, get it off to one side, and try to keep all the crates marked 'VEK' in the same general area if you can."

"Sure thing," Johnny replied as he walked back over to the rest of the gang.

Joe could hear some of the men yelling: "Magnifique... Petite Jean." Johnny was all smiles, as though he KO'd the heavyweight champ. As Joe laughed, he happened to look up to see Evrard talking to a man who had to be the captain. The captain pointed to Marcel the gang boss on the dock. A few minutes later, Evrard was out on the dock walking over to Marcel. They greeted one another with handshakes. They began speaking rapidly in French. Joe couldn't make out a word of it.

After he landed a load, Joe went over and asked Rémy, "Could you ask Marcel what he and my morbid friend were talking about, without arousing suspicion?"

"Of course... Marcel and I have no secrets. We go all the way back to school. I will ask for you."

Rémy walked over to Marcel and asked in French what had transpired between him and the visitor from the ship. They spoke for a few minutes. Rémy walked back casually and said, "The big visitor is a Frenchman named Evrard Molyneaux. He asked Marcel to load out his cargo tonight and he would pay double."

Evrard walked down the dock. Joe asked, "Where's he going now?"

"I think, he goes down the dock to one of the trucking

companies to see about a truck."

"Rémy, could you get me, you, and Johnny on that crew tonight?"

"Oui, bien sûr, Marcel and I know who you are. Charlie Anguine said to take care of you and Petite Jean. We will all be here together tonight—guaranteed. First we'd better unload the rest of this cargo. No?"

They continued unloading the cargo from the *Ponta Delgada*. The pace was fast. All that could be heard was the whine of the cranes, the clatter of jitneys moving freight off the docks and into the warehouses, and Marcel giving orders.

## CHAPTER SIXTEEN

MONTREAL
*Waterfront*

At the end of the workday Joe and Johnny headed back to the hotel. Walking along, Joe asked, "Well, how did you like it?"

"It sure is better than the coke plant in South Chicago. I can actually breathe at the end of the day."

"I worked as a casual, like you, while I was trying to go to college."

"College?" asked Johnny. "I didn't know you was a college guy."

"Well, for a couple of years anyway. Then my dad died and I had to drop out to support my mom and little sister."

"What school did you go to?"

"The University of Chicago," said Joe with a certain fondness... and pride.

"What?" exclaimed Johnny not believing what he just heard. "That's where Enrico Fermi was. He got the Nobel Prize, yuh know."

"Right on both counts."

"Italians were really proud of Fermi. They say he created the Bomb right there at the University of Chicago."

"Sort of, but the bomb wasn't built there, just the initial research," said Joe. "But that was quite a few years after I attended. I was studying law... going to become a lawyer."

"But you went with the longshoremen full time?" Johnny was confused.

"It was the most money I could get at the time after my dad's heart attack. Later, I started working for a lawyer, doing

192

investigations and research. Then some insurance companies and more lawyers. So I went out on my own. Then the war broke out."

"Yeah, I was doin' that stretch for the jewelry store thing. They give me a shot at the army for the balance of my sentence, and I ended up in the 4th Army Division, 12th Regiment. We was in the third landing on Utah Beach on D-Day."

"I read in the papers that Utah was the best out of the five."

"Yeah. First time I ever drew a long straw. At least that's what I thought."

"So Utah was bad like the rest?"

Johnny paused and said, "By the time my regiment got to the beach, the Germans had already been pushed back and the seawall had been breached. That let the vehicles reach the causeway points off the beach, but the Germans shelled the hell out of us from inland batteries."

"Our ships were shelling them right back, weren't they?"

"Hell yeah they did," said Johnny. "Our shells flew overhead like freight trains. You know, I could actually see 'em flyin'. Man, I was sure glad for those battleships."

Joe slowly nodded his head. "I'll bet."

"But later that week, the krauts let us taste their 88s."

"What are 88s?"

"88 millimeter canons. Them shells flew so fast, yuh couldn't even hear 'em comin' in. But the worst was the screamin' meanies."

Joe said, "I did hear about those: rockets fired by the dozen, in clusters."

"That's them," said Johnny. "But it was the sound that got yuh. See, as they flew in, they sorta 'moaned.' Scare the crap outa yuh."

"I can imagine."

"It got worse," replied Johnny. "A couple of days later, in Émondville—never forget that place—we lost three hundred guys. And that was just the beginning. Them damn hedgerows were murder, like fightin' in a maze." Johnny paused and added, "No other American division in Europe lost more men than we did."

Johnny got very quiet, a quiet tangled in sadness. The intensity of that experience is overwhelming and never quite lets you go. Joe said nothing.

Johnny said almost in a whisper, "I got the long straw... huh?"

The only sound now was their footsteps. After half of a block Joe said, "A wise old man told me 'It'll get better.' I hope he's right."

"Me too," Johnny said. "Tommy helps. I swore if I got through it all, through the war, I was gonna make a better life for me and my family." Johnny paused and then laughed. "The first day I got back, my wife asked me: 'You're gonna look for a job tomorrow, aren't ya?' They don't know."

"No they don't," Joe trailed off and repeated, "...No they don't."

"Things happened over there. Things I ain't proud of. Things I had to do."

Joe didn't say anything as they walked. He couldn't say anything, but he understood better than most. Joe's battles were fought alone, in the trenches and recesses of illusion, a place far more treacherous and frightening than any enemy in a uniform.

Johnny began to tell Joe about a day in Germany. "We was in Germany. I don't even know where. Near Saarbrücken, I think. They never told us the right names of the towns in case we were ever captured. We was coming out of these woods toward some town with a church way up on a hill. The krauts had their 50mm gun somewhere near that church. As soon as we come out of the forest, they let us have it. Ripped guys to pieces. We moved back fast, back into the woods for cover, and started digging fox holes like madmen. The krauts shot into the forest, big tree limbs were coming down—like spears—killing more guys.

"So, I'm hunkered down in my hole. I can hear the rounds hissing above my head. They got us pinned. A young lieutenant, straight from the Academy, jumps into my hole. He says to me... he says: 'Soldier, look up there and see where that fire is coming from.' I had a Luger I got off a dead German. I drew that Luger and pointed it at that lieutenant's head and told him: 'You look up there....'"

Joe was startled at first. "John—?"

"That lieutenant looked up," Johnny paused, a throb in his voice. This is a story he had never told and would never tell again. "...and a bullet went straight through his face."

Joe looked down at the sidewalk in a kind of mourning, a silent lament for what it takes to survive. The lieutenant would have court-martialed Johnny if he disobeyed his order, and Johnny would have been dead if he followed it. Either way, same outcome for Johnny.

"You chose life, John," trying to treat a wound Joe knew might never heal.

Softly, Johnny said, "Thanks...."

They walked toward their hotel, a silent covenant between them now. As if to complete their compact, Johnny asked, "You weren't over there, were yuh, Joe?"

"No—not like you think. I was doing something else."

"That's what I heard around."

"What's around, John?"

"Just you were gone for a while. Somethin' big."

"Big? Nobody knows yet. It may have all been for nothing." Looking straight at Johnny, Joe added, "There's things I've seen I can't even believe. But this much is sure: The next Hitler will have the power to destroy the entire world—if we don't do it first."

Johnny's eyes widened. He shook his head and said, "I don't wanna know." Sometimes silence was the best armor against the horrors of war.

Almost to the door of the *L'Enoteca* restaurant Joe said, "Let's get some dinner. What do you say?" Joe didn't really have to ask. He caught a glimpse of Zoé in the window on their way to the door.

"That sure sounds good," Johnny said as he opened the door. Zoé spotted them and dashed over to seat them.

"Bon jour, messieurs. You both look tired. Some coffee?"

Joe answered, "That would be perfect." Zoé led them to the other table by the window. When they were seated she left to get their coffees. Joe said, "Okay, you can pull your eyes back in."

"She's a beauty."

"That she is, but we have to go over our plans again for tonight. Rémy said the load goes out sometime after eight o'clock. That gives us about three hours."

Johnny woke from his trance and said, "Yeah, whatever you say, Joe. I was just—"

"I've had that look myself a couple of times. I hope it works out better for you than it did with me." Joe dropped that thought and said, "Now back to tonight."

"So, what do you want me to do?"

"We have to get me in that smaller crate and its contents into another. After I'm on the truck, Hamilton and his agents will track me from a safe distance."

"Where's your friend now?"

"He's right behind you."

Lawrence Hamilton hastily pulled up a chair and said, "Good afternoon, gentlemen." He shook their hands and continued, "Joseph, we have some disturbing news from London."

"What now?"

"An NKVD agent was found dead in some rubble not too far from Kemidov's hotel. The body was nearly bloodless and had been carefully dismembered."

Johnny gave Joe a sidelong glance and said, "Damn...." Johnny had encountered the NKVD while in Germany. One of his last details was guarding a German scientist in Berlin from possible abduction by the NKVD. Attached to the Soviet Army, the NKVD scoured Germany pursuing scientists and engineers to transfer to the USSR as war criminals. Once in custody, they could be persuaded to work for the Soviets.

Hamilton continued, "We suspect another NKVD may have killed him, but it could just as easily have been our General Kemidov."

Zoé returned to their table. "You have a guest." She poured their coffee and turned to Hamilton and asked, "Monsieur, would you care for coffee?"

"No, I'm afraid I shall be leaving shortly."

Zoé took Joe and Johnny's orders and left.

When Zoé was gone, Joe said, "I'm betting Kemidov killed the NKVD agent, maybe with the help of his associate. We got a good look at one of them today, a ghoulish-looking Frenchman by the name of Evrard Molyneaux. He was a passenger aboard the *Ponta Delgada*."

Hamilton asked, "Why do you think Kemidov eliminated the NKVD agent?"

"Whoever the dead NKVD was, he was making a move on Kemidov and got killed in the process. The only reason you cut up a body is to get it out of a place without anyone noticing it, like out of a hotel room."

Johnny added matter-of-factly, "The Outfit does it to warn everybody that they mean business."

"Good point," acknowledged Joe.

"I see," said Hamilton. "This would serve a dual purpose. It would certainly be a warning to whoever else was tracking Kemidov. In any event, these are dangerous criminals, Joseph. You must not be discovered."

Joe said, "Another thing: we found out Evrard's moving the swag tonight."

"I'm glad I brought this—" said Hamilton, as he reached down into his briefcase and pulled out a pack of Chesterfield cigarettes and placed them in front of Joe.

"I don't smoke."

Hamilton took the pack and said, "This is your transmitter. We can track you up to a range of five miles. Now, if you pull out this cigarette here at the opening, you may also speak to us."

Joe took the pack from Hamilton. "A little heavy but it looks like a real pack and Chesterfields to boot."

"I thought you would appreciate that choice, " Hamilton said with pride. "Now, there are two genuine cigarettes at the opening here as well, and you cannot smoke cigarettes without a lighter." Hamilton withdrew a somewhat oversized lighter from his briefcase.

"Fancy lighter," remarked Johnny looking at the plump Zippo with an American flag on it, similar to ones issued to GIs.

"Indeed, quite a lethal one as well. I hope you don't need this, Joseph—it's a gun. You open the lid like this." Hamilton opened the lighter's cover and explained, "Now, if you press the striking wheel it will fire a .22 caliber bullet from the chimney. It carries only two rounds."

"I'm still taking my .38."

"Just insurance, my boy."

Zoé arrived with their dinners. "Bon Appétit," she said, laying their plates down. She then turned and left, but shyly noticed Johnny gazing at her. She smiled to herself and headed to another table where a man sat alone.

Hamilton asked, "When are you off then?"

Joe answered, "Tonight... after eight."

"Advances our schedule," Hamilton said with hesitation. "Nevertheless, we shall be ready. The transmitter is on even now."

"I have no idea where they will be taking this shipment—and me—but it's sure to end up wherever Kemidov is."

"Agreed."

Joe said, "I have to get the drop on him and then call you in."

"My agents and I will then take custody of General Kemidov."

Joe looked sternly at Hamilton and asked, "You will provide an opportunity for a reunion between my client and her uncle?"

"Most assuredly. Indeed, I am counting on it. Even a reprobate, like Kemidov, sometimes can look beyond their own self-interests when confronted with the love of a family member."

Johnny listened and understood.

"I appreciate that, Lawrence," said Joe, realizing that all things behind the veil, in the world of mirrors, have benefits and costs.

"Of course, his inventory of art must be turned over to the Monuments Men," Hamilton added.

Joe looked quizzically at Hamilton and said, "Haven't heard of them. Who are they?"

Hamilton answered, "They are the men and women who quite possibly saved what was the most important aspect of Western Civilization—it's culture. The Nazis were not only the greatest murders in history, they were the greatest thieves. Even our Mr. Kemidov was no match for their rapacious avarice. They stole nearly everything of value in the occupied territories. This was industrialized looting on a scale the world has never seen before.

"The Monuments Men, a group of perhaps three hundred men and women from more than a dozen countries came together as the Monuments, Fine Arts, and Archives, the MFAA. Their mission was to preserve precious artworks in the battlefield and locate millions of artistic and cultural items stolen by Hitler and the Nazis. A school chum of mine Lt. Col. Leonard Maycott is with the MFAA and had loaned us the bait we used to lure our Mr. Kemidov, which is why it is imperative you locate those paintings in the small crate tonight."

"Thanks for the lecture, Lawrence. I feel like I'm back in your class again," said Joe. "And don't worry about your paintings, they will be returned."

Lawrence gave a little laugh but reiterated the importance of the paintings. As Johnny listened to Lawrence and Joe, he happened to glance over at a table in the corner of the restaurant. A man with pale skin sat alone, occasionally glancing in their direction. It was subtle but Johnny picked it up.

You develop instincts in places as dangerous as South Chicago. Johnny sensed something. "That guy over at that table... " Johnny motioned almost imperceptibly with his eyes.. "That guy has been eyeballing us for quite a while. Want me to go shake him up?"

Joe cautioned, "Don't bother. He may be a local. Here we are two guys from the US and another guy from England all talking.

He may just think we're amusing. Hell, he might not even speak English. Might be French Canadian. Besides, he doesn't look that dangerous."

"Let's not be too complacent, Joseph," said Hamilton as he lowered his voice. "Not all NKVD are sinister henchmen, you know. We have lost a number of MI5 agents to rather innocent looking operatives, including women."

Zoé came over to their table to freshen their coffee. She smiled at Johnny. He asked softly, "Zoé do you know that guy over there?"

"No, he is not a regular patron. He speaks French, though; but he is not Canadian. A visitor, maybe, like you and your friends." She smiled.

Johnny said, "Oh... I thought I knew him. Thanks."

Zoé cocked her head slightly but accepted his explanation and went about her duties.

Hamilton looked at Joe and said, "I see your associate is quite capable in these circumstances."

"Johnny's been on the streets all his life. He knows how to handle himself," Joe said. He looked over at the strange, pale man. "Damn—now you got me wondering about that guy."

"I'm tellin' yuh, Joe. There's something wrong with that guy."

"I must be off," Hamilton said meaning they should all depart. "When will you be boxed up?"

"I'd say no later than ten tonight."

Hamilton looked at Joe and shook his hand. "Good luck, my friend."

"Thanks—just don't be late when I play Jack-in-the-Box."

"Most assuredly. And good evening to you, Mr. Della Penna." Hamilton turned from the table and deliberately passed near the French-speaking observer on his way out to get a close look at him and file it in his photographic memory.

Zoé returned to their table to remove plates and asked, "Something sweet tonight?"

Johnny couldn't resist, "Just you."

Zoé laughed and blushed.

Joe rolled his eyes and said. "With that I'm going to the hotel and call Wilma. Have some dessert. I'll meet you in an hour."

"Thanks, Joe."

Joe stood up, left too much money on the table, and headed for the door. He looked back at the table as he left and saw Johnny and Zoé talking and laughing.

When Joe entered the hotel lobby, he waved to the desk clerk and headed straight for the phone booth. He placed a collect call to Wilma Murphy at the office. He heard her on the other end say, "Yes operator. Of course... Is that you, Joe?"

"Yeah, it's me."

"How have you been? How're the ribs?"

"They're still sore. I had to work on the docks all day today, but I'm okay. Any news?"

"Ludko and Benny are working that Skibinski case that you were supposed to start."

"Oh, yeah, I forgot all about that. It's just a tail job on a fiancé. Those two can handle it."

"...and Detective Donnelly called and said that things are heating up on the liquor heist. Oh, let me get my other notes." Wilma reached across her desk. "Here... he said Santori is fuming about stolen liquor winding up in one of his warehouses. He said he's going to bring Santori in for questioning. In his words: 'That ought to start a wildfire.' What does that mean?"

"It means everything is working out as planned."

"Tell Johnny that Tommy misses his dad. We haven't told Tommy anything, as if we knew anything anyway."

"That's the way it has to be for now. You understand."

"Sometimes I wish I didn't."

"Consider it a blessing." Joe happened to look out of the phone booth to see the pale man from the restaurant walking into the lobby. He stopped at the front desk and spoke briefly to the clerk. Joe turned his back. "Look, I'm going to be incommunicado for a couple of days, so don't worry."

"Joe, what's the matter? I can hear it in your voice. It's this Polina case, isn't it?"

"It's just more complicated."

"You be careful... hear me?

"Yes, my dear."

"I mean it, Joe," Wilma said shaking her head in disapproval.

"So long, sunshine."

"Bye, Joe." Wilma hung up the receiver and took a deep breath. The pale man was gone. Joe exited the booth and went over to the desk clerk and asked, "That fellow here a minute ago. Is he staying at this hotel?"

"Yes, he is a guest at the hotel. His room is just down the hall from yours, in fact. A Monsieur Gore."

"I thought I recognized him. He was at the restaurant across the street."

"Yes, many of our guests frequent the L'Enoteca. I eat there myself occasionally."

With that Joe headed upstairs. He checked the tape he'd placed on the door. Good. He unlocked the door and went in. He shocked himself when he looked in the mirror. Unshaven and dirty—Joe looked positively menacing. He checked his ribs. Entirely black and blue with complementary shades of green. He took a shower and shaved for the first time in days. He wrapped his ribs again and put on fresh work clothes.

Joe loaded the .38 Smith & Wesson and put extra cartridges in his pants pocket. He strapped on the shoulder holster and fitted the gun in it, then tried on his denim jacket. The jacket had enough bulk to conceal the bulge of the gun. He put his cigarette transmitter in the inside pocket of the jacket and his new gun lighter in his shirt pocket. Joe looked himself over in the mirror. *Not bad.*

Johnny Della Penna came in smiling and whistling. "Holly crap—I almost didn't recognize yuh. Wait'll Rémy and Marcel get a load of you."

"I look that good, eh?"

"Yeah, but you look like a cop now."

"That's exactly how I want to look."

Johnny laughed, "Yeah, you look sorta like a Clark Gable cop without the ears and the mustache, maybe a little Errol Flynn thrown in too." Joe frowned, and Johnny added, " Hey, I've got a date with Zoé after I get off tonight."

"Then you'd better get cleaned up too," suggested Joe.

"You're right." Johnny hurriedly showered and shaved. When he emerged from the bathroom he said, "Well, what do yuh think?"

"I think you're going to wow her."

"Thanks," said Johnny. Then, as if he remembered something, he added, "Ahh, you know, if things work out, I don't think I'm goin' back to South Chicago—I mean to stay. I'm gonna try to get something goin' up here."

Joe said, "I was sort of hoping you'd consider that."

Johnny lowered his eyes in thought, smiled then asked, "Oh, yeah?"

This had been Joe's backup plan—in case things *didn't* work out. If the liquor re-heist blew up, at least he would have Johnny safely out of their reach until he could engineer some other plan.

Joe let that question drop. "Wilma said that Tommy is missing his dad."

"He's asking after me?"

"That's what Wilma said."

"Yeah, I miss him too."

Joe flopped on his bed. "You know the funny guy at the restaurant?"

"Yeah."

"He's right down the hall from us."

"He might be legit then."

"Maybe. I'm going to catch forty winks."

"Okay, I'm gonna read this *Montreal Gazette*. It's in English." Johnny picked up the paper off the dresser and sat up in his bed reading.

Joe drifted off less than an hour. He woke with a start, "Hey, we got to get moving."

"Sure, Joe, take it easy. I was watchin' the time."

Joe sprang up. After making one more check of everything, they both left the room and headed down the hall to the stairs. Joe thought he saw one of the other room doors close just before they got to the stairs. They descended to the lobby and out the door. The tall pale man in the room down the hall fully opened his door. He followed Joe and Johnny at a discreet distance, holding to the shadows of the buildings along the street. Moments later, two other men emerged from the same room and walked to their car parked just around the corner from the hotel.

As Joe and Johnny walked the four blocks to Dock 17, Johnny asked, "Joe, if you don't mind me askin', how did you get hooked up with Lawrence Hamilton? What's his deal?"

"We met a while back when I was working a sort of government job. Lawrence was one of my instructors at a camp down in Toronto."

"I was just wonderin' how a guy from South Chicago gets with a guy like him."

"Someday, when I can, I'll tell you the story." Joe let that settle in and said, "Hey, tell me about your date. We're here only two days, and you've got a date already. I don't know what it is with you Italian guys."

Johnny smiled broadly and said, "We're just goin' down for a drink or two at that place down the block there."

"Well, I won't be back tonight, so...."

Johnny got it, but right away became concerned. "Joe, what do you mean you 'won't be back'? You aren't leavin' me here are yuh?" he said sounding like an abandoned child.

"I don't know what's going to happen. That's the thing about this business. When you're dealing with people, especially desperate people, you can only predict so much. The rest is up to a higher authority. Lawrence and I have worked together before. We know what to expect and what we can't expect."

"Got yuh."

They walked along silently. They felt uneasy, sensing something unnatural, but shrugged it off as anxiety. The haunts. As they approached Dock 17, Joe said, "John, I want you to stay on working here for a few days. Just work with Rémy and Marcel, and keep an eye out for Frankie Ferrel. I'm worried that we haven't seen his ugly mug yet."

"Maybe he knows somethin' we don't."

"Like what?"

"I'll ask him if I see him."

Joe let out a stifled laugh. "Don't make me laugh. My ribs hurt."

"Sorry," said Johnny glad that he got Joe to relax. "I'll watch for him."

They entered the gate at Dock 17, showed their cards and walked in. The pallid observer stayed well back in the shadows and watched them as they joined the other men. A car pulled up. The observer got in and nodded to the driver, and they disappeared into the night.

Marcel and Rémy were at the overhead door of Bay 6 of the warehouse. Joe and Johnny approached them. Rémy blurted out, "Sacrebleu—I do not know this man. This cannot be my *camarade* from this morning."

Marcel said, "I liked you better before."

"Thanks," said Joe. "Where's our anxious shipper?"

"I expect him any minute," assured Marcel. "Rémy, get the fork truck and locate all his crates. Put them near the truck dock."

"Oui... on my way."

It was getting dark. Marcel turned the warehouse lights on. Rémy was moving crates around to get access to Kemidov's cargo.

Joe said, "Johnny, let's find that smaller crate." They searched the warehouse and located the small crate, which earlier that morning Johnny had placed near an interior wall.

Joe went over to Marcel and asked, "I'm going to need an empty crate to transfer the cargo from that smaller one over there by John." He pointed to where Johnny was standing.

Marcel said, "You will need tools to open it. They are over in the tool room next to the office. I will find another crate for you."

Joe got a crow bar, a hammer, and some nails out of the tool room. He went to the smaller crate. He and Johnny carefully slit the seal with a pocket knife and opened the crate." They removed two trunks from the crate and placed them on the floor. To be sure he had Hamilton's bait, Joe opened the trunks to reveal the carefully wrapped paintings. He slowly unwrapped them. Joe recognized the styles of Van Gogh and Picasso, but not Renoir.

Johnny looked at them quizzically as Joe wrapped them back up. "That's what all the fuss is about?"

"Johnny, you're looking at probably $100,000 worth of art."

"Can't be," exclaimed Johnny in utter disbelief.

To help him understand, Joe said, "Long after you and I are gone, these paintings will still be here, still be admired. They represent the best of what man can achieve, his highest aspirations."

"And I laughed at this stuff in school. You know, back in high school, we took a trip downtown to the Art Institute. Maybe when I get back, I'll take another look."

Joe closed the trunks just as Rémy arrived with the extra crate on the forks of his fork truck. "Here is your crate, mon ami, compliments of Marcel."

"Thanks, Rémy," said Joe.

"Au revoir," and Rémy drove his fork truck back to where the loading would begin.

"Johnny, help me get these paintings into that other crate,"

"Sure," said Johnny. As he handed one of the paintings to Joe, he said to no one in particular, "A hundred grand?"

After they were finished, Joe went over to Marcel and said, "Someone from the Canadian Security Intelligence Service will pick up that crate as evidence. Please make sure it is protected until then."

"Of course, of course," assured Marcel.

Evrard Molyneaux backed his rented box truck into Bay 6 at the far end of the warehouse. Joe walked back over to Kemidov's emptied crate. He motioned for Johnny and said, "John, when I get inside there, put one nail in the center and fix the seal as best you can. Above all, load me last."

"Okay."

"If he even asks, tell Marcel I didn't feel good and that I went back to our hotel."

"Right."

Marcel took Evrard over to the office to go over the paperwork. When they went inside the office, Joe hopped inside the crate and Johnny quickly nailed it shut and smoothed the seal back down. Perfect.

# CHAPTER SEVENTEEN

MONTREAL
*Dock Warehouse, Bay 6*

It was dark inside the crate, with splinters of light leaking in, and the acrid smell of hardwood filled Joe's nostrils. He was so thankful it was cool and not the stifling heat of Chicago in late summer. From inside, Joe could hear orders in French and the clatter of the forklift driving around, jockeying crates to free Kemidov's illicit cargo. He could see the warehouse floor through the cracks between the slats of his crate. A couple of times, Johnny waltzed by Joe's crate and banged it and said, "You're almost loaded, brother."

Rémy moved large crates to the truck dock, and Johnny wrestled them into position inside, some as tall as he was. At some point Marcel asked Johnny, "Petite Jean, where is Monsieur Joe?"

"He left. He felt sick and went back to our hotel. Follow?"

"Oui... ah.... ah," said Marcel, stumbling for the correct words and finding them he smiled and added, "I gotcha."

Marcel and Rémy had been told to cooperate with Joe. Charlie Anguine, the business agent for the Longshoreman's Local Union, said Joe was there on important business for the union. That's all they needed to know.

Johnny patted Joe's crate and warned Marcel, "This one *has* to load last, comprendre?"

"Oui, I will tell Rémy," said Marcel. "Your Français is getting better."

Johnny resumed moving the crates inside the truck. At one point Evrard Molyneaux raised his hands in the air, pushing an imaginary box shouting, "Faire attention!"

Johnny understood, nodded, and answered, "Oui, je sais, je

sais" then moved the large crate very carefully, easing it toward the front of the truck.

Evrard inspected every single crate that was loaded. All sides, all over, including the seals and locks. He gave his blessing and the cargo would be loaded. Kemidov's shipment was scattered all over the warehouse, buried among other crates. Sorting them out took time. Evrard was growing impatient, so was Joe. From inside his hovel, all Joe could make out were flashes of light as the forklift passed by or when Johnny came by and tapped his crate.

"How many more, Marcel?" asked Johnny.

"Hmm..duo, trois. Yes, three," answered Marcel.

Rémy moved two large crates from deep inside the warehouse toward the truck dock. Then he went to pick up Joe. He landed Joe's crate clumsily on the floor nearer to Bay 6. He moved the other two crates to the dock edge, where Evrard inspected them thoroughly. Johnny wrestled them gently into the truck, being careful not to jostle the contents.

Rémy went and picked up the crate with Joe inside and drove toward the dock.

Evrard shouted, "Arrêter... geler." He raced over toward the dock edge. Johnny didn't need a translator. He started to sweat even in the cool of the night.

He was yelling something else in French and waving his hands. From inside the box, Joe sensed there was trouble.

Marcel ran from the office room on the floor of the warehouse toward Bay 6, toward Evrard. In rapid French, he was exhorting Evrard to sign more paperwork or he could not let the shipment leave that night. He motioned to Evrard and said, "Rapidement, Monsieur."

Evrard thought about it for a moment and decided he had inspected every crate loaded and thought *To hell with that little crate?* He changed direction and joined Marcel to sign the last bills to expedite the release of the freight to Evrard. Marcel looked over to Johnny and gave a wink.

Rémy saw the commotion and rushed the last small crate over to the truck. Joe felt every bump in the floor on his way to Bay 6. Rather than wait for Johnny to guide the crate into the truck, Rémy dropped it to the floor and used his forks to just push it off the dock floor into the truck. It dropped four inches and landed hard on the bed of the truck. Joe cursed under his breath: *Damn it, Rémy.*

Marcel and Evrard emerged from the office and returned to the truck, which was now loaded. Evrard looked inside and was satisfied. He slammed the back doors sharply and threw the latch. He turned to Marcel and handed him the promised wages including a generous bonus, and said, "Merci beaucoup."

Evrard left through the dock's exit door. He started the truck and pulled away from the warehouse toward the gate. He showed his papers to the attendant, who waved him off of the King Edward Quay. As he pulled on to the street and turned left, the truck hit the gutter and rocked back and forth, jarring its secret passenger.

Five blocks away in a customized ambulance, Lawrence Hamilton and two MI5 agents watched a distinct blip on a modified radar scope. The agent named Robert from the Canadian branch of MI5 said, "They're moving, sir."

"Very well," said Hamilton as he entered the driver's seat. "Let's keep it steady."

"Yes, sir." said Robert.

The other agent, one of Hamilton's operatives from London MI5, used a control to direct the aerial on the top of the ambulance to get a stronger signal. "The signal's getting weaker, sir," said Bradley.

"They are heading south," added Robert.

In his white driver's uniform and cap, Hamilton looked the part. He turned the ambulance and headed south. "How are we doing, Robert?"

"Fine, sir."

"The signal's still getting weaker, sir," said Bradley as he adjusted the antenna. "There... it's better now."

"Still heading south, sir."

Warning his men, Hamilton said, "Our road ends just up ahead. I will have to get us over on to the same road as our target." Hamilton took a hard left. That road came to a dead end too. "Drat!"

"Signal is definitely waning," said Bradley, listening with his headphones. Hamilton took another left at the dead end and increased speed to get to a through street. "I'm losing the signal entirely, sir." Hamilton sped up.

Robert said, "No visual either."

Hamilton floored the gas pedal and turned on the ambulance's siren and lights. He flew through two red lights when he heard Bradley say: "Got it back."

"They're headed west now," said Robert.

Hamilton took a left and asked, "Is the signal better now?"

"Good," reported Robert.

"Signal's strong, too," said Bradley. They followed almost parallel, a few blocks north of their target now, heading in the same direction.

Evrard noticed a car following his truck. He could see what looked like two men in the front seat, but it could have been a man and a woman, he wasn't sure. It was quite dark and hard to distinguish, but he sensed he was being tailed. They made the same turns that he made. Left, then right. Then right again.

Evrard had learned from the Gestapo in Paris how they would dog their prey. One more turn and Evrard would know. He made a sharp right, nearly tipping the truck over. Joe was tossed around inside the crate, banging his ribs and his head. *He's trying to drop a tail or test one. It can't be Hamilton. He's just paranoid.*

Joe could smell exhaust fumes. *Great,* he thought, *he must have knocked the muffler's tail pipe loose.* The truck had picked up speed, which meant the exhaust inside the box intensified. *I'm in my own gas chamber here. I got to get out.* Joe kneeled and got his back up on the lid of the crate. Using his legs he pushed up hard. The nail gave way. The lid flew open, and like a Jack-in-the-box, Joe was free. The lid slapped hard against the door.

Evrard heard it, but dismissed it, thinking the load had shifted in the back. He was more concerned with his pursuers. Joe put his face to the tiny space between the doors and took a deep breath. The fresh air smelled good. He looked through the crack for the pursuer.

No one there. This guy is crazy. Then it dawned on him: Okay, Einstein, how are you going to nail yourself back in this crate?

He took a few more breaths. He could see the street flying by through the crack between the doors. *He's going to kill himself—and me too!*

Evrard was satisfied he had lost his tail or it was never a tail at all. He slowed down. Joe was busy trying to get the nail out of the lid of his crate so it wouldn't be noticed. He used his .38 to pound the nail up and then used the trigger guard to pry it free from the wood. The truck took more evasive actions. Left. Right. Left again. Straight.

*Well, if it was a tail, he shook it,* Joe thought. He looked again through the crack between the doors. He saw what he thought was a church. They had passed by St. Joseph's Oratory, a Roman Catholic basilica on the west slope of Mount Royal in Montreal. The massive dome with its cross, bathed in artificial light made it look majestic and reminded Joe how long it had been since he'd been to Mass. *When I get through this,* he promised. Then, his mind jumped back to the follower: *Might have been Ferrel or NKVD.*

Exhaust fumes were building inside the back of the truck. *Maybe I'm not even thinking right in this gas chamber.* The back of the truck was so black, it felt strangely warm. He stayed close to the crack where the air was fresh. He could see street lights and dimly lit houses, big houses. After a few more turns, he felt the truck come to a stop. Evrard got out and unlocked what sounded like a huge gate. Joe heard it clanging free and squeaking as Evrard pushed it open.

The cab door closed again and the truck backed up. There were voices outside now, speaking French. *Maybe two guys,* Joe thought. He heard the voices say, "Qui est bon. Facile, facile.... Bon, arrêter!"

Recognizing the accent, Joe thought: *Got to be French Canadians.*

The truck stopped. By the sound of the motor, Joe could tell they must be inside a building, a garage perhaps. Evrard turned off the engine. *Thank goodness.* Joe heard Evrard get out and slam the cab door shut. He heard footsteps as Evrard walked to the back of the truck to give orders to the other two men. Joe couldn't understand what they were talking about, but soon they would open the cargo doors, so Joe carefully and silently took his place back inside the box and closed the lid.

Now inside the crate, Joe couldn't hear Evrard's voice anymore, just the two French Canadians. Evrard had gone up the nearby stairs and into the mansion to report to Yuri Kemidov and tell him all had gone well. Kemidov leased an impressive stone twin-peak Tudor-style mansion for the second phase of his operation. The grandeur of this two-and-a-half story mansion with its stone-walled, dual-stairway entrance and its balustrade veranda overlooking the front landscape was meant to impress the curators, wealthy collectors, and art dealers he would lure from the United States and elsewhere to his mansion gallery.

To surround his prey with luxury and comfort was all part of the charade. Kemidov had to dispose of these works expeditiously. The MFAA and INTERPOL were alerting governments around the world of art stolen by the Nazis. In Paris alone, nearly one third of all the art in private hands had been pillaged by the Nazis and collaborators, like "General" Yuri Kemidov.

Of course Kemidov did not consider himself an art thief by any means. Real art thieves were nothing more than thugs who never ventured into a museum except to rob it.

No, Yuri considered himself an aficionado, capable of the most discerning sensibilities. He believed he had rescued the so-called "degenerate" art from certain destruction at the hands of the Nazis. Besides, the Jews who once owned it were going to be eliminated anyway and had no more use for it. Better someone with his refinement, his sophistication, take possession of these works. The fact that he would make an obscene profit would merely justify the risks he had taken in acquiring it.

But time was running out, and Kemidov knew it.


The doors to the back of the truck opened. The two French Canadians prepared to unload its contents. The first crate was the smallest and at the very end of the truck. Joe was inside holding the lid down as the two men struggled to get it off. Complaining about the weight, the shorter Canadian said, "C'est lourde." Joe held the lid firm as they moved it off the truck. The taller man said, "Doit être statue," speculating that the contents had to be a statue. Joe felt his crate tip backward toward the little man. They struggled to place the crate gently on the floor.

Once on the floor, he listened as they slowly unloaded the rest of the crates. Joe didn't need be fluent in French to understand they were complaining about the work. He counted each crate placed on the floor, just as he'd counted every turn he made getting to the mansion gallery.

Cramped in the small crate, Joe thought: *Come on... shake a leg, would yuh?* He kept counting: *Ten, eleven, .......*

◇◇◇

After what seemed like forever, Joe thought: *Only one more to go. If they're going to start unpacking them, I've got to be ready.* Joe squirmed around to free the .38 S&W from his holster. *Now if they open up this Christmas present, I'll give them a great big surprise.*

With the last crate unloaded, Joe could hear the sound of keys jangling as that last crate was unlocked. Then he heard a pry bar and a hammer. The nails wailed as they were torn from the wood. The lid was removed and placed with a thud against a wall. The taller Canadian exclaimed, "Belle, belle."

They both gazed inside to see beautiful French Impressionist paintings by Renoir, Degas, Monet, and Pissarro. After their moment of rapture, they began the careful process of removing paintings, one by one, carrying each up a flight of stairs into the bowels of the mansion, toward an enormous dining room with three chandeliers and walnut-paneled walls.

Kemidov would use this space as his main gallery, displaying sculpture and paintings. Other rooms, more intimate, would serve as thematic galleries to focus on Post-Impressionist works and others rooms for moderns, like Braque and Picasso. Kemidov's mansion of art rivaled New York's finest galleries.

"They have definitely stopped moving, sir," said Robert. "We are about four miles from their location."

"Very well, then. We shall get within a few blocks, if we can, and wait for Joseph to call us in."

"Turn right up ahead," said Robert, and Hamilton made a right and travelled about a mile and then was told to make a left. "Getting closer, sir," said Robert. "Yes, sir, straight up ahead now. We are very near them." Hamilton pulled off the road and turned off the lights. Now, they had to wait.

Joe heard the two French Canadians coming and going. He timed their round trip. He had very little time to get out of that crate and get a fix on where he was for Hamilton and company. The two Canadians had just left, each with a painting. Joe slowly opened the lid of his crate. It squeaked like a coffin lid. *Oh, my God,* he thought, *I'm Dracula.*

Even though it was dim, the light hurt his eyes. *Now I know I'm*

*Dracula.* His eyes adjusted. He spotted a door at the back of the garage. *That door must lead to the rear of the house.* He had to get a description of the house, of its location, something for Hamilton to home in on. He noticed a late model Mercedes parked in the adjacent garage bay.

He flew out the door into the night. It was cool, almost cold. As he looked back, he thought, *This place is enormous. A mansion—it's Dracula's castle.* Joe moved over to the side fence bordering the property. Nothing but woods. A dog started barking viciously. Then another.

Joe started running away from the mansion toward the back of the property. He could hear the dogs getting closer. He looked back and caught a glimpse of them. *Dobermans!* They were gaining on him. He ran harder, his breathing rapid and heavy. His ribs ached as if they were breaking again.

Deep in the woods now, the undergrowth was heavy. Small branches lashed his face as he ran further into the woods. Briars tangled his feet. He reached the 15-foot high stone fence back fence, looked up: *Damn... Too high!.* He drew the .38 but didn't want to fire and give himself away. He turned and one of the Dobermans leaped for his throat.

Joe hit the dog's head hard with the butt of his gun. Rover One went down with a yelp, but not before Rover Two enthusiastically started in on his lower leg. With all his strength, using both hands, he slammed the dog on the top of his head with the gun butt. Knocked him out instantly, but not soon enough: Rover Two had mangled his lower leg. The first Doberman was regaining consciousness. He got another treatment.

Looking down at the two Dobermans, Joe whispered, "Somebody had to teach you boys some manners."

Joe checked his leg. It was bleeding now but no torn muscle, just a flesh wound. His work denims had protected him. The real pain would start in about a minute or two. He took a kerchief out of his coat pocket and tied it around his lower leg and rolled his pant leg back down.

He headed back to Kemidov's mansion. When he cleared the heavy underbrush, he saw someone standing on the back patio near the balustrade peering into the darkness, calling the dogs. The rear of the mansion had multiple French doors with light pouring onto the open patio.

Joe worked his way closer to the mansion, staying hidden in the wooded area. The dog caller gave up and went back inside through the glass doors. Joe got out his cigarette pack and pulled up the aerial. He said, "Okay... I'm in, but I don't know where I am. It's a huge house, a mansion, near a domed church. The house has two main peaks, nearly three stories tall, all stone, It's old, but in good shape. There's a front gate and a three-car garage on the uh..." He looked around to get his bearings. "...On the east side."

Bradley received Joe's transmission and repeated it, word for word, to Hamilton.

"That shouldn't be too hard to locate out this way," said Hamilton. "Let's have a look." He pulled the ambulance back on to the road.

"Signal's getting stronger now," reported Bradley.

"Still straight ahead, sir," added Robert. "I know where that church is, sir. It is St. Joseph's Oratory about a half mile from us."

"We are surely on the correct heading," said Hamilton. "There up ahead. Straight ahead. That must be it. We can observe the place from a safe distance here until Joseph's next transmission. Get your weapons ready, gentlemen." Hamilton parked the ambulance, and they waited.

Joe made it back to the rear garage door. He opened it a crack. He finally got a look at the two French Canadians he had only heard from his hiding place. The pictures he created in his mind didn't match the genuine articles—they never do. The short one was even shorter than Joe had imagined. Neither one was the dog caller on the back balcony. *That makes four now.* Joe was getting impatient. *Okay, come on, Shorty, get moving.*

Shorty and his partner were just then opening another crate and removing its contents. Joe would have to wait until they left with more art works before going back inside.

Finally, they were both gone. Joe waited just a moment more and entered the garage. He walked over to the same stairway that the French Canadians used to enter the mansion. He crept up the stairs to a dark hallway. He believed he was somewhere in the east wing  of the mansion now. He passed a another stairway, gun drawn. There were footprints in the dust at the bottom. *That's where Shorty and his partner must get into the main part of this castle.*

Joe continued down the hallway toward the rear of the mansion. Every step telegraphed the pain from where the dog had torn open his ankle. At the end of the hallway, he turned left. He saw another stairway leading up to the main floor. It was dark. Light leaked beneath a door at the top of the stairs. Joe waited in the stairwell for his two buddies to return for more paintings.

The two were talking as they headed back to the garage. Joe got a good look at them from the darkness of the stairwell. He thought: *Now's my chance to get on the main floor without running into those two.* He raced up the stairs and looked under the door. It looked like a pantry with some empty shelves at the bottom and a few canned goods just above and illuminated only by a single dim light. With a silent prayer, he tried the door handle. *Damn... locked.*

It was nearly black in the stairwell. Joe felt the door jamb near the handle. *It opens in!* He got out his pocket knife, unfolded it, and eased the blade between the stop molding and the jamb to pry open a slit between them. Someone entered the pantry. Joe stopped prying. He felt his heart pounding. He let out his breath slowly. He let go of the knife. It remained wedged between the molding and the door jamb. Joe dropped down to the bottom of the door to have look.

There—under the door—were a pair of boots. Joe pulled his .38 and silently moved down two steps, keeping his eyes focused on the boots. A moment that felt like an hour passed, and the boots walked away, out of the pantry. Joe slowly holstered his gun and went back to work on the door molding. His knife actions were more cautious now.

Joe pried the molding far enough away to permit his knife blade to reach the latch. Most latches will move even if the door is locked and the handles won't move. Joe eased the latch back without a sound, putting slight pressure on the door. It opened.

Like a practiced burglar, Joe entered the pantry, unlocked the door, and silently closed it behind him. He surveyed the room. It was huge with floor-to-ceiling shelves, crammed with boxes and cans of food, enough to feed a platoon. At the far wall, a door led to the kitchen. Joe edged over and looked underneath to see if the boots were in there. The kitchen was empty and dark. He got up and entered. The kitchen had two doors: one leading into the main dining room and the other into a hallway. He heard voices behind the hallway door.

He recognized Evrard's voice from the docks but not the other. They were speaking English. *Has to be Kemidov*, he thought. Now there was a third voice. He put his ear to the door leading into the hallway.

In a heavy French accent, a voice said "The dogs went off after a rabbit or a squirrel. I heard one yelp. They must be fighting over it."

"Very well," said Kemidov and waved his hand to dismiss the guard.

With four other men, Joe figured he would have to get the drop on Kemidov and get him to call off his human guard dogs until he could radio Hamilton. Joe's plan sounded good to him until he actually thought about it.


Through the crack in the kitchen door, Joe saw the short French Canadian from the garage carrying a small crate that must have been fairly heavy, judging by the way he labored with it. The man disappeared into a study just across from where they were taking most of the paintings, down a long hall from the kitchen.

Joe heard the crate being opened, the sound of nails squealing as they were pulled from the crate. Shorty left the room and headed back down to the garage.

After a few moments, he could just barely hear Kemidov say: "Look, my friend, the most excellent artifact in all antiquity." Kemidov removed what looked like a small mummy.

"A baby mummy, Yuri?" questioned Evrard. Joe could not make out what they were saying. He had to get closer. Shorty and his partner weren't due back for a few minutes. He saw a slightly opened door to a darkened room down the hall, adjacent to Kemidov's study. He made his move.

"Mummy? Not at all—even more valuable." Kemidov started gingerly unwrapping the little mummy.

Joe made it to the adjacent room and opened the door and entered. It was a large drawing room, carpeted with inset mahogany bookcases that held rows of beautiful leather-bound books that no one ever read or ever will. Double doors led to Kemidov's study. When he closed the hallway door, it made a slight click. Joe heard the two in the study stop talking. His eyes flashed. He looked directly at the double doors. His heart began pounding, his neck arteries throbbed, his ribs ached.

"Did you hear something?" said Kemidov.

Evrard said, "Must be those two bringing in the art things. Now what of this petite statue."

Joe let out his breath when he heard them talking again. He inched his way toward the double doors, his heart still racing from the click, his leg signaling each heartbeat with pain.

"Do not scoff at my little statue. It is worth more than that entire truckload of paintings and sculptures, my friend."

"Impossible," proclaimed Evrard in French. Then in English he added, " You said that the paintings were worth a million pounds."

"They are, indeed, " said Kemidov, "but beneath these wrappings is a solid gold bird covered with jewels." He paused admiring the bird and then with a flourish, he removed the uppermost wrappings. He exclaimed, "This is the legendary Falcon of Malta, the tribute paid to Emperor Charles V for his handing over Malta, Gozo, and Tripoli in 1530 AD by the Order of Hospitallers, the Knights of Rhodes."

Kemidov frantically unwrapped the statue to reveal the entire golden falcon, now gleaming and glinting in the light. "This... this is a piece of history!"

Thunderstruck, Evrard whispered, "Fantastique... c'est incroyable."

"Indeed, " agreed Kemidov. Then, like some maniacal professor giving his pupil an impassioned lecture, Kemidov sought to educate Evrard on his most prized possession, the crux of his obsession. "Every French schoolboy knows of the Knights Templar, a holy order, God's personal militia, a society so secret that its true purpose is still unknown. They were the heroes of the Crusades, the warrior monks who occupied Jerusalem's legendary Temple of Solomon, the richest most powerful military order in the medieval world."

He carefully placed the Falcon on the desk and continued, "By the beginning of the fourteenth century the Templars rivaled the Genovese, the Lombards, even the Jews as the controllers of currency. The Kings of France and England kept their treasuries in the Order's vaults. Even the Muslims banked with the Templars." Kemidov laughed. "Their unrivalled power would not last for very long."

There was a knock at the door. Kemiov covered the falcon clumsily with some of the wrappings. "Come in," said Kemidov.

Shorty entered and asked, "The large dining room is full, Monsieur. Where should we place the rest of the paintings?

"Paintings may go in the lounge and any sculptures in the library at the rear," said Kemidov still guarding the falcon.

Shorty noticed how strangely Kemidov was guarding the little covered item but left the room quickly before incurring his reprimand.

Kemidov uncovered the falcon and collected his thoughts. "Now where was I? Ah, yes, the Templars. Everyone knows that the Holy Wars were, in truth, a matter of loot, not unlike our erstwhile Nazi benefactors. Both the Templars and the Hospitallers preyed upon Saracens, amassing jewels and precious metals and ivories. Together they formed the bulwark of the Kingdom of Jerusalem. The Templars numbered in the thousands and thus had the lion's share of the spoils. With every victory their wealth increased, as did their unprecedented autonomy. The Templars constituted an empire unrivalled in Medieval history, with riches beyond imagination and power without limit. They answered to no one but the Pope.

"But they had something else, something even more precious. The Templars had discovered sacred treasures after their takeover of the Holy City. Sacred treasures and sacred knowledge."

Evrard said, "What good is centuries-old knowledge?"

"Knowledge, mon ami," intoned Kemidov, "is more valuable than gold, especially the knowledge they must have acquired in Solomon's Temple."

"What do you think they learned, Yuri?" asked Evrard.

Joe had been motionless so long his injured leg began to cramp. He wiggled his toes to get the blood flowing. Kemidov lowered his voice, as if to confide a secret. Joe opened his mouth slightly. It improved his hearing.

Kemidov continued, "In AD 70, the Romans under Titus and Tiberius Julius Alexander laid siege to Jerusalem and destroyed the famous Second Temple. The Jews to this very day mourn this in Tisha B'Av, an annual fast that commemorates the destruction of the First and Second Temples.

"Why is this important?" asked Evrard, growing weary of Kemidov's sermon.

"Because the Romans found little in the way of pillage. It had all vanished, which may explain the Roman's total destruction of the Temple. They were looking for the treasure and never found it."

His interest piqued by the prospect of such riches, Evrard asked, "Where did it go?"

"Apparently the Jewish priests spirited away the treasures of the Second Temple long before the Romans arrived. Fearing they might all be slaughtered by Titus, they most assuredly made a treasure map. I believe the Knights Templar found that map."

"Where is the map now, Yuri?"

"After almost two thousand years, surely it is lost; but the Templars left clues all over the world. On a small hill above Roslin Glen in Scotland is the Rosslyn Chapel or more properly the Collegiate Chapel of St. Matthew. Throughout the chapel are symbols of the Templars. In fact the layout of Rosslyn Chapel itself echoes that of Solomon's Temple. There are repeated images of two riders on a single horse in alcoves and niches throughout the chapel. That is the symbol of The Order of the Poor Knights Templar.

"In the United States, not too far from here, is the Round Tower of Newport, Rhode Island. The architecture and great age suggest that Scottish Templars voyaged there one hundred years before Columbus. Why?

"Here in Canada, in Nova Scotia, on Oak Island, three young men stumbled upon a round depression in the ground. This was in 1795, mind you. Well, these boys dug down ten feet and found a wooden platform. They dug down another ten feet and hit another wooden platform. They hit yet another platform at thirty feet down. At this point they needed more substantial tools to go any further. They reluctantly returned to the mainland, vowing to return and recover the treasure they knew was buried there, but they never did."

"This is the treasure of the Templars?"

"Quite possibly. Yes, in part. I want to explore these sites for clues to the Templars' treasure. Rumors of the treasure of Solomon's Temple ultimately led to the demise of Templars. You see, Evrard, in great wealth is great power, which foments even greater jealousy in one's rivals."

Kemidov cast a watchful eye toward Evrard and continued,

"The jaundiced Order of Hospitallers desired to share this outrageous wealth and power by petitioning the Pope to unite their two orders. They employed a renegade Templar, Esquiu de Floyrian, in their scheme. He impugned the Templars with charges of blasphemy, idolatry, sodomy, and devil worship. The Hospitallers brought these to Pope Clement V with the proviso that they would purify their ranks if only the Pope would unite the two orders. For his duplicity Esqui would receive a small share of the vast plunder.

"This effort failed, and the Hospitallers along with Esquiu looked to Philip the Fair, Philip IV, of France. Philip was deeply indebted to the Templars. He needed money for the English War, the Flemish revolt, and the costs of his self-indulgent government, so he seized this opportunity to rid himself of his creditors."

Evrard laughed, "Kill the banker, très bon."

"Yes, mon ami, and the Templars had immense landed estates in France, which Philip hoped to secure for himself. Thus, he had hundreds of Templars arrested on charges of heresy, homosexuality, denial of the cross, and devil worship.

"They were thrown into Philip's dungeons. While awaiting their dark fate, the Templars carved elaborate symbols on the walls of their dungeons, a secret language known only to them, the same ciphers used in their banking system.

"Applying severe torture, Philip IV and the Inquisition extracted confessions from all but three of the Templars. The Pope, powerless in the light of these confessions, issued a command to all Christian princes to arrest Templars in their lands.

"A few years later, Philip IV had the Master of the Order, Jacques de Molay, burned at the stake, and with that the Poor Fellow-Soldiers of Christ and the Temple of Solomon were destroyed. Pope Clement, a mere pawn of Philip, had their vast wealth passed to the Hospitallers."

"A fantastic story, Yuri."

"To be sure, and this golden falcon was one of the treasures of the Templars. The Hospitallers parlayed it to control Malta, Gozo, and Tripoli." Kemidov gazed at the Falcon as he polished it with his pocket square.

Evrard asked, "If the Templars were destroyed, why are you searching for treasure here?"

"Because, Evrard, thousands of Templars escaped," exclaimed

Kemidov. "Some fled to Switzerland and founded the Swiss banking systems, which rely on the utmost secrecy to this very day. Others vanished at night, on a fleet of ships from La Rochelle, France, to Scotland, the only country in Europe where the Papal bull did not run, since Robert the Bruce was excommunicated himself, and the whole country was under a Papal interdict. The treasures of the Templars sailed with them...."

As Joe listened, he could hardly believe the enormity of this case. The riches of Solomon... and the Falcon was only one of its jewels.

# CHAPTER EIGHTEEN

MONTREAL
*Kemidov's Mansion*

"Had things gone very badly in Paris, my friend, this little bird would have delivered us from the fowler's net. Indeed, it was our passport out of the clutches of the Nazis," said Kemidov. "However, I am relieved we did not have to part with it to save our lives."

"If they had found out you were giving information to the NKVD, this bird may not have been enough," Evrard pointed out.

"It most assuredly would. This precious statue would have gone directly to the Fuehrer for his personal museum, the one he planned in his hometown of Linz. And his gratitude, my friend, would have been unbounded."

"You think so, Yuri?"

"This golden falcon, once belonging to the Knights Templar, the guardians of the Holy Lands, the warrior monks, would complement the Holy Lance, the one used to pierce the side of Jesus, what the Fuehrer called the 'Spear of Destiny.'"

Evrard, intrigued by this revelation, asked, "What spear is this?"

"In Vienna, in the Hofburg Library, behind a glass case, was the Holy Lance that supposedly the Roman centurion Longinus used to smite the side of Jesus. When the Germans marched into Vienna, Hitler went to the Hofburg Library and removed the spear at once and said, 'I am holding the whole world in my hand.'

"The claim is whoever unlocks the secrets of the spear will rule the world. Hitler, you see, was a devout student of the occult. He believed in such things. Which is why he would believe my tale of the Falcon of Malta."

"What tale would you tell then?"

"Ah, you doubt me, Evrard? I would have convinced the Fuehrer that the Falcon was a relic of the Ancient Egyptians, discovered in Solomon's treasures by the Knights Templar. I would regale him with tales of the falcon god Horus, the god of war and hunting. I would show him these strange symbols upon the base. See here." Kemidov turned the Falcon upside down and showed Evrard.

"I would insinuate that these secret writings, when unlocked, and together with the Spear of Destiny, would place the fate of the entire world in the hands of the Nazis."

Kemidov looked almost parentally at Evrard. "No, Evrard, this Falcon of Malta would have guaranteed our safety. It is indeed a true wonder, a fabulous relic."

"Why did you not tell me of it before?" asked Evrard.

"As much as I trust you, I could not risk telling you for fear someone might learn of it during one of your inebriated celebrations. They would have killed both of us to obtain it."

"How did you come by it?" asked Evrard.

"As you are well aware, I have been in the Soviets' employ for many years. In my position as an art and antiquities dealer, I heard a story many years ago that a Greek dealer named Charilos Konstantinides had an object in his Paris shop whose description closely matched my knowledge of the Falcon. This was long ago, you understand. It turned out Konstantinides had been murdered and his shop was robbed of all its inventory.

"As luck would have it, the Falcon had been coated in thick black enamel paint and looked like so much kitsch. The thieves had no idea. I eventually discovered, through my underground contacts, who these criminals were. Once I had their names, I began tracking them down, one by one, all across Europe.

"Of course, they knew nothing and died because of their ignorance. The last thief I located actually had the Falcon sitting on his mantel. He went to his grave not knowing what he had, and now I have it."

"You mean we have it," said Evrard.

Kemidov noted that remark but reassured him, "Of course, of course, it will be our salvation in times of peril. Indeed, I have sold it any number of times since I acquired it, but only when my funds were alarmingly low."

Evrard then asked, confused by what he had heard, "Did you buy it back, then?"

Kemidov laughed. "I never delivered the genuine Falcon, only a skillfully crafted copy. My victim's greed and imagination did all the rest. I would claim I was in deep financial trouble, a Russian noble fleeing the communists. They seized upon my misfortune and made a trifling offer to purchase the priceless Falcon. I would gladly accept their offer, of course, and hand over the forgery. By the time they discovered the substitution, I would have a new location courtesy of the Soviets and sometimes even a new identity."

Evrard was thinking, a difficult task, and then asked squinting his left eye, "Have none of your victims sought revenge, Yuri?"

"Some, perhaps thought of it," said Kemidov, "but they surrounded themselves with the most unsavory types and often ended up killed by their cohorts desiring to possess the illustrious Falcon for themselves. Others met their demise when the forgery was revealed.

"However, there was one collector who did not quite fit the scenario I have just described. He located me in Lisbon many years back. I was in need of money—as always, it seems—and he offered an equitable price for the Falcon. I was truly surprised considering I had played the same drama of my impoverished state for him as I did the others, fully expecting the bargaining ploy on his part. Yet, he made no attempt to barter. In fact, he seemed quite pleased at having located and purchased the bird.

"I have always regretted that I did not ask much more from him. Interesting how things plague your mind. Regrets, I suppose. I still remember his name— Gore."

Kemidov paused for a moment lost in that thought and then added, "In any event, I eventually left Lisbon. As a fine art dealer, you can move all about Europe without raising much suspicion, especially if you have a moderate, but tasteful, inventory of paintings and sculpture. In fact you are often welcomed into your new community and embraced by its patricians. They all want to appear sophisticated and worldly. I provided that illusion for them—as I did the Nazis.

"Of course, people of money often have connections to officials in government and, thus, information, which I then sell to the NKVD or whoever it interests. I was already in Paris when hostilities broke out, a windfall for me with the NKVD. That is when I met you, my friend."

"Evrard tried to comprehend, as best he could, the stories Kemidov had revealed to him. "Will we sell the Falcon now, Yuri?"

"In good time, mon ami, in good time," purred Kemidov, who had no intention of ever selling his precious Falcon of Malta. So much wealth concentrated in such a small package would always be Kemidov's parlay, and Kemidov's alone.

"Evrard, what I am trying to create here in Montreal is a collection of modern masterpieces unrivalled even by the most prestigious galleries of New York and London, to put aside such contrivances as my Falcon ruse and enter the legitimate art world, as respected dealers.

"Here we will entertain the wealthiest, most powerful people in the world. You see, Europe, my friend, is no longer the capital of art."

Evrard answered with a tired, "No?"

"New York will emerge as the next art mecca, and from Montreal, I will become one of its major purveyors of impressionist and modern art. Our collection now surpasses most museums in Europe.

"We shall invite our guests to this mansion of art. Ours will offer exquisite accommodations, including sumptuous dining prepared by master French chefs, surrounded by the sights and sounds of Montreal and above all—Art."

With a brandish of his hand, gesturing around the room, Kemidov added, "Our mansion gallery will be unique in all the art world. Appropriating art from contemptible Jews is one thing, but disposing of it takes genius and vision.

Languidly, Evrard said, "Whatever your say, Yuri; but I am no art dealer."

"You are my trusted assistant. I cannot return to Europe as you know, so you will have to represent me periodically to inspect and take possession of new acquisitions I make. Yes, indeed, we shall have a fine gallery of impeccable works."

Swept over by all that he heard, Evrard turned his pocket-sized intellect to something he could grasp, his French Canadian wards. "I had better go see what is keeping those two in the garage." Evrard left the study.

◊◊◊

Joe had been watching through the crack between the double doors leading to the study and listened intently as Kemidov finished his fantastic tale. He saw Evrard leave the room. *Kemidov's alone.* Joe opened the doors.

"Don't make a move, General," growled Joe.

Kemidov gasped and turned toward Joe. His eyes grew wild, his mind raced trying to comprehend what was happening. The entire world he had fabricated for himself only moments before had come unraveled in an instant.

"Get your hands up," demanded Joe. "Now! Up! Up where I can see 'em."

Kemidov raised his hands slowly, calculating his options. "What is all this?" he asked, thinking of the absurdity of him actually being robbed. His thoughts flew to NKVD, a shakedown and now with this American accomplice. "I demand an answer."

"Well, here's your answer: You're under arrest for war crimes and profiteering."

No sooner had he said that, the cool muzzle of a gun pressed hard against the back of his neck. Instinctively, Joe swung around only to meet the barrel pointing right between his eyes... Evrard.

"Do not move, monsieur," Evrard ordered. "Put your gun on sa' table." Joe slowly relinquished his .38 S&W. "Now, move back."

Kemidov lowered his hands and in triumph demanded, "Now, where are the others?"

"INTERPOL could only spare me. Small budget."

"You are a liar. You are not INTERPOL. They have no sanction to apprehend war criminals. Now where are your NKVD accomplices?"

"I told you."

Kemidov moved over to the table and picked up Joe's .38, a midnight-black Victory model, so named for the "V" prefix placed before the serial number and represented "Victory" against the Axis powers in World War II. He looked carefully at it, pointed it at Joe, and said, "I know yours is a limited operation. A group of criminals operating as intelligence agents. It is too bad you will have to die by your own 'Victory' gun." Kemidov laughed at his joke. "For I assure you, I have every intention of killing you if you do not tell me where your colleagues are and how many guests I should expect."

Joe repeated, "I'm telling you, it's only me. They thought this was a simple arrest."

"Evrard, watch him, while I search our guest." Kemidov banged the .38 on the nearby table and roughly patted Joe down. He opened and searched his jacket. "You must complain to your *INTERPOL* tailor." He looked at the inside pocket and removed the cigarette pack.

"What is this? Somewhat heavy for cigarettes, no?" he said and inspected the pack, holding it up to the light and turning it with his hand. From his experience in espionage Kemidov recognized it was a signaling device. "Clever, quite clever," he remarked admiring the ingenuity. "I take it this is a transmitter, not also receiver? Too small, yes?" he asked. "I want you to contact your associates with this and have them come in." He handed the Chesterfield device back to Joe.

"I can't do that," said Joe as he glanced at his gun lying on the table.

"You can and you will," demanded Kemidov, "because otherwise I plan to make a hole in your skull," Kemidov turned and reached for Joe's gun on the table, "...with your own gun."

Joe warned Kemidov, "I don't think you'll do that."

As Kemidov turned back and pointed the gun right in Joe's face, he snarled, "And why not?"

"Because you'll get my brains all over your pretty paintings."

Evrard said through his teeth, "Let me carve him to pieces."

"You will get your chance, mon ami, but first we must draw the rest of them in." Kemidov shoved the .38 up to Joe's cheek bone and cocked the gun.

Kemidov then lowered the gun, and Joe pulled the small aerial out, which looked just like a cigarette. He waited a second.

"How ingenious. No wonder the Nazis lost," remarked Kemidov.

Speaking into the end of the pack, Joe said, "Joe Brooks calling in. They are under control. Come through the front door. I'll be waiting."

Kemidov laughed "How skillful of you, Mr. Joe Brooks, *INTERPOL man*—'I'll be waiting'— Now we have to let you live a little while longer. Your friends will be expecting you."

"Well, I was more concerned about your paintings," Joe replied with a smile.

"Evrard, wrap up the Falcon and take it to the car."

"Oui." Evrard immediately removed the golden bird, handling it with a newfound reverence. The two French Canadian art mules were still moving paintings into the gallery rooms across from the study. Kemidov looked smugly at Joe, still keeping the .38 pointed straight at him.

A few minutes later, Evrard returned. "What do you want me to do now, Yuri?"

Hoping for some kind of reaction that might give him an opportunity, Joe taunted Kemidov, "Why don't you just let me go, and we'll forget all about this, what do you say?"

"Shut up," said Kemidov and looked to Evrard. "Get the others and set up a crossfire around the front entrance. Tell them to wait until they are all inside before shooting. I don't want any of the NKVD agents to escape." Evrard left to instruct the other men.

Motioning with the cigarette pack, Joe said, "Hey, General, there's a couple of real cigarettes in here. Could I at least have a smoke before all the fireworks start?"

Kemidov reached brusquely for the Chesterfield pack. "Give me those. I shall see if there are genuine cigarettes in here." Kemidov investigated and found real cigarettes. "American," he said in admiration. "The very best. May I join you?"

"Why... will you shoot me if I say no?"

Kemidov gave Joe's gallows humor a wry smile and handed him a cigarette and took one for himself, all the while keeping the .38 trained on him.

Lawrence Hamilton had Bradley repeat Joe's message. "I want it exactly as he said it, so once more."

"Yes, sir. He said exactly this: 'Joe Brooks calling in. They are under control. Come through the front door. I'll be waiting.' And that is all, sir."

Hamilton paused and said, "Joseph's in trouble. He may already be dead."

"What makes you say that?" asked Robert.

"Joseph and I have used the name 'Joe Brooks' as a signal when composing coded messages. A 'Joe Brooks' is an American term for a well-dressed college student. It was his cover signal when there was trouble. His message is a code. He used the full name, plus two words—'calling in.' It must be a space holder, placing the word "they' in the fifth position. So, 'they' equals five. There are most likely five of them. Then he says 'Come through the front door.' We should do just the opposite. However, for appearances, someone must go through the front entrance as if Joseph had everything under control."

Robert said, "I'll take the back, sir."

"Then, Bradley, you will accompany me through the front door. We shall need to make a smashing entrance."

They started back on the road and headed toward Kemidov's Mansion of Art.

Joe took the cigarette and placed it between his lips. Then he went for the oversized Zippo lighter from his shirt pocket and flipped open the lid to light his cigarette. "Oh, my, I'm forgetting my manners. Allow me." Joe extended the opened lighter toward Kemidov, who still held the .38 aimed at Joe's chest.

Kemidov appreciated the gesture and said, "Why, thank you, Mr. Brooks."

Joe turned the lighter so its chimney pointed directly at Kemidov's head. Kemidov, keeping his eye on Joe, leaned slightly forward. Using his index finger, Joe turned the flint wheel and the .22 caliber round fired. Without a muzzle, the sound was deafening. The sound pierced the walls and could be heard all the way to the front entrance where Evrard was orchestrating an ambush. They all froze.

Joe reached for his gun as Kemidov fell backwards. The Zippo's .22 bullet had only grazed Kemidov's left cheekbone, but it stunned him. Joe followed him to the ground and got the .38 away from Kemidov with his left hand. Joe was up in an instant and turned off the lights and ran up the nearby stairs to the second floor. When he reached the top, Evrard and Shorty the French Canadian had already made it to the study. They searched for the light switch. The lights came on. Kemidov was lying in a small puddle of blood, but he struggled to his feet and yelled, "Get back to the front. Go! I am fine. Go!"

Joe eased his way down the dark corridor leading to the opposite side of the foyer. Each end of this Jacobean-style Tudor mansion had a sweeping staircase leading to the entrance foyer below. Joe had positioned himself on the upper floor in the dark at the opposite-side staircase. His heart was racing, his leg throbbing. *Where the hell is Lawrence? He should be here by now.......*

229

Outside, two NKVD agents emerged from the back of the dark woods, racing toward the rear patio. Kemidov's guard was patrolling the rear of the mansion. He hadn't heard Joe's Zippo discharge inside the mansion, but he heard something in the woods. He peered in the dark to see what it was, looking out over the elevated patio.

Robert had entered the grounds of the mansion over the side stone fence and was nearing the back patio stairs. Shots rang out. Kemidov's guard, the one who had been calling the dogs, fell over the balustrade, his gun clattering on the stones below. Robert watched him fall. Dead before he hit the ground. Thinking the battle had begun, Robert leaped up the stone stairs and headed toward the French doors leading into the mansion.

The two NKVD agents were right behind him. One of them bent down and checked the neck of Kemidov's fourth man for life. The other ran up the stairs. Robert heard the footsteps, turned in panic and fired. Missed. The NKVD agent fired off a shot and hit Robert below the left shoulder, knocking him back and to the patio stones. He was alive when the NKVD lead agent made it to the top of the stairs. The leader turned to his partner and said, "Ubyeite yego," and entered the mansion through the French doors. The other NKVD walked over to Robert lying there and aimed his gun at his head.

The NKVD lead man, now just inside the mansion, heard a shot from the patio and smiled in pleasure. The man outside, standing over Robert, fell hard on to the stone patio, a spinal cord shot from behind, just below his neck. He pinned Robert's legs with his lifeless body. Robert struggled to get his legs out from underneath the dead man. He didn't feel the pain of his shoulder wound yet. He freed himself from beneath the dead body and stood up. Confused, he turned and rushed inside. He could hardly see in the dark hallway. He noticed the lead NKVD man twenty feet ahead of him, making his way through a glass door into the heart of the mansion.

The lone NKVD turned his head to signal something to his partner, realized it was Robert, and turned abruptly aiming his gun. This time Robert didn't miss. His shot shattered the glass in the door and entered the lead man's heart. The NKVD man slammed hard into the wall, then slumped to the floor. Robert heard a terrible crash as Hamilton drove the Ambulance through the wrought iron gate with the siren blaring. Hamilton and Bradley flew out of the ambulance, up the stone stairs, and took cover at the corners of the entrance way. Hamilton shot out the glass that flanked the huge arched entrance doors, announcing their arrival.

Immediately Evrard came running back to the grand foyer joined by the little French Canadian. They hid in a study that flanked the foyer. A chandelier the size of a church bell hung directly above the foyer. Joe decided to drop it. From the second floor he fired three times trying to cut its hanger.

It crashed to the floor and shattered into thousands of pieces. That's all it took, Hamilton nodded his head to Bradley. In unison they kicked in the doors and rushed in and fell to the glass-covered marble floor, their weapons firing at everything.

Joe flew down the curved white staircase to where he could see Hamilton. Across the foyer, he saw Shorty taking aim. Joe fired and hit the little man in the chest. He fell instantly, writhing on the ground. Joe kept firing in that direction. Evrard ran through the drawing room adjacent to the study and into the labyrinth of hallways in the interior of the mansion.

The shooting stopped. Joe then made his way down the sweeping staircase to the foyer below, taking each step slowly. Bradley saw him through the blue smoke and raised his gun to shoot, then recognized Joe from photos at Hamilton's briefing.

But he didn't see the tall French Canadian emerge from the grand dining room where most all the paintings and sculptures were stored. From beneath the stairway, the Canadian glimpsed Joe's legs. He was about to swing around and shoot. Bradley saw the movement, took aim, and fired. He missed. Joe leaned over the handrail and fired. The bullet ripped into the French Canadian. He dropped to his knees, then down. His head cracked on the floor.

Bradley got up and ran into the dining room to clear that area. Joe flew down the staircase to the glass-strewn foyer and went to Hamilton and turned him over.

"Lawrence, are you all right?"

"Not at all, my boy." There was blood coming from the corners of his mouth.

"Damn!" Joe yelled.

With his voice garbled by blood, Hamilton said, "Take Bradley and get Kemidov." He paused, spat out some blood. "Take the ambulance. Don't let him escape."

There was no more gunfire. Bradley retreated slowly from the dining room and turned and saw someone kneeling over Hamilton. He pointed his gun and said, "Don't move."

Hamilton said, "This is Joseph." He could hardly breathe now.

Looking at Joe, "I'm sorry, sir. I thought you were on the stairs. I'm Bradley. I didn't know."

"Forget it," said Joe, as he loaded more cartridges from his pocket.

Robert, holding his shoulder, came into the grand foyer. "Where are they?"

"Two dead here," said Bradley.

"Two dead in the rear," said Robert. "I got one, was it you that got the other, sir?"

"No, I was upstairs... inside," said Joe wrinkling his brow, trying to comprehend what Robert just reported. "You're bleeding."

They heard the garage door open. The Mercedes went flying out of the garage, past the ambulance and over the damaged wrought iron gate with a clanking cacophony.

"Bradley, come with me," ordered Joe. Looking at Robert he said, "Stay here with Lawrence. We'll send help."

Bradley ran through the open entrance doors and down the stone stairway to the ambulance. Joe covered his back and followed behind. When he made it to the bottom of the stairs, Rover One and Rover Two were waiting—snarling and barking.

Joe snarled back, "What are you two doing here?"

The dogs heard gun butts in his voice. They whimpered and ran like greyhounds toward the back.

Joe jumped into the driver's seat, and Bradley hopped into the back where all their equipment was, and got on the radio. He called Operation Headquarters to tell them to send medical help immediately to 45 Cercle Belvedere. Joe threw it into reverse, pressed the gas pedal to the floor. When he hit the street, he slammed on the brakes, threw it into first gear, and floored it again, heading down Cercle Belvedere.

Robert was growing weaker from loss of blood. Hamilton was unconscious now. Robert sat down next to him. He examined Hamilton's wound, then his own. *Not good, not good at all,* he thought. His vision was blurred now. Down the long hall from the foyer, from deep within the mansion came a dark figure. Robert saw him but was too weak to raise his gun. He couldn't focus anymore.     ◊◊◊

Joe careened down Avenue Victoria trying to catch up to Kemidov and Molyneaux. They came to the end of the road. The cross street was Chemin de la Cote Saint Luc. "Which way?"

"Hard to say, sir."

"It's your biases that send you on the goose chase." Joe just sat at the intersection. "Well, left is back to toward Montreal. Right is toward what?"

"Toronto, sir," said Bradley in all earnestness.

"He's going to try for the states."

"Quite possibly, sir."

"Knock off the 'sir' stuff—it's Joe."

Bradley smiled and said, "Yes, sir."

Joe gave him a look. "I figure we go toward Toronto. He'll cross at Buffalo. That's my guess."

"Should I call ahead and alert the border men?"

"Why? Don't you think I'll catch up to him?"

"I have every confidence we will... Joe."

"Good—now call ahead." Joe made the right-hand turn and headed out of the area toward Toronto."

Bradley contacted MI5 Canadian Operation Headquarters again and had them alert the border authorities about Kemidov. They drove a circuitous route out of the Mount Royal area. After making a number of turns, Joe noticed a car following them.

"Bradley, I think we're being tailed. I'm not sure though. I'm going to make a few turns and loop back around on myself to see if they follow."

"Very good, Joe."

"I think I like the 'sir' better."

"Yes, sir. I hope Lawrence and Robert are doing well."

"So do I," said Joe as he made a turn. "I knew this might happen."

"In my briefing, Mr. Hamilton had us prepare for violence but doubted whether there would be any."

"Lawrence didn't realize the kind of money that was involved and what desperate people will do for money."

"Mr. Hamilton said this mission was to track down Kemidov and bring him into the system. Isn't that what we're doing?"

"I'm not sure what we're doing. I thought I was locating a lost uncle for my client, giving them a chance to reunite. Then it became something else."

"A noble gesture, nevertheless."

"Noble had nothing to do with it," Joe remarked and made another left-hand turn. The car behind was still following but at quite a distance. "One more turn and I'll know it's a tail." Joe turned left again and continued down the road, watching his mirror. The other car appeared.

"Hang on to your hat," Joe warned as he stepped on the gas. The road was rough, in need of repair. Bradley bounced all over the back of the ambulance. Joe took a hard right. The tail missed the turn and flew right on by. Joe drove about a half mile and turned off his lights and pulled to the side of the road slowly. He came to a stop. "I think we ditched them."

During Joe's rollercoaster ride, Bradley had accidentally hit the switch on the radio locator. It started to power up.

Joe asked, "You know, you're partner, Robert, said there were three guys shot outside the mansion. That makes two extra—I only counted five. The little French Canadian was down and so was the tall one. That leaves one—not three. Kemidov and Molyneaux are ahead of us, so who's been following us?"

"The other two may have been NKVD, as Lawrence had expected. Perhaps our tail is also NKVD," said Bradley.

"This just gets worse," said Joe.

Bradley noticed the scope light up and asked Joe, "Sir, do you have your cigarette transmitter with you?"

"No, it must still be back at that House of Horrors."

Bradley checked the scope and put the headphones on. "I believe you're wrong, sir. The cigarette pack is definitely moving... toward Montreal."

Joe laughed with delight. "Bradley, my man, I think Kemidov still has my cigarette pack on him, and he doesn't even know it." Wasting no time, Joe turned the ambulance around and headed back toward Montreal.

"Sir, I know a shorter route back. Turn left up ahead." Joe followed Bradley's directions, all the while keeping an eye in his mirrors for the tail. They made good time back to the city.

"Sir, they've stopped."

"How far away?"

"The signal is getting stronger. Let's see here," he said adjusting the antenna and watching the scope. "Yes, I would say perhaps three miles, perhaps less."

As they drove into the city, traffic increased. It was late, but the nightlife was just beginning. Bradley's directions led them to an industrial area—warehouses, truck terminals, fabrication shops.

"We are very close," said Bradley. "They are somewhere nearby."

The locator was a crude positioning system. It needed someone to guide them in. Joe cruised down street after street of warehouses and shops.

"We're headed away now, sir."

"Okay, I'll back track," replied Joe as he turned back to where the signal was strongest, looking for something—anything that would lead them to Kemidov.

Joe said, "They've pulled into one of these warehouses. A clever criminal has a backup plan and a safe place in case of trouble. They're going to lay low for a day or two and then take off."

Up one street and down another. The signal was equally strong wherever they went now.

"Signal's gone, sir."

"What do you mean—gone? Check your equipment."

"I don't hear anything or see anything."

Joe said in disappointment, "He found it."

"But he's within a two-mile radius of where we are right now."

"That's one big area," lamented Joe. They kept driving the same roads now. Then Joe said, "I've got an idea. The siren on this thing sounds just like the police. Nobody's in any of these places now. We'll just ride around and see if we scare up something or someone."

"Champion idea, sir."

Joe turned on the siren in each block, watching and waiting for something to happen.

# CHAPTER NINETEEN

MONTREAL
*Warehouse District*

They drove around for over an hour, searching for Kemidov's hideout. Joe said, "I'll do this all night if I have to."

"I was going to say the same thing," agreed Bradley.

Joe noticed the lights go off in one of the warehouses at the end of the block. "That's them. Right down there."

"What makes you say that?"

"Somebody turned their office lights off to get a better look at what's outside. Look at all these other places. Security lights still on. That's them alright."

"What now, sir?"

"I'm going to go maybe three blocks over and turn off the siren. They'll think it's a routine traffic stop. Then we'll pay them a visit."

"And then?"

"Hey, Bradley, I'm working on it." Joe drove three blocks north of the target warehouse. He stopped the ambulance and tried to think. "They might be heading out tomorrow. We have to get them tonight."

"You mean this morning."

"Bradley, don't pick those nits tonight."

"Sorry, sir. What do you suggest?"

"You drive this ambulance straight through the overhead door of that warehouse, right next to the office. If they're in there, they might get a little curious if a car crashes into their building. Drive as fast as you can and hit that door at full speed. This ambulance is built like a tank. You should barrel right through the door."

236

"Where will you be?"

"On my way home, if that's all right with you?" said Joe. "Where do you think I'll be?"

Bradley just looked at him.

Joe continued, "Look, I'm going to get close to the front of that place before you even get there. Then, when you crash through, I'll move in and surprise them when they bolt out to see what happened."

"I'll still be in the ambulance, sir. There are two of them, you know. Maybe more."

"Yeah, but I'm a good shot, and I'm fast. They'll never out gun me. When you do join me, we can take them all safely into custody."

"Appears workable, sir."

Joe drove within two blocks of the two-story warehouse on Brighton Street where Kemidov was holed up. "I'm going to get over there as fast I can. Give me two minutes and blast down that overhead door."

"Understood, sir. Good luck."

"Thanks. Drive carefully," Joe said and got out of the driver's seat and made his way toward the warehouse two blocks over. Bradley turned off the locator and got behind the wheel. He looked at his watch. And waited.

Joe did a quick survey of the warehouse as he approached. The office security lights were back on and there was movement inside. It was time.

Bradley put the ambulance in gear and drove over to Brighton Street and turned right and headed toward the warehouse, increasing his speed. He saw Joe already in position. Bradley made the turn into the truck entrance and stood on the accelerator. He hit the overhead door at nearly forty miles-per-hour.

The jar of the impact ran up Bradley's spine. The entire door crashed down on to the ambulance, ripped away from its supports. Bradley instinctively lowered his head as the roof caved in. He was thrown forward during the crash, his head and chest smashing into the steering wheel. A white flash went off in Bradley's head and he heard thunder. The headlights shattered into powder. He was motionless now. Eyes closed. Head turned awkwardly toward the driver's side window.

Joe rushed into the building and took cover behind some crates no more than ten feet from the office door. Evrard came out first with a gun in his hand. He turned to his left to see the overhead door on top of a vehicle. The dust and smoke obscured the ambulance. He thought the occupants were dead and lowered his gun.

"Hold it right there, Monsieur Molyneaux. Drop the gun. Now!" shouted Joe. Evrard put both hands up but kept the gun. He searched the dark warehouse for where the voice came from. There was nothing but rows of dim spaced bulbs. Then he spotted Joe. He lowered his gun hand slowly. "Throw it on the floor," demanded Joe.

Evrard threw the gun down behind some crates nearby. A split second later he dove for his gun, grabbed it, rolled behind some heavy crates, and started firing in Joe's direction. Joe returned fire. *Where the hell is Bradley?*

But Bradley wasn't going be any help. Joe maneuvered further back into the warehouse looking for a better angle. Shots were fired from the office door. Joe blindly fired back. His last bullet splintered the door jamb. Kemidov slinked back inside the office. Joe spotted a stairway one-hundred feet away that lead up to the warehouse mezzanine. He called to Evrard, "You'd better give up now. I have backup agents." Joe reached in his pocket for his extra bullets. His hands trembled as he loaded each one, the adrenalin racing through his body.

Evrard laughed, "You're sauveur is gone. It is only you and moi, mon ami. Your driver is dead in the automobile, and soon you will be too."

Joe ran up the stairs to the mezzanine overlooking the warehouse main floor. In the dark Joe saw Evrard moving from crate to crate to steel barrel, not offering even one clear shot.

In the dim warehouse light, Joe thought he made out a dark figure closing in on Evrard. Joe blinked hard, trying to pierce the darkness, trying to make sense of what he saw. *Is that a shadow? Bradley!*

There was the blinding flash of a gunshot and the sound ringing into silence. Evrard fell hard on the floor, shot in the back. Joe ran down the stairs toward Evrard, grateful that Bradley had shot him. He reached the body and checked his neck pulse. Dead. He picked up Evrard's gun and from behind he heard, "I'll take that, peeper."

Joe froze....

"And I was just starting to miss you," Joe said.

"Shut up and put his gun—and yours—over on that crate and step back," ordered Ferrel.

"You know, I underestimated you, Ferrel."

"Everybody does."

"What now?"

"Whatever the boss says," Ferrel said as he threw the guns away toward some crates in the back of the warehouse. "I'd prefer to drop you right here." Ferrel motioned with his gun. "Now move." Joe put his hands up and walked ahead of Ferrel back to the office.

Joe dropped his right hand cautiously to open the office door. Then he walked in with both hands raised. It took a few seconds for his eyes to adjust to the bright office lights. He squinted momentarily. As soon as his eyes grew accustomed to the light, his fears were realized.

He saw Polina with a gun in her hand pointed directly at Kemidov. All along Joe suspected Polina might be a NKVD agent. Then Detective Donnelly said something that made him think perhaps she might be someone from Kemidov's past. Either way, Joe planned to get to Kemidov first and hand him over to Hamilton and MI5. Now all he could do is look for some opportunity before they killed him.

"Polina!" Joe exclaimed. "What are you—? For God's sake that's your uncle."

Kemidov shouted in protest, "I have never seen this woman in my life. I have no niece." Then he pleaded, "Where is Evrard?"

"He's dead," said Ferrel, "just like you pretty soon."

Kemidov was shaking. "Dead?" He lowered his head. Polina walked over to him and slapped Kemidov hard with her gun, opening up the glancing bullet wound the cigarette gun had made on his left side earlier. He almost fell to the floor.

"Where is it?" she demanded.

"Where is what?" replied Kemidov.

She slapped him again, only harder. The side of his head was bloodied and swelling, his cheekbone cracked. "If I have to ask you again, I will have Mr. Ferrel cut your fingers off one by one until I get an answer."

"I don't know.... I don't know you.... I don't know what you are talking about. I—"

"You don't know me?" Polina said defiantly. "I'm Rhea Gutman. Remember that name: Gutman?"

Joe could now weave all the pieces together, staring at Polina now Rhea, the child mentioned by Detective Donnelly sent years ago to a mental hospital. The emotion on her face was grotesque. Rage, hate, vengeance. He had to think of something. Anything. Ferrel's gun was aimed right at him, close range, at his chest.

Kemidov stammered, "Gutman? I don't—"

Rhea said, "Kasper Gutman was my father. Do you remember him?" She viciously hit Kemidov again. Ferrel just smiled.

"No, I don't remember any— "

"You swindled my father out of $10,000 for a worthless falcon statue," Rhea said. "I am here to recover the authentic Falcon of Malta. Now, where is it?"

"Gutman?" muttered Kemidov, searching his memories. After a moment, "Ah, the fat man, yes, yes. Now I remember... I remember... but it was *he* who tried to swindle me. He made a ridiculous offer that he knew I could not accept. Then he sent his agents to coerce me into selling. And I let them of course. Oh, please, I will certainly return your father's money—with interest—but I no longer have the Falcon."

Rhea snarled, "You filthy liar. My father was killed because of that statue. Do you understand? Gunned down in the street like a dog when I was a girl. I want what belongs to me. Now!"

"But I told you, I don't have the Falcon," pleaded Kemidov.

"I tracked you all over Europe until the war broke out. I almost had you in Zurich, but you had help from the NKVD. They moved you to Paris, but then Paris fell to the Nazis.

"But that was no problem for a parasite like you. Your cover as Hugo Morand the art dealer let you procure paintings and antiquities for high-ranking Nazis, while at the same time collecting valuable intelligence from your Nazi plunderers and selling it to the Soviets. You made a fortune, didn't you *Hugo*?"

"I will pay you anything you want—any amount," pleaded Kemidov.

"I don't want your blood-stained money, you pig. I want the Falcon."

"I don't have it anymore. I sold it years ago."

"Oh, you have it, Yuri," said Rhea confidently. "I know you have it because I, too, was working for the Soviets. My control agent was also yours. Of course you did not know that, did you?"

"I don't believe you," said Kemidov.

"Ernst was my control," Rhea said with an unflinching Cheshire smile.

Kemidov gasped at the name "Ernst?" That was his London NKVD control agent. His real name was Nicky Rostov, a German Jewish refugee and devote communist. Kemidov sent his mostly notional accounts through a contact in Lisbon to Ernst. That contact was Rhea Gutman.

"I was your letter drop contact in Lisbon. I decoded all your reports using Thackeray's *The Four Georges*. Isn't that right, Yuri?"

Kemidov's shoulders slumped. "Yes... but how did you...?"

"Once I discovered your identity, I wormed my way into Rostov's organization. It was all the easier because I was part Jewish with a German name. I became an insignificant link in the Lisbon NKVD operation. I could care less about their stupid ideologies. I only wanted you.

"I read every one of your reports and discovered early on that they were as counterfeit as your identity. Eventually Ernst also became aware of your charade.

"Ernst came to Lisbon. We discussed your removal. I did not want them to kill you before I had the opportunity to locate the Falcon, so I offered to do the garbage disposal myself. At first Ernst resisted, not confident I could get the job done.

"But, I told him how I could get to Paris through my contacts in the Nazi Abwehr for a little vacation. I am very persuasive with men, you see."

"So, why didn't you kill me then?" Kemidov asked with the vaporous hope that he could somehow negotiate his way out of his predicament.

"I can answer that," said Joe, taking a chance.

"Shut up, peeper," snarled Ferrel.

"No, let him talk," said Rhea.

Joe continued, "See, Uncle Yuri, your niece here discovered you still had the Falcon, and if she killed you... well, she couldn't get her hands on it. So, she teamed up with rogue NKVD agents and regaled them with tales of your other art treasures."

From the corner of his eye, Joe looked for even a moment's distraction in Ferrel's gaze, but those dead eyes revealed nothing. Joe continued, "They all knew about Operation Overlord, the Normandy invasion. They knew France would soon be liberated, and the Germans would be on the run. So they just had to wait for your Nazi protectors to flee and for the Allies to take over. These NKVD agents would grab you at the opportune time and torture you into revealing everything. And *then* they would have killed you. Simple, isn't it?"

"But this dog got away," snapped Rhea. "He escaped to London with the help of a separate NKVD extraction unit. To cover your tracks, you had them kill Ernst, saying he was a traitor working with the Nazis. You were in a new theater and back in the espionage business, sitting on a fortune in art.

"I eventually tracked you down. I almost had you again at the Alhambra Hotel, Mon Général, but you slithered away from me and my associates. Not this time."

Trying to create an opening, using anger and indignation, Joe yelled, "No, this time you got me to hunt down your prey. You knew all along where Kemidov was headed, but you needed someone with connections in MI5 and the FBI. Where and how did you ever learn about me?"

"Settle down, gumshoe," growled Ferrel.

Rhea answered, "The NKVD has dossiers on Allied operatives. I learned about your service with your OSS, your Office of Strategic Services, and their links to the FBI. I know of your involvement with NKVD agent Kira Maslan and the bomb and what happened in that operation. You were perfect for my needs, and thank you for locating this vermin for me."

"You're not welcome."

Kemidov blurted out, "But, please, I do not have the Falcon. Your information was wrong. Yes, I have many valuable paintings, but the Falcon was sold years ago."

Rhea said with teeth clenched, "I would like nothing better than to hear your screams of agony as Mr. Ferrel cuts your fingers off one by one." Rhea looked over at Ferrel and said, "Begin now."

"Watch your peeper. If he moves, shoot him."

Rhea trained her gun on Joe. Ferrel holstered his weapon and unsheathed a hunting knife from beneath his coat. "This will be a pleasure."

Kemidov cowered in the corner of the office, falling over the desk and chair. "No, please, please. I beg of you," screamed Kemidov.

Ferrel walked slowly toward him.

Rhea jeered, "That must be how the Jews you betrayed in Paris must have pleaded to the Gestapo as they were being arrested and dragged away to the death camps. How does it feel, General?"

"Polina... Rhea... you can't do this," Joe insisted.

"I will avenge my father," Rhea said seething with emotion. "Kemidov set this all in motion and now he must pay. Continue, Mr. Ferrel." She backed further away from Joe, wanting to watch Ferrel mutilate Kemidov without giving Joe a chance to disarm her.

Kemidov was no match for Ferrel as he yanked him off the floor with one hand. He grabbed Kemidov's right hand and slammed it down on the desk, pounding Kemidov's hand with the rear bolster of the knife handle to open his clenched fist. As soon as it was opened, Ferrel jammed it flat with his full strength, nearly breaking his fingers. He slowly brought the knife blade to Kemidov's index finger, the blade slitting the skin, blood weeping, and....

"Stop...stop," shouted Kemidov. "I will tell you. I will tell you. Please. Please."

Ferrel let him go and said, "Where?"

"It is in a small box on the mezzanine floor in the back of the warehouse."

"Mr. Ferrel," Rhea said, "take the brave General Kemidov and get the Falcon. If it is not there, kill him on the spot, and we shall leave." Frankie Ferrel grabbed Kemidov, now shaking uncontrollably, bleeding from the temple and hand. He dragged him like a child out of the office to the same stairs Joe had used to get onto the mezzanine.

"What are you looking at?" snapped Rhea, as Joe looked at her.

"You don't have to do this."

"Do what?"

"You're going to kill him and me over a statue?"

"Not just any statuette, Mr. Ganzer—*this* is the Falcon."

"End this now. Let the authorities handle Kemidov."

Rhea said defiantly, "And who are the authorities—you?"

"I was working with them, yes." Joe took a half step toward her.

"That I knew and expected. Why do you think I chose you, Joe?"

"Nice...."

"And you're a fool, Joe Ganzer," remarked Rhea. "That made it so much easier, and you are an attractive man, so it was not all that unpleasant, you understand. And if you move another inch closer to me, I will kill you."

Joe waved his arm around the room. "All this because he cheated your father?" Joe inched closer to Rhea.

"My father was killed over that statue," she said, "shot down in the street by his lunatic boy gunman when the Falcon he spent fifteen years searching for turned out to be a fake, sold to him by General Kemidov. And to think, Kemidov has no idea what that Falcon truly is."

"I understand other people were killed as well, probably on your father's orders. I learned that a man named Thursby was murdered in San Francisco maybe by your father's little gunman. And Frankie Ferrel knew this Thursby, and Thursby knew about the statue. You're playing with dynamite here."

"What do you mean, I am playing with—"

The office door flew open and Ferrel shoved Kemidov through it into the room. He followed him in holding the little crate. He pushed Kemidov again to the back of the office by the desk, where he set the crate.

"Open it, open it," said Rhea.

Ferrel used his oversized knife to pry open the crate. It was filled with excelsior. He dug inside and removed the Falcon and set it on the desk. Ferrel moved back, pulled his gun out, and aimed it at Joe.

"This is it... the Falcon of Malta," exclaimed Rhea.

Rhea was spellbound, recalling all the many years she'd spent searching for Kemidov, now finding him, and at last possessing the Falcon, as if that could somehow avenge her father. The feelings of triumph engulfed her. She approached the Falcon as if it were an altar to God. She examined it carefully, leaning it back to reveal the bizarre symbols etched into the entire base.

"This is most truly the Falcon of Malta."

Like the strike of a cobra, Rhea's gun was now in Kemidov's hand, and his free arm was around her neck, nearly breaking it. With her as a shield, Kemidov shouted, "Stand back, I say." His eyes were wild with fear. "Drop your gun, Mr. Ferrel."

Frankie Ferrel pulled the trigger. The shot rang out. The room was filled with deafening noise and blue smoke. His .45-caliber bullet went through Rhea's heart and lodged in Kemidov's liver. He doubled over in pain, letting go of Rhea. They both fell to the floor. With lethal speed and accuracy, he shot again—putting a fatal bullet in Kemidov's chest.

Joe was already leaping across the small room at Ferrel, bolted, swinging his arm down as hard as he could to dislodge the .45 Colt. They fell together on top of the bodies of Rhea and Kemidov. Ferrel's gun bounced on the floor away from them, but Rhea's 9mm was still close by. They struggled to get to it. The blood made their hands slippery as each tried to grab the 9mm.

Ferrel got it first. As they rolled around on the floor, Joe tried to pry it loose with both hands. Ferrel pounded Joe in the head with his other fist. Joe kneed Ferrel in the groin. Ferrel reflexively convulsed, but he wouldn't let go of the gun. The gun came between them now.

The sound of the shot filled the room. The bullet penetrated Joe on his right side, through the lung, and lodged in his back. Joe rolled off Ferrel, who was still reeling from the knee he took. He shoved Joe over onto his stomach and got up. Ferrel loomed over Joe, breathing heavy. He was clearing his head from the struggle.

The Falcon lays on the floor lodged between the bodies of Kemidov and Rhea, covered in blood. The gold and the jewels and the red blood produced a grotesque abstraction of art and wealth and death.

Ferrel picked it up and smiled at his success. He had always planned to kill Rhea once he had the genuine Falcon. Kemidov's bold play only changed the timetable. The result was the same.

Ferrel saw Joe was still breathing. He walked toward him and moved the 9mm in line with Joe's head. As he bent forward to deliver the fatal shot, Joe rolled over and discharged his cigarette lighter gun. The bullet entered Ferrel's eye socket and pierced and shattered the orbital cavity, tore apart his eye, changed direction, splintered the bone, and careened off the inside of his skull and churned the killer's brains.

The Falcon crashed to the floor, and Ferrel collapsed heavily upon Joe.

Joe struggled to get Ferrel's body off of him, but he didn't have the strength. He could hardly breathe. He looked down at his chest soaked in blood. *This is bad.* He looked away from his chest, to ignore the horror of a hole in his body. He looked to his left. The bottom of the Falcon faced him. He focused on the strange symbols and then drifted unconscious....

Someone lifted Ferrel's body off of him. Joe's eyes flashed open in sheer panic.

He tried to focus. The ominous figure above him was tall, pale, and gaunt. Joe somehow recognized him. *Wait...no!*

The stranger said, "I am sorry...."

"Not, not *you*...."

He knew. This was Death come to claim him, like he'd read long ago in the *Appointment in Samarra*. He escaped Death before, but there could be no escape now.

In his delirium, Joe's mind summoned the ancient Babylonian myth of the merchant's servant in the Baghdad marketplace threatened by Death. The servant ran from Death and begged his master for his horse so he could flee to Samarra where Death surely could not find him. The merchant granted his wish and off he fled.

The merchant then went to the marketplace in Baghdad and confronted Death. "Why did you threaten my servant?"

Death replied, "I did not threaten your servant. It was a start of surprise. I was astonished to see him in Baghdad, for I had an appointment with him tonight in Samarra."


"...I am sorry that I am so late, but you eluded me with your driving skills back on Mount Royal. I am afraid I lost you for a time," said the stranger whose eyes were deep-set and melancholy. "Your injury is quite severe, Mr. Ganzer."

"What?" exclaimed Joe, now regaining his senses. "You... you know me? How?"

"For now, that does not matter. I need to check the others." The stranger rose and went to examine each of the others. All dead. He returned to Joe.

"I'm going to get my medical kit. I will return shortly." The stranger left the room.

It really didn't matter to Joe now. There is a quiet resolve that comes over a soldier when wounded and life is pouring out of him, a realization that nothing matters anymore, the despair of death.

The stranger returned. He bent down near Joe and opened up his kit. He placed a rolled up towel beneath his head and gently opened Joe's shirt. He examined the wound clinically, without emotion. He took battle dressings, which were large absorbent pads, and applied them to the site. Between the pain and the blood loss, the window to the conscious world was closing again. Joe was losing. He was on the edge of this reality, slipping into the next. He tried several times to rise.

"Please be still, Mr. Ganzer. I am nearly finished." The stranger applied medical tape to secure the pads to reduce the bleeding. He then reached around inside Joe's shirt checking for an exit wound. He couldn't find one. After the battle dressing was soaked, he removed it and began using an antiseptic solution to clean the area. He noted that the bullet entry was low on the chest and possibly the bullet missed the lung or only pierced the lower lobe.

Joe, bleary-eyed and disoriented, clenching his teeth and grimacing in pain, his voice garbled, "Who are you?"

To refocus Joe's mind while he cleaned the entry area, the stranger answered, "We are the Poor Travelers. I am one of many. I am Mr. Gore. We have searched for this Falcon a great long time. It belongs to us. And after all these years, it was *you* who was sent to recover it."

Joe tried to rise but was gently restrained. "So, you're Gore. Now I can put a face to the name . Where are your two friends?"

Mr. Gore smiled and said, "Forever the detective."

"You've been shadowing us since we crossed into Canada. Why?"

"Although we were sent as guardians, only you could free our precious bird from the fowler's snare. You see, this has always been your destiny, Mr. Ganzer."

Through the fog of pain Joe struggled again to sit up. " I don't undersssstaa..."

"Please, Mr. Ganzer. You must remain still." Mr. Gore guided him back down and said, "Let me explain. Once we had a great many such precious objects. They were lost in time or stolen. We were the victims of intrigue and base politics. For the Poor Travelers, the value of this statue lies not in its gold or its precious gems. The Falcon is the key that will unlock treasures of our Order hidden long, long ago."

As he reapplied clean dressing to the chest wound, Mr. Gore said, "Centuries ago our Order was held in great esteem for our service to the Father and his Son, protecting pilgrims to and from the Holy Land. We fought valiantly over the years to prevent the Holy Land from falling into the hands of the children of Ishmael."

Mr. Gore applied additional tape to the wound and continued, "We became the most powerful military order in the Middle Ages. At our pinnacle we numbered in the tens of thousands. Our empire was unrivaled in Medieval Europe, with riches beyond imagination. Our power had no limits, except those of the Pope.

"We created a banking arrangement for travelers to the Holy Land that became the very foundation for today's modern banking system. We were lenders to emperors, priests, nobles, and kings. The Order became wealthy, not only in terms of finance, but in knowledge and wisdom. Our clients were among the richest royal families, all seeking our protection and counsel.

"But scurrilous deceptions, greed, and lies destroyed our Order from without and within, and scattered our members to the four corners of the world. We have been maligned through the centuries for everything from devil worship to blasphemy and sexual immorality. None of it true."

He removed the bloody kerchief and began to clean the leg where the dog had mangled him. "This great war in Europe has provided an opportunity for us to re-establish our Order and protect the Holy Land, though not as before. Soon a new nation will rise. God will gather his people from all the nations of the world and return them after two thousand five hundred years to their promised land, and we shall be there to help make it possible."

Mr. Gore then carefully bandaged Joe's leg and said, "This is all I can do now. You need more help than I can provide. I wish that I had additional morphine in this kit to ease your pain."

"Some pain can't be relieved by morphine, but your story... it helps."

"For that I am glad. I must ask that you not mention what I've told you here today to anyone else, not that they would believe you in any event."

Joe almost smiled.

"I have already called for an ambulance, Mr. Ganzer."

Disguising the pain, his breath shallow, and his voice garbled by blood, "I'll be all right."

"We will be forever in your debt, Mr. Ganzer."

The Poor Traveler departed, cradling the Maltese Falcon.

# CHAPTER TWENTY

*Three days later*
MONTREAL
*General Hospital*

As the sedative released its grip, Joe saw a nurse hovering over him. "Mr. Ganzer, you have visitors, and then she left. Joe tried to focus on the figures surrounding his bed. He heard a woman's voice

"Damn you, Joe Ganzer. You gave us quite a scare. I just—"

"Wilma?" Joe said and blinked a few times, his vision adjusting to the bright lights. "Benny... Ludko!"

Ludko said, "It's good to hear your voice, Joe."

"Yeah," said Benny the Hat. "We thought you was a goner."

Through tears Wilma scolded Benny, "Don't even say that."

Ludko came to Benny's defense,"Yeah, but, Wilma, he's lucky to even be here." Ludko looked straight at Joe and said, "See what happens when you don't have me and Benny around to take care of yuh."

Joe smiled, his eyes blurred again, "It's so good to see you guys, so good. You don't know how much I've missed all of you, and I can't believe you came all the way up here."

Wilma said, "The Montreal Police called the office and said you were in critical condition. They said you'd been shot. That's all we had to hear."

Benny said, "Yeah, that's all."

Ludko's voice lowered, "Joe, if I'da known, I woulda never—"

Joe stopped him, "I knew from the start, Lud. I had to do this. You know that."

Ludko asked, "Yeah, but what went wrong?"

"Everything."

Wilma added, "I told you that woman was no good. You should have listened to me."

"Next time I might."

Ludko got serious. "Joe, is this thing over?"

"It's over, Lud, forever."

"What happened? How'd yuz get shot?" asked Benny.

"Frankie Ferrel shot me in a struggle over a gun," explained Joe.

"Ferrel's dead, Joe," reported Ludko, delighted to make the announcement.

"I sort of figured."

Outside the door of Joe's room, they heard the voice of a little boy. "Dad, can we go in? Is he really shot? Is he gonna die or something?"

Then, they heard a man's voice. "Tommy, we have to wait now. He can't have a lot of visitors."

Joe immediately smiled and called out, "Is that Tommy Della Penna, my ace detective?"

Tommy came bursting through the door with Johnny following after him. "I'm sorry, Joe," said Johnny.

"Hey, Uncle Joe, did you really get shot?"

"Yes, I did, Tommy, right under these bandages here."

"Wow! Are you gonna die?"

"Tommy!" scolded Johnny.

Joe answered, "No, not now that I've got my ace here to hold off the bad guys."

"I will too," said Tommy with fierce determination.

"How yuh doin', Joe?" asked Johnny.

"I'm a lot better."

"I shoulda gone with you that night."

"Not your problem John, but thanks."

"Hey, I'm still workin' on the docks," said Johnny proudly. "Marcel said he's gonna get me in the union up here."

"John, I could get the Chicago local to let you in."

"I'm movin' up here, Joe."

Joe was delighted. "Really? I thought you were kidding me before."

"No—Ludko told me there's no more charges on me for that liquor heist, and Zoé said she'd like for me to move up here, and Tommy will have a mom—"

"You don't mean?" asked Joe, knowing the answer.

"Yeah... well I'm hopin'.'"

"I guess you *were* serious before. I'm glad for you, John, real glad."

"I owe you another one," said Johnny.

Joe laughed and said, "Wilma, send him a bill."

"Come on, Tommy, we gotta let Mr. Ganzer rest. So long, Joe."

"See yuh, Uncle Joe," said Tommy. He waved as his dad picked him up and carried him out of Joe's room.

"See you, Tommy. Take care of your dad now."

"I will," he said as the door closed.

"He's a good kid," said Joe.

Ludko added, "There's no charges on Johnny, but it'll be good that he's away from those guys from now on."

Joe nodded. "What's happening with all that? You heard anything?"

"Yeah," said Ludko. "Rossi and Santori are almost in a gang war over that liquor."

"I hope they both lose."

"Speakin' of them guys. Yuh know who I heard died?"

"No, who?"

"Jimmy 'Mad Bomber' Belcastro."

"They whacked him?" asked Benny.

"No," said Ludko, turning to Benny. "I heard it was a heart attack."

Joe added, shaking his head, "His heart? Imagine that: a guy survives being shot five times in the head and body and ends up dying from natural causes."

Ludko looked back at Joe, raising his eyebrows, staring. "*Some guys* are lucky." He paused and asked. "Joe, how'd a missing person case end up like this?"

"It was never about a person. I was about a thing, a relic, a priceless little statue— the Falcon of Malta—solid gold and covered with jewels. It was truly a fascinating piece of art and history. That's what everybody was after, and *Polina* wasn't who she said she was, either."

Wilma blurted out, "I knew it."

"Joe, you sorta figured she wasn't on the level or you wouldn't've had us tailin' her," Benny said.

"I only had suspicions. Her real name was Rhea Gutman, the daughter of a fanatical art collector named Kasper Gutman.

General Kemidov swindled her father. He pulled a switch scam on him. Gutman gave Kemidov ten grand, and Kemidov gave him a fake statue. As it turned out, Kasper Gutman got himself killed over the thing by his own gunman. His daughter, Rhea, used me to find Kemidov, which I did. She intended to get the real statue and have Frankie Ferrel kill the General as vengeance for her father. Instead, Ferrel killed them both, and he almost killed me."

Benny was curious. "So how'd yuh get Ferrel if he shot youz first?"

"Lawrence Hamilton, God rest his soul—"

From across the room in the other bed a voice said, "A bit hasty in your eulogies, Joseph," said Hamilton.

Joe blinked his eyes again and looked over at the other bed and yelled: "Lawrence... Lawrence.... I'm so, so glad to—You can't believe—I thought you were... " Joe looked and said, " Wilma, Ludko, Benny meet my old associate from the British Isles."

They all politely offered their greetings.

Joe went on and said, "Honestly, Lawrence, I didn't think an ambulance would get to you in time. We called as soon as we took off, but I didn't think—"

"Robert didn't make it, Joseph," said Hamilton. "I almost didn't either. The strangest thing.... I saw a figure coming toward me after you and Bradley left. I must have lost consciousness, but the emergency crew said I was treated on site, so was Robert. But he lost so much blood there was no chance."

Joe listened in disbelief. He couldn't help but think it was one of the Mr. Gore's Poor Travelers. Then Joe asked, "What about Bradley?"

Hamilton said, "He is back on duty somewhere in London by now, I would imagine. He had a nasty bump on the head from that crash entry you had him do."

Still curious, Benny asked, "So how'd Lawrence help you shoot Ferrel?"

"Well, he gave me a cigarette lighter that was actually a gun, a gun I used on Ferrel. That's all I remember."

The nurse returned and said, "Alright, folks, he's had enough excitement for today. We will release him day after tomorrow if you don't wear him out tonight."

Wilma said, tears still in her eyes, "We're taking you home."

"Yeah, sure, coupla days, Joe," said Benny as he and Wilma turned toward the door.

Ludko couldn't look at Joe. He just waved as he averted his glazed eyes from him and headed to the door with a slight sniffle, disguised with a cough, and said, "Must be this cold weather up here."

They were gone. It was quiet now.

Joe looked across to Hamilton and said, "You lost your target."

Hamilton considered that for a second. "But I have my friend."

"I was just...." Joe let that go and then, "A guy treated my wounds that night, too. His name was Mr. Gore. He called himself a Poor Traveler." Joe paused. He was tired now but added, "He has that statue. Said it belongs to them."

Hamilton leaned back again in his bed and whispered, "The Poor Knights of the Temple of Solomon."

"Yeah."

# EPILOGUE

*Eight Months Later*
SOUTH CHICAGO
*Jos. Ganzer Investigations*


Friday, April 26, 1947 (Evening)


It had been a long week. Ludko and Benny had just left after helping finish up a difficult case involving a gruesome murder. For Joe it was just like it was before the war. He put his feet up on the desk and unfolded the last of his three newspapers, the *Chicago Herald-American*.

Joe liked this paper best. The antics of its reporters were sometimes more interesting than the news itself. They even made a screwball comedy based on the paper called *The Front Page* with Adolphe Menjou and Pat O'Brien. It was remade in 1940 as *His Girl Friday* with Cary Grant and Rosalind Russell—Joe's favorite of the two.

He read stories about the two presidential candidates Harry S. Truman and Thomas E. Dewey. When he got to page three, he stopped. He sat up straight, stunned by the headline at the bottom of the page on a single-column story.

## Six Poor Travelers Visit
## Aircraft Tunnels in England

Rochester, England--On the night of April 19, 1947, six young men contacted the co-workers of the Short Brothers' Ministry of Aircraft Production underground seaplane manufacturing works on the River Medway demanding a site observation. The six men identified themselves as "The Poor Travelers" and promised £5,000 (about $8000) to whosoever gave them a tour of the tunnels.

The tunnels were meant to house 75 new machine tools, as the existing works were at full capacity. Although the tunnels were more expensive than a surface building, they spared the Medway estuary.

The project involved excavating two parallel tunnels, each one a little over a football field long or 328 feet. These were linked by four adits almost 250 feet long. The tunnels were cut from chalk and lined with brick. Two ventilation shafts ran at 45 degrees to the surface.

Because of the war, the company built an extensive network of air raid shelter tunnels at the eastern end of the facility. These tunnels ran parallel to the cliff face, and each was 300 yards in length and had 14 crosscuts. These connected to the Shorts Factory tunnels by a single tunnel 1300 feet long with nine adits of varying lengths out of the cliff face.

The Poor travelers told the workers "Their inquisition was a high interest in the art of stone masonry and would like to see such work in progress". So on the 19th of April, six "Poor Travelers" had their first tour of the yet unfinished tunnels, from a man known only as Mr. Gore. The Poor Travelers, as well as their guide Mr. Gore, were never seen again.

Joe read the short article again and then again. *This is fantastic,* he thought. *Mr. Gore and the Poor Travelers are real.* He never trusted his memory of that night up in Canada.

Memory is such a poor journal. Pages get mixed up and out of sequence, especially after being shot. Joe's garbled memory prevented him from remembering everything, but he was able to piece together all the stories told by General Kemidov and Mr. Gore. What he needed were the details, which he found during his recovery.

After returning to Chicago, Joe spent nearly every day at the Chicago Public Library or at the Oriental Institute of the University of Chicago (his almost alma mater) searching for answers, answers to Mr. Gore and the Poor Travelers and the Knights Templar and the Falcon. For a time, this search gave him a reprieve from the dreams and from the things he wanted to forget.

Those questions sustained him during his long recovery. Where were the Poor Travelers from? Where are they now? What is next for Mr. Gore?

Joe thought he was onto something one day when a research librarian at the Chicago Public Library on Randolph Street and Michigan Avenue mentioned a story by Charles Dickens entitled *Seven Poor Travellers.*

Joe had to know more, so she took him up the Grand Staircase beneath the Tiffany Dome to the second floor of the library where she located the book for him. He read the story eagerly.

It told the tale of seven travelers all gathered for Christmas Eve dinner in the old city of Rochester at Watt's Charity, a sparse almshouse, where the six share their stories—the seventh traveler is the storyteller. None of the stories intersect or overlap in any way. The travelers just go their separate ways, and the reader is left to imagine what happened to them, where did they travel after that one night spent together, where did their lives end up.

That summed up Joe's feelings about Mr. Gore and his fellow travelers. His other research confirmed that the Knights Templar were the victims of conspiracy and betrayal. Their demise was the result of power games of the Royal House of France. In a monograph he found at the Oriental Institute, Joe discovered the Templars had indeed carved elaborate symbols in various castle dungeons where they were held and tortured. The symbols were similar to what Joe recalled from the bottom of the Falcon.

One of the last things he remembered was Mr. Gore telling him the Falcon was some kind of key. Joe reasoned it might be a cipher key, like the poem code.

He put down the paper, leaned back, and stared up at the metal ceiling tiles of his office. Joe smiled and nodded slightly. *God bless you, Mr. Gore... wherever you are.*

"It's late, Joe. I'm going home," said Wilma.

"Okay, see you in the morning. I'll be here awhile......."

# AUTHOR'S NOTE

## The Poor Travelers

The Short Brothers PLC (often called Shorts) was an aerospace company made famous in WWII for its manufacture of an effective anti-submarine patrol bomber—the Sunderland, a long-range and long-flying aircraft that closed the Mid-Atlantic gap between Iceland and Greenland, which helped end the Battle of the Atlantic. Shorts work on the Sunderland led to a contract for the Short Stirling, the RAF's first four-engine bomber.

During the Battle of Britain, the German Luftwaffe heavily bombed the Short Brothers' Rochester factory. The Shorts asked the Ministry of Aircraft Production (MAP) if they could build a new underground factory in tunnels excavated under chalk cliffs. MAP gave the go ahead and the tunnels were excavated. For a tour of the tunnels, search on YouTube for *"Rochester - Shorts Brothers Seaplane Factory and public air raid shelter."*

The connection between the Knights Templar and the Shorts Brothers' tunnels emerged after the war. Records briefly described the visit to the underground facility by six young men calling themselves "The Poor Travelers" accompanied by a Mr. Gore. The following is a link to the actual story:

*"The Templars and the Shorts"*

(http://everything.explained.at/Knights_Templar_in_England/)

# APPENDIX

## Cryptography

### Slater Telegraphic Code

The Slater Telegraphic Code was created for secrecy. It was first published in 1870, just after Her Majesty's government took control of the United Kingdom's telegraph system.

Slater's Code consists of a vocabulary of 25,000 words arranged 100 words to a page in two columns. The first 24,000 words comprise a dictionary in alphabetical order. The final 1,000 expressed proper names, geographic names and even names of deities and heroes (presumably because ships were often named after mythological characters). Each word was assigned a five-digit number from 00001 through 25000.

A copy of the Slater Code may be downloaded from Google Books using the following search: **slater telegraphic code**. The following is a sample page:

— 56 —

| TEX | ( 112 ) | THR | 224 |
|---|---|---|---|

| Word | No. | Word | No. |
|---|---|---|---|
| Textual ... ... ... | 22301 | Thing ... ... ... | 22351 |
| Texture ... ... ... | 22302 | Think ... ... ... | 22352 |
| Than ... ... ... | 22303 | Thinking ... ... | 22353 |
| Thank ... ... ... | 22304 | Thinks ... ... ... | 22354 |
| Thanked ... ... | 22305 | Thinly ... ... ... | 22355 |
| Thanking ... ... | 22306 | Third ... ... ... | 22356 |
| Thanks ... ... ... | 22307 | Thirst ... ... ... | 22357 |
| That ... ... ... | 22308 | Thirsting ... ... | 22358 |
| Thatch ... ... ... | 22309 | Thirsty ... ... ... | 22359 |
| Thaw ... ... ... | 22310 | Thirteen ... ... .. | 22360 |
| Thawed ... ... ... | 22311 | Thirteenth ... ... | 22361 |
| Thawing ... ... ... | 22312 | Thirtieth ... ... | 22362 |
| The ... ... ... ... | 22313 | Thirty ... ... ... | 22363 |
| Theatre ... ... ... | 22314 | This ... ... ... | 22364 |
| Thee ... ... ... | 22315 | Thither ... ... ... | 22365 |
| Theft ... ... ... | 22316 | Thorn ... ... ... | 22366 |
| Their ... ... ... | 22317 | Thorny ... ... ... | 22367 |
| Theirs ... ... ... | 22318 | Thorough ... ... | 22368 |
| Theist ... ... ... | 22319 | Thoroughfare... ... | 22369 |
| Them ... ... ... | 22320 | Thoroughly ... ... | 22370 |
| Theme ... ... ... | 22321 | Those ... ... ... | 22371 |
| Themselves ... ... | 22322 | Thou ... ... ... | 22372 |
| Then ... ... ... | 22323 | Though ... ... ... | 22373 |
| Thence ... ... ... | 22324 | Thought... ... ... | 22374 |
| Theodolite ... ... | 22325 | Thoughtful ... ... | 22375 |
| Theology ... ... | 22326 | Thoughtless ... ... | 22376 |
| Theory ... ... ... | 22327 | Thoughtlessly ... | 22377 |
| There ... ... ... | 22328 | Thousand ... ... | 22378 |
| Thereby ... ... ... | 22329 | Thousandth ... ... | 22379 |
| Therefore ... ... | 22330 | Thraldom ... ... | 22380 |
| Therefrom ... ... | 22331 | Thrash ... ... ... | 22381 |
| Therein ... ... ... | 22332 | Thrashed ... ... | 22382 |
| Thereof ... ... ... | 22333 | Thrashing ... ... | 22383 |
| Thereon ... ... ... | 22334 | Thread ... ... ... | 22384 |
| Thereunto ... ... | 22335 | Threat ... ... ... | 22385 |
| Thereupon ... ... | 22336 | Threaten ... ... | 22386 |
| Therewith ... ... | 22337 | Threatened ... ... | 22387 |
| Thermal ... ... ... | 22338 | Threatening ... ... | 22388 |
| Thermometer... ... | 22339 | Three ... ... ... | 22389 |
| These ... ... ... | 22340 | Threshold ... ... | 22390 |
| Thesis ... ... ... | 22341 | Threw ... ... ... | 22391 |
| Thew ... ... ... | 22342 | Thrice ... ... ... | 22392 |
| They ... ... ... | 22343 | Thrift ... ... ... | 22393 |
| Thick ... ... ... | 22344 | Thrifty ... ... ... | 22394 |
| Thicket ... ... ... | 22345 | Thrill ... ... ... | 22395 |
| Thickly ... ... ... | 22346 | Thrilling... ... ... | 22396 |
| Thief ... ... ... | 22347 | Thrive ... ... ... | 22397 |
| Thigh ... ... ... | 22348 | Thriving... ... ... | 22398 |
| Thin ... ... ... | 22349 | Thriven ... ... ... | 22399 |
| Thine ... ... ... | 22350 | Thrives ... ... ... | 22400 |

## *Poem Code*

The poem used for encrypting Lawrence Hamilton's message to Joe Ganzer was written by Leo Marks, the son of an antiquarian bookseller in London who introduced young Leo to Edgar Allen Poe's "The Gold Bug," a short story whose main character goes on an adventure after deciphering a secret message.

His early interest and facility with codes eventually led him to train as a cryptographer for the British Special Operations Executive (SOE) during WWII stationed at Betchley Park, an estate located in the town of Betchley, in Buckinghamshire, England. Decrypt teams at Betchley Park deciphered Germany's Enigma communications throughout the war.

Leo Marks was in charge of agent codes for Britain's spies. He abandoned using well-known preselected poems in the double transposition in favor of original poems. Well-known poems had significant disadvantages. They had limited cryptographic security and substantial minimum message sizes (short ones were easy to crack).

The poem "The Life That I Have" was a poem written by Marks, not for espionage, but for love. He had fallen in love with a woman who lived near him. She was killed in an air-crash. He wrote it for her.

Not too much later, Violette Szabo, an SOE agent on a mission to France, needed a poem for her codes. Marks gave her the lines he had written for his love. The poem is recited in the film *Carve Her Name With Pride* by actress Virginia McKenna playing Szabo. A clip on YouTube from the movie can be seen by searching for the title **Carve Her Name with Pride (Her Poem)** on YouTube. She would not reveal her poem even as she knelt before a Nazi SS firing squad at Ravensbruck.

That same poem was used by Lawrence Hamilton in *Return of the Falcon*. He chose five words from the seventh line of the poem as the key:

IS YOURS AND YOURS AND

The first step is to assign a number to each letter based on the letter's position in the alphabet relative to the others. As A is the first letter, it is assigned 1. The next A is assigned 2. The next are the Ds, ordered as 3 and 4. This continues until you have ordered the entire key.

| I | S | Y | O | U | R | S | A | N | D | Y | O | U | R | S | A | N | D |
|---|----|----|---|----|----|----|---|---|---|----|---|----|----|----|---|---|---|
| 5 | 12 | 17 | 8 | 15 | 10 | 13 | 1 | 6 | 3 | 18 | 9 | 16 | 11 | 14 | 2 | 7 | 4 |

## Double Transposition

*The following is a brief tutorial on double transposition by Fred Brandes, an expert in cryptography.*

SOE used a form of cipher known as Double Transposition. In brief the simplest form of a double transposition consists of writing out the message in rows with the number of letters in each row equal to the number of letters in the key phrase. The message is then re-written by taking the columns of the message in the order of the key phrase. This process is then repeated (thus the double of double transposition).

Here is a simple example using the keyword FREDBRANDES and the message:

*"An explanation of enciphering by double transposition for Don Satalic."*

The keyword FREDBRANDES has eleven letters. The first step is to assign a number to each letter based on the letter's position in the alphabet relative to the others. As A is the first letter it is assigned 1. B is second and assigned 2. There are 2 Ds and they are assigned 3 and 4 respectively. And so on until all letters have been assigned a number...

| F | R | E | D | B | R | A | N | D | E | S |
|---|---|---|---|---|---|---|---|---|---|---|
| 7 | 9 | 5 | 3 | 2 | 10 | 1 | 8 | 4 | 6 | 11 |

The message is then written out under the numbered keyword. Note that the message length must be a multiple of the key length and so the message is filled out with random letters (not so random in this case as THE END fits). For security (as in the case of SOE) the message should be of substantial length which is why 200 letters were the minimum when Marks arrived on the scene.

| F | R | E | D | B | R | A | N | D | E | S |
|---|---|---|---|---|---|---|---|---|---|---|
| 7 | 9 | 5 | 3 | 2 | 10 | 1 | 8 | 4 | 6 | 11 |

| A | N | E | X | P | L | A | N | A | T | I |
|---|---|---|---|---|---|---|---|---|---|---|
| O | N | O | F | E | N | C | I | P | H | E |
| R | I | N | G | B | Y | D | O | U | B | L |
| E | T | R | A | N | S | P | O | S | I | T |
| I | O | N | F | O | R | D | O | N | S | A |
| T | A | L | I | C | T | H | E | E | N | D |

| A | C | D | P | D | H | P | E | B | N | O |
|---|---|---|---|---|---|---|---|---|---|---|
| C | X | F | G | A | F | I | A | P | U | S |
| N | E | E | O | N | R | N | L | T | H | B |
| I | S | N | A | O | R | E | I | T | N | I |
| O | O | O | E | N | N | I | Y | O | A | L |
| N | Y | S | R | T | I | E | L | T | A | D |

The second transposition is accomplished in the same manner and produces the message that is actually transmitted, as follows:

PINEI EDANO NTPGO AERBP TTOTD FENOS NUHNA AACNI ONEAL IYLCX  ESOYH FRRNI OSBIL D

Of course the keyword or keyphrase indicator would be included (not necessarily at the start of the message for security reasons) and the total message text would be made a multiple of five because five-letter code groups is the accepted format for wireless transmissions. In addition, the SOE agents were instructed to make deliberate errors at certain points in the message as a means of assuring SOE that the agent had not been captured or otherwise compromised by the enemy. I've left these out as they are irrelevant to the example of encoding.

*End of Frank Brandes Tutorial*

## A Coded Message from the Author

To get a feel for the difficulties faced by SOE and OSS agents in the field, the reader might try deciphering the following message from the author. The key chosen for the message is DONSATALIC.

ENODF AROCG TEPCF TUJHA VEHSL YONEE EFYTR
OREAN EXHMJ OONND TIOLO ZTENS YHYER TUWRE

## Selected Bibliography

Kahn, David. *The Codebreakers: The Comprehensive History of Secret Communication from Ancient times to the Interent Scribner*, Rev Sub edition (December 5, 1996)

Marks, Leo. *Between Silk and Cyanide: A Codemaker's War, 1941-1945* Free Press; 1st Touchstone Ed edition (September 12, 2000)

Rosenheim, Shawn J. *The Cryptographic Imagination: Secret Writing from Edgar Poe to the Internet* The Johns Hopkins University Press (December 11, 1996)

# ABOUT THE AUTHOR

Mr. Satalic (suh-TAL-ik) has worked as a systems software engineer for the defense industry, as a fine art photographer, and as a structural iron worker.

He is author of

## The Dummy Case
(a sequel to *Return of the Falcon*)

## Tribute to Frank Marshall
### *America's Geppetto*
*An Essay*

## The Masque of William Shakespeare
*An Essay*

His books are available wherever books and ebooks are sold.

Mr. Satalic lives in the Chicago Metropolitan area and is currently working on a prequel to *Return of the Falcon*.